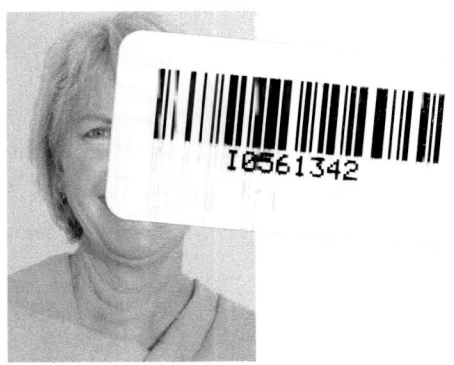

Karen grew up in a small country town in north-eastern Victoria, Australia. She spent her childhood riding horses through beautiful scenery of eucalypts, lakes, and snow-capped mountains and her love of landscape deeply affects her writing. She worked in a range of educational settings and holds a Ph.D. and M.Ed. (Hons) in the areas of fantasy. She is particularly interested in the power of the hero's inner journey which she explores through Deep Fantasy. Karen has travelled extensively overseas but enjoys nothing more than camping in the Australian Outback. She lives in Melbourne and now writes full-time. You can find out more about Karen and her books on her website.

Connect with K.S. Nikakis

Amazon: https://www.amazon.com/author/ksnikakis
Twitter: https://twitter.com/KSNikakis
Facebook: www.facebook.com/ksnikakis
Goodreads: www.goodreads.com
Website: www.ksnikakis.com
Email: author@ksnikakis.com

WORKS BY K S NIKAKIS

Non Fiction

Journey: Seeking the Sacred, Spirit and Soul in the
Australian Wilderness

Fantasy Novels Series

Angel Caste series:
Angel Blood
Angel Breath
Angel Bone
Angel Bound
Angel Blessed
Angel Caste – Complete 5 Book Series

The Kira Chronicles trilogy:*
The Whisper of Leaves
The Song of the Silvercades
The Cry of the Marwing
remnant hard copies only

The Kira Chronicles series:
The Whisper of Leaves
The Silence of Stone
The Secrets of Stars
The Thunder of Hoofs
The Crying of Birds
The Music of Home
The Kira Chronicles – Complete 6 Book Series

Fantasy Novels

The Emerald Serpent
Heart Hunter
The Third Moon
Messenger
I Heard the Wolf Call My Name
Finalist - Best YA Novel Aurealis Awards, 2019

Fantasy Short Stories

The Gift
The Tale of Prince Anura
Dragon Sprite
Glass-Heart
Finalist – Best YA Short Story Aurealis Awards, 2019

I HEARD THE WOLF CALL MY NAME

K.S. NIKAKIS

First published by SOV CONSULTING LLC - SOV Media Australia
2019
Amazon: www.amazon.com.au

Publisher: SOV CONSULTING LLC - SOV Media Melbourne Australia

Cover by AS Nikakis: http://asnikakis.com
Jozef Klopacka/Shutterstock.com
Olena Yakobchuk/Shutterstock.com
James Paul/ James Paul (font) - licenced

National Library of Australia
Cataloguing-in-Publication entry:
Nikakis, Karen Simpson
I Heard the Wolf Call My Name
ISBN 978-0-6482652-6-9

For those who search for their place

I HEARD THE WOLF CALL MY NAME

Glossary

I Heard the Wolf Call My Name draws on Maori, the language of the First Nation Peoples of New Zealand, and on the landscape of the Hawaiian Islands. Mythic and belief systems are entirely fictional.

Islands

Kawai Alanui (*kay-way alan-u-ee*) (also the Islanders' name for themselves) consists of four islands:

Iolana (*i-o-lan-a*) The largest. Dominated by a single peak (Tihi) (*tee-hee*). Sheer cliffs plunge in to the ocean on all sides
Rua (*roo-ah*) Second largest. Exploded ten years previously. Small mountains and gravel beaches
Pua (*poo-ah*) Small. Uninhabited in recorded history
Ke-one (*kee-wun*) Small. Uninhabited in recorded history

Iolana landscape - composed of five geographical bands:

Wairere (*way-ree-ree*) Tropical vegetation that sits atop coastal cliffs
Kohatu (*ko-hart-too*) Black volcanic stone with little vegetation
Makariri (*makka-ree-ree*) Permanent snow
Cloud Crown – A band of permanent cloud
Huna (*hoo-na*) Tihi's snow-capped peak

Off-islands

Makena (*mak-een-a*) A nation west of Kawai Alanui
Samarak (*sam-ar-rak*) A nation east of Kawai Alanui
Fayo Sea (*fai-o)* Between Makena and Samarak

Island Culture

Younger Ahi (*ar-hee*) From birth to around fifteen
Older Ahi – from sixteen to initiation at around nineteen to twenty
Ikaika (*ick-kie-ka*) Initiated Kawai Alanui
Elders – late thirties plus
Kuwaini (*Ku-wain-ee*) A select group of Elders responsible for community leadership
Kuwain (*Ku-wain*) Large ceremonial building where the Kuwaini meet
Awin (*ai-win*) Smaller buildings shared by friends and mate-pairs
Dream-travelers – Kawai Alanui who experience portentous dreams
Ohaku-sai (*o-hark-oo-say*) Pre-initiation rite consisting of trials
Ohaku (*o-hark-oo*) Initiation rite

I HEARD THE WOLF CALL MY NAME

1

Jax folded his arms across his chest and hunkered down in a vain attempt to fend off the cold. The chopper was one of the old MH-6's, like the rattlers he used to reconnoiter Arozi's desiccated landscapes on hot summer days. The trouble was, he didn't use MH-6's in the middle of the night, in the middle of nowhere, not that he had had any choice in finding himself a passenger in one. And Second Lieutenant Macy showed no signs of relinquishing the controls.

The chopper was open on both sides and Jax wondered whether the plexiglass had been taken out or had fallen out. He just hoped the rotors were in better condition than the cockpit. The wind roared through it, adding to his disorientation. It had been a normal day until the nameless officer had appeared in the garage's doorway to inform him he was being transferred, effective immediately.

Jax started as Macy nudged his shoulder to get his attention. 'The Zoaides,' bawled Macy, having to shout above the noise, 'otherwise known as *The Zoo*.' His teeth flashed in a smile as he stabbed his finger towards the hulking outline that loomed from the murk. Jax struggled to breathe but nodded and dutifully craned his neck. The peak was enormous and he made a show of scanning to either side, despite knowing there was no second jag of rock to make confetti of the rotors.

'Four of them,' bawled Macy again. 'That's the Big Island. Called *Iolana*. The mountain's Mount Matheson. The *flash-monkeys* call it *Tihi*. Means *peak* in their lingo. It is the only inhabited one. The others are Rua, Ke-one, and Puah.'

Spit pooled in Jax's mouth and he struggled to ensure his face showed only polite interest and not the dislike that burned up from his gut. He knew more about *The Zoo* than Macy ever would and not just because Rafi had sung their songs to him when Jax had first gone to live with him at the garage.

Then Macy banked the chopper away so sharply Jax was slammed against the cockpit's side. 'Exclusion Zone,' yelled Macy. 'Got to keep the Alanui *shifter-twisters* safe.'

'How big?' bawled Jax, now fighting to hide anger as well.

'Nautical mile above; three around.'

They had been a hell of a lot closer to Tihi than a nautical mile! Macy was either careless or incompetent. Jax concentrated on slowing his breathing and rested his head back against the seat. It had been a long day and he had no idea when it would end. He had not been told where he was being sent and he had learned not to waste breath asking. He did not want to think about his destination anyway, or that he had lacked the courage to turn for one last look at the garage that had been home since he was fourteen, and at the man who had loved him as his own.

Jax stretched his legs as far as the cockpit allowed in an attempt to ease his muscles. The cockpit had been designed for an average-sized Off-islander and Jax was neither. He wanted to sleep, but the racket made it impossible and he fixed his gaze on Wessel's bright pulse instead. *Whetu's* a voice in his head countered, and spit pooled in his mouth again.

Wessel made the surrounding stars as dull as gravel but after a while, even its brilliance failed to stave off his weariness, and his eyelids drooped. He had no idea how long he had slept before a change in the chopper's chug woke him. He jerked upright, fearing they were going down, but Macy seemed unconcerned.

He was bent forward over the flight panel, his face bathed in its greenish light as he searched the ground. Jax peered down too. A blotch of gold appeared in the darkness, disappeared, and appeared again. If it *were* a landing pad, its owner did not want to advertise the fact.

'Almost there,' yelled Macy, his gaze glued below. Jax nodded and subtly extended his senses. He heard nothing above the chopper's thud but he smelled the moistness of forested land beyond the cockpit's odor of oil and rusty metal.

Seeing Tihi again was bad enough, but this was worse. The scent embedded itself in his memory like a fish-hook, and with a jag of pain, jerked him back to the time he had spent ten years fighting to forget.

Macy took the chopper down in a series of jags, like a spider falling on a line of web, and as the trees closed in, Jax's tongue slid

2

along his lips to taste the air.

'We part ways here,' bawled Macy as soon as the skids touched the ground. 'The base is through those trees. Enjoy.' His teeth flashed in another smile and Jax nodded as he grabbed his kit-bag, swung his legs out, and dropped to the ground. He ducked the rotors but the chopper already powered away, leaving him a farewell gift of grit.

Jax sleeved his face and peered about. It was a relief to escape the chopper's brutal roar, to have the earth under his feet again, to be surrounded by silence, although nowhere was ever completely silent. Even on the stillest nights, creatures bred and burrowed beneath the earth, fluffed their feathers in woody nests, or slid through the night on hunt.

He flared his nostrils. The air carried the sweet scent of rokai and he saw its waxy flowers on the edge of the landing pad, as pale as milk against its leathery leaves. He crossed the open ground and ran his fingers over their velvety petals, then dropped his hand and spat. As if he could rid himself of the memories so easily, he thought, as he eyed the spittle in disgust.

He swung his kit-bag over his shoulder and strode off through the trees. Bats chittered and he recalled they fed off rokai blooms or at least *peka* bats did. His gut tightened. He did not know how long he had slept, but if these *were* peka bats, he had a pretty good idea where Macy had dumped him.

It was too dark to catch more than a glimpse of the bats and peka were not easy to mimic. It did not help he was as rusty as all hell either. He stopped and without really knowing why, sent out a tentative *tchk-tchk-tchk*. It was a male courting-call but too high. He swore under his breath and tried again. It was closer this time but he did not expect to be mobbed by excited females and he was not. His third attempt was *true* and he waited. Nothing happened but he resisted the urge to repeat the call and was rewarded with the flick of brown bats past his face.

They *were* peka and his gut knotted again. Peka might frequent all sorts of places he had never heard of, he reasoned as he went on, but their presence *here*, his abrupt re-assignment, and Macy's less than detailed explanation of *where* Jax had been off-loaded painted a pretty unappealing picture.

He had no escort and as the cluster of buildings emerged from the trees, he saw there was no perimeter fence either and no obvious guards. He scanned as he approached, half-expecting a challenge or the gleam of a weapon thrust in his face, but there was nothing. What was he supposed to do? Walk up and knock on the door? There seemed to be plenty of lights on, their yellow glow visible through the windows of the largest building, so he supposed it was exactly what he would do.

But his feet slowed and he took a breath and opened himself. He heard owls off in the distance and the chitter of bats, distant now too, and he heard the faint sound of human voices inside the buildings. He smelled the remains of a meal, the smoke of dead coals, soap and the peppermint of toothpaste.

His surroundings tasted strongly of the trees but there were traces of aviation fuel too. His skin tested the dewy air which told him dawn was close, and as his vision sharpened, he saw the base had six buildings.

Macy had set him down near an unguarded base which told Jax he was expected and given his lack of escort, its commander did not expect him to abscond. He grimaced. Either there was nowhere to abscond to, or his recent history of compliance was well-documented. Hardly a surprise given *everything* about him was well-documented.

He quickened his pace again but stopped when the door of the closest building opened and yellow light slashed the ground. A man's shadow joined it and Jax's heart thundered. It was a reaction to strangers he had battled for years but had yet to defeat. Every instinct urged him to *shift* but he remained rooted to the spot.

The shadow's owner advanced and Jax struggled not to lash out in self-defence. The man held the advantage of being in shadow while Jax was in light and to add to Jax's turmoil, he knew the man saw his fear.

'Welcome to URZOL, Jax,' the man said softly.

Jax recognised the voice and his panic grew. 'You are dead,' he whispered.

'Yes, and . . . no,' said the man cryptically, and Jax sensed a smile. 'Come inside, Jax. We need to talk.'

2

*J*ax remained frozen in the slash of light, and for the third time that night, threw open his senses. It *was* Matiu, despite his voice carrying the deeper tones of a man. Memories stormed back of a wall of flame that had threatened to devour Jax as it had already devoured Matiu, and he wiped his mouth.

'You have had a long day,' repeated Matiu. 'Come inside. You need to eat and we need to talk.'

Matiu turned slowly, exposing his back in a gesture of trust and Jax followed him over the threshold into a small ante-room. Its yellow lights dazzled him and Jax drew on his other senses as he followed Matiu on through a second door.

There were smells of cooked meat, vegetables and beer; warm air tinged by wood smoke; a slight give to the floor that told him it was built on stumps; and the sound of murmured conversations in other rooms. The stench of Off-islanders was heavy in the air and while he had grown used to it over the years, Matiu's Kawai Alanui scent threw it into sharp relief.

The light revealed Matiu's birth-form to be that of a military Off-islander, where training created muscles suited to heaving packs over difficult terrain, not to *shifting*, as Jax's Kawai Alanui slenderness did. He scanned with habitual caution and noted the fire in the grate, the couch and lounge chairs, and the low table set with food. It might look like a pleasant place to relax but it reeked of an interrogation space.

'Sit, Jax,' said Matiu, and poured coffee into a couple of mugs. Jax obeyed, his gaze on the opaque window in the wall opposite. There would be another room beyond it with observers. He had first been in a room like this as a bewildered twelve year old, still wrapped in the rescue boat's silver therma-blanket, but he had been in plenty of them since.

He cleared his face of expression but then Matiu raised his as he handed Jax his coffee and Jax struggled to maintain his blankness. The left side of Matiu's face and neck were rucked with scars, as was his left hand and wrist where it protruded from his military-issue shirt-sleeve.

'It is good to see you, Jax,' said Matiu, lifting his mug in toast. Habit made Jax mirror the Off-island gesture of camaraderie and he sipped his coffee as Matiu did, even though he detested its taste. Matiu's eyes were the same green Jax remembered and despite the scarring, he simply looked like an older version of the boy Jax had known.

'So, tell me what you have been doing with yourself these last ten years,' said Matiu, his smile still firmly in place.

Matiu was military and would know *exactly* what Jax had been doing, but Jax dutifully recited the potted history of his life since the day the fireball had annihilated everyone and everything he had loved.

'I was sent to a training-home for boys of *unknown parentage* in Sawquorn Prefecture,' he said, and took another sip of his coffee. Even now the phrase *of unknown parentage* was like a kick in the guts. 'When I was fourteen, I was sent to Arozi, where my *Alanui traits* could be put to *good use*. At eighteen I was sent to Nakoda Base to complete my Service to Country. I trained as a chopper pilot. I was sent back to Arozi and piloted choppers for the military's flora and fauna reconnaissance. Now I have been sent here.'

Matiu piled a plate with cornbread, corned beef, and chillie greens, and Jax politely nodded his thanks. It was typical military fare and like other Off-island food, quelled his hunger pangs, which was all he needed.

He started on the bread and Matiu watched him eat. 'Arozi's desert country, Jax,' he said after a while. 'Didn't you miss *moana*?' Jax kept his attention on the food and as the silence stretched, Matiu changed tack. 'Were you told only two of us survived that day?' he asked. Jax shook his head, intent on the chillie greens. 'What *were* you told?' pursued Matiu.

'That Rua was gone and I was being sent to Sawquorn.'

'Is that all?'

Jax glanced up. Matiu actually looked shocked and Jax shrugged. 'What did they tell you?'

Matiu poured himself more coffee and topped up Jax's. 'I was in the Naraven Base Infirmary for almost a year, and they mainly told me to lie still and take my meds.' He smiled ironically. 'I think they forgot about me really. I was just the kid in the corner bed and by the time they got me up and about again, interest in Rua had waned. The ash cloud had gone and Rua being in the Exclusion Zone prevented any real investigation as to why it had exploded. I stayed at Naraven and did my Service to Country there, and then I was sent to Rilo Base, and then here to URZOL.'

Matiu relaxed back in his seat and folded his hands behind his head. 'Didn't you feel tempted to go back?'

'Rua's gone,' said Jax, uncurling his own legs.

'Iolana's still there,' said Matiu softly. Jax said nothing and Matiu leaned forward again. 'We are *all* Kawai Alanui, Jax, regardless of island. We are *all* connected. All you had to do was *shift* and fly home. Or swim,' he added with a forced smile.

'All *I* had to do? That's all *you* had to do too, yet here you are, a proud member of the military!' Jax forced himself to still, annoyed he had revealed his feelings to the spies beyond the window.

'The military gave me a home,' said Matiu quietly, 'but that wasn't the only reason I stayed.' He held up his scarred hand. 'The blast cooked half my body, Jax. I can't *shift*.'

Saliva pooled in Jax's mouth and the need to spit was overwhelming. He gulped and then coughed to disguise the gesture. 'Rua's gone, Matiu,' he said with a shrug, 'and you have made a life here. It doesn't matter.'

Matiu's face was suddenly a hand span's from his. '*Don't* tell me *shifting* doesn't matter!' Jax stared straight ahead and Matiu got to his feet. 'I will show you to your quarters,' he clipped out. 'Tomorrow Commander Keli will brief you on URZOL and your duties here.'

Jax said nothing, just picked up his kit-bag, and followed Matiu out.

Keli lounged back in his chair, his gaze on the empty room beyond the window and Connel was the first to speak. 'So, this is our real live, *fully*-functioning *shifter,*' he said.

'Yes,' said Keli thoughtfully, as he considered the exchange. 'The only one we know of outside the Zoaides and not happy to be here amongst the despised *military Off-islanders*.'

Connel flipped open the folder on the desk in front of him. 'His record suggests he isn't happy to be *anywhere*. Absconded six times during his service training.' Connel glanced up. 'He spent a lot of time in the cells.' There was a pause as he read the close-set print. 'Offered no reason for his actions, in fact, refused to speak of them at all. He has been clean of misdemeanors in the two years he has been back in the desert.' He read on for a moment. 'A competent pilot but one who prefers to be left alone, by the sound of it.' He peered across at Keli. 'Why was he sent to Arozi in the first place? He was just a kid.'

Keli rose and rubbed the back of his neck. 'I'm not sure. Rua blew only a few years after the war. People were pretty jumpy and no one wanted to risk *appearing* to break the Exclusion Zone. There were only two survivors anyway, both picked up east of the islands. Matiu was pretty banged up, which solved the problem of what to do with him, but Jax was not injured.'

Keli wandered around the room and came to a stop, hands on hips. 'There was no Rua to return him to and Iolana was off limits. From what I can make out from the records we *do* have, the military knew of an old mixed-blood out at Arozi, name of Rafi, and when Jax turned fourteen, somebody had the bright idea Jax would be happy with him. No one seems to have checked whether he was.'

'Jax returned there after his Service to Country and has lived with him since, so it sounds like it worked out,' said Connel thoughtfully. 'I suppose it was better than the Boys' Home.'

Keli rubbed his chin. 'I've had a lot to do with Matiu over the years, but have never been too sure how typical he is. You are the expert on the Alanui, *Professor* Connel, what do you think?'

'*No one* is an *expert* on the Alanui, Commander,' said Connel. Keli's eyes narrowed and Connel cleared his throat. 'The inhabitants of the Zoaides are more properly known as the *Kawai* Alanui, which is also how they name their islands. *Kawai Alanui* means *water-road* which supports the theory they were a single people originally spread over the four islands.'

'One now,' said Keli tersely.

Connel nodded. 'And two for years before Rua blew. Ke-one and Puha haven't been inhabited in recorded history, although the Kawai Alanui might still sing of them.' Keli's eyebrows rose. 'They store their history in songs,' explained Connel.

'Matiu doesn't seem to know *any* Alanui histories. Would Jax?'

'Unlikely. Alanui lore seems to be passed on at initiation.'

'Which is when?'

'Late teens to early twenties. The Elders decide when each *Ahi*, or pre-initiate, is ready. They are known as *Ikaika* afterwards, which means *strong*. No one knows whether initiation brings about a physical change, but like all initiation rites, it certainly brings about a psychological one.'

'So neither Matiu nor Jax have been initiated,' muttered Keli.

'No, which might explain Jax's behavior. He sounds a lot less compliant than Matiu.'

'Most likely because Matiu grew up on a base and learned discipline.'

'Initiation isn't about *discipline*, Commander, at least in the way you mean it,' said Connel mildly. 'But being part of the military probably gave Matiu what he missed out on from not being initiated. The purpose of initiation rites is to connect the young to their communities so their communities survive after the old die off.'

'Or Jax's defiance might simply be a personality trait,' said Keli tersely. 'With only two in our Alanui sample, it is hard to draw *any* conclusions. Jax wouldn't be the first conscript to buck orders and he won't be the last.' Keli threw himself back into his chair. 'What do you make of what we have just seen?'

'Jax is twenty-two, I believe,' said Connel, glancing at the folder again, and Keli nodded. 'For that age, he is *very* controlled. He has just been wrenched from the only family he has known for the last eight years, flown through the night, and dumped in an unfamiliar place. Then he has come face to face with someone he probably thought was dead. Instead, that *someone* is part of the military, or what the Kawai Alanui more broadly term *opala*.'

'*Opala*?'

'Their word for *trash*.'

Keli grimaced. 'I thought Jax would look more like Matiu, for some reason,' he admitted.

'From what I understand, Jax is more typical of the Kawai Alanui than Matiu. They tend to be tall and lean, and he must be six two.'

'Six four,' said Keli, '*and* with wolf-eyes.'

'It is interesting you should use that term, Commander. The white-wolf is one of the *skin-spirit* animals the Kawai Alanui connect with during initiation.'

'You mean like a totem animal?'

'Not exactly.' Connel gazed at the folder thoughtfully. 'Green seems to be the most common eye-color on the islands but blue, brown, grey and amber aren't unknown.'

'And his hair? Do the Alanui go grey in their twenties?'

'Not that I know of. It could be a result of the trauma he suffered, or he might have simply inherited unlucky genes.' Connel smiled briefly. 'As you have pointed out, Commander, our research sample is rather small.'

There was a knock and Keli went to the door and took delivery of a tab. 'Vision of Jax's arrival,' he said briefly, holding it up before he clipped it into the vid. 'I ordered Macy to drop him at the old pad. The trees there are thick with sen-cams. I wanted to see Jax's reactions.'

Connel flicked off the lights and dragged his chair closer, and for a while they watched in silence, then Connel's breath hissed. 'He is sensing,' he said excitedly, as Jax's shadowy outline stopped and flared brighter.

'Sensing?' All Keli could see were the usual colors of body heat against the darker trees.

'Like we do but more powerfully. He knew we observed him tonight because he looked straight at the window when he came in, but even if he hadn't, he probably would have *smelled* us, or *felt* us. And that is another Kawai Alanui trait.' said Connel, jabbing his finger at the screen as Jax spat.

'What? Spitting?'

Connel nodded. 'The Kawai Alanui spit for very specific reasons.'

'Such as?'

'To rid themselves of unwanted images or memories.'

'But isn't that the same for us when we spit in contempt?'

'There is a subtle difference. Jax was shocked by Matiu's scarring just now, but he suppressed the urge to spit. It's—' Connel stopped. 'Now that *is* interesting.'

'What is?' demanded Keli in frustration.

'Can you increase the sound?'

'Yes, but it's only bats. They are thick there this time of year. They feed off the rokai.'

'No, it is him, Jax. He is calling the bats to him using mimicry.' Connel's excitement was palpable. 'I have read of this. Can you replay the vid?'

Keli did as he was asked and forced himself to focus on it. Connel was right! 'Why would Jax bother calling bats?'

Connel shrugged, not taking his eyes from the screen. 'For fun, to test himself, who knows? But the skill goes beyond summoning bats. The Kawai Alanui can mimic whole languages: words, gestures, the most subtle of nuances. It makes them pan-lingual. You saw how he mirrored Matiu?'

'Mirrored?'

'It is a way of building rapport by repeating a person's gestures back to them, but I don't think Jax tried to build rapport. I think he used it to reduce what he saw as a threat.' Connel's finger jabbed at the vid. 'You see how his body-heat changes as he nears the base? How his stride changes? The way he holds himself? They are all classic fear reactions. Let's watch it a third time.'

Keli was keen to oblige and this time he saw Jax's sureness in the dark, his skill in bringing the wild creatures to him, and how he countered his fears. 'He is exactly what I need,' he said, as he flicked on the lights.

'He has shown no interest in his heritage *or* in us,' said Connel. 'He isn't likely to cooperate.'

'Not *willingly*,' acknowledged Keli. 'But every man has his vulnerabilities.'

'Jax is *Kawai Alanui*,' Connel reminded him.

'Who have *very* specific vulnerabilities, which is why I had you re-assigned to URZOL.'

Connel stared down at the folder for a moment. 'You want me to break Jax?' he asked heavily.

Keli smiled grimly. 'Whether I issue that particular order will depend on him.'

3

*A*nahera heard the Off-islander machine thud overhead, but shut it from her mind and tightened her grip on the cliff-face. It was a long way down. She should have shed her whitiki and para before she climbed or *shifted*. In fact, *she should not have climbed at all*. She shrugged off the bizarre notion and scowled as she almost slipped. Moving at all was a *very* bad idea but there was no point following Tamati if all she saw were tree-tops.

She flexed her numb fingers and searched for a better hold. Whetu blazed in the sky and its fluorescence showed a crevice to her right. It looked shallow but might be enough *if* she could reach it. She pressed herself against the stone, slid her foot along the ledge, and stretched. Her muscles trembled but she wedged her fingers into the crevice, grinned, and edged her way forward.

She could see the display platform now where generations of shia had raised the earth above the forest floor and kept it clear of creeper- and stringer-vines. The surrounding track was dense, for shia favored a woody circle to mark their territory *except* she was pretty sure the shia gathered below were not birth-form birds but *shifted* Ahi.

They still milled about so she had not missed anything, she realized in relief. Tamati should have told her what he planned, or Malo, or Nikau, but the older Ahi males had grown secretive lately. Her lip curled. As if Tamati or Malo could fool her! Maybe she had grown secretive too, she conceded, and glanced up at Whetu's reassuring presence.

Miru spoke of the Ahi altering before they *died* and of Iolana growing more dangerous for them, and Anahera licked her lips. Iolana was the same; *she* was the same, so how could things grow more dangerous? Her uneasiness was caused by knowing she had been a fool to climb the cliff in birth-form *and* clothed although she could not entirely dismiss Miru's claim. Miru was a Dream-traveler, and Dream-travelers saw things denied to even the wisest Elders.

She shrugged off the mysteries of Dream-travelers and counted the birds below. There were five but distance made it hard to tell which Ahi males had *shifted*. They looked identical as they jostled for position, their plumage flashing crimson and emerald in Whetu's light.

It could take a long time for a shia alpha to claim the lead in a display and given the shia's blade-sharp leg-spurs, the claim could involve a very bloody fight, but even as she watched, the shia formed the arrow-head of dance.

The speed of the transformation confirmed they *were* Ahi in shift-form *and* that either Tamati or Malo were missing. It was just as well. Their rivalry might just tempt them to fight and being injured so close to ohaku would be catastrophic.

A hush descended as it always did before a display began and only moana's voice filled the silence as its waves dashed against Iolana's cliffs, and then the shia's first calls sounded, as guttural as snow-goats in rut. No shia danced in silence, whether in birth-form or *shifted*, and her heart quickened as the alpha strutted forward, gold crest erect, crimson tail-feathers splayed. Tamati, she guessed, given the extravagance of its early display.

The shia's music was discordant, as the lesser shia jostled for position, but then the cacophony settled into a rhythmic beat as the birds found their places and fanned out behind the leader. The alpha led in more ways than one. The rise and fall of its clawed feet, the bow and thrust of its chest, the spread and snap of its wings, all created a pattern for the lesser birds to follow. The alpha might claim the right to *dictate* the dance, but it remained part of the dance, for no Iolani danced alone.

Anahera had watched many birth-form shia displays and knew how the cock-birds danced together, not just to claim first right to display to the hens, but to strengthen male bonding. The lesser males learned from the alphas, and the intricacy of the dance meant birds must accommodate the steps of their companions. The display might be about individual male beauty and potency, but it was also about flock unity.

Shia were not the only of Iolana's birds to display, but their dance was the most intricate and, to Iolana's males on the verge of Ikaika, the most dazzling. Anahera was dazzled too and as her blood surged back and forth in rhythm with the dance, she wondered whether her skin-spirit was a shia and not a white-wolf after all. The thought was fleeting. She had always known that one day, deep in the Cloud

Crown, she would hear a wolf call her name.

The prospect was so intoxicating she stared up at the pale swirl that ringed Tihi's slopes. Neither the sun nor Whetu's brilliance penetrated the soft, grey cloud that encircled the mountain, but the minds of Dream-travelers did *and* the Ahi who survived Tihi's perilous climb. Days after they set out, they would die there and be born Ikaika, new to Iolana but knowing more than their Ahi kin confined in Wairere's valleys below.

Anahera licked her lips and brought her attention back to the display. The alpha strutted backwards and forwards, head low then thrown back in challenge, its blue throat-feathers as brilliant as the lightning that danced across moana in summer storms. The lesser birds followed the alpha's lead, but Anahera was barely aware of them. It no longer mattered whether the alpha was Tamati or Malo, or a shia in birth-form. The cock-bird's beauty reduced the lesser birds to shadows even as Tihi's soaring majesty reduced Iolana's smaller peaks to hills.

The shia's music built to a crescendo and Anahera's blood pounded as the alpha held its wing displays longer and longer, feathers extended to their uttermost breadth, and then a throbbing staccato erupted overhead, far closer than the last Off-islander machine. It jarred Anahera from the dance's all-consuming trance and she lost her grip on the stone. She clutched at the cliff-face in desperation and missed, and then she was falling, a scream torn from her throat as she plunged into oblivion.

4

The scream slammed into Tamati's birth-form consciousness like a lightning bolt and he sprang from the display mound and cleared the trees in a single wing-beat. But then his shift-form awareness kicked in to create a lethal mix. He was overwhelmed by the need to save the falling Iolani but his shift-form senses still exalted in his alpha potency, and for a crucial moment he hesitated. And then the Iolani smashed into him and he crashed back into the trees.

His wings clamped the Iolani close as the impact sheared branches from the brack but not all gave way and the sturdier ones flung him sideways to where the land fell away in a sheer drop to moana. His birth-form senses screamed warning but there was no time to *shift* before he too was falling, tumbling over and over through the cool night air, until it disappeared and he slammed into the water.

Anahera gasped as it closed over her head and as she plunged deeper, she tore off her para and whitiki and *shifted*. Panic thrust her instinctively into *hiri*-form and her flippers propelled her back to the surface so fast she arced through the air and had dived again before she righted herself to surface more gently. Waves surged around her, a flash with Whetu's light, but empty of her rescuer.

'Tamati!' The name was clear in her head but in shift-form came out as a harsh bark, and she dived again, using her rear flippers to power her ever deeper. Moana's darkness revealed nothing and in desperation she took a deep breath, *shifted* back to birth-form and then to *wheke*, needing their keen eyes. And then she saw him, still in shia-form, wings rising and falling in a parody of flight as he drifted with the current.

Her tentacles pulled him close as she jetted back to the surface, then bobbed there, using her suckers to keep his head above the water while she searched Iolana's cliffs for a wave-washed rock to make landfall. There was nothing.

Had she been alone, she would have *shifted* to bird-form and flown to safety, but Tamati lay senseless on moana's surface, trapped in shift-form by injury, and she scoured her memory for ways to keep him safe. Snow-goats scaled Iolana's cliffs but not carrying sodden

15

shia on their backs, and to avoid being smashed to pieces, she must *shift* to snow-goat-form the moment she made landfall in birth-form, and she doubted she had the strength.

There *was* a way to get him to safety but she dreaded using it. Maybe her arms cradled only a shia, she thought hopefully, and she could fly away and leave the bird to its fate, but all her senses told her it *was* Tamati who had burst through the trees to save her, and that now she must save him.

She glanced around, relieved to see no *taniwha* fin slice through the waters towards her but taniwha had excellent noses for trouble, especially the troubles of others, and she needed to get Tamati out of moana. She tightened her arms about him, gathered the last of her strength, and jetted southward. She kept her senses trained on keeping his head clear of the waves as she scanned the rocks for the tunnel's opening and when she found it, she dived.

The last time she navigated the tunnel's darkness she had been in hiri-form, as had Malo, who she had chased. She had been infuriated by his goading and so determined to catch him to prove she *was* the swifter, she had been a long way into the blackness before fear had replaced anger. A current had pulled her in as well and she had swum on, too panicked to *shift* from hiri to a water-breathing-form, and had finally emerged breathless and trembling into a large cavern.

Malo had not been there because, as he had later boasted, he had *shifted* to silver-fish-form and swum out under her very nose, but the cavern had been so astonishing, she had not noticed his absence. It was above moana's level outside and fed with fresh air from cracks in the ceiling, but most surprising of all, it had a beach like those that had once girdled Rua.

Anahera was not thinking of Rua now, or of the day it had ceased to exist, but of getting Tamati out of the water. She feared she dragged a corpse behind her but as she jetted on, a greater fear consumed her: that she would be too late to release him from shia-form.

Her wheke eyes saw the dull sheen on the water above and she powered upwards, broke the surface, *shifted*, and staggered up the beach, hauling Tamati with her. He lay motionless on the coarse gravel, but at least his sodden chest-feathers rose and fell, which meant he lived.

She crouched over him, panting from her multiple *shifts* and the speed of her swim. 'Tamati!' No response. She shook him violently. 'Tamati!' Nothing. She licked her lips knowing that Tamati's senseless Iolani brain might have already succumbed to his shia one. He had been in the middle of a display when she had fallen; a cock-bird at the peak of its power, and the potency of that state would be hard for him to reject, perhaps *too* hard.

It was a danger the Elders warned of, but there were always younger Ahi who became *wairua*, ghosts so seduced by the snow-hawk's flight or the white-hare's beauty, they had been unable to leave it behind.

'Tamati!' she screamed, aware that every passing moment increased the risk of losing him forever. To pull him back to birth-form, she had to give him a reason to return, and she had to do it fast. She was already naked, which helped, and she *shifted* to shia-form, straddled the shia's prone body, and brought her wing tips gently across its chest. It was the first caress of an intricate courtship dance that ended in a mate-pair and she had seen shia perform it countless times before.

Her Iolani brain knew exactly what she did and *why*, but as she repeated the caress lower on the cock-bird's belly, her shia-blood thrummed. She leaned in closer, so her crest pressed against its and a throaty *chrrr-ee* escaped her beak as she took in its magnificence. The cock-bird might lie unmoving but its breathing quickened even as hers did and then, as she gently smoothed her crest-feathers along the curve of its beak, its eyes opened, and it came to its feet in one smooth motion.

Its wings curved about her, its nearness as heady as rokai scent on a summer's night as it strutted forwards and backwards, swept its head low then thrust it high. She mirrored its steps, the harsher *krrr-ee* of its pleasure-song answered by her lighter notes. Her birth-form senses receded as its brilliant eyes held hers, its gaze unwavering as it wove its courtship-dance about her, the feathery kisses of its wing-tips making her blood trill.

Their necks entwined and its eyes suffused with an amethyst as deep as night, the change so glorious that almost she was caught. Her shia-form yearned for the sweet rush of their joining but as it slid behind her she summoned the last of her strength and *shifted*, the

17

wrench so violent she stumbled forward to her knees.

The cock-bird cawed in fury and she threw herself over in time to see it launch at her, lethal leg-spurs slashing.

'Tamati! No!' she shrieked and flung up her hand. It swerved away with such force its wing-tip hit the beach and it cartwheeled along the gravel and lay still. Anahera scrambled up and sped to the tangle of broken plumage but it was Tamati who lay there now, chest heaving, eyes amethyst-drenched and unseeing. 'Tamati!' She crouched over him and the amethyst drained away to leave his eyes their usual green.

He was on his feet in an instant, his fury undiminished despite being in birth-form. 'How—dare—you!' he ground out. 'Is this all a game to you? Spying on display? Joining a courtship-dance?'

Anger fumed from his every pore and Anahera dropped her eyes, only to see that he was erect, and she shifted her gaze to her feet instead. The gravel crunched as he swung away to hide his arousal and, she knew, to avoid looking at her. It was usual for young Ahi to be naked in each other's company but they were no longer *young* Ahi. Her whitiki and para floated somewhere in moana and she shrugged her hair forward. It fell to her hips and made an adequate enough covering for the time being.

'I . . . I didn't mean for any of this to happen,' she said, having to speak to his back. 'I just wanted to see a shia display.'

'You *knew* what you watched!'

He was still angry and she grimaced. 'Yes.'

There was a long pause. 'If you intended to spy, you should at least have had the sense to *shift* to bird-form.'

'Yes,' she repeated grudgingly. The concession galled her but she did not want another argument. They had clashed in the past but knowing how close he had come to wairua made their quarrels seem petty. He turned around and she was careful to keep her eyes on his face. It was no hardship. He was the most beautiful of the older male Ahi and he knew it.

'You should find something to serve as a whitiki,' he said curtly, even as his eyes roved over her.

'So should you,' she retorted, annoyed to feel her face warm. 'But nothing grows here.'

He stared around for the first time. 'Where *is* here? Where *is* this place you have brought me?'

His tone was faintly mocking but she refused to be riled. 'If it has a name, I haven't been given it,' she said evenly. 'You were senseless and I needed somewhere safe for you to *shift* back.'

'*If* it is safe,' he said, his gaze on the cracks in the roof.

'It's safer than the waters around Iolana's cliffs,' she retorted, annoyed he had not acknowledged her efforts in saving him, let alone thanked her.

'Where we ended up because of *your* stupidity,' he said, green eyes burning into hers.

'Well, you don't need to put up with *my* stupidity a moment longer,' she snapped. 'I suggest you *shift* to something you can *shift out* of again, and given the tunnel's length and darkness, choose something that breathes water. I will see you back in Lani *or not*,' she added under her breath, and headed for the water.

'Anahera!' She came to a reluctant stop but refused to turn. 'How many times did you *shift* to bring me here?'

'Four,' she muttered.

'And then to shia and back again,' he added, 'which makes six. And now you think you have the strength to safely *shift* again *and* swim out along a dark, airless tunnel?' His voice was scathing. 'Use your brains, Anahera.'

'What I can or *can't* do, is no concern of yours,' she retorted, and stepped into the water.

'It *is* a concern of mine. Ahi are one, or has that slipped your mind along with respect for display?'

The cold water lapped her ankles, its blackness unrelieved by Whetu's life-giving spark and tiredness gnawed at her muscles. 'We are going to die soon anyway,' she murmured, unable to drag her eyes from its darkness.

There was a splash and she started as his arms came around her. His chest and belly were warm against her back but it was the scent of his maleness that set her blood pounding. She wondered whether her senses still carried the shia-taint from the courtship dance, and whether his did too. He had never held her like this before.

'To die we must be strong,' he said softly, 'and to be strong, we must rest.' She said nothing and he released her, leaving her intensely aware of his absence. 'And while we rest here, *on the beach*, you can tell me how you discovered this place.'

5

*K*eli grunted as he stared down at the fat folder on his desk. He had asked Connel to select data only relevant to Operation V but it had still taken Keli most of the morning to read through it. God knows how much more material the *Professor* had accumulated if this were a *selection*.

He wondered irritably why Connel had made his life's work the study of obscure islands in the middle of the Fayo Sea. It said something about Connel's personality, he supposed, as did Connel's repugnance at the prospect of being *disrespectful* to a shifter. Keli's lip curled. Like most civilians, Connel had little understanding of the fragility of the peace he enjoyed or of the realities that kept him and his fellow citizens safe.

Keli scowled as he considered the pages he had trawled through. In Connel's defence, it would have thinned the wad had Keli been more explicit about Operation *Vesuvius*, but his orders had not allowed it.

Keli took a quick turn around the room knowing he needed a run or a long session at the gym, and that there was time for neither. He came to a stop at the window and peered out. There was not much to see, just a collection of timber buildings set amongst long overgrown gardens. URZOL's budget did not stretch to gardeners, but it suited the military for URZOL's facilities to look ramshackle and *unthreatening*.

The Unit for Research into the Zoaides Oceans and Lands bore all the hallmarks of an under-funded, lip-service payment to the *extraordinary* fauna and flora of the Zoaides' four islands, now three, that had the misfortune to lie smack bang in the middle of two warring nations, and thanks to the last peace deal, off limits to both.

He scratched at his stubbly jaw. URZOL served as a handy front for Rilo Base that sat ten miles behind it, deep in the Rilo Valley, but no one was really fooling anyone. Samarak had bases all along its western seaboard in addition to Rilo, and if it were not for the Zoaides in between, Keli could almost have seen the sun shining off Makena's military installations along its *eastern* seaboard.

At least neither Samarak nor Makena had lobbed missiles at each in the fifteen years of uneasy peace since the last *engagement*, and his orders were that it stayed that way. Easier said than done, he conceded, when you dealt with shifters.

He took another turn around the room. He still found it hard to believe that humans *could* re-arrange their flesh and bone into the shape of another creature *and* in a matter of seconds. It was probably why the few Samaraks who had heard of the Zoaides' strange inhabitants, relegated them to the same bizarre tales as the famed female warriors of Amazonia. But the Amazonians, *if* they had existed outside myth, seemed to have been fully human, whereas the Alanui . . .

It would have been comforting to conclude that any *alleged* Alanui *strangeness* resulted from the toxins that rained down on them from the weapons that streaked overhead, and even without exposure to poisonous fumes, there were documented cases of genetic mutations that produced humans covered in hair or with feet split like bird-claws. And the glimpse of a *hirsute* human, or bird-like prints in the sand, could prompt all sorts of wild tales.

A great theory, *Commander Keli*, he admonished himself, but where did that leave *Senior Airman Matiu*? Matiu had been stationed at Rilo Base when Keli had taken command of URZOL, and Keli had immediately requested his transfer to URZOL. In the years since, Matiu had *done* nothing to suggest he was other than completely normal, or as normal as anyone could be whose entire way of life had been wiped out in a single cataclysmic blast, *and* who had spent years recovering from its burns.

Keli had interviewed Matiu multiple times and Matiu had never denied the Alanui's ability to *shift*. His cooperation also meant Keli had never had cause to discipline him, but answering his commander's questions and *volunteering* information were very different things. It meant the commander had to know *what* questions to ask, and it had not been until Matiu's incidental use of the word *we* one day, that Keli discovered the existence of a second survivor.

The lingering effects of the war's aftermath meant records of the other Alanui survivor were scant, and it had taken Keli close to six months to track Jax down and another three to convince his superiors to transfer him to URZOL.

Their reluctance to station Jax anywhere near a sensitive area like an Exclusion Zone was understandable, given Jax's military record, and they had made it very clear that Jax would be removed at the first sign of *trouble*.

Keli's lips thinned. It was not a question of whether *Airman* Jax would cause trouble, because his record said he would. It was more a question of whether Jax's value to Operation V outweighed his potential to scuttle it, and the answer to that, like so much else about *Airman* Jax, remained unknown.

Keli glanced back to Connel's sheaf of close-packed print. It referenced research from the turn of the century, before the latest round of wars, when anthropologists had made landfall on Rua. No researchers seemed to have braved the big island's cliffs even then, so there were no records of how Iolana's *natives* lived. It was simply assumed that, given their shared ethnicity, the Iolani's cultural practices would be the same.

Keli had skipped over the accounts of first contact but noted Connel's high-lighted text that it had been peaceful. He had only scanned the long-winded descriptions of initiation rites too, but he had read the sole description of an Alanui *shift* multiple times.

It was unclear whether the *shift* had been for the benefit of the *Off-island* visitors, was normal Alanui behavior, or whether indeed the shifter had been Ahi or Ikaika, and Keli had no idea whether any of it mattered. In truth, he struggled to believe a *shift* had taken place at all. The researchers would not have been the first to falsify their data to accelerate their careers, although they would have been fools to choose something so bizarre.

According to the *eye-witnesses,* the *shift* had started in the man's chest area, extended to his head, shoulders and arms, and then to his lower body and legs. It had been extremely fast, *in the blink of an eye*, in fact. The Alanui had become a snow-goat and then *shifted* back, this time his human head had appeared first, followed by his neck, torso, arms and legs.

Keli snorted. His military training told him it was ridiculous but it also told him to weigh the evidence and reach a logical conclusion. Matiu had answered Keli's questions on *shifting* along with his questions on Alanui food sources, housing, and cultural beliefs, but again Keli wondered whether he had asked the *right* questions. And even if he had, the fact remained there was no evidence such as a vid to confirm *shifting* existed.

He considered the exchange between Matiu and Jax the previous night. Keli had never seen Matiu angry but he had been angry when

Jax suggested that *shifting* did not matter. It added weight to the premise that *shifting* existed, but muddied the waters about Matiu and Jax's relationship.

Keli did not know whether Jax meant *shifting* did not matter to *anyone*, or to Jax, or whether he had simply tried to soothe Matiu's upset over his lost ability to *shift*. If he had, it had backfired spectacularly.

According to Connel, Ahi were as close as *blood-brothers* and Keli had hoped Matiu would quickly bring Jax onside but last night the two looked anything but close. He supposed their exchange contributed another puzzle-piece to how *shifting* worked, but there were still plenty of holes to plug in his understanding.

If scarring prevented *shifting,* as Matiu implied, then maybe any injury prevented it. Or was it burn injuries in particular, given the inelastic nature of scar-tissue. But the *location* of injuries might be important too. Keli's heart quickened as he considered Matiu's words: *the blast cooked half my body.*

He grunted. Matiu's problem might be the *extent* of his injuries or the destruction of his symmetry, or both. Connel's notes told him Alanui foraged, gardened, and hunted to live, and while foraging and gardening were safer than hunting, none of them were risk free. The Alanui must suffer injuries like anyone else although not extensive ones to *one* side of their bodies.

Keli had read Matiu's medical file and seen photos of his burns. The blast that had wiped Rua from the maps had caught the left side of his body and even quick medical aid had not saved him from scarring. Scar tissue did not stretch like normal skin but *normal* skin did not stretch to accommodate a massive chest or tail, or shrink to fit the skeleton of a bird or fish.

Keli struggled with the urge to dismiss the whole concept. *Assuming* it existed, something as extraordinary as *shifting* must be central to the Alanui's culture, and if it were, it would be as important to Jax as it was to Matiu. So why had Jax suggested the exact opposite?

Keli grabbed Jax's file out of the cabinet and settled back into his chair. Information on Jax's Service to Country was thick with reports of his AWOLs including his refusal to divulge where he had gone and why. Jax had served his time in the cells, returned to his unit, and been the obedient Airman *until* the next time.

All his AWOLs had been in the second half of each year, Keli noticed and frowned, and on an impulse, he retrieved the lunar phases for the same time. There was no correlation between moon phases and the dates and he snorted. He really was grasping at straws if he thought Jax were some sort of werewolf!

He flipped through the rest of Jax's service record in case he had missed something. Jax's psych report put him in the normal range, which was not surprising given the Alanui's supposed ability to mimic *anything*, including being *normal*. Jax's sociability rating was in the normal range too although there were no records of close friendships or sexual relationships. Keli read on and frowned. Jax did not seem to have enjoyed sexual liaisons at Arozi either.

Connel did not know much about Alanui sexual practices but Jax was a good-looking young man by any measure, and Keli was surprised he was celibate, given his Service to Country had been in a mixed unit. There were female Airmen at Arozi too.

He wondered whether sex was prohibited before initiation and retrieved Matiu's file. Rilo was a mixed base but, like Jax, Matiu did not seem to have enjoyed sexual relationships either. Keli sighed. As Connel had pointed out, a sample of two was next to useless. For all Keli knew, life on the big island might be one long orgy, *or* sex might only be allowed after the Ahi had become Ikaika and, if that *were* the case, Jax and Matiu were doomed to celibacy for the rest of their uninitiated lives. Of course they might spurn sex with Off-island *trash*, or simply be horribly shy, and in Matiu's case, his disfigurement might discourage physical intimacy.

Keli glanced up at the wall clock, its broad yellow face in keeping with the dated building. Almost time. Matiu was punctual and Keli went to the window and peered out, careful to stand where he could not be seen. And then right on cue, Matiu appeared on the path with Jax.

Keli was keen to use what he had learned from Connel and kept his attention on Jax. The shifter had adopted the more upright posture of the military, but Keli saw the slight movement of his head as he scanned, and then the flare of his nostrils as he glanced at the window. Keli was obscured from outside but he knew Jax had sensed his presence, almost as if Jax had smelled him.

Irritation washed over him *and* wonder. Jax could be even more useful to Operation V than Keli had thought *if* he cooperated. Keli's attention switched to Matiu. His demeanor was very different from last night, and Keli's attention on him sharpened. Matiu had been angry with Jax but he was not now. He glanced at Jax often, even though Jax kept his gaze straight ahead, and he walked so closely that their hands brushed.

They disappeared from view but Keli remained where he was. Matiu's affection for Jax might be the Ahi closeness Connel had described, or it might be something else. And if it were *something else*, things had just got a whole lot more complicated.

6

Jax made his way back to the building where he had met Matiu the previous night. The sky was a clear-washed blue but he took no pleasure in it. He had not slept well despite the luxury of a bedroom to himself, and a bathroom and small kitchen he shared only with Matiu, something Matiu had briefly pointed out before his bedroom door had slammed shut.

Jax had experienced many angry Off-island males and it made no difference Matiu was Kawai Alanui. Jax's memories of his life on Rua were like an old photograph, robbed of color and form, as if faded by the sun. He barely recognized those in the picture, or where and when it had been taken. It was like looking at something that had never really existed.

His life was in the Arozi Desert now, where he could see to the horizon no matter which way he turned; where the air smelled of sand and yellow grass; where desiccated things fought for life and often failed. There was no water there except that which was drilled, and it tasted of nothing that grew, especially when the wells ran low.

Arozi was an easy place to lose himself in, like Rafi had years before, when his Off-island father had taken his Kawai Alanui mother there and abandoned her, deep in its emptiness, to raise Rafi alone. And it had not been long before Rafi *had* been alone, his mother taken by death, his Kawai Alanui memories as faded as Jax's.

At some point in the years after Jax's nights had ceased to be filled with smoke, and every blink with the flash of Rua's destruction, he had decided Arozi's emptiness suited him. He had worked with Rafi in the ramshackle garage to repair the broken trucks the equally broken locals brought in, and after his Service to Country, had returned to work for the military. His pay cheque gave Rafi an easier life and his Kawai Alanui sensibilities allowed him to present to others whatever they wanted to see.

The desert's emptiness provided nothing to disturb the void inside but he was no longer in the desert. He was in a place where trees crowded close and the air held the faintest tang of salt, and he was with a male who, despite the overlay of soap and toothpaste, bore a scent that threatened to resurrect things that Jax needed to remain dead.

Matiu walked closely beside him but Jax ignored him. He neither wanted Matiu's friendship nor needed it, but he *did* need to know what this new commander wanted so he could deliver it to him and get back to Arozi's blessed emptiness.

'I'm glad you are here, Jax,' said Matiu, as they neared the door of the building.

Jax made no sign of having heard him, just kept his attention on the windows. There did no t seem to be watchers on *this* side of the building and he slowed his pace to let Matiu enter first. It was not any sort of strategy; Matiu's insignia told Jax he ranked higher.

Once inside, Matiu headed for the door directly ahead, knocked once, and when the order was given to enter, led the way in. Jax noted the window where the watcher had stood, the coffee table and lounge chairs to his left, and the desks to his right, the largest occupied by a black-haired officer.

Jax turned in its direction, came to attention, and saluted, but the officer's gaze was on Matiu.

'Wait outside, Senior Airman,' the officer ordered. Matiu's eyes slid sideways to Jax as he passed and Jax heard the door close behind him. Then the officer's attention swung to him. 'I am Lieutenant Colonel Keli, Commander of URZOL. You will address me as Commander Keli.'

'Yes, Commander Keli.'

'Do you know what URZOL is, Airman?'

'No, Commander Keli.' The commander had lounged back in his seat and Jax stiffened his spine to emphasize his subservience.

'URZOL is an acronym, Airman, for the base I command. It stands for the Unit for Research into the Zoaides' Ocean and Lands. And do you know why you have been transferred here?'

'No, Commander Keli.'

The commander eyed him sardonically. 'I am sure you can guess, Airman.'

Jax said nothing. Keli had not ordered him to answer *yet*, but he would. Jax had served under males like Keli during his Service to Country, whose notions of leadership revolved around power and control, and Jax had submitted as long as he could. But there had always come a time when to survive, he must escape to the most isolated place he could find.

And so he had run, and when the storm inside had subsided, had returned to be the obedient Airman the military demanded, *until* the next time. It had been hard to endure the interrogations that followed his *desertions* but the incarcerations, especially in solitary confinement, had aided his recovery.

Keli's hard gaze still considered him and Jax tensed as Keli thrust his chair from his desk and strode past. Keli's footsteps stopped behind him and Jax's heart thundered. Keli could strike him with little risk of repercussions, given his superiority and lack of witnesses, but Keli had no reason to strike him, unless he enjoyed violence. Jax extended his senses and his heart slowed as Keli's breathing revealed he stood near the door, *out of striking range.*

'Are you aware you are one of just two survivors from the island of Rua?' asked Keli from behind him.

'Yes, Commander Keli,' said Jax, although until last night, he had believed himself the *only* survivor.

'And yet you can't guess why you have been transferred to URZOL?'

The commander's tone was mocking but Jax held his silence. Matiu had been here for a while so Keli knew as much about Rua, the Kawai Alanui, and probably Iolana, as Matiu did. Maybe Keli distrusted Matiu and wanted to use Jax to trap him in some lie or other, but Jax had not sensed antagonism when Matiu had spoken of the commander.

'Tell me, Airman, how you came to survive when everyone else on Rua, bar one, was killed.'

'I do not know why I survived, Commander Keli.'

'I didn't ask you *why* you survived, Airman. I asked you *how*,' barked Keli. He was still near the door which meant he could not see Jax's face *unless* there were cams in the room. The patch of ceiling Jax could see without moving his head looked clean but it had been a mistake not to check when he had entered.

'Answer me, Airman!'

'I wasn't on Rua when it blew, Commander Keli.'

'Where were you?'

'Out on the Fayo Sea, Commander Keli.'

'On a boat?'

'No, Commander Keli.' Jax's mouth filled with saliva as he fought to keep the memories at bay.

'Were you in animal-form?' Keli's tone was now belligerent, as if he resented having to ask such a ridiculous question.

Jax swallowed convulsively as he recalled how he and Matiu had argued, how Matiu had *shifted* to redgull, how Jax had pursued him in sun-eagle-form on and on over moana's tossing waves, and how Jax had speared skywards to drop on Matiu as sun-eagles dropped on redgulls when the world had disappeared into a blaze of white. Saliva spilt from his mouth and he wiped it away with the back of his hand.

'Answer the question, Airman! That's an order!'

Jax kept his gaze on the wall in front but it seemed as if he were no longer in the room *or* on Rua, but caught between. Rua's Elders warned Ahi of the perils of straying from Rua's shores and if he had heeded their wisdom, he would be with them now, not marooned here.

He heard the staccato of Keli's boots as Keli strode back and flinched as Keli's angry face appeared in front of him. 'Your insubordination has been noted, Airman,' he clipped out. 'You are confined to your quarters until further orders. Dismissed!'

'Yes, Commander Keli,' said Jax, vaguely aware Keli was back at the door again barking orders at Matiu. Jax saluted, heard the door slam shut behind him, and then he was out in the cool morning sunshine again.

Keli came back to his chair and stabbed at the intercom on his desk. 'Completed?' he demanded.

'Yes, Commander,' came the staticky reply, and Keli's breath hissed in relief.

'You have done well,' he said, clicked off the intercom, and sprawled back in his seat. Jax's reaction to his aggression had been predictable but he had stuck in his heels sooner rather than later and had not budged, despite his stress-response of salivation.

It would be interesting to see whether he now tried to abscond. There were no drinking-holes within walking distance of URZOL to skulk in, although plenty up the coast *if* he turned into a bird and flew. Keli grunted. He still had no proof *shifting* was even possible.

A knock at the door turned out to be Connel with the tape from the ante-room's cam, and Keli snapped it into the vid. It would have been useful to have cams in his office but there had not been time to organize them as well as the mics in Matiu and Jax's quarters, and he had chosen the latter.

They watched the tape in silence and it was easy to see Matiu's distress. The tape came to an end but Connel's brows remained drawn in thought. 'You were *really* shouting at Jax,' he said finally.

'It was mainly for Matiu's benefit. I stood near the door.'

'*Behind* Jax?'

'Jax faced my desk. Would that have worsened his stress?'

'Would an aggressive superior behind you worsen *your* stress?'

'He wiped his mouth,' said Keli, ignoring Connel's disapproval.

'Before or after you ordered him to answer your question?'

Keli considered for a moment. 'Before, which is odd. You said last night spitting is stress-related.'

'I said it was the Kawai Alanui's way of ridding themselves of unwanted thoughts or memories, but if you triggered things Jax wanted to avoid, it would have the same effect.'

'About him *shifting*?' asked Keli.

'*Or* about the form he was in when Rua exploded, *or* why he and Matiu were so far from home, *or* the explosion's aftermath, which must have been horrific.' Connel glanced at him. 'But wasn't today's little experiment about whether their feelings for each other constitute the *vulnerability* you need?'

Keli nodded. 'Matiu remembers nothing about the day of the explosion or his first weeks in the Infirmary. He and Jax were picked up by different boats and ended up at different bases. In the mayhem that followed, no one thought to tell them that the other had survived, and to survive in the first place, they had to have been a long way from Rua.'

'Which itself is unusual,' said Connel. 'The Kawai Alanui don't stray from home and the key purposes of initiation is to tie them even *more* closely to their particular island.'

'Through the totem animal?'

Keli saw Connel suppress a sigh. 'The premise behind a *totem* animal, or spirit-animal as they are sometimes called, is the existence of a special link between the animal and a particular individual, or between the animal and an entire community. For instance, a *totem* animal would not be hunted or eaten, and might be deemed protective of the individual or community, or might serve as a conduit to the spirits or gods. Data on the Kawai Alanui is a long way from complete but *skin-spirit* animals seem only to strengthen the individual's link to their island.'

'How?'

Connel shrugged. 'Have you asked Matiu?'

Keli shook his head. 'It never seemed important.' Connel suppressed a second sigh and Keli's irritation grew. 'Now you are here, *Professor*, you can ask him yourself,' he said brusquely, '*if* there is time, and given the urgency of the situation, there might not be.' He stared at the blank vid for a moment. 'I have had mics installed in Jax and Matiu's quarters.'

'Is that *permitted*?' asked Connel in surprise.

'URZOL's brief extends to the flora and fauna of Samarak's coast,' said Keli smoothly. 'The Fayo Sea washes up seeds and nuts from the islands that take root here and sometimes animals even survive the swim to struggle ashore. And of course, the crossing is easy for birds, despite the Fayo's infamous storms. It is why there are sen-cams in the trees all the way to Rilo Base. It is also useful, *research-wise*, to know which Zoaides' fauna might adapt to human habitats such as buildings. Mics can pick up all sorts of scratchings and squeaks to add to our data.'

'Or human voices,' said Connel acidly.

'No,' said Keli with a cold smile. 'Alanui ones.'

7

*A*nahera sat on the beach's gravel, her chin on her knees, her gaze on the water. She had described how she had discovered the cavern and Tamati had told her to sleep and gone off to explore, but Anahera was too cold to sleep.

The light was as gloomy as it had been on her first visit but she had no idea what time of day it was outside. Tamati prowled around the cavern behind her but all he would find were bigger chunks of the black stone and dull red pebbles that made up the beach.

She shivered. The tunnel robbed the water of warmth and while she dreaded the biting cold of the return journey, she hated sitting around waiting too. The crunch of gravel behind her fell silent and she peered over her shoulder. Tamati had stopped at one of the ceiling cracks, probably to search for peka bats or moko, as she had on her first visit, but the cavern was as empty of bats and lizards now as it had been then.

She shivered again and struggled to her feet. Sitting around just made her colder and she wanted to get the return swim over with. 'I am going back to Lani,' she called to Tamati.

'You need to sleep,' he tossed back, his attention on the roof.

'I will sleep at Lani,' she said and headed off down the beach.

He strode back over the gravel and stopped in front of her. '*If* you make it. You have done enough fool-hardy things for one day, Anahera. Don't add to the tally.'

'Thanks for the advice,' she said, as she side-stepped him. 'I will keep it in mind the next time I am tempted to do something as *fool-hardy* as saving you.'

He shook his head impatiently. 'We both know Ahi need sleep after multiple shifts.'

'I am too cold to sleep.'

He ran his hand down her arm. 'You *are* cold,' he said in surprise.

'Of course I am,' she retorted, shrugging back her hair in irritation. 'Do you think I am a liar as well as a fool?'

She expected an equally bad-tempered response but his expression became unreadable and her attention flicked to his stance. He leaned in but not in aggression and she blinked in confusion.

'I have thought you *many* things Anahera, but never a liar or fool, especially of late,' he added. She was still trying to decipher his words when he spoke again. 'Exhaustion makes it harder to stay warm,' he said briskly. 'Remember that when you are in the Cloud Crown. As for now, the problem is easily solved. I will provide you with a nice warm bed.'

'What . . .' she began, but he had already started to *shift*. The muscular chest in front of her was replaced with a mottled grey one, then a torso that extended to haunches and a tail at one end, and to powerful fore-paws, muscled neck and broad head at the other.

He lowered himself onto the beach, his amber eyes watching her expectantly. A snow-goat's fleece would have been just as snug but Tamati offered her a white-wolf's pelt, the animal she sensed was her skin-spirit. She hesitated but supposed it did not matter while they were both Ahi and she dropped to her knees and curled up in the curve of his body. The gravel crunched as he shuffled closer and the fur of his chest and belly enclosed her naked back.

After being chilled for so long, his warmth was exquisite, as was his scent. 'Thank you, Tamati,' she murmured, and was asleep so quickly she was not aware of his cool muzzle on her neck, of his moist breath as he snuffed her hair, or of his gentle mouthings on her shoulder. Nor did she know of the point at which, close to dawn, he brought his paw over her to lock her close, gave a satisfied whine, and slept too.

Lani was quiet, its awins' window blinds shut against the night's dew. Moths chased midges through the rero, only to be snatched from the air by the scarlet tongues of frogs, but the bats' chitter had faded as they retreated to Wairere's darker places ahead of dawn's slow march.

Lani's only light came from the Kuwain's windows where it spilled past the blinds from the cup-wax lamps inside. The Kuwain sat at Lani's heart, where its soaring beams of carved barim and sides of patterned shingles, dwarfed the surrounding awins of weave and thatch.

Miru barely noticed the sweetness of the cup-wax lamps or the scents of barim and seeli-grass matting as she eased her aching bones on the mat. She preferred her chair of fragrant mina-wood but that was back in her awin. The rites of *ohaku-sai* demanded the oldest traditions be observed and that meant sitting on the floor.

She glanced at her fellow *Kuwaini*. Davi's stern face told her his bones protested as much as hers, and Shenrin's probably more so, given her age, but her face, like Sairin, Anbros and Cheren's betrayed little. It was their rigid backs that revealed their discomfort.

'Shall we make a start?' asked Davi, pulling his cloak closer about his shoulders. The air that seeped past the blinds brought the first hints of winter and Miru rubbed her bare arms. The days would stay fine for a while longer but the perfumed heat of summer was gone.

The Kuwaini nodded and Davi's deep tones filled the Kuwain's cavernous space as he sang of the Kuwai Alanui's beginnings. The song started every ohaku-sai and Miru had heard it countless times before. It told how Whetu's light had guided their ancestors' rafts safely over moana's far reaches to Iolana; of how Whetu had granted them the means to scale Iolana's soaring cliffs; of how Whetu had gifted them oneness with the creatures that made the island their home so that the Kawai Alanui would truly belong too.

He sang of Rua, Ke-one and Puha too; of Tihi's majesty; of the unfathomable mysteries of the Cloud Crown; and of the skin-spirit links that kept the Kawai Alanui whole, regardless of island. Miru's eyelids drooped as Davi's resonant voice carried her across the ocean, deep into Iolana's lush valleys and up Tihi's soaring slopes, and she felt again the terror of her own ohaku journey. And then she was somewhere else, the sky choked with smoke as black as night.

Her eyes flew open but years of practice kept her still, despite the sweat that wove its salty trails down her back. Davi still sang and the Kuwaini's attention was on him, except for Shenrin, whose gaze was on Miru. It was no surprise. Shenrin was a Dream-traveler too, and felt the ripple of Miru's dreams, even as Miru felt hers.

Davi fell silent and there was a sigh as the Kuwaini released their breaths. 'I thank you, Davi,' said Anbros, 'for reminding us of Whetu's gifts and of the task before us.' The rest of the Kuwaini nodded their thanks, as they always did when a song was gifted.

'How many have *chosen to die*?' asked Miru, voicing the ritual question.

'Nine,' said Shenrin and began to sing, her voice crackly with age as she told of the death of Ahi in the Cloud Crown and the birth of Ikaika, so that the ways of the Kawai Alanui continued, at one with all Whetu had gifted. The song ended and again the Kuwaini acknowledged her gift, then looked to Davi once more.

'The nine I know of are Maia, Airini, Malo, Tamati, Hemi, Nikau, Hana, Rawiri and Anahera,' he said. 'Do the Kuwaini know of others?' The circle exchanged glances but no one spoke. Miru held her silence too but her thoughts were not on Iolana's Ahi but on Rua's. The brief dream had reminded her that Rua's Ahi had once completed their ohaku on Iolana as well.

'Are there any of the nine you would exclude before the trials of ohaku-sai begin?' continued Davi. The question was asked at the start of every ohaku-sai and the silence was longer this time, as the Kuwaini considered each Ahi in turn. 'Let us share our thoughts then,' said Davi, when the Kuwain remained quiet. 'Maia?'

'She was strong as a younger Ahi and her strength continues,' offered Cheren. 'She enjoys many friendships and few squabbles.'

'Airini?' asked Davi.

'Strong like Maia,' said Cheren, 'but spends much time alone. Her joy is in solitude rather than the company of others.'

'Malo?' asked Davi.

'Malo,' snorted Anbros. 'We might as well discuss Tamati at the same time and end our ohaku-sai early,' he grumbled. 'The number of times I have had to stitch him.'

'*And* Nikau,' said Shenrin acidly.

'All three are strong,' said Miru diplomatically.

'As are snow-goats,' muttered Shenrin.

'Especially in rut,' added Anbros, 'when they lack *all* fore-thought, like the three we discuss.'

'The nature of older male Ahi is well known,' said Davi smoothly, 'and some of us might remember the passions that drove *us* as older Ahi, and that, by Whetu's grace, became the strengths that drive us as Elders and Kuwaini to keep the Kawai Alanui strong.'

'Are the three ready?' asked Miru quickly, keen to keep the discussion on track as the ache in her hips grew.

'More than ready,' grunted Shenrin.

'Which brings us to Hemi,' said Miru.

'Strong *and* sensible,' said Shenrin. '*He* has friendships rather than rivalries.'

'Hana?' asked Davi, pressing on.

'Very similar to Airini,' said Cheren. 'Strong as a younger Ahi and remains strong. She has many friends.'

'Because she talks non-stop,' said Sairin.

'Rawiri?' asked Davi.

'Strong *and* sensible,' said Shenrin. 'It is a pity more of our males aren't like him.'

'And Anahera?' asked Davi.

'Strong and—,' began Miru and stopped as new sweat pricked her back.

'And?' asked Sairin.

'As goat-headed as our bothersome male threesome,' grumbled Anbros.

'Have you dreamed her?' asked Shenrin, her rheumy eyes on Miru. The rest of the Kuwaini looked too.

'No, but I *am* troubled,' admitted Miru.

'Do you feel she is unready?' asked Davi. Miru shook her head. 'Would you delay her ohaku?' he pursued. The Kuwain hushed and Miru became aware of the chatter of Kawai Alanui beyond the blinds. The sun had breached Tihi's shoulder and people emerged from their awins to draw water for cooking.

There was good reason why the Kuwaini remained silent. Separating an Ahi from their friends risked a type of *wairua*, someone who belonged to neither the new Ikaika or the younger Ahi who followed. And without the care of their friends, Ahi were prone to recklessness. Many of the wairua who haunted Wairere's remoter valleys had been trapped in shift-form when far from their friends' company and care.

But recklessness could also be a sign of frustration, as if an Ahi denied the chance to become Ikaika, chaffed in their present state. She considered Anahera's fall from Tihi, in birth-form *and* clothed, but she also considered *the four*.

'I would not delay her ohaku,' said Miru finally, but even as the words left her mouth, sweat started afresh.

The Kuwaini's relief was palpable but Shenrin's craggy face remained intent on her. 'The trials of ohaku-sai are yet to start,' said Davi comfortingly, 'and as we know, the final decision as to who is ready for ohaku, comes *after* their completion. There is plenty of time.'

8

*A*nahera was cold again when she woke but the gnawing fatigue had gone and she sat up. Tamati was back in birth-form pacing up and down the beach, a sure sign he was impatient to be gone. That suited her; she had delayed in the gloom long enough.

'We take wheke-form,' he said, when he saw she was awake. 'Once we reach the surface, we use shia-form and fly to Hapua. There are plenty of casberries there and pan-reed.'

Anahera bristled at his smooth assumption of control. Food for his belly and pan-reed for his modesty *and* hers, she thought acidly. 'It would be better to *shift* to redgulls to clear moana,' she said. 'It takes a lot of strength for shia lift off from water.'

'Shia aren't vulnerable to sun-eagle strike.'

'Redgulls can out fly sun-eagles,' she countered.

'Only sometimes and only at *full* strength,' he said, hands coming to his hips. 'It is a long time since either of us ate and you have too many *shifts* behind you. Find a wave-rock if you must, but for once in your life, Anahera, show some sense.'

Anahera scrambled to her feet to deliver a stinging retort, but managed to bite it back. She had argued with Tamati *and* Malo countless times over the years, but never over her safety and she wondered whether the ending of being Ahi was to blame for Tamati's sudden obsession with it. Miru warned that Iolana got more dangerous for Ahi as they neared Ikaika but maybe it was the Ahi who drew danger by becoming reckless. The idea was far from comforting.

Tamati waited, his eyes an intense green in the cave's grey light and it struck Anahera that the cavern's light had not changed in the time she had slept. A shiver ran over her skin that had nothing to do with cold. 'Let's go then,' she said tightly.

She sensed his surprise at her lack of argument but his voice betrayed nothing. 'You go first,' he said.

He wanted her ahead of him, *safely* in vision-range, and she grimaced and stepped into the water. It was as cold as she feared and a new current tugged at her legs. She *shifted* when she was waist deep and dived. It was an easier swim out because the current pulled her in the direction she must go. Now she did not have to worry about hauling Tamati along, she was aware of how her wheke skin picked up the smallest sparks of light. Even so, she was relieved to see the shimmer of moana's waves above.

She surfaced, *shifted* to birth-form, then to shia, but her sodden plumage dragged her down as she had predicted. She struggled to flap her wings in the water and then somehow managed to get airborne. It was dawn, the sky pink-tinged but she barely had the strength to stay aloft let alone enjoy her favorite time of day *or* check that Tamati followed.

She headed north, skirted the cliff's ribbon waterfalls, and turned into the Hapua Valley. It was lush like the rest of Wairere and she forced herself on until Hapua's gleaming lagoon appeared below her, then stilled her aching wings and glided.

She had intended to beat them again as she neared the ground, but the effort was too much and she landed heavily and was thrown forward into the pan-reeds. Her shia brain cried out for rest while her birth-form brain hammered her to *shift*, but Tamati was right. Too many *shifts* and too little food were a dangerous combination and she flapped deeper into the comforting shelter of the pan-reeds, and let her eyes close.

Tamati watched in horror as Anahera disappeared from the sky and angled sharply into a dive to land on the lagoon's shores but there was no sign of her. He threw back his head and trumpeted in alarm and upslope, a rero's branches exploded as shia burst from them.

Tamati *shifted* to birth-form, even as the shia did, but fear for Anahera blunted his surprise at Malo and Airini's presence. 'Anahera's here somewhere, probably locked in shia-form,' he told them urgently. 'We *must* find her.'

'We heard a crash but thought it was hawklings squabbling,' said Airini quickly. 'It came from those pan-reeds,' she added, gesturing behind them.

'We sweep, starting at the shore-line,' ordered Tamati. 'A shia would go to ground.'

For once Malo did not argue and they hurried into the reeds, took up position an arm's-length apart and moved forwards together, their senses trained on their surroundings. Pan-reeds grew densely and the old growth near the ground was the same mottled cream, grey and brown as a hen-bird's plumage.

They had completed one careful sweep and started on a second, when Airini's nostrils flared and she stared to her left. 'I have found her!'

Malo and Tamati hastened after her deeper into the reeds and all three bent over the prone hen-bird. She was motionless, eyes shut, wings splayed in a protective shield. 'We need to bring her back,' said Malo urgently.

'You aren't telling me anything new!' snapped Tamati, as he considered how best to do it. He did not want to use sexual bait to reclaim her as she had reclaimed him because they were too close to Ahi's ending *and* Malo was there.

Airini's gaze flicked between them. 'Leave her to me,' she ordered.

'We don't have much time,' said Tamati. 'We need to—'

'You aren't telling me anything new,' said Airini tartly.

Malo moved away back towards the lagoon and Tamati reluctantly followed until a thick stand of pan-reeds separated them from Airini and the senseless shia. Neither Tamati nor Malo spoke, just listened for the smallest sounds that would confirm Anahera was safe.

Tamati guessed Airini would *shift* to shia-form and use song to tempt Anahera back. Shia hens built bonds through harmonies rather than display and it was not long before cooing started and he exchanged glances with Malo as Airini interspersed higher notes with those that thrummed in her throat.

'When I heard you had plunged into moana, I feared the worst,' whispered Malo after a little.

'I am very much alive, as you can see,' muttered Tamati, straining to hear that Anahera was too.

Malo's hand turned Tamati's face to his. 'For which I am grateful.'

A dapple of sunlight turned Malo's eyes to honey and Tamati's heart quickened. 'You worry too much,' he said softly.

'Or not enough,' said Malo. He slid his hand under Tamati's hair and drew him close. 'We are running out of time, *aroha*,' he whispered, and rested his forehead against Tamati's. 'Soon—'

The shia song stopped and Tamati's heart pounded, then they

both turned as the reeds rustled and Airini stepped through. She had shrugged her hair forward to cover herself which told Tamati her concerns were for Ahi conventions now, not Anahera, and his gut unclenched.

'All is well,' she confirmed 'but Anahera needs to rest and then eat. We will join you at the casberry grove later.'

Airini disappeared back into the reeds, and Tamati and Malo set off in the opposite direction. They did not go far before they stopped in a stand of reeds, lush with new growth, harvested a selection of stems and leaves and then settled on the lagoon's shores to fashion whitikis. *Shifting* often meant the loss of clothing, but Ahi were adept at making new paras and whitikis and clothes of ceremonial importance remained safely in Lani.

They worked for a while in companionable silence, stripping the reeds of fibre, plaiting them into loin-straps, and weaving in skirts of leaves at the front. 'I am going to wash off moana's salt first,' said Tamati when they had finished.

Malo nodded and followed him into the water, his slow strokes mirroring Tamati's as they swam out into the lagoon. Hapua's waters were silken after moana's buffet and when Tamati reached the lagoon's centre, he flipped onto his back and floated. The air was warm and the sunshine bright, and he let his senses roam. Pulses of sweetness came from samora on the eastern shore and the placid chirp of silvercrests confirmed no screech-cat hunted nearby.

'Tell me what happened after you plunged into moana,' said Malo, as he floated alongside.

'I don't know exactly,' said Tamati, intent on the cloudless sky. 'I was knocked senseless by the trees.'

'Those you led in display said Anahera caused the accident.'

'Did they?' said Tamati noncommittedly.

'And they wonder, given her foolishness, whether she is ready for ohaku.'

Tamati rolled onto his belly. 'As *older* Ahi, they should know it is the Kuwaini who decide who is ready to enter the Cloud Crown, not them,' he said tersely.

'So, what happened?' pursued Malo. 'You have been gone more than a day.'

'Anahera *shifted* to wheke and kept me safe until I came to my senses. Then we *shifted* to shia and came here.'

Malo's puzzlement was clear. '*Kept you safe*? In wheke-form? How?'

'Ask *her*,' muttered Tamati and struck out for shore. Anahera had found the cavern when she pursued Malo into the tunnel but apparently Malo had swum out before *he* had discovered it. Ahi rarely kept secrets from each other but knowledge of the cavern might be the preserve of the Ikaika, or the Elders, or solely of the Kuwaini, in which case, Tamati had no right to speak of it.

He padded from the water, donned his whitiki, and watched Malo don his. Malo's water-sleeked body gleamed and Tamati's blood fired again, but then his gaze was drawn to Tihi. 'Not long now,' he said hoarsely.

Malo kissed him tenderly but Tamati returned the kisses hungrily. 'Sometimes I want nothing to change,' he growled, 'and sometimes I can't bear the sameness a moment longer.'

'Your beauty won't change,' said Malo, as he stroked Tamati's cheek. 'Whatever ohaku brings, that will be the same.'

'*Whatever ohaku brings*,' muttered Tamati, and stared up at Tihi again.

The Kuwai Alanui were born in its shelter and as they grew, climbed higher up its slopes. Like his friends, there had come a time when Tamati had left Wairere's emerald valleys and crystal waterfalls behind for Kohatu's band of black stone, and then for Makariri's snowlands, but that was where his journey and those of his friends had ended.

They could not enter the cloud that circled Tihi like a second sky until ohaku, and only then, when their skin-spirit tethers were safely in place, could they look upon Tihi's peak, Huna, and know who they truly were.

'We are still Ahi, Tami,' Malo reminded him, 'and I am hungry. Let's eat.'

Tamati forced a smile. 'You being hungry all the time won't change either,' he said, 'and nor should it,' he added quietly.

'The casberries,' prompted Malo, and they set off along the shore.

9

Jax strode back to his quarters, barely aware of Matiu by his side. This base was no different to Arozi or Nakoda, he told himself, and he had survived Off-islanders like Keli at both, *except* at Nakoda, men had soon lost interest in his *Zoaides* heritage and at Arozi, he had lived off-base and been left alone to carry out his duties, whereas here, Keli had made his *particular* interest in Jax very clear indeed.

URZOL: the Unit for Research into the Zoaides Oceans and Lands, *and* into *shifter-twisters* like *him*? Was that why he had been transferred? To serve as a research specimen? He had a vision of dogs with muzzles taped shut and chimps with wires jutting from their veins, and spat to one side. Even worse, Matiu was part of this outfit!

'What is your role here?' he demanded, keeping his gaze straight ahead.

'I am an Airman like you.'

'You aren't like me!' Jax wrenched open the door to their quarters and would have slammed it in Matiu's face had Matiu not thrust his boot out.

Matiu followed him across the small kitchen. 'We need to speak, Jax.'

'Not if you are part of *them*!'

'Sit down, Jax.'

Jax stopped, his hand on the door to his room. 'Is that an order, *Senior* Airman?'

'Yes.'

Jax turned back to the table and threw himself onto a chair and Matiu sat opposite. Jax knew he needed to present the same calm, compliant exterior to Matiu as he did to other Off-islanders but Matiu *was not* an Off-islander and the understanding was like a knife in the gut.

'I have been ordered to stay with you today,' said Matiu quietly.

'In case I abscond?'

'I am not privy to Commander Keli's thoughts.'

'Are there cams or mics in here?'

Matiu looked at him in surprise. 'Of course not.'

'What makes you so sure?'

'It is against regulations to covertly monitor military personnel in their quarters.'

'*Human* military personnel but we are *flash-monkeys*.' Matiu grimaced and Jax leaned forward. 'Don't like *that* term, *Senior* Airman? How about *twister-shifters* then? Is that any better?'

'We are Kawai Alanui, Jax.'

'You might be. I've been nothing since Rua blew.'

'We belonged to all four islands and still live on Iolana. Why didn't you go there?'

'You asked me that before.'

'You didn't answer.'

'And I'm not answering you this time either. You can note that down as my *second* act of insubordination for the day, *Senior* Airman.'

'Why wouldn't you tell Commander Keli the shift-form you were in when Rua exploded?'

Jax stared straight ahead and Matiu sighed and went to the sink. Jax heard him fill the kettle but the sound echoed moana's slide over Rua's gravel beaches and he winced. To survive, he *had* to banish memories of his old life.

Matiu returned with mugs of coffee and Jax nodded his thanks and sipped the bitter brew. The daylight showed the full extent of Matiu's burns, his dark brown crew-cut pocked with coin-sized bald patches and the side of his forehead, cheek and jaw, ridged with hard white lines. But the daylight also revealed the emerald-green depths of his eyes, the curve of his jaw, and the shape of his lips. Jax's gut churned and he shifted his gaze to a point beyond Matiu's shoulder.

'Don't do that, Jax,' said Matiu softly. 'Don't pretend our time in Rua didn't exist.'

'Is that an order *Senior* Airman?'

'It is a request.'

Jax kept his gaze beyond Matiu's shoulder but he started to sweat and Matiu's warm hand closed over his. 'Jax ...'

Jax wrenched his hand free and there was a long silence before Matiu rose again. He went to the window this time and stood staring out. The line of Matiu's shoulder and flank were hauntingly familiar but his Off-islander muscles, like his scars, were also obvious in the light and Jax struggled to swallow the bile that rose in his throat.

'I have no memories of the day Rua exploded,' said Matiu softly. 'The blast caused a concussion that lasted for weeks and I was medicated to control the pain of the burns.' He swung back. 'I want to know why we were so far from Rua.'

Sweat soaked Jax's shirt and Matiu came back to the table. 'Why won't you tell me? *You* escaped injury! *You* are whole and unmarked.' He leaned forward over the table. 'Nothing prevents *you* from living whatever life *you* choose, either here *or* on Iolana, while I am confined here. *I* have no choices, Jax! You owe me an answer!'

Matiu's hand slammed down on the table but Jax kept his gaze straight ahead and Matiu's mouth twisted in contempt. 'You know where I am when you remember what it means to be Kawai Alanui, Jax, *and* honor it.'

Matiu strode away and the door to his room slammed shut but Jax remained frozen. Then, as the bile surged again he scrambled to the sink and vomited. He continued to retch and sweat dripped from his forehead. '*Aroha*,' he whispered, and shut his eyes.

Keli's intense gaze flashed to Connel. 'Did you catch that word?' he asked sharply.

'It was too soft. It sounded like *mahoha*,' said Connel doubtfully.

'Do you know what it means?'

'No. But it is interesting the rest of the exchange was in English. I thought they would speak Kawai Alanui in private. I presume it has been taped for *research*?' Keli nodded. 'Can we hear it again?' Keli replayed the tape and concentrated on the nuances. At least he had learned to do that much from the *Professor*! He preferred a visual to an audio any day but that might be pushing his luck with his superiors *and* the regulations, a bit *too* far.

The recording came to an end but Connel still gazed into space and Keli's fingers drummed the desk. 'Jax vomited after Matiu left,' he prompted.

'Yes,' said Connel.

'So his stress levels were extremely high? Connel nodded. 'Then why not answer Matiu's questions? They seemed reasonable enough.'

'They spoke English which suggests they are estranged,' said Connel slowly. 'The Kuwai Alanui are very close, especially as Ahi, but no culture is immune from conflict.'

'Just my luck to have the only Alanui outside the Zoaides who hate each other's guts,' muttered Keli.

Connel shook his head. 'Matiu was reaching out to Jax.'

'How do the Alanui view homosexuality?' asked Keli abruptly.

'They don't.'

Keli's brows shot up. 'What do you mean?'

'They differentiate life-stages very formally, but everything else, including sexuality, seems to be irrelevant. The Kawai Alanui are either young Ahi, or older Ahi, or Ikaika, or Elders. I am guessing that when you can *shift* between human and animal forms, your sexual preferences in *any* form are irrelevant.' Connel considered him thoughtfully. 'You think Jax and Matiu are gay and their stand-off is a lover's tiff?'

'Their files show no sexual liaisons.'

'They might be more discreet than the average Airman,' said Connel dryly. 'I understand that homosexuality is legal in the military though hardly celebrated. Anything else you have noticed?'

'Matiu walks so close to Jax he touches him.'

'That could be a Kawai Alanui trait *or* you could be right about their relationship.'

Keli took a quick turn around the room to counter his frustration. 'Did Jax and Matiu break some sort of Alanui law by leaving Rua?'

'Young Kawai Alanui are warned against straying and the purpose of their initiation rites, as I have said, is to tie them more closely to the islands. But as far as I know, there is no actual punishment for Ahi or Ikaika who choose to leave.'

'Yet none of them *choose* to leave, do they?' said Keli, throwing himself back into his chair. 'Why so much emphasis on staying, Connel? Even when the four islands were inhabited, they hardly offered a rich or varied life-style, especially to the young.'

'To our Off-islander sensibilities perhaps,' said Connel. 'In a way, the Kawai Alanui remind me of the military.'

'How?'

'When men and women join the military, they become part of a family which understands and supports them. They live in the same way, obey the same rules, and face the same dangers. They might lose individual freedoms but they gain a *very* strong sense of belonging.'

'Perhaps,' said Keli noncommittedly, rocking back on his chair. 'What else did you get from the exchange?'

'That Matiu is wrong about Jax and that we probably are too.'

Keli's chair thumped back to the floor. 'In what way?'

'Matiu said Jax had *escaped injury* and was *whole and unmarked* and Matiu is correct, *if* he refers to Jax's body not his mental state.'

'Jax's psych and social reports put him in the normal range,' Keli reminded him.

'Which is where *our* mistake might lie,' said Connel. 'The military's medical systems are designed to measure *human* attributes, not Kawai Alanui ones.'

Keli shrugged. 'Matiu obviously sees Jax as *normal* or he wouldn't be so angry with him.' Keli paused. 'I have never known Matiu to lose his temper over anything or anyone before.'

'Which supports my contention that he is wrong about Jax too. He expects Jax to act like a Kawai Alanui, or an Ahi, and when Jax doesn't, he concludes Jax is being bloody-minded. But *if* Jax *were* playing some sort of power game, he wouldn't have vomited.' Connel paused to let his words sink in. 'It is also instructive how Jax describes himself.'

'What?' asked Keli, grappling with the implications of dealing with a shifter who might also be mentally ill.

'When Matiu reminded him he was Kawai Alanui, Jax said, and I quote: *You might be. I've been nothing since Rua blew.*'

Keli rubbed his hand through his hair. 'What did he mean by that?'

'That he doesn't see himself as Kawai Alanui anymore *or* as an Off-islander.'

'Which makes him what?'

Connel shrugged. 'Nothing, I suppose, which is a dangerous state to exist in.'

'But his psych and social reports didn't pick up a damned thing,' said Keli in exasperation. Hell and Purgatory! His plans for Jax's role in Operation V were unravelling like rotten rope right before his very eyes.

'They wouldn't. As I have said before, the Kawai Alanui are expert mimics. Think of Jax as a mirror, Commander. He gives back to the observer exactly what they expect to see, but it hasn't taken much to crack the glass. I suspect the desert was a good place for him, because it demanded so little but then he was brought here and came face to face with Matiu. *If* I am right, that would have been Jax's worse nightmare. Matiu belongs to a time so painful that, to survive, Jax has severed all connection to it.'

'He could throw in his lot with the military *trash*,' said Keli tightly.

'Committing to the *opala* isn't an option for him either.'

'Which leaves us where?' demanded Keli.

'Probably with a young man who needs the therapy he should have received ten years ago when he was pulled out the Fayo.'

Keli paced around the room again. 'There's no time for that now,' he said, glancing at the grubby clock on the wall. He needed a shifter who could *shift*, who was committed to the Zoaides, and who could be trusted not to betray his Off-islander comrades. He had hoped Jax would fit the bill, but that seemed increasingly unlikely, *unless* Keli altered his approach.

'Are things so urgent?' asked Connel carefully.

Keli nodded. 'I can't wait for Jax to *decide* to cooperate,' he said. 'There is too much at stake.' His breath sifted between his teeth as he considered his options. 'I'm sending him to Rilo,' he said abruptly.

'You mean the base in the Rilo Valley?'

'Yes.'

'Why there?' asked Connel.

'If Jax won't respond to persuasion, we will try force.' Keli smiled grimly. 'Rilo has a very demanding training course.'

'Jax's issues are mental, Commander, not physical.'

'I am aware of that, *Professor*, but pushing a man to breaking point *physically*, can bring about some interesting mental changes. Jax might decide that life at URZOL is preferable to Rilo's *requirements*.'

'Or *shift* and fly away.'

'There is no evidence he has *shifted* since Rua exploded but we will be prepared. If *Airman* Jax decides he wants out, he won't be going *anywhere* except the cells.'

10

Airini waited until Tamati and Malo's footsteps had crunched away through the reeds before she returned to Anahera and knelt by her side. Anahera stared straight ahead, but her eyes were their usual amber, not the shia's gold and Airini smoothed the hair from her face. It was the same red-brown as a sun-eagle's breast and Airini sang the sun-eagle's song as she finger-combed it.

Anahera sighed as the song came to an end. 'I could stay here all day,' she murmured.

Airini smiled. 'That is a very good idea. You need rest and it is peaceful in the reeds.'

'You like quiet more than me,' said Anahera, making the reeds rustle as she sat up, 'and I am ravenous.'

'There are plenty of casberries in the grove or there were. Malo and Tamati have probably gorged them by now but I know something you will enjoy. Stay here.'

She slipped away to the lagoon's shore, *shifted* to otter-form, and dived. Water chestnuts grew thickly and she piled them up on the mossy shore, *shifted* back and washed them free of the rich, dark mud. A quick weave of pan-reeds served as a basket and she hastened back, relieved Anahera remained where she was.

'Eat,' she said, setting the basket between them. Anahera needed no further encouragement and for a while the only sound was them crunching their way through the chestnuts' sweet white flesh.

'Did you come here with Malo?' asked Anahera.

'I came here to collect samora flowers for my hair but you know Malo.' She smiled ironically. 'He can't stand his own company.'

'And then me and Tamati crashed in on you.'

'*Crashed* is a good way to describe it,' said Airini, looking at her sideways. 'Malo was worried about you *and* about Tamati. Word of your fall and of you both ending up in moana is all over Lani.'

'I lost my footing, that's all. It's not the first time I've done something stupid.'

'Even Ikaika are prone to such moments,' said Airini diplomatically.

'Though not Tamati or Malo,' muttered Anahera.

'Only in their own minds,' added Airini with a grin. 'It will be interesting to see how we change after ohaku.'

'The newest Ikaika don't seem much different,' said Anahera, as she finished off the last of the chestnuts.

'Really? They know their skin-spirits, they gaze on Huna, they court. Some have even mate-paired.'

Anahera brushed the crumbs from her belly. 'Apart from that.'

'Isn't that everything?' asked Airini, finger-combing her own hair.

'I don't know.' Anahera's eyes flashed to hers reminding Airini of her own fears and of Malo's, although he did not admit to them.

'Miru says Iolana grows more dangerous as ohaku approaches, but I don't see how,' said Airini.

'I've been thinking about her words too,' admitted Anahera. 'She's a Dream-traveler,' she added uneasily.

'Yes, but a cliff is still a cliff and moana's currents don't suddenly change direction,' said Airini. 'Maybe Miru means Ahi change, that we take more risks, like you did cliff-climbing in birth-form.' She half smiled to soften her words. 'It's as if we forget the nature of Wairere and Kohatu and Makariri; as if we forget our *own* natures. Maybe it's some sort of preparation for the Cloud Crown, where we lose everything we know to become something new.'

Anahera stared at her. 'That is an odd thing to say.'

'Yes,' said Airini, and concentrated on the golden-flies that hovered nearby.

The flies' lives seemed simple compared to hers, she thought enviously, and felt Anahera's hand on her knee. 'Odd, but probably true,' said Anahera, 'although I can't imagine *you* doing anything stupid. You see more deeply than me. My gut ties itself in knots and you calmly explain why.'

'Not *calmly*.'

Anahera struggled to her feet. 'Those water chestnuts were delicious but I keep thinking of casberries. Let's sort some clothes and get to the grove before Malo and Tamati *do* eat it out.'

They searched out a suitable stand of pan-reeds, and Anahera stripped out the fibre for whitikis, while Airini fashioned paras. 'It would have been useful had Whetu made us like other creatures with no need of clothing,' grumbled Anahera, as she looped the fibres around her toe to keep them taut and started to plait. 'Or made us males, so we only needed whitikis.'

'Do you really want to be like Malc and Tamati?' asked Airini as she worked. 'Strutting around at the head of display? Having to prove yourself faster and stronger and smarter than other male Ahi?'

'Not really,' said Anahera, although her face suggested she did.

'Here,' said Airini, handing her a para. 'Let me help with the whitikis. You have yet to regain your strength.'

'I feel completely normal,' said Anahera, not pausing in her plaiting.

'I will gather samora blooms then,' said Airini, and headed off towards the stand. Most of the blossoms were spent but the last few of summer clung to the branches. The next time they blossomed she would be Ikaika, she realized in wonder.

She breathed in the blooms' heady scent as she searched for colors to complement her and Anahera's hair then made her way back. Anahera had finished the whitikis and looked more cheerful. 'I will groom your hair, then you can groom mine,' said Airini, slipping on the whitiki and fastening the para around her breasts.

'It might be the last time we groom with these,' said Anahera, as she fingered the blossoms.

'Yes,' said Airini, lifting Anahera's hair forward over her shoulder and starting to braid. 'It will be good to wear pearl shell. The Ikaika look so much more *mature* and shell lasts longer than flowers.' She wove in the samora blooms as she worked, choosing the paler colors for Anahera, then tied off the braid.

'Are you really looking forward to wearing shell?' asked Anahera, starting on Airini's hair. The crimson and purple blooms glowed against Airini's black hair which, with her grey eyes, made her as striking as Tamati.

'I would be if I didn't have to complete ohaku first,' said Airini, pulling a face.

Anahera laughed, finished Airini's braid and stood back to admire her handiwork. 'You look beautiful.'

Airini clasped Anahera's hands. 'So do you, as is fitting for Ahi females on the verge of Ikaika. I wonder if our *handsome* males will notice how lovely we are, or whether they will be too busy proving which of them is stronger.'

'Or quicker at filling their bellies,' added Anahera dryly.

'Probably the last,' said Airini.

'Come,' said Anahera. 'I'm keen to fill mine too.'

Tamati was relieved to see Anahera in birth-form and now she had replaced her whitiki and para, he did not have to avert his gaze. The females had groomed too, and the braid made Anahera look more Ikaika. She had changed since last winter and although she was just as impatient, she no longer challenged *everything* he said, although she still did fool-hardy things like climbing cliffs in birth-form. At least Whetu had ensured she had crashed into *his* arms although given his near-drowning, he could probably do without Whetu's meddling!

Malo was appraising Anahera too and Tamati resisted the urge to shift to snow-goat-form and use his horns to remind Malo which of them was stronger. Instead he made a show of lowering his head to formally welcome both female Ahi before he focused on Anahera again. 'Are you recovered?' he asked her.

'Of course,' she said, acknowledging Malo with a nod. 'You have made a good harvest, I see,' she added dryly, her gaze on the strew of casberry pips.

'For all of us,' said Tamati smoothly, and gestured to the pile of casberries behind him. 'Sit and eat.'

'Airini gathered water chestnuts for me,' said Anahera, as they settled on the moss. 'Otherwise you would have to fight me for them.'

Tamati scooped up a handful and offered them to her. 'No need for fighting,' he said with a smile. His hands brushed hers as he delivered them, but she simply passed half to Airini.

Malo continued to eye her as she ate. 'Tamati says I should ask you how you kept him safe in moana when you were in wheke-form,' he said.

'Did he?' said Anahera, busy with the casberries.

'Well?'

'You know what wheke are like, Malo,' she said, licking casberry juice from her fingers. 'They have eight legs: two to hold up a senseless Ahi in shia-form and six to swim with. More than enough to solve the problem.'

'Swim *where*? You were gone over a day.'

'Which means I should get back to Lani,' she said, scrambling upright.

Tamati rose too. 'It is getting late. We should—' he began, but at that moment, a shia swept overhead, circled back, and came into land.

It carried a whitiki in its claws and there was a blur as Rawiri's head appeared, followed by the rest of him. He turned away, pulled on his whitiki, and turned back. 'Miru sent me to find you,' he said without preamble. 'The Kuwaini summon those who have *chosen to die*. You are to come now.'

11

*A*nahera kept her gaze on the lush valleys below as they flew back to Lani. They had *shifted* to shia-form and Tamati led with Malo and Rawiri to either side, and she and Airini between them. Tamati had insisted the configuration was the safest, from what, he had not said and Anahera had not bothered to ask. Neither had anyone else. Maybe like her they found his new obsession with safety as annoying as his old one with winning.

The evening air held pockets of warmth and scents that were sweet and spicy, and nearer moana, laced with salt. Twilight smudged the stands of brack, rero and barim, the paler patches of seeli-grass and the drifts of creeper- and stringer-vines a flower with purple blooms. It silvered the narrow streams and aqua lagoons too, and the ribbon waterfalls' snowy fumes where they fell to clash with moana's grey.

It was all so beautiful that for a moment Anahera was overcome with fear she would lose it and her wingbeats faltered. Airini's bright shia-eyes flashed to hers but then Anahera righted herself. The Kuwaini ensured that all those who set out for the Cloud Crown lived to return.

Anahera carried her clothing in her talons, as did the rest of the group and when Tamati, Malo and Rawiri descended to land in the brack on Lani's perimeter, Anahera and Airini flew on to the rero.

'Tamati has changed,' said Airini as they dressed amongst the trees.

'You mean his latest obsession with safety?' said Anahera. Airini nodded. 'He went on about it after I fell off the cliff too, but it will be something else tomorrow. You know Tamati; he always wants to be the leader. The next thing will probably be explaining why white-wolves make better skin-spirits than sun-eagles.'

'No skin-spirit animal is superior to any other,' said Airini. 'They all gift belonging.'

'Ah, but the white-wolf is so beautiful,' teased Anahera. 'So swift and strong, and with a pelt like moana in storm. Surely the white-wolf is superior to the redgull?'

'Redgulls know moana as well as Iolana. They fly closer to Whetu and see further than the white-wolf,' said Airini quietly.

'You are right,' said Anahera, nonplussed she had never considered the redgull's attributes.

'What you say of the white-wolf is true though,' continued Airini. 'Which is why Tamati will seek it, and Malo, and you. But remember, it is the *creature* who chooses us, who binds *us* to the Kawai Alanui, not we who choose the creature, and it all unfolds in Whetu's realm.'

'Why do you think Tamati, Malo and I will seek the white-wolf?' asked Anahera, rankling at being lumped together with the sparring males.

'Because it is so beautiful, and swift, and strong,' mimicked Airini.

'So is a sun-eagle,' countered Anahera. Airini said nothing and Anahera tucked a stray lock of Airini's hair back amongst the samora blooms. 'I always wished I had your black hair,' she said.

'And I always wished I had your amber eyes,' returned Airini with a smile.

Anahera glanced up at Tihi. 'Soon none of it will matter.'

'Ahi friendships will always matter,' said Airini, her gaze on the peak too.

'Are you frightened?' whispered Anahera, her thoughts on *the four*.

'Of course not. Are you?'

'Of course not.'

Their arms came around each other and they held each other tight. Airini's hair was soft against Anahera's face and its samora blossoms fragrant, and she closed her eyes.

'The Kuwaini are waiting for us,' said Airini, but neither moved, and then a wolf howled, high above the Cloud Crown, and Anahera shivered. 'Let us go,' said Airini, and hand in hand, they made their way through the trees to Lani.

Miru eyed the last of the Ahi as they filed into the Kuwain. It was predictable Tamati, Malo and Anahera had been in some far flung valley but she was surprised Airini had been hard to find as well. Airini held Anahera's hand which confirmed that, despite Anahera's more thoughtless escapades, she was as anxious as the rest. Ohaku marked the death of the old self and the birth of the new, and no one pretended that was easy, or the Cloud Crown anything other than perilous.

Airini and Anahera settled with the other female Ahi and the male Ahi sat together too. They could sit anywhere on the seeli-grass mats but it was the same with every group on the verge of ohaku.

Davi said the males sought solace in those they had displayed with, and the females with those they had groomed and shared song with, but Miru believed there was more to it than that. The trials of the ohaku-sai marked the first step towards Ikaika, when the Ahi's primary attachment transferred to Iolana, so it was natural they clung together for as long as they could.

The Kuwain hushed as Davi began the song of endings and beginnings, and Miru closed her eyes as the music washed over her like the cool air from the window. The song spoke more of shia chicks high in their woody nests than the shia bones that crumbled on the forest floor, but it was fitting. The songs of death came later, when the Ahi trekked away from Lani for the last time.

Her gaze roved over those who had *chosen to die*. She had seen them born and overseen their first clumsy *shifts*, and now she prepared them for death. The Ahi gathered in the Kuwain were uncharacteristically solemn, but as the song went on, their straight backs relaxed a little and their gazes wondered. Miru watched *where* their gazes wandered, as did the rest of the Kuwaini. The Ahi who stared up at the Kuwain's carved beams or down at the seeli-mats told a different tale to those who gazed straight ahead or at other Ahi.

Ahi friendships and rivalries were intense and sometimes destructive, but after Ikaika, both must serve Iolana. Friendships united the Iolani and kept them strong and the passions generated by rivalries could too, *if* channeled towards Iolana's protection, but they had the potential to fracture groups as well, especially where mate-pairs were involved.

There were four females and five males in this group and the Iolani needed children from at least some of them. The last group of Ahi had generated three mate-pairs from eight males and seven females, but two of the mate-pairs had been male. The remaining males and females could be waiting to mate-pair with Ahi from *this* group, Miru comforted herself, or an earlier group might court *them*.

55

Hemi stared straight ahead, as did Hana, but Maia's eyes flicked to Rawiri more than once, and his to her. It was a good sign. Both were sensible and would make strong parents. Nikau's gaze drifted around the hall and he plucked at the seeli-mat as if already bored with the ohaku-sai, and Miru suppressed a sigh and shifted her attention to Airini and Anahera. They still held hands and the matching blooms in their hair told her they had lately groomed.

It would be a surprising mate-pair *if* they joined. Airini was quiet and introspective while Anahera was anything but, yet sometimes opposite traits were complementary. She turned her attention to Malo and Tamati. They also sat closely but there was no mistaking where their gazes went.

It would be convenient if one paired with Airini and the other with Anahera but Whetu was seldom *convenient*. The storms that tore the brack down were not *convenient* nor the tides that battered Iolana's cliffs, and Miru wondered whether the unease she felt when she considered Anahera, flowed from Tamati and Malo. They had spent a lot of time together but over the last couple of years, Anahera had made their twosome into a threesome, and threesomes seldom augured well.

Davi's song came to an end and Sairin cleared her throat. 'The Kuwaini welcome those who have *chosen to die*,' she said formally. 'Dawn marks the start of the trials of ohaku-sai the journeys you take in preparation for your ohaku. You will not complete the ohaku-sai trials alone. We, the Kuwaini, will guide you so that when you set out on your final journey of ohaku, you will know the way.

'The first trial of ohaku-sai is this: at dawn you will go to Kohatu. You must journey there alone but you may choose company for your return. When you reach Kohatu, you will select something to bring to us. You will not eat or drink during the journey. Nor will you *shift*.'

Sairin dipped her head as did the rest of the Kuwaini and the mats rustled as the Ahi filed out. They looked relieved, as Ahi always did when they discovered the first trial was to a place they knew well and wouldn't inflict great hunger or thirst.

Some would already be planning the fastest route, others the easiest, but the Kuwaini had no interest in how quickly or cleverly the Ahi completed the trek. They were interested in what they *chose* to bring back. Kohatu's black shattered stone looked much the same to the younger Ahi eye, but what it looked like to an Ahi on the verge of Ikaika, *should* be a very different thing indeed.

12

ax was woken by a rap on the door. He had spent the night slumped at the table and he hauled himself upright. It was not yet dawn and he had a feeling the news was not going to be good. It was Macy but it might have been a stranger for all the recognition the *Second Lieutenant* showed, and Jax snapped to attention.

'Get your kit, Airman,' ordered Macy. 'You are being transferred.'

'Yes, sir.' Jax headed for his room even as Matiu's door opened. Matiu did not look like he had slept either. Jax swung his kit-bag onto the bed, thrust his jacket in and went to the bathroom to retrieve his toothbrush and soap. Kawai Alanui did not grow beards like Off-islanders so he had no shaving gear and he did not use tooth paste or deodorant either, unable to bear their stench.

If he extended his senses, he could hear what was being said in the kitchen but he did not bother. He was growing used to being tossed about between military bases. What he *could* hear suggested the familiarity of friends and that, despite the disparity in rank, information was being exchanged.

They fell silent when Jax re-appeared but Matiu's anxiety was obvious and when Jax followed Macy out, Matiu fell into step beside him. They took the same route Jax had on his arrival but it was morning now and Jax swallowed as the dew sharpened the rokai's scent.

'You are going to Rilo Base,' whispered Matiu in Kawai Alanui. 'It won't be easy, Jax.' Jax ignored him and Matiu leaned in closer. 'I *need* you here,' he hissed. 'Remember what I said last night.'

Rafi's Kawai Alanui language had been corrupted by English but Matiu's was pure and Jax clenched his teeth. He strode on, gut as tight as a drum, eyes straight ahead and was relieved when the chopper emerged from the trees. It looked like the same rattler that had delivered him and he climbed in and belted up. He did not look down at Matiu as they lifted off but he could not stop himself staring west.

A haze hinted at where moana might lie, but Macy turned east towards the mountains. Their westward slopes were creased with valleys and in less than ten minutes, Jax was peering down at the buildings and perimeter fencing of Rilo Base. The chopper pad was at the edge of a tarmacked square where a Training Instructor drilled men, their formation precise despite being at double time. It told Jax they were not new recruits, snatched from their former lives for two years of Service to Country, but older and more skilled. There was an obstacle course too, a ropes course, and a large warrior tower.

It won't be easy, Matiu had warned, and now Jax understood why. Keli's punishment for insubordination was not to be the cells like Nakoda, but hard physical training.

'Follow me, Airman,' ordered Macy, and Jax squared his shoulders and marched behind him along the square's perimeter towards the buildings. Bases had similar lay-outs and his time at Nakoda and Arozi gave him a good idea of which buildings were sleeping quarters, ablution blocks, kitchens, stores, and offices.

Macy headed towards the offices and Jax kept two paces behind him as Macy led the way inside, past cubicles of ground personnel busy at their desks, and through a door into an office. A female Airman glanced up from her work, and pressed buttons on the intercom.

'Second Lieutenant Macy is here with Airman Arozi, sir,' she said.

Permission was granted to enter, but Jax was barely aware of following Macy in. The military had solved the problem of his missing last name by assigning him the name of his former base. It was probably administrative convenience or maybe they thought it would make Jax feel more at home, but he would *never* be *opala*!

There were two men in the room: a commander seated at a desk and a training instructor standing against the wall. His occupation was easy to pick given he had the same bull-neck and muscle-bound shoulders as Nakoda and Arozi's TI's.

Macy saluted the commander and handed over an envelope and Jax held himself to attention while the commander pulled out a sheet of paper and read. Jax guessed it was orders on how he was to be treated given Keli would have already passed on details from Jax's file, including his history of *insubordination*.

The commander finished reading and glanced up at Macy. 'Dismissed Second Lieutenant,' he said, and Macy saluted, turned on his heel, and the door closed behind him.

The commander's pale eyes came to Jax. 'I am Major Giles, commander of Rilo Base,' said the commander. 'You will address me as Commander Giles.'

'Yes, Commander Giles.'

'You are a native of the Zoaides?'

'Yes, Commander Giles.'

'Which island?'

'Rua, Commander Giles.'

'The one that blew its top?'

'Yes, Commander Giles.'

'Why didn't you blow up with it? Everyone else did.'

'I don't know, Commander Giles.'

Giles' eyes narrowed. 'I have heard the natives of the Zoaides can change themselves into all sorts of animals. Is that true, Airman?'

Keli had not questioned the Kawai Alanui's *ability* to *shift*, but everything about Giles reeked of contempt and Jax blinked to convey confusion. 'I don't know, Commander Giles.'

'You don't seem to know very much, Airman.' Giles' pale eyes swept over him and he leaned forward in his chair. 'You lived there, Airman. Answer the question!'

Jax blinked again. 'I was twelve,' he said hesitantly, and frowned as if he fought to remember. 'There was an enormous explosion. It deafened me . . . and then I was in the Fayo. I thought I was going to drown.' He gulped convulsively. 'There was darkness and fire, and choking smoke.' Jax half shook his head. 'And then I was at the Sawquorn Training Home for Boys.'

The intercom buzzed but Giles had it muted and Jax only heard half the conversation. 'Can't it wait?' the Commander demanded. He scowled as he listened. 'Very well. Five minutes.'

He stabbed at the intercom again and his eyes came back to Jax. 'You have a history of insubordination, Airman, which makes you unsuitable for Rilo Base, *and* any other base that relies on the integrity and teamwork of its men to get the job done. But as you are under Lieutenant Colonel Keli's command, ultimately that isn't my problem. You are here because he wants to know what you are capable of *physically*.' His lip curled. 'He already knows what you are *in*capable of *mentally*.'

He gathered the papers on his desk and stood. 'Training Instructor

Briggs here will take you through our program,' he said, nodding to the second man. 'Our training courses are acknowledged as the most rigorous in the military and take anywhere from four to six weeks to complete, depending on the individual's *attributes*.' He smiled sourly and slipped the papers into a folder. 'Rilo tolerates *no* insubordination, Airman, remember that, *unless* you want your time here to be even *more* testing.'

Briggs turned out to be worse than the TI thugs Jax had detested at Nakoda and Arozi Bases. There was no way Jax could escape the sour vapor of his aggression and having to mimic subservience for hours on end, sent Jax's stress levels sky high.

Seeing Rilo's training course up-close also confirmed it was at a whole other level, unsurprising given the men Jax joined were not a bunch of naïve recruits but seasoned veterans who sought entry to specialist units. They had been at Rilo a full week too, which meant friendships *and* enmities had already formed.

The men shared a billet and Jax found being confined with twenty Off-islanders as wearing as Briggs' bawling orders a hand span from his face. There was no time alone to claw back equilibrium and the close-packed bodies filled the air with the stink of *personal hygiene products*.

Jax took the bunk nearest the door which was always unpopular given men visited the latrines at night to create an endless stream of drafts, but the bursts of fresh air suited Jax as did not having Off-islanders on both sides.

The men were too busy striving to excel at the tasks Briggs set to be friendly *or* hostile but that would change when Briggs formed them into teams. Nakoda and Arozi had taught him that military Off-islanders hated nothing more than being compromised by weak team members.

When Jax was not being screamed at by Briggs, who drilled them for hours mostly at double time, he was being berated as he ran. The running routes were initially through the flatter parts of the Rilo Valley and Jax might have found them bearable had he run alone. He had run Arozi's sandy wastelands countless times, mostly at night to avoid the company of others, and the desert's star-lit expanses had dulled the savage emptiness inside. His Kawai Alanui build made him suited to long distance running too, but Briggs would soon increase the weight of their packs, as TI's always did.

Jax ran at the back of the men to keep Briggs' expectations low and, as the runs grew longer, panted and stumbled until Briggs ran at his shoulder and bellowed insults in his ear. The men covertly tallied his strengths and weaknesses, as they did each other's, but Jax felt the hard gaze of one man in particular.

The man's physical bulk made him imposing but he moved quickly and Jax began to think of him as the *Taniwha*. Jax did not know his real name because Rilo replaced names with numbers as Nakoda had during Jax's Service to Country. Jax had still been raw from Rua's loss and had hated the last of his identity being stripped away but he welcomed the anonymity now.

Being RN21 made him more like RN20, RN19, RN18 and the rest of them, though it did not disguise the fact, that the other men were older, stronger, and more determined. And having been at Rilo longer, they were more hardened.

They ate together and Jax responded courteously to any comments that came his way but few went beyond the quality of the food, the state of the men's aching muscles, and speculation about Briggs' next set of *challenges*.

Jax was the tallest of the group but the lightest and many of the men lifted weights after hours to prepare for the obstacle course. Jax did not. He had been determined to avoid developing the bulky neck and shoulders of Off-islander military males and that meant he would soon refuse Briggs' orders to build them by training on the obstacle course.

Nakoda had punished his insubordination with incarceration and URZOL by sending him here, but how would Rilo punish him? Giles hinted it would be through an even more brutal training regime, but if Jax refused to comply? Bases prohibited physical violence but Briggs' verbal violence never seemed far from crossing the line.

Choppers thudded overhead as they ran and Jax guessed they enforced Samarak's territorial claims on the Fayo. He did not know whether *Senior Airman* Matiu piloted one because he did not know whether *Senior Airman* Matiu's duties extended to Rilo.

Matiu claimed Jax had more choices than him but Matiu could

work his way up through the military's ranks, stay as he was, serve in a special unit, or leave and work in civilian life, while Jax's choices had narrowed to giving Keli whatever he wanted or absconding *permanently*. But disappearing amongst Off-islanders was almost impossible.

The civilian and military worlds both had the man-power to hunt down fugitives and while he could dye his hair, mimicry could not disguise his height and eyes. And even if he did somehow disappear, he would need to work to feed himself and to send money to Rafi.

Jax stared into the darkness as he lay on his bunk that night, sleep a long way off despite his exhaustion. Briggs had smilingly informed them they would be doing *a little climbing* in the morning, and that meant the obstacle course. Jax loathed obstacle courses, not because of their barbed-wire tunnels, but because their hurdles, bars and towers demanded Off-islander muscles.

He had barely slept since his arrival at Rilo and now the knot in his gut made breathing hard as well. Even if he *did* somehow meet Rilo's *requirements*, the best he could hope for was to be sent back to URZOL. His heart thundered and he screwed his eyes shut as, for the first time, he doubted he had the strength to maintain the façade that allowed him to exist outside Rua.

A draught of chill air cut the billet's fug as someone entered but the footsteps did not continue past Jax's bunk and Jax's eyes jerked open to see the dim silhouette of the taniwha's head and massive shoulders loom over him.

'I'm RN08,' the taniwha whispered, 'but you can call me Carter.'

Carter extended his hand and Jax forced himself to shake it. 'RN21 or Jax,' he managed to say.

'I know. You couldn't be anyone else. You are Kawai Alanui,' said Carter, and before Jax could react, gently brought the backs of his fingers down Jax's cheek. If Carter had called him a *flash-monkey* or *shifter-twister*, Jax could have pretended ignorance, but Carter knew exactly what he was.

'A friend asked me to check in on you,' Carter continued softly. 'The friend flies reconnaissance over the Fayo, but can do no more than look down on you from the skies. The friend worries about you, Jax.'

Jax resisted the urge to sit up in case Carter saw it as a challenge and Carter's caress added to Jax's confusion. Jax had not experienced such tenderness since Rua blew. His mouth filled with spit but he managed to swallow. 'Tell the *friend* I am no longer his concern.'

Carter's calloused hand briefly enclosed Jax's. 'Love is not so easily discarded,' he said, and slipped away.

13

Anahera paced up and down in the predawn light, the moss cool under her feet. She had hardly slept and it was a relief to be out under the trees. The Kuwaini prohibited them from setting out before dawn but Anahera was tempted to leave anyway. She suspected Malo and Tamati had already left but she had no idea which route they would take or her own route for that matter. It was not a hard journey to Kohatu; all they had to do was climb.

The air carried winter's tang and she rubbed her arms. She was more excited than cold but she would be cold on ohaku because Makariri's snows had to be crossed to reach the Cloud Crown. A shia's calls finally heralded the dawn and she set off and as the land steepened, passed the streams and lagoons where the Iolani bathed and collected water.

The earthy scent of turned soil announced the gardens and she went on until the path gave way to an overgrown track and then to grasses. Her legs were soon wet with dew but she resisted the urge to harvest a handful to drink. The ohaku-sai prepared Ahi for the rigors of ohaku where food was forbidden and water might be scarce.

The trees thinned as she climbed and rokai blooms sweetened the air. The smell reminded Anahera of how she had groomed with Airini at Hapua and she wondered how high Airini had climbed. Tamati and Malo would be higher, no doubt, and she quickened her pace.

Moana's glittering expanse stretched to her right and she looked up to where a sun-eagle circled above the waves. Airini claimed no skin-spirit creature was superior to another but surely it would be better to be the hunter rather than the hunted, and for all the sun-eagle's beauty, Anahera still preferred the white-wolf.

The Iolani *shifted* to many creatures but needing to keep birth-form consciousness meant no Iolani fully understood how a white-wolf thought, or a sun-eagle, or a wheke for that matter, and yet Anahera remembered the thrill of powering through moana's depths in wheke-form and how her wheke-skin had sensed Whetu's spark.

She toiled on, watching the moko emerge to warm themselves in the sun. She was glad of the sun too. It suggested the day was the same as every other day, not the start of something that would end her Ahi life forever.

Anahera stopped to catch her breath when Wairere's lushness gave way to Kohatu's black stone. The sun was high but the stone looked all the same to her and as she squinted at it in the sun's glare, she wondered what the Kuwaini expected her to choose. She just wanted to grab something and get back before Tamati and Malo, but the Kuwaini did not set simple tasks for ohaku-sai and she picked her forward.

A flash of green caught her eye, stark against the black, and she made her way over. Little grew here but the wind swept up leaves and seeds from Wairere's forests that lodged in the crevices and sometimes grew *until* their roots reached the unforgiving stone beneath.

It was what a young rero had done, and she crouched and caressed its leaves. It would not grow much taller if left there and on an impulse, she eased from the crevice, cupped its roots carefully in her hands, and set off downslope.

As soon as she reached Wairere, she packed its roots with soil and wrapped them around with plani-leaves but as she turned towards Lani, she worried that the Kuwaini had wanted her to search Kohatu for something *special*, and that she had just failed her first ohaku-sai.

Miru considered the nine objects lined up on the Kuwain's seeli-mats. All of the Ahi had returned with black stone, except Anahera, who had presented them with a rero seedling.

'What are your thoughts?' asked Shenrin, hobbling to Miru's side.

'That I would feel happier about Anahera's readiness for ohaku if I looked upon *nine* pieces of stone instead of eight. The rero belongs in Wairere and I suspect Anahera still belongs there too.'

'My nights have been empty,' said Shenrin. 'Whetu sends me no guidance.'

'Nor me—yet.'

'But you remain troubled,' murmured Shenrin and Miru nodded. 'There is still time to think on Anahera's readiness. At least the other eight offer no cause for concern.'

'No,' agreed Miru. Airini had found a smooth, egg-shaped pebble, no small feat given Kohatu's *shattered* stone; Maia one that was perfectly symmetrical and Hana one that resembled a hiri. The male Ahi had returned with stones mottled with the lichen that grew on Kohatu's northern-most rim, as males usually did, keen to prove their readiness to journey on further to the Cloud Crown.

Davi made his way over to join them. 'Anahera asks whether she might have the rero seedling back to plant it,' he said. Kohatu's tokens could be reclaimed by their owners but most did not bother and Miru nodded. 'It is a strange thing to bring back,' he said, as he picked it up.

'Our thoughts also,' said Shenrin.

'She retrieved something that would have otherwise died,' he murmured, as he went out.

Miru glanced at Shenrin. 'I hadn't thought of that,' she admitted.

'Nor me. Death is usually not so easily avoided,' she muttered. 'And saving the rero is a more comforting possibility than the one we discussed,' she added.

'Indeed it is,' said Miru. 'It will be interesting to see what the second ohaku-sai reveals.'

Anahera cupped water in her hands and carried it to the seedling. She had planted it in a sunny clearing created where a storm had brought a brack down. It was a far kinder place for the seedling than in Kohatu.

'I thought we had enough rero,' said Malo behind her, making her start.

'You can never have enough rero,' she said, turning back to the lagoon for more water.

Malo settled on the brack's trunk and watched her deliver another double handful to the seedling. 'True,' he said. 'But carting one from Kohatu seems a tiresome way to increase our supply of building and burning wood.'

'It's more useful than carting rocks,' retorted Anahera.

'That is true too.'

Anahera looked sideways at him. 'You are unusually agreeable.'

Malo shrugged. 'Quarrels are for younger Ahi, not for those of us on the verge of Ikaika.'

'The *verge* of Ikaika? We have completed *one* ohaku-sai, Malo, and I am guessing it was the easiest one.'

'We have completed our first step *away* from the Ahi, Anahera.

There is no going back.' Anahera said nothing and he smiled. 'Don't look so worried,' he said, as he slid from the trunk. 'You are strong. You won't have any trouble completing ohaku.'

'I never said I would,' she retorted, flicking back her hair. 'But none of us know what the Cloud Crown holds.'

His cool fingers stroked her arm. 'That is true,' he said.

'Three truths in a row,' she said dryly. 'That must be a record for me.'

'For the Anahera of the Ahi, perhaps but not for the Anahera of the Ikaika.'

'I—' she began, and ducked as a sun-eagle swooped low. Sun-eagles did not frequent Wairere and she wondered if it were injured, then grimaced as she noticed it carried a whitiki. It landed, and Tamati's head appeared followed by the rest of him before he stepped behind a rero to dress.

'This *is* a surprise,' said Malo.

'Yes,' said Tamati pleasantly as he emerged. 'I didn't expect you to be planting reros on the first day of ohaku-sai, Malo.'

'It is Anahera who is planting reros,' said Malo tersely.

'Then I am not surprised,' he said, switching his attention to her. 'Anahera is capable of all sorts of extraordinary things.'

'Planting a rero is hardly *extraordinary*,' she retorted, sick of being caught up in their sparring. 'But now it *is* planted, I am going back to Lani. And I don't want company,' she tossed over her shoulder as she strode off. But she did not go far before she turned upslope again, having decided that the peace of Shani's waters was preferable to Lani's chatter. Elders and Ikaika took a keen interest in those *about to die* and Anahera did not want to explain her choice of rero a second time. Explaining it the first time to the Kuwaini had been hard enough.

As dusk thickened the air, the cicadas' rattle gave way to the hum of flicker-bugs and the croak of scarlet-tongues in the moister dips. Anahera went slowly, weary from her quick trip to Kohatu but when the lagoon's waters emerged from the trees, someone perched on its shores.

Anahera stopped but the person turned before she could retreat. It was Airini. 'Anahera! Come sit with me.'

'I don't think I'll make very good company,' said Anahera advancing reluctantly.

Airini grinned. 'We can be silent and sulky together.'

'You mean like Malo and Tamati?' asked Anahera, settling beside her.

'Sulky yes, but have you ever known those two to be silent?'

'Not recently.'

Airini glanced at her sideways. 'They compete for you.'

Anahera rolled her eyes. 'They just want to beat each other.'

'To be *first* to *you*.'

Anahera gazed at the water. 'I can't think of anything beyond ohaku,' she muttered.

Airini's hand closed over hers. 'It is natural to be afraid.'

Anahera shrugged. 'I never said I was afraid, just that I can't imagine a life beyond being Ahi.'

An owl called further up the valley and Airini paused to listen to it. 'The Ikaika don't speak of the time before they died,' she said, her gaze on Shani's waters too. The surface dimpled where slip-fish hunted golden-flies and Anahera felt Airini's grip on her hand tighten. 'The Kuwaini won't let any of us set out who aren't ready.'

Anahera's gut churned. The prospect of staying Ahi while her friends became Ikaika was worse than entering the Cloud Crown.

'Let's spend the night here,' said Airini suddenly. 'We can *shift* to kirirua and fill our bellies with water-snails, then sleep in the brack. There is plenty of stipplefern to keep us snug.'

Anahera nodded, glad to delay her return to Lani. They shed their clothes, waded into the water, and *shifted*. A kirirua's vision was poor but Anahera forgot her fears of the Cloud Crown as Airini's sinuous form slithered along in front and the delicious smell of water-snails filled her kirirua senses. Her keen kirirua nose uncovered countless snails *and* blackwing grubs, and they were soon well-sated.

They *shifted* back to birth-form, donned their clothes, and made their way deep into the brack. 'Being a kirirua would be good,' said Anahera as they pulled the stipplefern over themselves.

'Unless there were hawklings about.'

Anahera curled up on her side and stared into the night. 'I prefer hawklings to the Cloud Crown even in kirirua-form,' she muttered.

The ferns rustled as Airini's arms came around her. 'Sleep,' she said softly, and kissed Anahera's shoulder. 'Whetu watches over us.'

14

Briggs began the day with the marching drills the military used to build teamwork, but marching was the opposite of how Jax ran and swam in birth-form, and had run and swum *and* flown in shift-form. It meant keeping his steps to a precise length and speed instead of varying them according to the flow of his strength and, even worse, it meant being hemmed in on every side by Off-islanders.

He had countered the effects of marching at Arozi by slipping away at night to run the desert but there was no escape at Rilo. Briggs bawled orders for hours on end, taking them from single to double time, to rest position, to attention, and back to double time. Jax kept formation but his sweat-drenched shirt had nothing to do with exertion.

After days of Briggs' verbal and physical intimidation, the temptation to *shift* was unbearable, but Jax had not shifted since he had chased Matiu from Rua. And even when he had fled Nakoda's torments, he had done so in birth-form. *Shifting* belonged to the same faded photograph as Rua, a version of himself that was dead and gone like everything else.

Briggs finally gave the order to fall out and they returned to the mess hall to eat. Jax lagged to make sure he was at the end of the food queue and the tables were full. It meant he could sit by himself but he had scarcely settled with his tray of food when Carter's tray clunked down opposite. Jax focused on eating but it was hard to choke down anything at all.

'A friend tells me the Kawai Alarui find it hard being confined amongst Off-islanders,' said Carter, keeping his voice low. Jax said nothing and heard Carter take a swig of his coke. 'The friend doesn't believe you will survive Rilo,' he continued. 'Do *you* believe you will survive Rilo, Jax?' Jax kept his gaze on his food and shrugged. 'Is that affirmative or negative?'

The silence stretched and Jax glanced up. The daylight showed Carter's chiseled jaw and the roped muscles of his neck and shoulders, but it also lit his eyes. They were green, not the deep emerald of Matiu's, but green enough to jolt Jax.

'Negative,' he heard himself say, and sensed Carter relax slightly.

'I agree,' said Carter. 'The friend believes a request for a transfer back to URZOL would be granted.'

'I'm not going back.'

Carter eyed him shrewdly. 'You don't believe you will survive Rilo and you won't go back to URZOL. The friend tells me you have ruled out returning to the Zoaides too. Doesn't leave you with many options, does it, Jax?'

Jax concentrated on his food again and sensed Carter lean over the table. 'You aren't thinking of a more *permanent* solution to your problems, are you, Jax?'

Jax's knuckles whitened on his fork. Carter alluded to the Off-islander practice of *suicide*, a notion so alien Jax had at first struggled to believe it existed. Only Whetu gave and took life and yet, as time had gone on, Jax had come to understand the temptation of a more final escape.

'Jax?'

He had no idea why the Off-islander bothered to pass on Matiu's messages but Carter's voice held real concern and Jax forced himself to look up. 'Tell your friend I haven't forgotten Whetu.'

Carter nodded as if he understood Whetu's significance. 'I can help you while you are here, Jax, but only for a while. Once the training picks up . . .'

'I don't want Off-islander help!'

'It is a favor for a friend.'

Jax lowered his voice to a hiss. 'Why help Matiu? Why help *any* flash-monkey?'

Carter smiled. 'There are many things that make someone an outsider, Jax, apart from being Kawai Alanui. And as I've said, love isn't an easy thing to discard.'

Carter's military muscles marked him as anything but an outsider, but if he had been Matiu's mate-pair, even temporarily, it might explain his behavior. But surely Matiu wouldn't—

'I had thought Matiu beautiful until I saw you,' murmured Carter. 'He has made a life for himself in Samarak. You could too.'

Jax shook his head and Carter's voice sank to a harsh whisper. 'You are only *just* surviving, Jax. Matiu discovered life could be so much more, with the help and *love* of friends.'

Jax thrust his chair back and strode away from the table. Exhaustion made it hard to mimic nonchalance and he was aware the men stared after him. A wind had sprung up outside and it chilled his sweat-drenched shirt as he forced himself on past the cluster of buildings, over the square and sward of tussocky grass, to the perimeter fence.

It was the usual wire mesh topped with razor-wire and Jax hooked his fingers through the links and sagged against it. The faintest taint of salt reminded him that moana was close and that it lapped Samarak's shores and Rua's ruined ones as well.

'Jax?'

Jax jerked around, shocked he had not sensed Carter's approach. Carter had stopped several lengths away which confirmed he understood *some* Kawai Alanui sensibilities. 'Time to go,' he said and headed back to where the men were assembling. Jax stumbled after him and forced himself into line, then Briggs marched them to the far end of the base where hurdles marked the start of the obstacle course.

Carter's attention was on him but Jax was beyond mimicking calmness. It took all his strength to march in time as his fear built, not of the obstacle course, but of losing of control. Seeing Matiu again, smelling moana's salt, enduring Briggs' brutal regime had combined to erode the version of himself that filled the abyss between being Kawai Alanui and being Off-islander, and with it gone, there was nothing to stave off the horror of Rua's annihilation.

Briggs' bawled numbers to divide them into teams and Jax shuffled into place and feigned attentiveness as Briggs yelled instructions on how the obstacle course was to be completed. It consisted of the usual low pole-jumps, logs in ladder-form and laid end to end, towering walls, bridges and climbing-nets of rope, and a tunnel of barbed wire, but it was longer and its walls higher than those at Nakoda and Arozi.

Briggs shouted an order and the first two men set off, their comrades urging them on. Jax knew he should study the men's techniques but even if he survived the course, Briggs would devise something worse, and Jax stared beyond the perimeter fence instead. Forests clothed the valley's sides enclosing places that were quiet and dark *and* hidden, and he kept his gaze on them.

The men around him dwindled but he was barely aware of it and then it was his turn. The shouting was so loud he had no idea which team led; he simply ran for his life. He sensed the men's surprise at his speed, and Briggs', as he vaulted the lower walls without breaking stride, sprinted along the logs and threw himself at the wall. His speed gave him the momentum to get a grip halfway up and he clawed his way to the top, taking the skin from his hands and knees, half slid down the rope designed for descent and let go to land with a jarring thud.

He scarcely registered the pain as he navigated the net, aware of cheering as he ran on over the rope bridge, and then he was at the final obstacle, the tunnel. The other man was hard on his heels and Jax used his hands and knees not elbows and belly. The barbs tore through his shirt and back but the pain was far away too, his head empty of everything but the sanctuary beyond the fence.

He exited the tunnel and ran on past the end of the course, heard the cheering give way to stunned silence, and then to the boom of Briggs' bawled orders. He did not stop, just hurled himself at the fence as he had hurled himself at the wall. He reached the top and scrambled into the razor-wire.

It trapped him like a bird in a net, and his body burned with searing slashes as he struggled to break free, and then his blood-soaked shirt tore loose, and he fell to the grass on the other side, struggled to his feet and ran, aware of nothing more than the need to escape.

Keli broke off his conversation with Connel as the phone rang and listened in silence. Giles' report was short, to the point, and left nothing to the imagination. 'I want to know *immediately* he is located,' barked Keli, 'and I want the Infirmary prepared.

'That means a *secure* bed, Giles. And I shouldn't have to remind you he's a shifter. Wait,' he snapped and swung back to Connel. 'Would injuries Jax suffered in human shape manifest in animal shape?'

'I don't know but it's unlikely that shifting heals—'

Keli turned back to the phone. 'Brief your men they might be searching for an injured animal too.' He slammed the phone down and swore.

'Jax has been hurt absconding?' asked Connel.

'Absconding?' growled Keli. 'He fled in full sight of everyone, over the perimeter fence and into the Rilo Valley.'

Connel stared at him in shock. '*Over* the perimeter fence? How badly cut is he?'

'Enough,' said Keli and swore again. 'I gave Giles *explicit* instructions to report *any* deterioration in Jax's mental state.'

'Jax is a mimic,' said Connel tightly.

Keli's hands came to his hips. The Rilo Valley had hundreds of hiding places for a man, and in animal form, Jax could sustain himself indefinitely. But if he had lost the quantity of blood Giles suggested, he would be weakened, and a weakened animal might simply crawl into a hole to die.

Keli swung back to Connel. 'Do the Alanui think like animals when in animal form?'

'I don't know that either, but the Kawai Alanui warn of the dangers of staying in animal form too long, which suggests they retain human consciousness at first and lose it as time goes on.'

Keli's breath hissed. If Jax stayed in animal form *or* died, Keli would only have Matiu, and Matiu did not have the strength for Operation V.

'There is no evidence Jax has *shifted* since Rua exploded,' said Connel. 'My understanding is he was in human form when he absconded previously.'

'Correct,' snapped Keli.

'Given he went through the razor-wire this time in *human* form, he is most likely *still* in human form.' There was a short silence. 'Do you know what triggered his flight?'

'That is no longer relevant.'

'With respect, Commander, *anything* I can learn about the Kawai Alanui *is* relevant. Jax has been at Rilo close to a fortnight. I would have expected him to run before this. It would be useful to know exactly what happened.'

'I expected him to abscond earlier too,' admitted Keli. 'I had extra patrols put on the perimeter fence and on the gates. The last thing I expected was him to take off in daylight, in full view of everyone.'

'*And* over razor-wire,' added Connel grimly. 'You wanted to push him to breaking point, Commander, and it seems you've succeeded.'

'We won't know his mental state until we find him,' said Keli tersely.

'*If* we find him.'

15

'The next ohaku-sai isn't that bad,' muttered Anahera, as she followed the Ahi out of the Kuwain.

'No,' agreed Airini. 'And we don't even have to complete it alone. But I wonder what the Kuwaini want us to discover. Even younger Ahi have circled Iolana multiple times.'

'Not in one day and in land, sea and air shift-forms,' muttered Anahera. The smoke of the cooking fires added to dusk's soft purple and her stomach rumbled as she smelled roasted fish.

'Yes,' agreed Airini, as they went on through the awins. 'Miru was very precise about the shift-forms.'

'They want us to choose the *best* shift-form for each part of the journey,' said Tamati, coming level.

'Or the *swiftest* shift-form,' said Malo, appearing at Tamati's shoulder.

Anahera shrugged. 'Same thing.'

'I don't think so,' said Airini. 'Circling Iolana isn't about speed, it is about what we see and that depends on the shift-form we choose for each part of the journey *and* on our pace. Go too fast and you don't see anything.'

'It depends on the route we choose too,' said Tamati, his gaze on Anahera. 'The Kuwaini obviously want us to travel together to sharpen our observations. Two sets of eyes see better than one.'

'It depends on whose eyes they are,' said Malo dryly.

'Saying we *can* travel together, doesn't mean we have to,' said Anahera, already considering how fast she could travel on her own.

'Journeying alone is risky given how late it is in the season,' said Tamati, and flared his nostrils. 'A storm is coming.'

Malo glanced up at the clear sky. 'So now you are a weather-reader as well,' he goaded.

Airini flared her nostrils too. 'Tamati's right,' she said. 'It's probably why the Kuwaini offered us the choice of staying together.'

'If there were any danger they wouldn't be sending us off,' said Anahera.

'They don't have any choice,' said Malo unexpectedly. 'Once the ohaku-sai begin, they must continue uninterrupted until ohaku. They can't postpone them *or* the ohaku.'

The others looked at him in surprise. 'How do you know that?' demanded Airini.

'Ari told me,' said Malo, naming an Ikaika who had entered the Cloud Crown several years before. 'He was one of *the nine*.'

Silence fell as they considered the nine Ahi who had set out, and *the four* who had not returned. A terrible wind had assailed Tihi, bringing storms and snow, and four Ahi had perished. It had been the worst loss of life on ohaku in living memory and Anahera licked her lips as she realized she, Airini, Malo and Tamati were also four of nine. 'The four who died were together, so being together didn't help *them*,' she said thickly.

'They weren't together at the start,' pointed out Tamati. 'You can only journey together on the return trip from Kohatu.' There was a short silence. 'The Kuwaini do nothing without reason,' he added carefully. 'Perhaps this ohaku-sai is to hone skills not honed by solitary journeys.'

'Such as?' demanded Anahera, still rattled.

'Cooperation, teamwork, trust . . .' He smiled at her. 'I think we should travel as a foursome.'

Anahera snorted. 'We don't have time. We will still be arguing over who is to lead, the route to follow, and the shift-forms to take when the sun sets.'

'I am guessing such decisions are called *teamwork*,' said Malo sardonically.

'It might be fun to travel as a foursome,' said Airini unexpectedly.

'The Kuwaini don't set ohaku-sai for *fun*,' said Anahera, annoyed Airini had sided with Tamati.

'The *joy* of being Ahi *is* important,' said Tamati. 'It is possible the Kuwaini want to remind us of it as we near Ikaika.'

'*Anything* is possible but being together will be distracting and we might miss whatever it is we are supposed to see,' said Anahera.

'Or see it *because* of our fellow Ahi,' countered Tamati.

'Or don't see it because we are staring *at* our fellow Ahi,' said Airini meaningfully.

Tamati scowled at Airini but Anahera's belly rumbled again as Elders raked kumara from the ashes of a nearby fire. 'We could argue about this all night but we need to eat and sleep.'

'So we make our decision now,' said Tamati smoothly. 'Like Airini, I think we should journey as a foursome, so unless someone objects, we meet back here at dawn.'

Anahera nodded briefly and headed for her awin. She had no idea whether journeying as a foursome would be useful because she had no idea what the Kuwaini wanted, but she did sense she needed to make a better impression on them than last time.

Anahera slept badly and knowing she could not plan her shift-forms *or* route added to her bad temper the next morning. Despite Malo's much vaunted notion of teamwork, she was pretty sure he and Tamati had already decided which way they would all go *and* in what form.

It was still dark but she clambered from her sleeping-mat, glad no one shared her awin that night and she had no one to disturb. Tamati's determination to get his own way was matched only by Malo's, she concluded irritably, as she yanked a comb through her hair.

She had watched them lock horns as snow-goats and fight as shia-form alphas but at least that would soon end; Ikaika *cooperated* to keep Iolana safe, not competed. Her mood was not helped by Airini's claim that Tamati sought her. Tamati simply goaded Malo over who was closest to their *female* Ahi friend and Anahera was heartily sick of it.

Dawn heralded a grey sky and blustery wind but Airini already waited at the edge of Lani and gave Anahera a hug. 'Still feeling anxious?' she asked, as she smoothed back Anahera's hair.

'I am mainly feeling annoyed I agreed to journey with Tamati and Malo,' said Anahera. 'They probably want to take some complicated route to prove how strong and fast they are while I just want to get it over with.'

'Then *we* choose the route instead. Which way would you like to go?' asked Airini. Anahera shrugged. 'Moana first in water-breathing form?' suggested Airini. 'Or in air-breathing form? Or would you prefer to start in bird-form?'

'I don't know because I don't know what the Kuwaini want!'

'They might not know either, except for Miru and Shenrin,' said Airini soothingly.

'Dream-travelers,' muttered Anahera, her gaze on the reros' tossing crowns. Moana would be angry too and flight near its surface hazardous. 'I wonder what they *really* see.'

'Not the worsening weather or they wouldn't have started the ohaku-sai.'

'Nothing wrong with the weather,' said Malo, appearing with Tamati. 'We can swim beneath it or fly above it.'

'I need to warm up,' said Anahera, her teeth beginning to chatter. The ohaku-sai were completed without cloaks to harden Ahi to the Cloud Crown and Huna afterwards and she was chilling fast.

'If we start in bird-form, we can complete most of the journey hugging Iolana's shores, which will be quicker, then shift to a water-breathing form for a while, and then to a land-form for the last part of the journey back,' said Tamati.

Tamati's plan was a good one except it was *his* plan and Anahera remained tight-lipped. 'Are we going to be able to see enough?' asked Airini doubtfully.

'We will see through the eyes of three shift-forms, one for each of air, water and land, as the Kuwaini require,' said Malo.

It was obvious Malo and Tamati had decided the route together *and* how to counter objections, and Anahera exchanged glances with Airini.

'Are we agreed?' asked Tamati.

Anahera shrugged. 'I am using redgull form,' she said.

'It would be safer for *all* of us to use sun-eagle form,' said Tamati.

'Sun-eagles aren't agile enough close to the ground,' said Anahera, 'especially in this wind.'

'We don't need to fly *close to the ground* or to moana,' said Tamati evenly.

'We do if we want to see anything,' said Anahera, glaring at him, 'which is the *whole* point of the ohaku-sai.'

'We don't *all* need to be in sun-eagle form,' said Airini hurriedly.

'It would be safer if we were,' said Tamati, his hard gaze on Anahera.

'Safety isn't my main priority,' retorted Anahera.

'Then maybe you shouldn't be doing ohaku,' snapped Tamati. 'Iolana needs Ikaika, not dead Ahi.'

'The Kuwaini decide who completes ohaku, not you, and *you* don't decide what shift-form *I* take and what route *I* follow either,' said Anahera angrily. 'In fact, *I* have just decided to complete this ohaku-sai alone!' She stormed off, ignoring Airini's call to wait, found a dense stand of stringer-vines and plunged in. Airini hurried past and Anahera tore off her clothes and *shifted* to snake-form. She had not taken snake-form since her experiments as a younger Ahi, and few older Ahi favored snake-form either. Snakes were vulnerable to owls, stoats and sun-eagles, and their cold-blood slowed them, especially on days like today.

Anahera did not intend to stay in snake-form long and she skirted Lani, then set off towards moana, her tongue tasting the shells of dead hummer- and stinger-bugs, the delicious fragrance of fern-mice, scarlet-tongue frogs, and then a topaz-moko as she went.

Her belly felt the rough and smooth of the ground she slid over and the squelch of dips where moisture pooled, and she let her senses roam until the tang of salt heralded the end of Wairere's green. Then she stopped, *shifted* to birth-form and then redgull.

The wind's buffet sent moana's fume high into the air and though she had intended to hug the cliffs, she battled not to be dashed against them. Redgulls sought safety in numbers as did blackgulls but only a few wheeled in the distance, probably because of the wind.

She struggled on and then a jag of shift-form consciousness made her glance up. Three sun-eagles rode the winds above. Tamati, Malo and Airini, she concluded bad-temperedly. It was typical of Tamati to encourage the others to ignore her wishes to complete her ohaku-sai alone.

The wind's batter continued and she wondered if it would be easier to fly just above the water but moana's waves were high and she risked being caught in their clash. Clouds dimmed her shadow over their surface and then other shadows crossed hers. The sun-eagles were all about her! A bolt of pure terror speared through her and she dived.

The impact would have made a birth-form redgull easy pickings but fear drove her deep into moana's depths. Sun-eagles were known to pluck prey from below moana's surface and she paddled her wings to gain depth and then, as suffocation threatened. *shifted* to birth-form, sucked in a lungful of water, choked and *shifted* to taniwha. She had never taken taniwha-form before, the choice had been instinctive, as if the terror of being prey had triggered the need to be a predator.

Her vision cleared and her hearing and sense of smell grew as she sliced through moana's grey-green swirl. The wind-tossed world above seemed a long way away and the thrill of her new-found power grew as silverfish ran before her. She could see far into the distance and smell other creatures too whose vibrations sparked the water like lightning and set her blood on fire.

She powered on, faster and faster, the want to seize and tear and devour growing with every flick of her lithe body. The understanding that she *could* snatch life from any creature she chose was intoxicating and when she sensed a young hiri at play on the water's surface, she launched upwards.

Its blubber was already pungent in her shift-form mouth but at the last moment her birth-form consciousness slammed home and she swerved and rocketed out of the water beside it. She glimpsed its liquid eyes filled with horror, and then she was back in moana's depths, her horror scarcely less than its.

She swam on, barely aware of what she did, and when she found a wave-washed rock, shifted to birth-form and clawed her way onto it and huddled there, wetted by waves that broke over it, pulled back, and broke again.

The Iolani sometimes hunted hiri, as they trapped stoat and white-hare, and even the youngest Ahi knew that life meant death, but knowing it and *feeling* it were different things. The want for such power surged afresh but taniwha took life only to fill their bellies, and she had not been hungry.

She brought a shaking hand to her mouth. The want to kill had come from her birth-form and she sensed that Tamati had seen what the Kuwaini already knew, that she was not fit to undertake her ohaku. And as the consequences swept over her, she cradled her face in her hands and cried.

16

Jax ran, his breath torn from his throat in scalding sobs, his body afire with pain. There was no easy lope like his runs in Arozi's arid emptiness, just a shambling stagger driven by a desperate need to escape. He stumbled down slopes into shallow valleys and clawed his way up their sides. The trees wavered as if under water and when he wiped the sweat from his face he found that it was blood. His arms wept blood too, and his torso, and legs, and in the reaches of his brain that still functioned, he knew he must rest if he were to *survive*.

Survive Briggs, *survive* Keli, *survive* Arozi, *survive* Nakoda, *survive* Sawquorn Training-home for Boys, *survive* moana's icy embrace; *survive* the blast that had torn his old self apart. His mind ran backwards in a bizarre inversion of time he was powerless to stop, and he wondered if it were because he had no future.

But he had no past either, not beyond the blast; he existed only here in this time of pain and endless running. He came to a stream and stumbled to a stop on its banks. He knew its rush, its glassy slide over river-stones, the smell of its moss and wet reeds, and he knew where it came from: its silent seep, its silver stream, its shining waterfall.

It lived in his memory, before the blast, when there had been songs and Kawai Alanui he had loved and who had loved him. The stream's birth lived there too in a quiet place, where leaf-fall and bark-fall, flesh and feather and bone, rotted down to a soil that fed new life.

He lurched into the stream and fell to his knees. He had swum in pools and lagoons; felt waterfalls pound his shoulders; watched their rainbows arc into space. The stream swirled around him, tugged at him, pulled him apart, and he collapsed forwards, face down, and let himself go.

Keli paused only to toss back a cup of cold coffee as he paced around his office. Connel's eyes were closed, his head resting on his chair-back but Keli was in no mood to sleep. Briggs had brought in the tracker dogs but it had been more than twelve hours since Jax had torn himself to pieces on the perimeter fence and disappeared.

The foul weather had not helped. Torrential rain brought a thick night that had grounded the choppers and washed away Jax's blood and scent. It had marooned Matiu further north at Brachnall Base too. He was on his way back by vehicle but would not reach Rilo before dawn, presuming the roads stayed open.

To add to Keli's frustration, the latest reconnaissance confirmed things were far from well in the Fayo. Keli swore but resisted the urge to send the trash can flying with a well-aimed boot. He was running out of time and if Jax died, out of options. He considered using Matiu again, and again dismissed the idea. Matiu was not strong enough, but more crucially, he could not *shift*.

Keli needed Jax! His hands came to his hips as he considered Connel's advice to tell Jax *why* he needed him. As if that would make any difference! Keli was limited in what he could reveal anyway, which did not help build empathy, even with Connel.

But he did concede it had been a mistake to send Jax to Rilo. The only person who could bring Jax onside was Matiu, but Keli did not have the two or three months it might take. Even one month might be too late to avert a second catastrophe.

He threw himself into his chair and read through Jax's files yet again, in the hope of finding something new and when he did not, rubbed his eyes and read through Connel's thick folder. If there *were* anything useful in either, he was either too blind *or* too tired to see it.

He joined Connel in using his chair as a bed but it seemed only moments later the phone rang. The room was bathed in the dawn's grey light and he cranked his head from side to side to unkink his neck as he listened to the staticky update. 'We'll come up,' he said, and slammed the receiver down.

Connel jerked awake. 'They have found Jax?'

'They have found blood.' Keli wrenched on his jacket and headed for the door. 'We will meet Matiu there. Grab a coat, Connel. The weather's as foul as yesterday's.'

Keli gripped the cold metal of the grab-handle as the jeep reared and pitched its way up Rilo's narrow tracks, the journey infuriatingly slow. He had run many of the tracks before the demands of Operation V had eaten his time, and the military used them to access the valley for training and reconnaissance. Even so, large swathes of rugged terrain remained untouched, *surplus to military requirements* and off limits to civilians like much of the adjacent coast.

Keli had enjoyed his runs, the air crisp and the narrow ravines ashine with rushing streams. The tracks were rutted from military vehicles and the unused ones deep in leaf-litter but they were all slick when it rained and it rained now. It might not be yesterday's deluge but it was enough to keep the choppers grounded.

Keli turned up his jacket collar to fend off the drips that flicked in through the windows, but his legs were chill where it wet his trousers. The cold did not bode well for a man weakened by blood loss, he concluded grimly.

'How much further?' asked Connel, having to bawl from the back seat to be heard above the engine.

Keli held up fingers to indicate five minutes but it was closer to ten before they rounded a bend and stopped in a small turn-out. It was crowded with vehicles, wet airmen and dogs. The truck that had brought Briggs' search party was there, and the jeep Keli hoped had delivered Matiu, and an ambulance, with the silhouettes of medics huddled inside.

The jeep came to a stop and Keli slung the walkie-talkie pouch over his shoulder and clambered out. Connel followed, swearing as mud closed over his shoes, but Keli's attention was on Matiu. He appeared from behind the truck with Briggs, his face pale but expressionless and Keli shifted his attention to Briggs' report. Blood had been found further down the ridge and a party of men and dogs had searched its slopes but found nothing since.

Keli dismissed Briggs and pulled Matiu aside. 'You've had time to look around?' he asked. Matiu nodded, his scarring stark in the grey light. 'What are your thoughts?'

'There is rero here, Commander Keli, which grew on Rua, and the streams are similar too. But it's nearly ten miles from the base. That is a long way to run for an injured man,' he added and swallowed.

'Would Jax have *shifted* to animal form?' pursued Keli, ignoring Matiu's distress and Connel's disapproval.

'No, Commander Keli.'

Keli's eyes narrowed. 'You seem very sure.'

'A friend saw him caught in the razor-wire. If Jax were going

83

to *shift*, he would have *shifted* then.' Matiu swallowed several more times and wiped his mouth. 'When Jax rejected the Kawai Alanui, he rejected *shifting*,' he added, and was forced to spit. 'I … I beg your pardon, Commander Keli.'

'There's no need,' snapped Keli. Matiu looked on the verge of collapse but Keli pressed on. 'Would Jax keep running or search for shelter?'

'I don't know, Commander Keli. I don't know him well enough to judge.'

Keli gripped Matiu's shoulder and wrenched him close. 'You know him better than anyone living, *Senior Airman*, and that makes you our best hope of saving him! And make no mistake, I *need* him saved, not for your sake or his, but for the sake of your islands. They are under threat and I *need* Jax alive.' Keli released him and took a deep breath. '*If* Jax got this far, where would he go?'

Matiu swallowed convulsively but Keli was relieved to see his military training kick in. 'The lands around the base are green like Rua was and the air smells moist. There are chika bats too.' His brows creased in thought. 'The land *here* steepens like Rua and you can hear water.' Then his eyes flashed to Keli's. 'Rua's streams and falls were slender and fast flowing *like those here*,' he said quickly. '*If* Jax made it this far, he would seek them out.'

Keli's mind raced. He knew this part of the Rilo well from his runs and given where the blood had been found, there were three or four ravines Jax might have ended up in. He strode back to Briggs and snapped out orders to search the three nearest the blood, but even with Briggs' men *and* dogs, the searchers were spread thin. He would search the more easterly ravine with Matiu and Connel.

They set off upslope in silence but Matiu scanned, sniffed the air, and licked his lips. 'Can Alanui sense other Alanui?' asked Keli.

'The Kawai Alanui have a greater awareness of each other than Off-islanders have of each other, Commander Keli.'

Which was not an answer. 'Could you sense Jax's presence without seeing him?' he demanded. The slopes were heavily wooded and the last thing he wanted was to walk on past Jax lying unconscious in some thicket.

'I don't know, Commander Keli. We have been apart a long time.'

They reached the top of the ridge and started their descent, Keli ordering Matiu to lead in the hope even a tenuous connection might aid their search. The misting rain made the slope slippery and they grabbed onto bushes to stay upright. He followed Matiu to the bottom and sleeved the rain from his eyes as Connel came level.

The stream rushed along a rocky bed that curved away past dense stands of trees in both directions, restricting their view to a few lengths. 'Which way, Senior Airman?' he demanded.

'Upstream, Commander Keli,' said Matiu. Keli countered a surge of hope as he followed. He could have made the same decision with a flip of a coin. It was quiet in the ravine, the stones shining under a patina of moisture and the air aromatic with wet foliage. It was not a bad place to die, concluded Keli dourly, and then Matiu gave a cry and rushed forward.

Keli dashed after him but for a maddening moment Matiu blocked his view and then he saw what Matiu had: Jax's body, face down in the water. The pale skin of his back was slashed with vivid red wounds and he rocked gently in the current.

'Don't touch him!' ordered Keli, as Matiu fell to his knees beside him.

Keli crouched on the other side and his heart leapt as he saw Jax's cheek rested on stone. It had kept his mouth and nose clear of the water, or so Keli hoped.

'Is he alive?' panted Connel, hurrying up.

Keli felt for a pulse on his neck, found nothing and searched again. Matiu's face was agonized, but Keli focused on his search and was rewarded. 'Yes,' he confirmed, 'but we need to get him out the water. 'You take his legs, Senior Airman,' he ordered. 'Connel and I will take his shoulders.'

Keli rolled Jax onto his back and Connel gasped. The slashes were even worse on his front and his trousers saturated with blood. At least his face had largely escaped, thought Keli grimly, as they maneuvered him onto the bank. Matiu had already shrugged out of his jacket and Keli nodded approvingly. 'Warm him, Senior Airman, while I summon the medics.'

Connel hovered nearby and Keli wrenched the walkie-talkie from its pouch and strode off along the bank, relayed Jax's condition to the medics first, and then contacted Briggs to organize the retrieval.

It would not be easy to get the stretchers down or Jax up, and even once he reached the ambulance, it was over an hour to the Infirmary. Keli cursed the low cloud again but even had the skies been clear, the terrain made it hazardous for choppers.

He turned back to where Connel waited and stopped. Matiu had stripped off his shirt and jacket and pulled Jax into his arms, and Connel had wrapped the clothing over them both. It was standard military practice to use skin to skin body-heat to warm the injured but that was not what rooted Keli to the spot. It was that Matiu sang.

Keli knew the Alanui used songs to pass on histories, but this was something different. Matiu's voice was soft but Keli heard the word the mics had picked up in Jax's quarters. It was not *mahoha,* as he and Connel had thought, but *aroha*, and Matiu sang it over and over again.

Keli felt for Jax's pulse again, relieved it had not weakened, and while Matiu watched him anxiously, his singing did not falter. 'You are doing well,' said Keli encouragingly, then gestured Connel to follow him back along the bank. 'I'm guessing Matiu's not passing on Alanui histories,' he said softly.

'I think he is begging Jax to live,' said Connel.

'Do you recognize anything?'

'*Aroha*,' said Connel, and cleared his throat. 'It is an important word in the Kawai Alanui culture.'

'And means?'

'Love.'

17

*A*nahera stopped on the edge Lani and scanned the night-shrouded awins. She had delayed her return until long after Whetu's brightness filled the skies to avoid explaining herself to her fellow Ahi, Elders or Ikaika. Confessing her failures to the Kuwaini was going to be awful enough.

She slipped between the awins, detoured around the fire circles and stopped at the Kuwain's door. It was as silent as the awins but the Kuwaini were within. They waited for the last Ahi to return either from ohaku-sai or ohaku, and their long vigil for *the four* who had perished had been remembered in song.

Tears threatened again and she blinked hard. Eight Ahi would set out for the Cloud Crown not nine and the sooner she told the Kuwaini the better. They slept on their seeli-mats with coverings tossed over them but Davi kept watch and he struggled to his feet when she appeared.

'Welcome, Anahera,' he said. 'We feared for you.' Anahera nodded, her throat too tight to speak, and seated herself on the floor while Davi nudged the Kuwaini awake. There were grunts as they struggled to sit and Anahera flinched as six pairs of eyes fastened on her.

'You are very late, Anahera, and we are glad of your return,' croaked Shenrin. 'Tell us what you have discovered.'

Anahera's hands clenched on her knees. 'I have discovered I am not yet *ready to die.*'

No one spoke but a breeze woke outside and the cup-lamps flickered. 'It is the Kuwaini who decide who is ready to die,' said Davi gently. 'Tell us what you have discovered.'

Anahera bit her lip as she considered her quarrel with Airini, Malo and Tamati, her blindness to the sun-eagles' threat, and her enjoyment of power over other water-breathing creatures. 'I discovered I care more about myself than my fellow Ahi; that I am ignorant of things I should know; that I enjoy power and might use it to destroy.'

She dropped her head and it was Miru who next spoke. 'Tell us how you discovered these things, Anahera.'

Anahera falteringly described her refusal to complete her ohaku-sai with her fellow Ahi; her arrogant assumption about the sun-eagles; and her near-attack on the hiri. Silence fell again but she could not bring herself to look up to see the Kuwaini's knowing nods that their doubts had been vindicated.

'There is a third ohaku-sai to be completed before the Kuwaini decide who is *ready to die*,' said Miru. 'It is late now, Anahera. Eat and rest. You will be summoned again when it is time.'

No one spoke after Anahera had gone but Miru was grateful when Davi fetched a pot of *fela* and filled their bowls. Silence was usual after an Ahi returned from ohaku-sai, as the Kuwaini pondered what the Ahi had discovered compared to their fellow Ahi and those who were already Ikaika.

'Does anyone require more time?' asked Davi after a while, and when they shook their heads he sang the song of thanking for Anahera's safe return.

The song ended and Shenrin cleared her throat. 'The Ahi have discovered the beauty of Iolana in all its variety; the importance of its lowliest creatures; the boundlessness of its soil, air and water *and* their smallness; the strength that comes with working with others *and* its limitations; and how to see afresh what they have seen a thousand times before,' she said croakily. 'These discoveries are important. To safe-guard Iolana, Ikaika must understand how truly precious it is,' she finished, and coughed. 'But there is one Ahi who seems to have discovered none of these things.'

'Anahera discovered other things,' said Davi.

'Are they things Ikaika must know to keep Iolana safe?' rasped Shenrin.

Davi shrugged helplessly and Anbros stirred. He rarely spoke and Miru hoped the healer was about to offer an insight. 'She might be right to judge herself unready for ohaku,' he said, and Miru swallowed her disappointment. It would be easy to take Anahera at her word and exclude her but it was the Kuwaini's responsibility to decide who entered the Cloud Crown and who waited.

'Both Anahera's ohaku-sai have been different to those of the other Ahi,' acknowledged Miru, 'but different doesn't mean inferior.'

It was one of the insights the second ohaku-sai was intended to elicit, and one she sourly concluded had eluded Anbros during his ohaku-sai.

'*You* expressed concerns about her readiness before her first ohaku-sai,' said Shenrin, and coughed again. 'What do *you* make of her discoveries?'

Miru resented being reminded of her doubts and knew if she agreed with Anbros, the Kuwaini would withdraw Anahera from ohaku without further discussion, but she also sensed it would be the wrong decision.

'Anahera's discoveries distressed her,' she said thoughtfully. 'It is natural she doubts her readiness for ohaku. But consider this: she discovered flaws in herself *and* admitted them, and she discovered the intoxication of power and *resisted* it. Anahera made worthy discoveries, and I see no reason to exclude her from ohaku.'

'Yet,' croaked Shenrin.

Anahera loitered near her awin, reluctant to enter in case Airini, Maia or Hana were inside or perhaps all three. It was common for Ahi to share awins but Anahera wanted solitude, and she was considering other *empty* awins when a shadow detached itself from the darkness.

'Where in Whetu's name have you been?' It was Tamati, his voice edged with real anger.

Anahera stared at him dumbly, unable to think of anything that would not reveal the hurt inside.

'Anahera?' His voice had gentled as he moved closer but it made it worse. 'Tell me what happened.'

'I can't,' she said thickly.

'Did you complete ohaku-sai?'

'Yes,' she mumbled and looked away.

'Have you eaten?' he asked. She shook her head and his fingers brushed the top of her hand and when she did not withdraw it, took it. 'I have roasted kumara at my fire. Come and eat with me.'

He led her off to the awin he often shared with Malo, squatted by the fire circle and heaped coals over the kumara. The orange glow lit his face, beautiful as always but for the first time, she wondered if she *really* knew him. This was the male she had played with as a younger Ahi and quarreled with as an older one, but things seemed strange now, including him.

'If you have just returned, you must have taken a very long route,' he said, glancing sideways at her. She shook her head and when the silence stretched, he got to his feet. 'I'll make us some fela,' he said, and retrieved a pot of water and drinking bowls from his awin. He set the pot on the coals, and glanced at her again, then up at the stars. 'At least the rain has cleared,' he said.

She looked up too and as the knot eased in her gut, closed her eyes and opened her other senses. She could smell the rero-tinged smoke, feel the soft pulse of the fire-warmth, hear the rustle of scarlet-tongues away in the brack.

'Anahera?' His voice was tender and as his arm came around her, she let the tears come, a wet sliding down her cheeks then cooler splashes onto her chest. He pulled her close so that her face rested in the curve of his neck and his hair brushed her face. He did not speak but she felt the strong beat of his heart and something changed in hers.

'Tami,' she whispered in wonder, and touched his cheek. His heart quickened and she tilted her face to meet his kiss.

Ahi kissed each other often, sometimes in fun, sometimes in passion but this was different. His lips only brushed hers then moved over her cheek like the dance of golden-flies but he stirred a hunger for more and she kissed him hard on the mouth.

He returned her kisses with equal passion but she was not surprised when he drew back as Ahi always did. What did surprise her was when cradled her face between his hands. 'You are the most precious of all Ahi to me,' he said. 'And you will be the most precious of all Ikaika. I want to be the most precious of all Ikaika to you as well.'

The declaration was a request for a mate-pair but only Ikaika could mate-pair and she blinked in confusion. He waited and she licked her lips. 'Ohaku changes everything,' she said unsteadily. 'You don't know *what* will be precious to you after that.'

'I know this.'

She jerked her face free. 'My ohaku-sai was poor, Tamati. I might not enter the Cloud Crown.'

'Is that what the Kuwaini said?' he asked sharply.

'They said to wait to be called.'

She heard his exhalation of relief. 'The Kuwaini are wise, Anahera. You need to trust them.' His fingers caressed her arm and he smiled. 'You should have stayed with me, Malo and Airini,' he said lightly. 'We had no difficulties.'

'Yes,' she said slowly. 'I should have stayed with you.' The confession seemed to please him, as if she had learned some sort of lesson, but acknowledging her mistake simply reinforced her belief that, when her friends entered the Cloud Crown, she would not be with them.

18

$\mathcal{J}$ax was aware that he dreamed, that the suck of moana up and down Rua's gravel beach was a dream, like the wheel of redgulls against Rua's blue skies, and the sound of Mati's laughter beside him, but he questioned none of it, greedy for more. Mati slung his sun-warmed arm around Jax's shoulders and even in the dream, Jax delighted in Mati's touch, and scent, and nearness.

They stood on Rua's northern shores and stared up at Iolana's soaring peak with its ever-present circle of cloud and as Jax's focus on the cloud narrowed, the understanding that he dreamed faded. He still heard Mati's voice as they joked about how one day they would climb Tihi and return to Rua as powerful Ikaika, but the words blurred. He was aware only that Mati boasted he would still be faster than Jax, and that irritation had flared.

And then Mati was running, as if to prove his point, and the sunny day dimmed as Jax sprinted after him along the gleaming shore. Mati tossed words over his shoulder that Jax could not quite hear but that fed an anger that roared like fire, and then he was a sun-eagle far from Rua, Mati's shift-form a long way below, and then everything was white: the air, the ribs of the boat that hauled him from the water, the fluorescent tubes overhead.

Jax opened his eyes. It was white here too. The light, the ceiling, the pillow he glimpsed to either side. He still heard Mati's voice but Jax's head was too heavy to turn and his body a dead weight. He shut his eyes again, relieved to leave the white behind.

The light was gentler the next time he woke. The ripe sun of evening, he thought vaguely. He stared at the stripes on the wall in front and after a while deduced that sunlight streamed through a barred window behind him. He tried to ease himself up but could not, and cranked his head from the pillow to peer down.

He was pinned to the bed by webbing straps. They looped over his chest, stomach and legs, and more of them around his wrists ensured the drips in his arms stayed firmly in place. Bandages bound his chest and limbs too, adding to his feeling of constriction and being unable to mimic even the smallest Off-islander gestures deepened his horrible sense of vulnerability.

'Welcome back, Jax.' It was Matiu's voice and a chair grated as Matiu shifted into Jax's line of vision. For a moment Jax saw the boy from the dream: green eyes dancing, teeth flashing in a smile, and then Matiu's scarred face replaced it. He looked tired, his green eyes infinitely sadder. 'I thought I was going to lose you,' he whispered. 'You came close to dying.'

Matiu used Kawai Alanui, as he had in the dream, and Jax stared at the barred shadow on the wall. 'Shame I didn't,' he said in English.

Matiu's hand closed over his and the straps prevented Jax shrugging it off. 'Don't,' he ordered harshly, but Matiu's hand remained.

'I need you, Jax,' he said, reverting to English, 'but it's more than that. The Kawai Alanui need you. They are under threat.' Jax stared at the ceiling and Matiu leaned forward. 'Doesn't that mean anything to you, Jax? That our people are under threat?'

'*Our* people? You've thrown in your lot with the opala,' said Jax, refusing to look at him. 'Why would you care?'

'Because I remember the cooking-fires on Rua; the songs of the Elders; the chase of younger Ahi through the awins. I remember the sunlight on the lagoons, the hiri at play along the beaches, the voice of the wind in the rero. I remember the Ikaika who raised us, the smiles of our Ahi friends. I remember the sun's pink blush as it rose over moana, the gold of its setting, and how Whetu painted Rua as bright as Tihi's snow.'

Jax swallowed several times. 'Not even the mighty opala can stop a volcano blowing its top.'

'Rua didn't explode because it was a volcano,' said Matiu quietly.

'The whole *Zoo* is volcanic,' sneered Jax.

'You are correct. Iolana, Rua, Ke-one and Puha *are* volcanoes but *extinct* volcanoes, and even were they only dormant, no volcano erupts without warning. Tremors, quakes, smoke, fumes, changes in currents and sea-water temperatures: you don't need an Off-islander's instruments to notice those.'

Jax looked at him for the first time. 'What are you saying?'

'I am saying that Rua didn't blow up because it was volcanic, and that Iolana is under threat. It is why Commander Keli transferred you to URZOL, and why you need to go back there.' Matiu's grip tightened on Jax's hand. 'You need to go back to URZOL and work with Commander Keli to save Iolana.'

'I am not *working* with the *opala,* even if it means spending the rest of my days in a cell.'

'Do you think I am lying, Jax?'

Matiu had adopted the reasoned tone Off-islanders used to convince their adversaries through logic, and Jax strained against the straps in an effort to escape, then slumped back in frustration. 'I think you have been lied to!' he gritted.

'For what purpose?'

'For the usual purpose! The opala play games, Matiu. Stir a nation up here, nudge a few skirmishes along to a full-blown war there. It's the way they sell more of their stinking weapons!' Jax laughed mirthlessly. 'But I forgot you are part of *them,* part of the commerce that keeps it all ticking along.'

A buzzer sounded and Matiu rose. 'You need to sleep now to heal. I will be back to speak with you when you wake.'

'Don't bother. We have nothing to say.'

The door opened and a medic appeared with an instrument tray. 'Rest, Jax,' said Matiu, and gave his hand a final squeeze. The medic lifted the hypodermic from the tray, and tapped it with his fingers.

'I don't need to sleep,' growled Jax, straining against the straps again, but he was powerless to stop the needle sliding into his vein.

Keli clicked off the recorder but neither he nor Connel spoke and a few minutes later, there was a knock at the door. 'Enter,' called Keli, and Matiu came in and saluted. He looked just as haggard as when Keli had briefed him after Jax's retrieval, and that was four days ago. He gestured Matiu to the couch. 'Sit, Senior Airman.'

Connel poured him a coffee and Keli waited until he had gulped it down and some color returned to his face. 'We heard the exchange, of course,' said Keli, 'but we didn't see it. And even had we been present, we don't have your understanding of Alanui ways *or* of Jax.'

'I'm not sure I can claim to understand Jax,' admitted Matiu. 'We were twelve when we were last together.'

Connel leaned forward in his chair. 'What was he like then?'

Keli glanced at Connel in irritation. Matiu looked done in and Keli did not want to waste precious time on things that no longer mattered.

'Beautiful as he is now,' said Matiu. 'Happy, exuberant, competitive, as Ahi males often are. And loving,' he added softly.

'Competitive?' broke in Keli. 'Is it possible Jax is competing with us now? We want him to do X and Jax wants to beat us by *not* doing it?'

Matiu shook his head. 'Ahi males are competitive but they never intentionally injure each other or themselves, even in shift-form.'

'But Jax might have injured you *unintentionally*,' said Connel thoughtfully.

Keli and Matiu stared at him. 'What do you mean?' demanded Keli.

Connel's gaze on Matiu gentled. 'You were a long way from Rua when it blew up,' he said. 'The most obvious explanation is you raced each other. You suffered burns, Jax lost everything he loved. You can't remember the blast, but Jax can, and he remembers *why* you were so far from home. So he carries the guilt for the injuries inflicted on you *both*.'

'We raced each other many times,' said Matiu slowly. 'We were the fastest Ahi amongst our friends.'

Keli rose and prowled the room. 'Interesting,' he muttered, 'but I don't see how it helps us now.'

'Neither do I,' admitted Connel.

'But it explains so much,' said Matiu in wonder. 'The Kawai Alanui are one people. Four islands but one people. We should have been there, Jax and I. We should have died.' He glanced up at Keli. 'No one leaves the islands, Commander Keli. We share our name with our homeland for good reason, and yet Jax and I ended up here.' He took a shuddering breath and Keli and Connel exchanged glances. 'But I was luckier than Jax. I don't remember anything while Jax remembers *everything*.'

'Which is why he no longer sees himself as part of the Alanui,' said Connel.

'But he doesn't see himself as an Off-islander either,' said Keli tersely. '*You* managed to make a home amongst Off-islanders, Senior

Airman. Why didn't Jax? Or is your *apparent* ability to fit in mimicry?'

'I was in the Infirmary for over a year,' said Matiu, 'and cared for by those at Naraven Base. Airman, medics, nurses, cleaners, ground staff. Males and females of all ages became my family. Jax told me he was sent to a Boys' Home.'

'He later lived with an older man who was half Alanui,' said Keli, feeling obliged to defend the military. 'He returned there voluntarily after his Service to Country and was with him until he was transferred here. It seems to have worked out.'

'Just one person,' murmured Matiu, almost to himself, then looked up. 'The Kawai Alanui live as a community, Commander Keli. Younger Ahi, older Ahi, Elders; all together.'

'Which leaves us where?' said Keli in frustration.

'It leaves us probably knowing more about Jax's motivations,' said Connel. 'When Jax absconded previously, where did he go?'

'No one knows,' said Keli. 'There were no sightings of him off base and he wasn't apprehended. He was gone seven or eight days each time and returned to take his punishment. But we *do* know where he went this time,' he added grimly.

'Yes. To a place with a passing resemblance to Rua,' said Connel, and glanced at Matiu for confirmation. Matiu nodded. 'So,' continued Connel, 'on one level at least, it appears Jax wants to return to the islands.'

'*If* he goes back, it will be under my orders and for a very specific purpose,' said Keli shortly.

'Without knowing the military's exact requirements concerning Airman Jax,' said Connel carefully, 'it might be useful if Jax returned to the islands *before* the operation commenced. It would reconnect him to the Kawai Alanui and give him a powerful reason to work in their best interests.'

'Not possible with his record,' snapped Keli. 'After the latest incident, I was on the phone for over an hour fighting to keep Jax at URZOL. There are many who would prefer to see him as far from the Exclusion Zone as possible, and most of them happen to be my superiors.'

'Perhaps I could perform the duties you have in mind, Commander Keli,' said Matiu.

'If you could, you would have been assigned them months ago,' said Keli bluntly, 'but thank you for the offer. I need a shifter who can *shift*, and unfortunately, Jax remains the only candidate.

Jax had no idea how much time had passed before he woke again. He was aware he had not dreamed, at least of Rua, but he had dream-like memories of being unstrapped and turned, of being bathed and dressings changed. There were the sting of hypodermics and jabs of pain where catheters were jolted, and then he was on his back again, smooth white sheets cool against his skin, straps holding him to the bed.

Drugs dulled the pain of the slashes but nothing eased the horror of being held motionless. It was a constant reminder of being trapped between Kawai Alanui and the Off-islands and the room's empty whiteness added to his distress. He craved the view from the window behind him, which might show something, *anything* green, assuming he was at Rilo Base. All he could do was stare at the shadow of bars on the wall, and they reinforced his status as prisoner.

Medics adjusted his drips and checked his temperature and blood pressure, but they did not speak and Jax wondered if their silence were part of his punishment. It would only be a small part and given his record, he probably faced a dishonorable discharge. It would end the pay cheque for Rafi, but free Jax to work another job.

Hope kindled and died. Keli was not about to reward Jax's insubordination by setting him free. He grimaced as he considered Matiu's claims about Rua and Iolana. They could be a pack of lies except the Kawai Alanui did not lie, *except* as military, Matiu would do as he was ordered.

None of it made sense. There was no reason for Off-islanders to blow-up Rua, although Off-islanders did not always need reasons. Sometimes they did things simply because they could. There had been wars where opposing forces had destroyed whole communities, even whole countries unrelated to the conflict, to threaten, or punish, or prove their might.

Had Jax been at Arozi, he would have run deep into the desert to scour the appalling idea from his head, but he was tethered here, with nothing to do but dwell on the possibility that Off-Islanders had obliterated Rua on a whim.

Saliva flooded his mouth and as he fought the straps, bile surged. He tried to swallow but being flat on his back, choked, struggled to drag in air, and choked again. The door was flung open, which told him the room had mics, and then medics were all around him. Matiu was there too. 'He can't breathe,' he cried. 'You need to sit him up!'

The straps were loosened and he was hauled upright and his head held over an instrument tray. He spat and sucked in air, the relief of being free, even briefly, overwhelming. The medics were muscular and straps still tethered most of him to the bed, but they hurriedly fastened the straps again as if they expected him to flee. Matiu hovered anxiously but did not speak again until they were alone, and then only to ask if Jax still felt nauseous.

Jax made no reply. It was pointless explaining the toll it took to suppress memories and he pushed at the straps again. The constriction might have been bearable had he not been horizontal. All he could see was the endless white of the ceiling, the shadow bars on the wall, and Matiu.

He turned his head and looked at him properly, the dream-image of Matiu's unscarred younger self still clear in his mind. 'Let me go, Mati,' he said softly.

Matiu took his hand again. 'I can't.'

'No. It would be a massive black mark against your *exemplary* military record, wouldn't it?' sneered Jax, and stared at the ceiling again.

'You are all I have.' The words were Kawai Alanui and Jax shut his eyes. 'If I took the straps off, where would you go?' continued Matiu softly, in English. 'Through the razor-wire again? And if you survived that, what life would you have? You were always a fast runner, Jax, and still are according to my friend, but you can't run forever, and when the military caught up with you, as they inevitably would, there would be more cells, and more of this,' he added, gesturing to the room.

Jax had concluded the same thing during Briggs' training course, but hearing Matiu voice it woke his anger. 'So you want me to build a nice shiny career with the opala like you.'

'I want you to help Commander Keli stop Iolana suffering the same fate as Rua.'

'Why should I?' demanded Jax.

'Because you are Kawai Alanui like me, and they are our people.'

'I am *not* Kawai Alanui!'

Matiu stood and Jax thought he was going to storm out but he caught Jax's jaw and forced Jax's face to his. 'It isn't your fault Rua blew up. It isn't your fault I was scarred. It isn't your fault you lost everything you loved. We were racing because it was something we always did. We were far from Rua because we competed, as *all* younger Ahi males compete. You aren't responsible for *anything* that happened!'

'Let go of me,' gritted Jax.

'No! The time for running is over, Jax. You aren't responsible for the past, but you *are* responsible for the future, for *Iolana's* future. Ahi become the guardians of *everyone's* future when they die and are born again as Ikaika. You *have* to go back! You have to go back and die so you can stop what happened to Rua happening to Iolana. It isn't a choice, Jax! It's your responsibility.'

Jax's chest heaved but he did not wrench his face free even when Matiu loosened his grip. He simply stared into Matiu's green eyes, as he had so many times before, but this time he saw Rua's verdant valleys and the deep emerald of its lagoons.

Tears seeped from his own eyes but he let them come and then Matiu's mouth came to his, his lips soft, the kiss fleeting. 'I love you, Jax,' he whispered in Kawai Alanui. 'But I can't do this for you. *You* have to do it for all of us.'

19

Anahera hugged herself in an attempt to still her shaking but it was no use. Tamati shook beside her, and Malo and Airini, in fact everyone who had *chosen to die* shivered. They sat in a circle, shoulder to shoulder in Makariri's snow, and stared at each other.

No one said anything but Tamati was the first to *do* something. He put one arm around Anahera and the other around Malo on his other side, and feeling the warmth increase, Anahera put her arm around him and the other around Airini on *her* other side, and it was not long before the rest of the Ahi followed suit.

Their inter-laced arms tightened the circle and as they shuffled forward and their thighs came into contact and warmed each other, they tightened the circle again until their feet all but touched in the centre.

It was fortunate the weather was still or they would have been even colder, concluded Anahera, as she considered the blustery winds of the previous days. The snow was brilliant against the blue sky, but it was still freezing and her backside was numb

The third ohaku-sai required them to sit together in Makariri, Kohatu and Wairere and they had decided to visit Makariri's snows first, before they grew tired. Anahera was glad to be with her fellow Ahi but the ohaku-sai puzzled her. The Kuwaini had not stipulated how long they must sit or what they must do, though she guessed it was not to stare at each other in silence.

The Ahi's faces told her no one wanted to be first to suggest they leave, but as she scanned the group, Maia sagged sideways against Nikau. 'Maia!' she called in alarm. 'Are you unwell?'

Maia said something but her head had fallen forward and her words were unintelligible. Nikau shook her and she managed to raise her head. 'She is all right—' he began but Tamati cut him off.

'She isn't all right and we have been here long enough,' he said, and struggled to his feet.

'Whether we have been here *long enough* is a group decision,' said Hemi.

'And should have been taken before Maia sickened,' retorted Tamati. 'Is anyone else feeling ill?' His gaze searched the group and fastened on Rawiri.

'Just cold,' said Rawiri, but his words were slurred and Anahera's heart missed.

'We need to descend to Kohatu,' said Tamati, and Anahera, Malo and Airini struggled to their feet.

'It needs to be a *group* decision,' insisted Hemi, not moving. '*I* don't feel overly cold.'

'My concern isn't for Ahi who don't feel *overly cold*, but for those who are frozen,' snapped Tamati.

Hemi opened his mouth to respond but Airini got in first. 'This is why the Kuwaini sent us here,' she said.

'To make half of us ill?' asked Malo tersely.

'To see if we can act as a group. The Ikaika work *together* to keep the Kawai Alanui safe, but here we are, bickering over whether we should stay because some of us still feel strong, while others are already unwell.'

'Ikaika protect the vulnerable,' said Hemi slowly. 'Tamati is right. We should *all* descend.'

The group clambered to their feet but Maia could not walk and Tamati took one arm and Hemi the other, and they half carried her between them. Malo helped Rawiri, who insisted he was well, but he did not shrug Malo off. The rest followed with their arms about each other, greedy for warmth.

Kohatu's black stone felt as warm as moana's summer waters after Makariri's snow, and Anahera unclenched her arms from around Airini and sighed in relief. Most of the group sought out the largest, flattest stones and sunned themselves like moko, but Tamati and Hemi still supported Maia and Anahera hurried over.

'I am feeling better,' muttered Maia, as they lowered her down, but it was clear how unsteady she was.

'I will sit with her,' Anahera told Tamati, knowing female Ahi preferred female company when ill.

Hemi moved off but Tamati lingered. 'Call if you need help,' he said, and Anahera nodded. She put her arm around Maia and pulled her close, and Maia rested her head on Anahera's shoulder.

'I don't want to enter the Cloud Crown if it is like Makariri,' muttered Maia.

'I don't think any of us want to enter the Cloud Crown whatever it is like.'

'The male Ahi seem unconcerned.' Anahera made no reply, her attention on the slow circles of a sun-eagle, and she shivered as she recalled her second ohaku-sai. 'Are you cold too?' asked Maia, raising her head.

'No, it is warm here.' Anahera smiled humorlessly. 'I've never liked Kohatu but it is positively lovely compared to Makariri.'

Maia managed a smile. 'It is now my favorite place too.'

Kohatu's broken stone meant they could not sit closely but they shifted to stones where they could face each other, and for a while simply enjoyed the warmth. As usual, Malo was the first to grow restless. 'Anyone have any idea what the Kuwaini want us to discover here?' he asked.

'That stone is better than snow?' suggested Rawiri ironically.

'Or simply different,' said Hana. 'Both are part of Iolana and both important. Makariri's snows feed Iolana's springs and streams, while Kohatu's stone . . .' She trailed off.

'Exactly,' said Malo. 'What *is* the point of Kohatu's stone?'

'It has no point,' said Nikau, and sighed as he stretched out his legs.

'So why ask us to sit here?' asked Airini.

'The Kuwaini set ohaku-sai for a reason,' Tamati reminded them.

'But trying to work out the reason feels like a game of seek,' said Rawiri.

'It's a lot more important than a game of seek,' said Tamati. 'Anyone have any thoughts?' No one spoke and Tamati's gaze settled on Anahera. 'What about you?'

'Maybe the point is there is *no* point, at least for us. We are sitting here discussing what is important to *us*. But we are only one of Iolana's creatures. Kohatu is important to countless *other* creatures, including moko and snakes, and to sun-eagles who prey on both. Maybe the Kuwaini want us to understand Iolana doesn't just belong to us.'

'I don't know *what* the Kuwaini want us to understand, but what Anahera says makes sense,' said Airini.

'As much as anything makes sense during ohaku-sai,' muttered Malo.

'Have you got a better suggestion?' challenged Tamati.

Malo shrugged. 'That the Kuwaini want to remind us parts of Iolana differ from each other as *we* differ from each other; that Iolana has a heart of stone you can only see here; that *where* we are in Iolana is irrelevant, it is being together as Ahi for the last time that is important . . .' He grimaced. 'Shall I go on?'

'You probably will anyway,' muttered Nikau.

'All these things might be true,' said Maia thickly. 'Maybe the Kuwaini want us to realize that questions don't have to have a single correct answer.'

No one said anything and Malo got to his feet. 'I'm not sure there is anything more to be gained from staying here, given everyone has warmed up. Are you all right to walk, Maia?' Maia nodded. 'Then unless anyone objects, I suggest we go back to Wairere.'

Anahera sensed the group's tension lessen as soon as they reached the trees. Nikau and Malo chatted amiably, Maia had color back in her cheeks, and Tamati had stopped frowning. But they had yet to decide where in Wairere to sit and she dreaded another argument.

'I would have preferred to do this final ohaku-sai alone,' said Airini, coming level, 'or with you,' she added. 'It is so much harder for a group to decide *anything*.'

'Yes, and the Ikaika decide *everything* as a group.'

'So do the Kuwaini. And yet, despite their wisdom, it is difficult to believe they never argue. They are all so different. Miru and Shenrin Dream-travelers, Davi thoughtful, Anbros quiet, in fact, you wonder if he even listens when you describe your ohaku-sai. Cheren and Sairin barely speak either.'

'We are all different too,' said Anahera, 'which is why we argued today.'

'It would be dangerous if we were all the same,' said Airini unexpectedly. 'We might agree on something without proper discussion and be completely wrong. There is a better chance of a good decision if we disagree.'

'So let's hope the Kuwaini disagree about who is ready for ohaku,' said Anahera.

Airini looked at her in surprise. 'But we are all ready.'

Anahera said nothing and Airini caught her hand and locked fingers. 'It is normal to have doubts, as I have said before. In any case, in a few short days, our Ahi doubts will be behind us and we will be *wise* Ikaika,' she added with a grin.

Most of the group wanted to sit on Iolana's cliffs over-looking moana and Anahera thought it was fitting to be reminded that moana shaped so much of their lives. They perched on stones next to each other, but their eyes were on the sea. Moana could be as grey as the Cloud Crown, with huge rolling swells, or as still as glass, with waters as green as Wairere's valleys, *and* all the moods and colors in between.

But it was quiet now, bathed in the afternoon's golden light, its crests as bright as Makariri's snows. Red- and blackgulls wheeled above the waves and Anahera instinctively searched for sun-eagles and was relieved to find none.

'Any suggestions what the Kuwaini want us to discover here?' asked Malo.

'That we are capable of enjoying moana in silence?' suggested Airini.

'Anything else?' pursued Malo, ignoring Airini's tone.

'That moana makes us what we are, namely Kawai Alanui, not *Off*-islanders,' said Tamati.

'*And* what it means to be Kawai Alanui,' added Nikau.

'And what *does* it mean to be Kawai Alanui?' goaded Malo.

Nikau shrugged. 'If you don't know by now there isn't much point me explaining it to you.'

'It *is* an important question, given that as Ikaika, we must protect Kawai Alanui ways,' said Tamati unexpectedly.

'We can *shift* form,' said Hana. 'Off-islanders are stuck in birth-form all their lives. *Shifting* gives us an understanding of our fellow creatures, unlike the Of-islanders. Maybe that is why they are war-like.'

Silence fell and Anahera wondered whether they recalled how the Off-islanders' weapons had streaked overhead to explode with roars louder than lightning bolts. They might not, having been very young but they would all remember when Rua had blown up; the fear the world had ended etched into their memories.

'You look serious,' said Tamati, settling beside her.

'I was thinking about when Rua blew up which was very serious,' she said, forcing a smile.

'So is mate-pairing. I hope you have been thinking about that as well.'

Tamati made no effort to lower his voice and even the Ahi further along the cliff looked at them, except for Malo, who positively glared. 'I haven't been thinking about mate-pairing,' she said, annoyed Tamati used her to goad Malo. The Ahi still stared and she shrugged. 'Becoming Ikaika changes everything. No one knows what they will want then.'

'*I* know what I will want.'

'Then you are fortunate,' snapped Anahera, sick of his game-playing. She got to her feet. 'Are we ready to go back to Lani or do we need to speak some more?' she asked of no one in particular.

'I think we have *all* said enough for one day,' said Airini, and set off through the trees.

Miru lay motionless until the dream's horror had faded. She had not dreamed since ohaku-sai had begun and it was ominous she dreamed now. She peeled back the cover and eased herself up, careful not to disturb the other Kuwaini. She needed the star-filled air to ponder the dream but as she picked her way through the sleeping bodies, Shenrin struggled upright too.

Miru's lips compressed but the journeys of Dream-travelers could not be hidden from those who trod the same paths and they made their way out and settled next to the fire. The coals glowed softly but Miru stared up at the stars' cold light. The fire reminded her too much of Iolana's sky when Rua had disappeared.

'It might *only* be Rua you dreamed of,' croaked Shenrin after a while.

'Rua has been gone ten years and I haven't dreamed of it before. No, we both know this is about ohaku.'

'About *Anahera's* ohaku,' corrected Shenrin. 'What will you do?'

'It is a question of what the *Kuwaini* will do,' countered Miru.

'We will take your advice.'

But Miru did not know what advice to give. She had been troubled by Anahera's first two ohaku-sai but there was nothing unusual about the last one, and even an unusual ohaku-sai did not necessarily bode ill. Younger Ahi grew as their spirits dictated but differences faded as they matured into older Ahi, and when they became Ikaika, they must put their differences aside to serve Iolana.

She stifled a yawn. It had been a long day listening to the Ahi recount their feelings at being with their fellow Ahi in Makariri, Kohatu and Wairere, and Anahera's account had roused no uneasiness, but Miru had not felt uneasy when *the nine* had set out either and nor had the Kuwaini.

'We have another day,' said Shenrin soothingly when Miru failed to speak, but Miru feared another day would not be enough.

20

*J*ax watched the barred shadows fade on the wall. It was the first time he had noticed the light changing which told him the medics pumped fewer sedatives into him, as did his increase in pain. Fighting the straps had not hurt before but it did now. And reducing his medication did not mean they would not return to knock him out for the night and once they had, he would not be going anywhere.

He had not *shifted* since Rua had blown but shifting was as natural as breathing. What made his gut churn was not knowing how birth-form injuries affected a shift-form. If he was just as badly cut up in shift-form, his chances of escape were nil.

There was only way to find out. He needed a shift-form that could shed the drips and catheters, slip through window bars, and get him through the perimeter fence, and assuming he was still at Rilo, he knew the route to take. Rats, moko and snakes came to mind but none could cross moana to Iolana which meant he would need a second shift-form.

Shifting took strength and younger Ahi were warned against *shifting* multiple times without resting in between and Jax was already weak. He would just have to rest when he reached Iolana *if* he reached it.

He took one last look at the ceiling and felt the familiar slide, as if he slipped into one of Rua's cool lagoons, then pain jagged. He had a moment of panicked confusion before his birth-form brain realized the tubes and catheters had ripped from his body, then the pain stopped and as shift-form consciousness grew, he slithered from the bed.

He reached the window, reared upright, and slid through the bars. The window did not lead to outside as he had supposed, but to a corridor, and he cursed his stupidity. No military building had exterior windows open to the weather. He turned along the corridor and set off, flicking his tongue as he went. The floor reeked of antiseptic and he was slowed by its lack of traction.

He craved the cover of bushes but vibrations told of the thump of military boots instead and he took refuge under a trolley parked against the wall. The vibrations dwindled and he went on, hugging the skirting board and seeking deeper shadows where he could but the sense of threat grew and his shift-form consciousness yearned to strike.

Off-islander voices boomed and his muscles bunched but then a sharp drop in temperature told him a door had opened to the outside. He tasted sweat on the air and the vibrations increased but he launched himself forward, the boom of voices like thunder and the air moving as men leapt aside, but there was earth under his belly now and he sped on.

He wove through the bushes at speed, skirted the square, and reached the grass beyond it. Leaves scraped his scales and he slowed as he tasted frog and mouse on the air His shift-form consciousness urged him to seek them out but his birth-form consciousness hurried him on. The perimeter fence was blurred but its metallic smell was strong and its links rasped his scales as he slid through.

He went on through the trees to the deeper shadows and rested for a moment below the spreading branches of a tree. It was a relief to be beyond the fence but then he sensed movement and looked up. The darkness was smudged by the gold eyes of an owl and then he heard wings scythe the air as it swooped.

Keli stared up at the grimy clock on his office wall and wondered sourly how his life had come to be ruled by its decrepit hands. Time had hammered him since his arrival at URZOL but the blows had ramped up in the last few months. He had fought time to track down Jax, to have him transferred, to be broken by Briggs, to put him back together and finally, to gain his cooperation, although the last had yet to be confirmed. And meanwhile, reports of Makena's covert activities in the Fayo continued to flow in. Makena had the jump on him, and as a runner, Keli hated to start behind.

At least he had a shifter now, or would have in a few days. Keli had sent Matiu back to his regular duties and would let Jax be for a while. Being held in isolation, strapped flat on his back, should reinforce the benefits of the *cooperation* Matiu had persuaded Jax of *emotionally*. In any case, *Airman* Jax needed more time to heal.

Time again! Keli clicked on the tape of Matiu and Jax's latest exchange. He and Connel had questioned Matiu about it afterwards and dissected the tape in minute detail since, but the parts in Alanui still troubled Keli and he regretted he had not insisted Matiu translate them. In truth he had been so relieved at Jax's apparent agreement to cooperate, he had not pushed the matter.

Connel's keenness to respect Alanui *sensitivities* had not helped but Keli worried the words whispered in Alanui might not be as intimate as they sounded, but a secret message from Matiu on how to circumvent Keli's demands.

He stood and stretched as the tape ran on. He had no reason to doubt Matiu's loyalty to the military *or* to him, but it was never wise to ask a man to choose between his leader and his lover.

The time for running is over, Jax. You aren't responsible for the past, but you are responsible for the future, for Iolana's future. Ahi become the guardians of everyone's future when they die and are born again as Ikaika. You have to go back! You have to go back and die so you can stop what happened to Rua happening to Iolana. It isn't a choice, Jax! It's your responsibility.

Keli's breath hissed as it had when he had first heard the tape. There was no time for the niceties of initiation rites. Jax could become a *man* in Alanui terms afterwards, if there were an *afterwards*. Right now he was a serving member of Samarak's military and would do as he was ordered, and that was to ensure Operation V's success.

Keli clicked off the tape and wandered to the window. The night was clear but the weather report told him another of the Fayo's howlers was on its way and he went to the cupboard and pulled out his running gear. It had been too long since he had felt the distance slip away under his feet and his heart pound with exertion, and if he had to run at night, so be it. There would be no time for running, or anything else, in the weeks to come.

Jax's *shift* back to birth-form was pure instinct and the owl clipped his shoulder before it swerved away. He sagged against the tree, too shocked to move, despite knowing he was visible from the fence. Blood oozed from his slashes where the stitches had given way and he suspected every *shift* would worsen the damage.

He had thought he would use a water-breathing shift-form to cross moana, but blood drew taniwha, and taniwha even attacked each other if the prize were big enough, and whatever form he used, he must first reach the coast.

The razor-wire glimmered in the starlight and he winced and hauled himself into the deeper shadow of the tree's lee, then let himself slide to the ground. If he *shifted* to sun-eagle he could clear the forests *and* moana without *shifting* again, but a sun-eagle's night vision poor. Whatever he did, he must do before Briggs came after him with men and dogs.

He forced his weary brain into gear. He needed a shift-form with keen night vision, speed, and no predators and his mouth twisted as he considered a screech-cat. Not the most beautiful of Whetu's creatures, but it fitted the bill.

The shift was painless this time, despite his wounds, and he sped off through the trees. His eyes pierced the denser shadows and his strength made every turn, leap and landing graceful, and it was not long before anxiety over Briggs' pursuit gave way to enjoyment of his power.

He streaked along, guided by shift-form instinct, pausing only to quench his thirst at streams. Running had never been so effortless nor the world so sparkling, every leaf and stone picked out in brilliant detail, and it came to him that no one would find him if he stayed in screech-cat form.

Rua's Elders warned against the seduction of certain shift-forms for good reason but he could not recall them warning against screech-cats, probably because their flattened faces, hulking shoulders and ruthless killing made them an unpopular *shift* choice. Staying in screech-cat form wouldn't make him a screech-cat anyway but a wairua.

He slowed when the trees gave way to coastal scrub and continued on lowered haunches, head coursing from side to side as if on hunt. Military installations were thick along Samarak's western seaboard, and he did not want some military hothead making a trophy of him. Whetu's rising increased the risks as well, its light so bright he threw a shadow.

He came to the cliff edge and stopped. Moana stretched away before him, but he did not shift, despite making an easy mark for a night-time hunter. His birth-form consciousness badgered him with questions as to why he was there, and he snarled as he prowled up and down. It had taken ten years to bury the memories of his first twelve, and he did not know whether he had the strength to resurrect them or even whether he wanted to.

The night air was full of the scents of creatures of soft fur and softer flesh and as the urge to hunt threatened to overwhelm him, he *shifted* back to birth-form and fell to his knees. Blood oozed down torso and he yearned for some dark hole to crawl into and sleep, but there was no time, just Briggs behind him and moana in front.

Sun-eagles were the only bird with the strength to reach Iolana without resting on moana's waves and he gulped down air and *shifted* again. The relief was immediate but he knew the *shift* had cost him, and he dreaded *shifting* back at the end of his flight. The stars were hazy through his shift-form eyes, but kept his gaze on them as he leapt into the air, and powered away over moana's dark expanse.

Keli's sense of well-being evaporated the minute he set foot back in his office. The answering machine's blinking light told him he had missed multiple calls and his language deteriorated as he listened to the messages.

He snatched up the phone and ordered Connel and Matiu to his office, and then the sen-cam footage from the surrounds of Rilo Base. It was close to dawn but he was in no mood for a shower. He toweled off the sweat, pulled a sweater over his wet tee-shirt, and brewed some coffee. He was on his second cup when Connel appeared, and his fourth when Matiu reported.

Connel looked like he had thrown clothes over his pajamas but Matiu did not look like he had slept and Keli's suspicion escalated. Matiu saluted but Keli was in no mood for formalities. 'Jax has absconded, Senior Airman,' he snapped, 'and I want an explanation.'

Matiu visibly paled. 'After I spoke to him, Jax understood the need to aid Iolana, Commander Keli.'

'Absconding is *not* aiding Iolana!'

'I believe he has gone there, Commander Keli,' he said, and swallowed convulsively.

'Believe or *know*?'

'Jax has to—' he began.

'I want to know *exactly* what you said to Jax in Alanui,' interrupted

Keli, and clicked the recorder on. 'Here,' he said, and paused it.

'I told him he had to stay.'

'Your *exact* words, Senior Airman!'

'*You are all I have.*'

Keli snapped the tape back on and they listened in silence until he paused it again. 'And here?'

Matiu licked his lips, his gaze straight ahead. '*I love you, Jax, but I can't do this for you. You have to do it for all of us.*'

'And *doing* it *for all of us* means following orders, *not* absconding,' grated Keli.

Connel cleared his throat and Keli's gaze swung to him. 'You have something to add, *Professor*?'

'Something I would like to clarify with Senior Airman Matiu, with your permission.' Keli nodded abruptly and Connel turned to Matiu. 'We discussed this after your last interview with Jax, but I want to make sure I understood you correctly. When you told Jax he had to go back to Iolana and *die*, you referred to the transition from Ahi to Ikaika. Is that right?' Matiu nodded. 'So you meant Jax couldn't help the Kawai Alanui until he was Ikaika?'

'Yes, Professor Connel.'

'Which means he has to go back and initiate before he can perform the duties of Operation V?' Matiu nodded, and Connel softened his voice. 'And yet you were shocked just now when Commander Keli informed you Jax had gone. Do you think Jax has reneged on his implicit agreement to help the Kawai Alanui?'

'No, Professor Connel.

'Then what?'

'Jax is terribly injured. It is too soon.'

'How do injuries affect *shifting,* Senior Airman?'

Connel's tone had not changed but Keli sensed his excitement at the prospect of adding to his research, and Keli wanted to know too. It would be useful if Jax could make it back to URZOL even if he were shot.

'I am unsure, Professor Connel, especially in my own case, but *shifting* requires strength.'

'And Jax is already weakened,' said Connel, and glanced at Keli.

There was a knock and Keli strode to the door and came back with a vid. 'Let's see if Rilo's sen-cams can shed any light on Airman

Jax's whereabouts,' he said, and slotted it into the machine.

They pulled their chairs closer but the early footage revealed only darkened trees, the flit of bats, and the occasional sound of owls. 'How did Jax escape the Infirmary,' asked Connel as they watched.

'He changed into a snake,' said Keli.

'A snake?' repeated Connel in astonishment.

'To fit between the window-bars,' said Matiu softly.

'Precisely,' snapped Keli, his gaze on the screen. '*And* he was seen, although no one thought a snake in the Infirmary was worth reporting.'

'Jax couldn't reach the coast in snake-form; it is too far,' said Matiu. 'He would have to *shift* again.'

'Two *shifts*,' said Connel. 'A lot considering his injuries.'

'*Three shifts*,' corrected Matiu. 'You can't *shift* directly from one animal-form to another. You must return to birth-form in between. It means—'

'What the hell was that?!' exclaimed Keli. He slammed the stop button, and the tape whirred as he re-wound it.

'It looks like a jackal,' said Connel. 'Can we see it again?' Keli obliged but the animal's speed reduced it to a blur.

'It is a screech-cat,' said Matiu suddenly.

'A what?' demanded Keli.

'Like a cougar but with heavier forequarters. They lived in Rua's mountains and probably still do in Iolana's. They aren't something you want to tackle,' he added with a poor attempt at a smile. 'They are fast and very aggressive.'

'Just what you need if you want to get from point A to B quickly without being challenged,' muttered Keli.

'But not if you need to cross water,' said Connel. 'Jax would have to shift again when he reached the coast. That would be *five* shifts,' he said and glanced at Matiu. 'Would it be too many, Senior Airman?'

'Not if he rests.'

'And will he rest?' asked Keli.

'Jax has absconded before and knows what it is to be hunted. No, Commander Keli, Jax won't rest.'

2/

$\int$henrin sang, her voice failing on the high notes and throaty on the low, but Miru was glad. Shenrin had not sung for the last few years. Sunlight streamed in dusty shafts through the windows but the Kuwain seemed gloomy. Today they must decide which Ahi were fit to start their ohaku and it was never an easy decision. The Ahi who set out must return as Ikaika, able to receive the songs of the Kawai Alanui's past and present, and later make songs about the future.

But if they returned with their own wants and needs intact then they returned without the means to keep the Kawai Alanui safe. Miru felt old suddenly, and glanced down at her hands, as gnarled as rero roots where they rested in her lap. All Whetu's creatures died, it was the natural way of things, and all the Kuwaini could do was keep the Ahi safe. But nothing was without risk and the Kuwaini might still send Ahi to their deaths as they had before.

Tihi's slopes were perilous beyond Kohatu and the storms seeded by the winds' sweep around the islands could be lethal. Miru stared at the bright sky beyond the window for reassurance, but blue skies could turn grey with shocking suddenness and water to ice in Tihi's higher pools.

Shenrin's wavering song ended and Miru joined the Kuwaini in thanking her. The Kuwaini were equal to each other, as were the Elders, Ikaika and Ahi, but Davi usually led the proceedings, and the Kuwaini's gazes drifted to him.

'We have had time to dwell on the natures of those who have *chosen to die*, on what they perceived about their ohaku-sai, and what *they* think it means,' he began. 'And we have observed them too and dwelled on what *we* think it means. Now we must decide who sets out for the Cloud Crown at dawn and who, if anyone, remains in Lani.'

Davi could prompt the Kuwaini to respond in any order but he always left Shenrin and Miru until last. Dream-travelers could offer extra insights, but as Davi worked his way around the gathering, Miru struggled to think of anything to say at all.

Davi, Sairin, Anbros and Cheren agreed that eight of the nine had completed successful ohaku-sai, and noted that while Anahera's experiences had been different, and she was less confident than the others, they believed her ready to set out. Shenrin's view was the same, and then the Kuwaini's attention settled on Miru.

'I agree with the Kuwaini that Airini, Maia, Nikau, Hana, Rawiri and Hemi give no cause for concern,' began Miru. 'I might have said the same of Malo and Tamati, except I find it hard to separate them from Anahera, and Anahera *does* trouble me.'

'More than she troubled you at the start of ohaku-sai?' asked Davi.

'No, but my unease persists.'

'Do you think it stems from Malo and Tamati's competition for her as a mate-pair?' asked Anbros.

'That they continue to compete should make us *all* uneasy,' rasped Shenrin. 'They are virtually Ikaika.'

'From what is told, Tamati's pursuit is genuine,' said Davi.

'I have heard the same,' said Sairin.

Formal courting was the preserve of the Ikaika and conducted in private but Kawai Alanui roamed Wairere and things were seen, and heard, and gossiped about.

'He seems to have acquired a taste for safety too,' said Davi. 'It suggests a readiness for Ikaika.'

'And Malo?' asked Miru.

'Many of our finest Ikaika were similar to him as older Ahi,' said Davi, 'but we are asking for *your* thoughts, Miru.'

Miru half shook her head. 'I can say no more. The unease I felt about Anahera remains. My feeling are less clear about Tamati and Malo.'

'What of your dream?' asked Shenrin.

Miru had not wanted to share the dream, but the Kuwaini had a right to know. 'I dreamed of Rua's destruction,' she confessed, 'but I don't know whether it shadows the lives of those about to enter the Cloud Crown. I had *no* dreams before *the nine* set out.'

'You are the best judge of your dreams,' said Davi, 'although it seems strange Rua's ending should return to you now.' There was a pause as uneasy glances were exchanged. 'It is close to noon,' continued Davi, 'and we must decide whether we summon nine to the songs of departure or eight.'

'I won't deny Anahera the right to journey with her friends,' said

Miru, which was not an endorsement exactly but the best she could do.

Davi nodded. 'All nine will be summoned then,' he said, and taking a deep breath, began the song that marked the ending of ohakusai. The Kuwaini joined him, as was customary, but Miru found it hard to sing. Being a Dream-traveler gave her special responsibilities and she feared she might have just failed them.

Miru returned to her awin to eat and rest and it was dusk before she went back to the Kuwain. She had not sought guidance in dream, or in speech with other Kuwaini, that time had passed, but Shenrin had sat with her in the awin, her knobby hand meshed with Miru's, and Miru had been glad of her company.

Voices hummed outside the Kuwain as the nine Ahi arrived one by one and settled on the mats. It was their final evening as Ahi and the Kawai Alanui gathered outside the Kuwain to embrace and farewell them as they passed. These were the children they had seen born and helped grow, who left now, never to return.

Anahera looked tense but so did the others, and Miru imprinted their faces on her mind as she thought of *the nine* who had sat here and of *the four* who had not returned. They had been beautiful, as the young always were, as *these* nine were. Graceful in birth-form and skilful in *shift*, they would make strong Ikaika, strong mate-pairs, and strong parents.

Then why did dread sit like Kohatu's stone in her chest? She had made her decision, she reminded herself, and if worse came to worse and only eight returned, it would have to be enough.

Anahera struggled to empty her mind as the Kuwaini's songs swirled around her. The Kuwain sat in the heart of Lani and she had heard the songs spill from its windows when Ahi embarked on ohaku and when Kawai Alanui died. The songs for those who would never tread Wairere's lush valleys again and those who would never tread them again *as Ahi*, were the same. Death was final for both.

Maia sat to her right and Hemi to her left but she wished she had timed her entry to sit near Airini, or Tamati, or Malo. She needed

Malo's sardonic sideways glance, or Airini's comforting hand, or Tamati's *accidental* brush of his arm or leg against hers. It was normal to be anxious, she reminded herself, and she sensed the rest of the group were too, but that in a few short days they would all be back here as Ikaika to enjoy the songs of welcome.

The Kuwaini fell silent and Davi stepped forward and gestured to Maia, and she went to him and bowed her head as he put his hands on her shoulders and spoke to her quietly. Some of his words were for Maia's ears alone, such as where she must start her ohaku and the route she must take, but others were the same for everyone.

They could drink but not eat or *shift* until they had found their skin-spirit and gazed on Huna. They could eat and journey together once they reached Kohatu again, if they wished, but once they reached Lani, they must go straight to the Kuwain to receive the songs gifted to Ikaika.

Maia stared straight ahead as she went out and Shenrin stepped forward and summoned Anahera. The Kuwaini was unsteady and Anahera braced as Shenrin all but fell on her.

'You will start at Hapua and go directly north,' whispered Shenrin hoarsely, clutching Anahera's shoulders. 'The Cloud Crown is perilous and you must not delay after you discover your skin-spirit. Look on Huna and come directly back. If you see others returning, return with them.'

Anahera nodded and waited for Shenrin to loosen her grip before she made her way out. To start her ohaku at Hapua meant she must leave Lani in shift-form well before dawn and she wondered whether it would be best to go there now and sleep beside Hapua's peaceful lagoon. Her belly was full of kumara and whitefish so there was no reason to delay but she lingered outside, reluctant to leave without farewell.

She nodded to Hemi and then to Hana as they came out and then Tamati appeared. He did not say anything just waited with her, and they acknowledged Nikau and Rawiri as they went past, and then Malo appeared followed by Airini. They were not permitted to speak of their ohaku but they moved off together to one of the more private fires. They did not sit, just stood and stared at the coals.

'And so it ends,' said Malo finally.

'And begins,' said Tamati. 'And the weather isn't going to be kind.'

They looked to where shreds of cloud streamed in to veil Whetu's light. 'At least if it rains, we can open our mouths and stare up at Whetu to quench our thirst,' said Airini.

Anahera burst out laughing and Malo and Tamati grunted their enjoyment. 'I *do* love you,' said Anahera, wrapping Airini in an intense hug. Tamati's arms came around them, and Malo's, and they stood enclosed until Airini eased herself free.

'We have a hard few days ahead of us,' she said. 'Time for rest. Stay safe my friends,' she whispered, eyes glistening in the firelight.

'You too,' said Anahera, and gave her a final hug. Airini disappeared back through the awins and silence fell. Anahera guessed Tamati wanted to speak to her alone but Malo showed no signs of leaving and she gave a small smile. 'Time for me to rest too,' she said, and her throat tightened as she embraced each in turn. 'Stay safe,' she managed to say and headed off after Airini.

But she did not go far before she looped back towards the reros. The stand provided good cover to strip off her para and whitiki and *shift*, but Tamati appeared before she had a chance to do either.

'This isn't where your awin is,' he said.

'I didn't say I was going to rest in my awin '

He did not say anything but she saw him sift the possibilities. Heading for the reros meant her ohaku starting point was distant enough to require a *shift*.

'I wanted to farewell you properly,' he said, 'and remind you to be careful. There is no need to delay in the Cloud Crown once you discover your skin-spirit, or at Huna, especially given the coming weather.'

Tamati echoed Shenrin's warning but it was sensible advice the Kuwaini probably gave to everyone after *the four*. Anahera felt like flinging back that he should be careful too, but his face was tender. 'I have a gift for you,' he said, and slipped something over her head. It was cool against her skin and she peered down. It was a wolf's head skilfully carved out of pearl shell. 'I don't know your skin-spirit or mine,' said Tamati, 'but the white-wolf is beautiful like you.'

Gift-giving was part of Ikaika courtships not Ahi friendships and she had trouble meeting his eyes. 'I don't know what is to come, Tami. Neither of us do,' she muttered.

'It is a gift, Anahera, nothing more.'

It would be churlish to refuse it and Anahera nodded but she doubted even Tamati believed his own words.

22

Jax had not been airborne long before the wind picked up, buffeting him from the side so that he struggled to hold his course. The Kawai Alanui did not question the winds that battered their shores but Jax knew from the military that the strait that separated Samarak from Makena funneled air as well as oceans. Makena's row of extinct volcanoes along its eastern seaboard did not help the wind's turbulence either.

Cloud obliterated Whetu's light but sun-eagles had made Kawai Alanui their home for time uncounted and its location was imprinted on every hatchling's brain. He flew on, aware of an ominous creeping fatigue in birth-form and knowing he would end his days in the black waters below if his shift-form strength failed too.

The wind grew and as he fought to stay aloft he was enveloped in smoke. His exhausted brain feared Iolana had blown up then his heart thundered as he realized it was Tihi's cloud collar. The cloud band was for Ikaika, not for Ahi like him but as he angled his body sharply downwards, the wind thrust him back up into the cloud and he lost all sense of direction.

A shadowy tree emerged from the murk and he swerved, clipped another, and was flung sideways into a third. The shock took the last of his vision and he was aware of falling, of stinging foliage, and of a bone-shattering thump. He was wet, but had no idea whether it was water or blood, just used his last shreds of consciousness to *shift*. He screamed as pain tore through him and then darkness stole his other senses too.

Miru gasped and sat up. Wind thumped the blinds against the Kuwain's sides and Davi's dim outline moved along the walls as he secured them. All but one cup-lamp had blown out but there was enough light to see those around her still slept snug under their covers.

She hauled herself upright, and Davi nodded his thanks as she helped him rekindle the cup-lamps. 'It would be good to be as deaf as our fellow Kuwaini,' he said dryly. 'They sleep well.'

'I wasn't woken by the wind,' said Miru.

Davi paused over a cup-lamp, his face bathed in skull-like shadows. 'Do you wish to speak of it?'

'No, but I think I must.'

'Shall I rouse the Kuwaini?'

Miru shook her head. It would be pointless to disturb their sleep too; the nine could not be recalled no matter the dream. Rain joined the wind's howl outside and they settled at the small table in the corner.

Davi waited with his usual patience, but Miru wished it was Shenrin who sat opposite. 'I dreamed of a death in the Cloud Crown,' she said.

'One of the nine?'

'Of a sun-eagle but not a sun-eagle.' Miru knew she was unclear but dreams were not of the waking world and were hard to describe with the waking-world's words.

'Of a Kawai Alanui in shift-form?'

Miru nodded and Davi contemplated her. 'Only those on ohaku can enter the Cloud Crown and they aren't permitted to *shift*,' he said. Miru nodded again but could think of nothing to add.

'The dream seems to suggests one of the nine will break their ohaku by *shifting* and die in the Cloud Crown in shift-form,' said Davi thoughtfully, 'or an Ikaika will return to the Cloud Crown in shift-form and die there.'

'Or already have,' said Miru, aware time functioned differently in the dream-world.

'Ikaika have no reason to go to the Cloud Crown,' said Davi. 'Do you sense the dream concerns Anahera?'

'The Kuwaini know Anahera has troubled me from the start, but I do not sense it is her.'

Davi's eyebrows rose. 'Who then?'

'I don't sense it is *any* of the Ahi *or* the Ikaika, and yet it must be.' Miru sighed. 'Maybe I am simply poor at understanding what Whetu sends.'

Davi patted her hand. 'Once the weather eases, we will ensure Ikaika are accounted for. As for the nine who depart at dawn, all we can do is hope Whetu keeps them safe.'

Anahera left Hapua as soon as there was light enough to see. Wind roared through the brack and she was soon plastered with wet leaves but Shenrin's route saved her from the worst of the rain. There would be no shelter once she reached Kohatu and she thought of Tamati, Airini and Malo, and of the others who braved Tihi's storm-battered slopes. They were strong, *she* was strong, she reassured herself. No harm would come to them.

It was no lighter when Wairere ended and she surveyed Kohatu's hard blackness. Rain struck the stone and sent up fine mists before forming torrents between the crevices. Anahera had never seen Kohatu in storm before and the haze seemed as threatening as the Cloud Crown. She wanted to stay in Wairere's safety but forced herself to search for the best route up. There was not one and she gritted her teeth and set off.

The rain hit her as soon as she left the trees: hard, chill, and unrelenting, and the stone was so slick, she had to use her hands to haul herself up. A moko could run the distance in half the time, she concluded grimly, as she struggled on. The stone finally gave way to Makariri's snow and she broke into a jog. Running warmed her but she kept her attention on the snow. It had turned to slush and it would be easy to turn an ankle.

Her breath heaved in and out, and then soft grey streamered over the white and she stopped and palmed the water from her eyes. The tangle of mist-clothed vegetation looked like Wairere and she heard and smelled nothing unusual. She advanced cautiously, nerves a tingle, and when the bushes gave way to trees, stopped in their shelter to rest. She had thought entering the Cloud Crown would be terrifying it but it was a relief to be out of the rain.

The trees were dense, with rero hard up against brack, and there were creeper- and stringer-vines, and vines with glossy leaves and tendrils as thick as her wrist. But the cloud sat like a sheet of ice between her and her surroundings making it hard to see anything clearly and she opened her other senses.

The cloud distorted the bird-calls so that birds that seemed distant were suddenly close, and she jumped as blue-chuffs burst from the branches overhead, except they were blue-chuffs with yellow, orange and crimson breasts not just the usual blue! The Cloud Crown seemed like a different version of Wairere, as far as she could see, which was not far. An immense moko rested on a brack, and she hurried past, and glimpsed silver-crests with gold and bronze crest-feathers.

There was no sign of screech-cats or anything worse but if the land had not sloped upwards she would have lost her sense of direction. Her legs ached and having to clamber over rotten timber did not help. Logs and branches littered the slope, thick with yellow and cream shelf-mushrooms, as well as Wairere's usual orange.

She searched her surroundings as she went, and strained for sound, but saw and heard nothing to alarm her and wondered whether the Cloud Crown's dangers emerged at night. She guessed it still rained outside, despite only drips penetrating the Cloud Crown's canopy, but the light had started to dull.

Anahera licked her dry lips and grinned as she recalled Airini's quip about drinking the rain as they walked. The memory cheered her and she sent a silent entreaty to Whetu to keep Airini and the others safe.

Frogs sang beyond the rain's drip and knowing frog-song meant water, Anahera set off in their direction. It was only a rivulet but she cupped her hands and drank. The frogs had fallen silent at her approach but started up again after she settled on the moss to rest.

They sounded like scarlet-tongues but when she finally spotted one, its tongue was yellow. The Cloud Crown seemed to hold *more* of what Wairere held, she pondered, as she went on, but the rain was the same and she needed somewhere dry to sleep.

'Easier said than done,' she muttered. Everything was wet, from the thick moss underfoot to the blanket of clammy air. It was not a place a white-wolf would favor either. They needed over-hangs or shallow caves as lairs, but even as the thought crossed her mind, she glimpsed a flash of silver through the leaves and froze.

Every instinct told her it was a white-wolf and her hope of seeing one and it *knowing* her was about to unfold. White-wolves were not aggressive, unless under threat, and while they were not timid, they did not seek human company. She remained motionless and so did it and her confusion grew.

She began to wonder if she were mistaken, but it was definitely a white-wolf's pelt she saw, though not its eyes, ears, or snout. Its back then, but unmoving. White-wolves sunned themselves like moko but not on wet ground, in wet air, and she wondered whether it was ill or dead.

She circled cautiously and stopped. It was not a white-wolf but the back of a male's head! The wild idea came to her he was one of *the four* who had perished but they would have been bones years ago and she breathed again.

Despite his grey hair he was young and she gasped as saw his body was covered in horrendous slashes. None of it made sense! His short hair marked him as an Off-islander but as she edged around to get a better view of his face, she noticed broken rero branches and looked up. They had been torn from a rero, all the way down from its crown, and that told her he had plunged from the sky and *must* be Kawai Alanui.

His chest rose and fell but his sprawl told her he had not moved since he had hit the ground, and she picked up a branch and prodded him. 'Who are you?' she asked. He did not respond and she jabbed him harder. 'Who are you?' she demanded, then felt a wave of shame. No Kawai Alanui treated others so, especially the injured, and she dropped the branch and crouched by his side. His face was beautiful and she stroked his wet cheek. 'Who are you?' she repeated softly.

His wounds gaped as he breathed and she wondered if they had been inflicted by some sort of Off-Island weapon. She needed to *shift* to warm him but that would breach her ohaku, in fact, even being with him might breach it!

Her heart thundered and she willed him to wake so she could go on her way, but his breathing was too low for sleep and he might have other *hidden* injuries caused by his fall. Regardless, he would die unless she did *something*.

She stared sightlessly into the gloom, desperate to know what the Kuwaini would advise but the murk told her nothing. All she knew was Kawai Alanui did not abandon each other and for all his strangeness, this male was Kawai Alanui. Tears slid down her cheeks as she removed her clothes and the wolf-head from around her neck. 'I am sorry, Tamati,' she mumbled, as she put it aside.

She *shifted* to white-wolf because the stranger needed warmth but as her shift-form consciousness grew, so did the urge to clean his wounds. White-wolves licked injuries to aid healing and she worked her way over the stranger's body, starting with the scratches on his face and ending with the gashes on his legs. She hoped his eyes would open but he did not stir and when she had finished, she lay down and covered him with as much of her pelt as she could.

The light faded but it was dangerous to sleep in shift-form even without whatever lurked in the cloud-shrouded trees. She heard owls call and smelled white-hare and stoat but there were no snarls of screech-cats and as time went on, her tension eased and she was rewarded by the sound of the stranger's breathing shifting to the lighter rhythm of sleep.

23

*M*iru set off up the path to Shani, needing to stretch her legs. Food was delivered to the Kuwain during ohaku, so the Kuwaini had no reason to leave until the last new Ikaika returned, but after a day and two nights of rain, Miru was keen to escape its confines. It was not a frustration shared by the rest of the Kuwaini, who still slept, except for Davi who breakfasted.

Frogs were in full voice as they always were when it rained and Miru gazed at the water-silvered trees as she walked. The nine should have reached the Cloud Crown by now, and some gone beyond it. Male Ahi traveled quickly and were less discerning of the skin-spirit they chose while female Ahi tended to linger in the Cloud Crown.

It was hard not to think of Anahera after the dream but Shenrin had not dreamed of Anahera *or* the other Ahi on ohaku, *or* sensed Miru's latest dream, and Miru wondered if her dream of sun-eagle death was no more than that.

All Whetu's creatures died, taken by other creatures, storms, or time, so why dream of a sun-eagle? It was the biggest of Kawai Alanui's birds and the fiercest. Every moko, snake, stoat and gull were at risk when the sun-eagle hunted.

Miru stopped on Shani's banks and gazed at its shimmering water. A fine rain peppered the surface sending ripples to join other ripples in endless patterns. Miru was part of such patterns as were those whose bones lay under Iolana's soil, as were those who died as Ahi to be born as Ikaika, as was *everything* Whetu brought into existence, yet despite the insight, she felt blind.

She had always thought her dream-travels a gift but lately she wondered whether they simply bequeathed her a poor night's sleep. A shadow flicked over the lagoon's surface and she glanced up to see a sun-eagle disappear into the clouds. For a brief moment, all else ceased to exist, and then she bowed her head. 'Now I see,' she muttered, and turned back towards Lani.

It was too late for haste and when she reached the Kuwain, only Shenrin still lay snug beneath her cover. 'She sleeps,' said Davi quietly, as he poured Miru a bowl of fela.

'No,' said Miru, and knelt by her friend's side. Shenrin's eyes were open, as if she gazed on a place far beyond Kawai Alanui, and Miru gently closed them.

The Kuwaini hushed and it was Davi who helped Miru rise. 'How did you know?' he asked.

'I dreamed it,' she said, her gaze on Shenrin, 'though I didn't understand what I saw.' Skin-spirits were not shared but there were no secrets in dreams. 'Fly well my friend,' she murmured, and then let the tears come.

Jax's back was cold and his front warm and the mystery was enough for him to drag his eyes open. A wolf straddled him, its muzzle a hand span from his face and he gasped, expecting an attack but it withdrew, taking its warmth with it. There were steps behind him and he tensed but had not the strength to raise his head, and then a young woman knelt by his side. She had the wolf's eyes and his head swam.

'Who are you?' she demanded in Kawai Alanui.

'Jax,' he croaked.

She shook her head impatiently. '*What* are you?'

'Kawai Alanui.'

'If you were Kawai Alanui, you wouldn't be here.'

By *here* she meant the collar of cloud, he supposed. It was a special place and Jax wondered if that were the cause of her anger. 'I didn't mean to be *here*,' he said hoarsely and coughed to clear his throat. 'I got caught in a storm. I am from Rua.'

Her eyes narrowed. 'Rua exploded. Everyone was killed.'

'Not everyone. Two of us survived.'

She glanced away as she struggled with his claim and he had time to look at her properly. He had been twelve the last time he had seen a female Kawai Alanui and it was hard not to stare. She had straight brows, a full mouth, and very long, very thick auburn hair that fell forward, but he glimpsed a chest covering woven of leaves, and the barest of loincloths, also of leaves. A *para* and *whitiki*. It was so long since he had used the words, they sounded alien in his head.

She looked back to him, her amber eyes piercing, and he realized it was not her hair or clothes that made her different to Off-island females but her direct gaze. She looked straight at him, not to intimidate or flirt, but to understand him. 'Where is the other one?' she demanded. 'The one who survived with you.'

'Matiu is in the Off-islands.'

'Why didn't *he* come? Why didn't you *both* come straight after Rua exploded?'

'He was hurt.'

'Why not come on your own? Why stay with *them*?'

It was Jax's turn to look away. 'I was hurt too.'

She touched his chest next to a gash, her hand gentle despite her anger. 'Like this?'

He shook his head. 'Inside.'

'Did *they* do this to you when you tried to leave?'

'I did it to myself.'

She scrambled up and left his line of vision. 'You shouldn't be here,' she said, from away to his left.

Jax searched his memory for *anything* he knew about the cloud that covered Tihi's higher slopes. Ahi went there to complete the rite that changed them to Ikaika, but he had been too young to take much interest in it. *Ohaku* was something he and Matiu would complete in the far flung future.

'Are you on your ohaku?' he asked tentatively.

'I *was*.' And he being here had interrupted it. He struggled to sit but the trees swung sickeningly and he slumped back. 'You need to rest,' she said, beside him again.

'I need to leave . . . to speak to your . . . Elders. Then you can . . . . continue your ohaku.'

'My ohaku is finished. Those who *choose to die* must be solitary until they reach Kohatu on the return journey.'

Jax did not understand everything she said but the damage of his intrusion was clear. 'You should have ignored me and kept going.'

She blinked in confusion. 'The Kuwai Alanui don't abandon each other,' she said, but she was still angry.

The ground was cold and he needed to get himself off it, into shift-form, and to the Iolani settlement, wherever *that* was, but even keeping his eyes open was an effort and as shivers racked him, he let them close.

He felt her touch again. 'You need food and rest. Don't try to leave. I will come back for you.'

I will come back for you. The words ebbed and flowed in Jax's head and he groaned as his wounds throbbed. Why would she come back for him? He had ruined her ohaku. *The Kawai Alanui don't abandon each other.* He thought of Rafi, a man as lost as Jax, who had taken a sullen fourteen year old into his house and into his heart. Now Jax had abandoned him.

The frogs' sang as they had on Rua and for once, his head did not fill with choking smoke, but with memories of Rua's beauty. He had fought for ten long years to lock the memories away but now he let them come. They took his mind off the pain.

Anahera *shifted* to shia, streaked over Kohatu, swerved west to Hapua, *shifted* to birth-form and then to kirirua. She feasted on water-snails to shore up her strength then *shifted* back to birth-form to weave a basket for the casberries she harvested, *shifted* back to shia and streaked back, carrying the basket of casberries in her talons.

She could not save her ohaku but at some point in her flight, she realized she could save Jax, *if* she were fast enough. She did not know how long he had lain senseless in the cold and wet, but combined with his injuries, it could be fatal. Everything about him told her he was Kawai Alanui but *nothing* about him made sense. The Kuwaini's wisdom would solve the puzzle, she consoled herself, but first had to keep him alive.

Only his shivering told her he still lived and she *shifted*, dressed and shook him hard. His amber eyes opened, framed by his short silver hair, and almost it seemed she looked upon a white-wolf after all.

'You came back,' he said hoarsely.

'Of course I came back. You must eat then I will warm you.' She placed the basket of casberries next to him but he was too weak to sit and she had to prop him upright and feed him. After a little he recovered enough to feed himself but she still had to support him.

'They are sweet,' he mumbled. 'Off-islander food is bitter.' He looked at her. 'Aren't you having some?'

'I ate at the lagoon.'

'Rua had lagoons,' he said and stopped eating.

'Eat *all* the casberries,' she ordered. 'Then I will *shift* to warm you.'

'Don't. I have caused enough trouble.' He rubbed his face. 'I didn't intend for *any* of this to happen, and I don't even know your name.'

'Anahera.' She gazed up at the rero. 'Maybe this wasn't my time,' she said slowly, and shook her head, to rid herself of the thought. 'Whatever Whetu's intentions, you must be warmed.'

'Then *I* will *shift*.'

'You can't even sit by yourself,' she snapped, 'and tomorrow we must start back.'

'To where?'

'Lani, where the Kuwaini are.'

'Is the journey long?'

'In birth-form at least two days given we must go slowly.'

'I will *shift* to sun-eagle,' said Jax, his voice thick with exhaustion. 'It is how I came here.'

'Shifting takes strength. It is too dangerous for you.' She grimaced. She sounded like Tamati! Jax shook his head and her temper flared. 'We are *both* Ahi,' she said in exasperation, and swallowed as the truth of her words sank in.

He still stared at her blankly and she reminded herself he had been with the opala a long time. She knelt in front of him, took his face between her hands, and kissed him. He did not pull back but he did not return the kiss either and she kissed him harder. 'We are *both* Ahi, Jax. Do you understand what that means?' He said nothing and she kissed him again, more softly this time. 'Ahi are one, *we* are one. Remember that.'

24

*A*nahera *shifted* to white-wolf again and licked Jax's wounds before enclosing him in the warmth of her pelt. Wolves used saliva to heal their injuries but the act was intimate, given he was naked, and she had kissed him too.

He had been kissed by drunk female Off-islanders and by *sober* ones who had offered him affection as well as intimacy, but kissing had meant something else on Rua. He and Matiu had kissed as younger Ahi but Ahi kissed less as they matured, at least until they mate-paired as Ikaika. Older Ahi clothed themselves too which was why Anahera never *shifted* in front of him, and he flushed at his own naked state.

The consequences of her failed ohaku nagged at him as well. She probably had friends who completed their ohaku while she was stuck here with him. He guessed it was why she had been angry when he had first woken, but her anger had given way to concern for him. *Ahi are one, we are one. Remember that.*

Her care of him, a stranger who had destroyed her ohaku, made no sense at all. Rafi had done his best for Jax, but Rafi had been alone a long time and had never lived on Kawai Alanui. And then there was the military. It called itself a family but one for Off-islanders, not for the likes of him. The desert had been easier where there had been less need to pretend he was an Off-islander, but at least he had the skills to, whereas here, he had no skills at all.

It was as if he were that twelve year old boy who had chased Matiu along Rua's beach. He did not know how older Ahi behaved or how Ikaika and Elders behaved, and he wondered if it were possible to reclaim the years he had lost. The possibility he would end up wairua, neither Kawai Alanui nor Off-islander, suddenly seemed very real.

Jax felt stronger when he woke, which was not saying much, he conceded sourly, and the cloud meant things remained gloomy. Anahera *shifted* to shia again and disappeared into the murk to retrieve food but she took so long he worried she had come to harm. Rua had had screech-cats and he assumed Iolana did as well and there might be other creatures that preyed on the unwary. He did not need military training to tell him the lack of visibility made them vulnerable and he was relieved to hear her fly in.

This time she carried a whitiki as well as casberries and he struggled upright and waited for her to emerge from the trees. She approached from behind, as she usually did, her face creased with worry. 'I didn't realize the slashes on your back were even worse,' she said. 'I should have cleaned them too.'

'You have done more than enough for me'.

She shook her head impatiently, a gesture he was becoming familiar with. 'We are Ahi. I don't know why I must keep saying it.'

'Because I have forgotten what it means,' he snapped, fear of becoming wairua putting him on edge. 'I was twelve when Rua blew and spent two years in a Boys' Home. Off-islander boys, Anahera, with no past and no future, just like me. Then I got sent to live with a man who was half Kawai Alanui, but had never been here. He loved me but I didn't have any love to give back. Then I went into the military to give him money to make his life easier.

'You need money to trade for food and shelter in the Off-islands, things Kawai Alanui gift for free,' he said bitterly. 'Then I got sent to another base and met Matiu again.' Jax stared at the trees as he fought to steady. 'I thought he had died when Rua blew. He was happy to see me, but I wasn't happy to see him. If I hadn't chased him in sun-eagle form we would be with those we loved, not marooned here, neither Kawai Alanui nor opala. It was my fault we survived.'

Anahera came to him but he could not bring himself to look at her. 'It was Whetu's will,' she said softly.

'And was it Whetu's will Rua blew?' he demanded savagely.

'No one knows why Rua exploded.' Jax doubted it given Keli's behavior and Matiu's hint; it was the reason he was here. 'Eat,' she said. 'I made you a whitiki too, but first I will clean your wounds.'

Jax did not bother to argue and she disappeared again to reappear in white-wolf form. He sat and ate while her warm tongue moved over the gashes on his back, and then she licked those on his front again for good measure. The sweep of her warm tongue eased the knot in his gut, and when she reached the gashes on his chest, he stroked the pelt of her face, and she stilled, her amber eyes intent.

He had not experienced such tenderness since Rua had blown,

although Matiu had tried, and he rested his forehead against hers. She nuzzled his face then padded away and he sighed and struggled into the whitiki. It was scratchy after Off-island underwear but he felt more Kawai Alanui and less like a naked intruder.

He was still on his feet when she returned and her clear eyes appraised him. 'It is good you can stand,' she said, 'but sit and rest now. We leave tomorrow.'

'You said last night we would leave today.'

'You are weaker than I thought. We will travel faster if you build your strength.'

It was pointless arguing with the obvious and he slumped back onto the moss. 'Won't your people worry about you?' he asked.

'*Our* people know ohaku can take many days. Sometimes the skin-spirit is found early, sometimes it must be searched for.'

'What skin-spirit did you search for when you found me?' he asked, starting on the casberries.

'Skin-spirits aren't shared.'

The reprimand was a slap in the face and reminded him how little he knew of the people she insisted were his, and he stared at the trees again.

'Eat, Jax,' she said more gently, and he started on the casberries, tasting nothing. 'On ohaku, the Ahi journey to the Cloud Crown to discover their skin-spirits,' she explained. 'Then we continue up Tihi to gaze on Huna, the peak, before we return to the Kuwain to receive the songs of the Kawai Alanui. Then we are Ikaika.'

He did not need to hear her voice thicken to be reminded he had de-railed her ohaku, and she was stuck as Ahi, like him. 'Will the Elders give you a second chance?'

'A *second chance*?'

'Will they let you undertake another ohaku?'

She shrugged but her eyes glistened. 'I don't know of anyone failing their ohaku, except *the four*.'

'The four?'

'Years ago, nine Ahi set out on their ohaku and only five returned. The songs say Tihi was battered by terrible storms, but the Cloud Crown is perilous.' She shivered and gazed about. 'Not even the Kuwaini know what dwells here.'

'The Kuwaini?' She had used the term before.

'The Elders who prepare us for ohaku. They set the ohaku-sai, trials to ensure we are ready. Nine of us set out this time on different routes. We must travel alone until we reach Kohatu on the return journey. We aren't permitted to eat or *shift*.'

But she had *shifted* to save him. She looked away and he resisted the urge to comfort her. It had been a long time since he had reached out to anyone. 'So, the other eight are somewhere in this cloud?'

'Probably fewer. Tamati and Malo would have reached Huna.'

'They are the fastest males?'

'The most competitive, although . . . ' she paused. 'As Ikaika, they must put that aside.' She fingered the carving at her neck and smiled. 'Tamati will find that hard.'

Her expression and the pendant told him a lot about her relationship with *Tamati* but after Jax's blunder over skin-spirits, he did not ask. It was none of his business anyway.

Anahera was right about him needing to rest. The Cloud Crown might be dangerous but it was a measure of his weakness he let her keep watch while he slid into oblivion. He had never slept easily, even at Arozi, but he slept solidly now and was sorry when bird-calls roused him the next morning.

She was not there but he knew she would be back with the usual supply of casberries and that after he had eaten, they would set out for Lani. He dreaded the prospect. He had no idea what to say to the Kuwaini because he had left Rilo knowing nothing more than Iolana was under threat. But it would be harder for Anahera.

I don't know of anyone failing their ohaku, she had said, but it was worse than that. The other eight, presumably her friends, would be Ikaika, while she remained Ahi. And then there was the male called *Tamati*. Jax had not taken much interest in mate-pairing as a twelve year old, or in the courtship that preceded it, but he remembered mate-pairs could not be formed as Ahi. His crash into the Tihi's cloud had not just robbed Anahera of her ohaku, but Tamati of his mate-pair and the loss would be permanent *unless* the Kuwaini allowed Anahera a second chance.

They set out, but it did not take long for Jax to tire, despite the downwards slope. They rested frequently and drank from streams and Anahera even found him buri-nuts to eat, but he was exhausted long before the cloud shredded and the trees gave way to snow. He slumped onto a mossy log and surveyed the frozen whiteness. The cloud had kept the worse of the cold off but now it returned with a vengeance.

'How long does it take to cross?' he asked, hugging himself.

'We will reach Kohatu mid afternoon if we keep a steady pace. Once we start, we need to keep going. There isn't anywhere to rest.'

'Kohatu is where Lani is?'

She shook her head. 'Lani is in Wairere.'

Rua had just been Rua but Iolana was many times bigger, Jax told himself.

'From Huna you descend to the Cloud Crown, then to Makariri, where we are now, then to Kohatu which is mainly stone and then to Wairere and moana of course.'

'Rua didn't have mountains as mighty Tihi,' said Jax wearily, 'or snow, or bands of stone. It was lush with growth, lagoons and falls. It gave us all we needed.' His voice cracked and he dragged in air.

'It sounds like Wairere,' she said, and took his hand, but he jerked it free. He had caused enough trouble without muddying the waters with her mate-pair. 'We should go,' he said, his gaze on the snow. 'You lead.'

She set off but following her troubled him as much as her touch. She had the Kawai Alanui's height and slenderness and the whitiki left nothing to the imagination. She was not an Off-island female, he reminded himself, and amongst the Kawai Alanui, nakedness had nothing to do with sex.

She glanced back often, her amber eyes intent, but he concentrated on her prints. His feet were numb and hers were scarlet which told him she suffered too, and he started to imagine lying down in the snow and not getting up.

'Almost there,' she called over his shoulder, and then the snow ended as suddenly as it had started and he was staring at stone. Compared to the snow it was deliciously warm and he collapsed onto a broad slab and closed his eyes.

'I'll *shift*,' she said, but he managed to catch her wrist.

'You are tired too. Rest.'

Her face was suddenly very close to his. 'Ahi are one, Jax! How many times must I say it!'

'I am just an opala intruder who has ruined your ohaku,' he gasped. 'I don't want to ruin your mate-pair too.'

Her eyes narrowed. 'What are you talking about?'

'The Ahi called Tamati. He gave you the wolf-head you wear, didn't he?'

'Yes, but that doesn't mean—'

'Your face softened when you spoke of him.'

Anahera grunted. 'My face would *soften* if I spoke of Malo and Airini too although with Tamati, it is just as likely to fill with irritation.' She leaned in closer again. 'You have been with the opala a long time, Jax. You need to remember what it is to be Kawai Alanui.'

'I don't know if I can,' he admitted, and swallowed several times.

Her fingers stroked his cheek and he closed his eyes as her mouth came to his, the kiss long and gentle, and then he heard a guttural snarl and jerked upright. And in the instant he had left, he tore off his whitiki and *shifted*.

25

*M*iru lingered in the last of the evening light, reluctant to follow the Elders back to Lani. The rain had gone but the scent of turned earth remained. Shenrin had lain in her awin for the last three days, snug in her shia-feather cloak, and the Kawai Alanui had sang her praises, laughed over her foibles, and wept. And then they had brought her here in solemn procession, to lay amongst her friends.

Miru sighed as she considered those who rested in the trees around her and whose laughter she still missed, and now Shenrin was gone too. Peka chittered overhead and she turned back towards Lani, going slowly, the burden of Dream-traveling seeming heavier now she must bear it alone.

There would be other Dream-travelers, she reassured herself, who had yet to make themselves known but searching for Dream-travelers was less urgent then finding Elders whose wisdom could be added to the Kuwaini's and, before that, the Kawai Alanui's histories must be sung to the nine.

Dawn marked the fourth day since their departure and despite the rains, the first of them should return on the morrow and the rest over the following few days. And until the last one arrived and the last song been sung, there would be little rest for the Kuwaini.

Miru had less time to wait than she thought. Airini appeared later that evening, exhausted but calm as Ahi always were who knew their skin-spirits and had gazed on Huna in all its beauty. The Kuwain's blinds were secured, for these songs were special and not for the Ahi who might wander outside.

The Kuwaini sang some songs together and others alone, and Whetu's light had filled the skies before they kissed Airini on the forehead and formally welcome her to Ikaika. Airini went to her awin and the Kuwaini snatched sleep until Tamati and Malo arrived, and then Nikau. The songs and welcome were repeated, and it was evening again before Maia, Hemi and Hana reached Lani, having journeyed together from Kohatu.

The night passed uneventfully and gave way to a bright, clear day, but the mood in the Kuwain was somber. Two Ahi had yet to return and it seemed ominous that one was Anahera.

'She might travel with Rawiri,' said Davi to Miru as they ate together that night, 'or one or both be slowed by injury.'

'Or I shouldn't have allowed her to go,' muttered Miru

'It was the *Kuwaini's* decision.'

'But *my* dream,' she said, and drained her bowl of fela.

'And one Shenrin didn't share. She saw no cause for concern.'

'Perhaps she was too close to death,' said Miru as she wiped her mouth. 'Something else I failed to sense.'

'Whetu sends guidance, not answers,' Davi reminded her. 'There is time yet.'

Tamati stirred the coals of his awin's fire back to life but was too restless to enjoy their warmth. Dawn was close and neither Anahera nor Rawiri had returned. Tamati's care must be for all Iolani now but he could think of nothing beyond the missing Ahi

They would aid each other if one were injured, but what if both were injured, and in different parts of Kohatu, assuming they were not dead. Dawn marked the seventh day and new Ikaika returned in five or six, unless skin-spirits proved elusive. The wonder of finding his own washed over him again, and then he spun as he heard footsteps.

It was Rawiri and he was alone. He acknowledged Tamati with a nod, but limped on towards the Kuwain and Tamati resisted the urge to demand news of Anahera. Rawiri must receive the Kuwaini's songs to complete his ohaku and Tamati did not have the right to delay him.

His heart leapt as a second figure emerged from the gloom but it was Malo. 'Rawiri is back,' he said.

'I saw him,' said Tamati. 'Slowed by a sprain, by the look of it.' He stared at the fire for a moment, then his eyes flashed to Marlo. 'If she isn't back by dawn, we search.' Malo said nothing and Tamati's regard intensified. 'The *Ikaika* would search.'

'But not interfere.'

'Aid is allowed once Ikaika reach Kohatu.'

'Anahera is Ahi until she receives the songs,' pointed out Malo.

'Well I am going to search, even if won't,' said Tamati.

'I never said I wouldn't search,' snapped Malo. 'But we are Ikaika, Tamati. We can't act like Ahi.'

'It sounds as if you are,' said Airini mildly, coming to the fire. Malo took a steadying breath and Tamati resumed his fascination with the flames. 'Becoming Ikaika broadens Ahi friendships, not erases them, so that we care for everyone now, including Rawiri and Anahera.'

'Rawiri is back,' said Tamati shortly.

'With no word of Anahera?' she asked sharply.

'I didn't ask,' said Tamati. 'He was on his way to the Kuwain.'

'Given it is seven days since she set out, it is reasonable we visit Kohatu to ensure she isn't in need,' said Airini.

'At first light,' said Tamati, and Malo and Airini nodded.

'First light,' repeated Malo grimly.

Jax's *shift* to screech-cat was pure instinct but it was his military training that triggered his swift reconnoiter of the terrain. The other screech-cat was downslope, which gave Jax the advantage, and Jax snarled. It was the military equivalent of a show of force but the second screech-cat continued its advance.

It looked young and so might be keen to challenge, but Jax knew he might have accidentally invaded its territory. He snatched a glance over his shoulder and was appalled to see Anahera had not *shifted* and then he forgot about her as the screech-cat leapt onto the stone below.

Jax sprang, slamming into its chest, and sending it tumbling. It was on its feet in an instant, ears flattened and Jax braced. His birth-form consciousness wanted it gone but his shift-form consciousness wanted to tear it to shreds.

Jax advanced, hackles erect, teeth barred and it lowered its body and slid backwards, but he sprang again, fastened his fangs in its neck, and shook it savagely. The screech-cat shrieked and as soon as he released it, turned tail and fled.

The taste of blood was intoxicating and Jax battled the urge to pursue it, *shifting instead.* Pain surged through him but he managed to pull on his whitiki before he collapsed back onto the stone next to Anahera and sit with his head hanging forward. 'You should have *shifted* to bird-form,' he gasped.

'Why?'

She was angry again but he had no idea why. 'Because you would have been safer in a form a screech-cat couldn't get at,' he explained with insulting slowness.

'It was scarcely more than a cub and would have left if you hadn't challenged it.' Her face hardened. 'There was no need to attack it.'

Jax was surprised by how much her disapproval hurt. 'I am opala,' he said bitterly, his gaze on the sprawl of black stone. 'It's what opala do. We hurt things.' She said nothing and he hauled himself upright. 'Time to go.'

'You need to rest.'

He felt her hand on his arm and shrugged it off. 'I need to get to Lani,' he said and stumbled away but navigating the stone cost him everything and it was not long before he staggered to a stop and slumped down.

'I am sorry, Jax,' said Anahera, settling beside him.

'*You* have no reason to be. It was *I* who ruined everything for *you.*'

Her hand rested on his thigh, its comfort like a balm. 'It isn't just about you. I am impatient and impatience brings anger and thoughtlessness. None of these are Ikaika traits.' She shrugged back her hair. 'I know you *shifted* to screech-cat to protect me. I am sorry I spoke as I did.'

Jax could not recall anyone apologizing to him *ever* and he lay his hand over hers. 'At least Whetu is the same,' he said, staring up at it.

'You need to rest.'

'Not many beds around here,' he said with a poor attempt at humour.

'I will make a nice snug one.'

'You always do.'

'What? No argument?' she teased. 'That is unlike you.'

He brought her hand to his lips and kissed it. 'Maybe I am learning to be more Kawai Alanui.'

Her mouth kinked in a smile. 'Maybe.'

It was Anahera's sudden movement from his side that woke Jax and he wondered groggily whether the screech-cat had returned. He sat up and grimaced as pain burned. The gashes within vision range had started to seal but they were a long way from healed.

Kohatu's stone was just as gloomy in the early morning light but he kept his gaze on it until Anahera re-appeared in birth-form. Her attention was on the sky and he followed her gaze to where a sun-eagle circled.

'Tamati most likely,' said Anahera, as the bird descended.

Jax hauled himself upright, needing to meet Tamati on his feet. The Kawai Alanui were not violent but Tamati would not be happy at the loss of his intended mate-pair. The sun-eagle landed on a nearby stone and *shifted* but a blur of long black hair told Jax it was a female and he turned away.

There were footfalls behind him then Anahera's voice. 'Jax?' He braced knowing a female friend of Anahera's would not welcome him either. The new-comer was tall like Anahera but with black hair and grey eyes. 'This is Airini,' said Anahera. Jax nodded but Airini's appraisal was so intense he was annoyed to feel himself flush. 'Jax is from Rua,' added Anahera.

Airini blinked. 'Rua?'

'I have lived with Off-islanders,' said Jax.

'But—' Airini's eyes widened as she took in his gashes.

'I found Jax in the Cloud Crown,' continued Anahera. 'He is Ahi *like me.*'

Airini's breath hissed. 'Are you saying you *didn't* complete your ohaku?'

'Jax needed aid.' Airini's shocked gaze remained on Anahera but Anahera glanced skywards. 'We have company.'

'Malo and Tamati,' said Airini distractedly. 'We separated to search for you.'

Jax swayed, feeling the effects of his *shift* to screech-cat and lack of food. Anahera had not made her usual foray to Wairere for casberries because he had stormed off. 'Sit, Jax,' she ordered. Jax wanted to be on his feet when Tamati arrived but the stone tilted and it was Airini who caught his arm and lowered him down. She did not speak but kept a steadying hand on him.

The sun-eagles landed a short way off and Anahera waited for them to dress before she made her way over. Jax watched them. He did not need ten years of mimicking emotions to recognize their shock and anger.

Anahera led them back and Jax struggled to his feet again. The brown-haired male's hands came to his hips but Jax guessed the black-haired male was Tamati, which Anahera confirmed. Tamati hid his anger as Off-islanders did but the set of his shoulders gave him away.

They had the same build and direct gazes as Anahera and Airini but Jax had learned to avoid eye-contact with Off-island males, especially military ones, and found it hard to break the habit. Standing was hard too and he swayed again, something Tamati noticed. 'We need to get him to Lani,' he said to Anahera. 'You go ahead to the Kuwaini and tell them what has happened. We will bring Jax.'

'I stay with Jax,' she said, coming to Jax's side.

Tamati's brows drew. 'You need to—'

'You are *all* Ikaika,' she said fiercely. 'Jax and I are Ahi! Ahi stay together!'

Anahera could not have set up a better competition for her affections if she had tried, but Jax did not think it was deliberate. It was more a public declaration of her failed ohaku than anything else.

'*I* will go to the Kuwaini,' said Airini quickly. 'It will better if Tamati and Malo use their *male* Ikaika strength to help Jax to safety.'

26

Tamati and Malo put their arms under Jax's shoulders and all but carried him over the stone and Anahera followed. Tamati was angry with her and Malo probably was too, but the Ahi owed care to each other first, unlike the Ikaika, who owed care to the Iolani equally.

They journeyed in silence, apart from the occasional words of encouragement Malo and Tamati offered Jax, and turned west as soon as they neared Wairere. Anahera guessed they headed to Puru Lagoon to rest, where there were buri-nut palms, and snug shelter in the pan-reeds.

It was close to midday before they settled Jax in the reeds on Puru's shore and then Tamati's hard eyes swung to her. 'Malo will help Jax drink while we collect nuts,' he said, and strode off before Malo had a chance to argue.

Anahera followed but Tamati did not speak until they reached the palms and then he made no effort to hide his anger. 'You were wrong to abandon your ohaku!'

His anger was expected but his words took her a back. 'I didn't have any choice.'

'There is always a choice! Jax might have recovered and made his own way to Lani.'

'You see how weak he is, even now. He would have died.'

Tamati prowled up and down, kicking at the detritus. 'He *claims* to be from Rua and even if he is, why didn't he come ten years ago when Rua exploded?'

'He said he was hurt. He wants to speak to the Kuwaini.'

'He doesn't belong here!'

'Do you think Jax is an Off-islander?' she asked in confusion. Tamati shrugged and Anahera's temper flared. Tamati was Ikaika and Ikaika owed protection to *all* Kawai Alanui. 'Do—you—think—Jax—is—an—Off-islander?' she demanded.

'He shouldn't be here!'

'He has as much right to be here as I do! As *you* do! As *all* of us do!' Tamati made no reply and her voice dropped to a hiss. 'I don't know what you found in the Cloud Crown, Tamati, but I know what you lost, and that was your understanding of what it means to be Kawai Alanui!'

'Breaking ohaku doesn't just affect you,' he ground out.

Anahera wrenched the pearl shell wolf-head from around her neck and thrust it into his hand. 'It does now,' she said, and strode off.

Jax knew they had argued as soon as they re-appeared through the reeds. Tamati's body reeked of anger and Anahera no longer wore the pendant. Tamati nodded to him briefly and moved off along the lagoon's banks with Malo, but Anahera plonked down beside him with the nuts.

The male Ikaika had stopped to speak, standing closely as friends did, and Jax's thoughts went to Matiu and then back to Anahera. 'I am sorry I ruined your mate-pair,' he said.

'There *is* no mate-pair,' she snapped.

'Tamati thinks there is.'

Anahera followed Jax's gaze. 'Tamati thinks lots of things that aren't true,' she said. 'Eat, Jax. It is still a long walk to Lani.' Jax started on the buri-nuts, enjoying their sweet flesh. He remembered them as like coconuts but their taste was quite different. 'Why did you come to Iolana?' Anahera asked abruptly.

'To speak to your Elders.'

'But why now? You said you had just discovered Matiu had survived. Didn't you want to stay with him?'

The nut-meat balled in Jax's throat and he struggled to swallow. 'Matiu told me Rua didn't blow because it was a volcano. He said there was a risk to Iolana.'

'What sort of risk?'

'I don't know. I *shifted* and left.' He stared out over the lagoon. 'I wanted to complete ohaku. I thought being Ikaika would help me do whatever needed to be done.' He glanced back to her. 'I am twenty-two, Anahera. I should have been Ikaika two or three years ago.'

'Being Ikaika hasn't helped Tamati,' she muttered. 'It would have been better had you found out what the risk was *before* you came.'

'I feared that if I didn't leave then, I wouldn't have the courage to leave at all.' He smiled sourly. 'I have spent ten years fighting to forget

144

I was Kawai Alanui, Anahera, and that if I hadn't chased Matiu from Rua that day, we would be with our people.'

'You *are* with your people!'

'It doesn't feel that way.' He shrugged. 'Maybe I have lost too much time. Maybe there *is* no way back.'

'You *are* Kawai Alanui,' she said fiercely, and kissed him on the mouth.

The male Ikaika were on their way back but she kissed him again, and stroked his face. 'Eat the buri-nuts, Jax, then get some sleep,' she said, and with a final kiss, moved away with the males back along the shore.

Tamati and Malo walked in silence and Anahera grimaced. 'Jax needs to rest,' she said eventually.

'It will be easier to journey in the light,' said Tamati shortly.

'He will sleep for however long he needs to sleep,' said Anahera. 'It doesn't make any difference whether we reach Lani tonight or tomorrow.'

'Not anymore,' said Tamati, and Anahera's irritation stirred. Malo still said nothing, in fact, he refused to look at her.

'I am going for a swim,' she said, wanting to be quit of their company, and quickened her pace to the next stand of rero, undressed and slipped into the water. It was silent beneath the surface but she resisted the temptation to *shift* to kirirua in case her irritation with Tamati and Malo tempted her not to *shift* back again.

She came back to the surface, snatched a breath, and dived again, but her worries grew. Despite what she had told Tamati, she wanted Jax in Lani as soon as possible, so Anbros could salve his wounds.

She broke the surface, sucked in air, and dived deeper this time. This was the realm of the water-snail and kirirua, where the forest's detritus swirled down to join the rich mud on the bottom. A shadowy form jolted her from her reverie and she powered back to the surface. Taniwha did not frequent lagoons but she flinched as the water erupted beside her.

It was Tamati. 'I felt like a swim too,' he said.

'What about Malo? Is he down there as well?'

'I persuaded him to stay on the bank.'

Tamati broke Ikaika conventions by approaching her when they were naked and a glance down confirmed her floating hair did not hide much at all. It was probably why he kept his gaze on her face as they trod water. 'You shouldn't be here,' she said.

'I needed to return this.' He held out the pearl shell pendant. 'It was a gift, Anahera, from one Ahi to another.'

Tamati's water-sleeked hair high-lighted the line of his check and lips and she wondered what his skin-spirit was, and Malo's, and Airini's. She had hoped to find a white-wolf but had found Jax instead.

'It was a gift, Anahera,' he repeated more softly.

'It was never a gift, Tamati,' she said slowly, 'and I shouldn't have taken it. I told you at the time we didn't know how ohaku would change us.'

'*I* am the same but Jax seems to have changed you.'

'You *are* the same, Tamati, and that is the problem. Ikaika are supposed to be different,' she said, and swam away.

The Kuwaini listened to Airini's tale in shocked silence and it was Anbros who seemed the only one capable of speech. He asked Airini to tell Malo and Tamati to bring Jax straight to his awin, and had gone off to prepare salves.

Miru rued Anbros's absence because with Shenrin gone, there were only four of them to consider the strange turn of events. The Kuwaini's attention settled on her as the sole Dream-traveler and she licked her lips. 'I didn't sense this,' she confessed.

'You were uneasy,' Davi reminded her, 'and thought it stemmed from more than Anahera.'

'Yes, but I didn't sense Jax.'

'How could anyone sense the arrival of a survivor from Rua?'

'At least Anahera is alive,' said Sairin.

'Yes,' said Davi. 'We have much to be thankful for.'

'Do we?' challenged Cheren. 'Anahera failed her ohaku. What will become of her now?'

'The rites of ohaku weren't intended for events such as these,' said Davi in surprise.

Cheren's brows bristled. 'They are clear in requiring Ahi to remain solitary until they reach Kohatu on the return journey.'

'Anahera gave aid to a badly injured Ahi,' said Davi heatedly. 'We should be proud of her, not be thinking of ways to punish her!'

'None of it changes the fact she failed her ohaku,' retorted Cheren.

'She did the same thing on her first ohaku-sai,' said Miru suddenly.

'What?' asked Davi, turning to her.

'Don't you see? She retrieved a rero seedling from Kohatu that shouldn't have been there and would have otherwise died.'

'And this Ahi from Rua shouldn't have been in the Cloud Crown,' said Davi heavily.

'So why *was* he there?' demanded Cheren.

'That we have yet to discover,' said Miru.

Jax slept until mid afternoon and only needed Anahera's occasional steadying hand as they went on. It meant they made good time but Anahera's dread grew. Malo and Tamati walked ahead, conversing together in low voices, but she did not try to listen in. Malo had barely spoken to her all day and she wondered if the remainder of the nine would shun her too.

It was dusk when they reached Lani and Airini waited for them. At least her smile was welcoming. 'The Kuwaini request Jax be taken straight to Anbros's awin,' she said, 'and that Anahera goes to the Kuwain.'

Anahera nodded and gave Jax a quick hug. 'Anbros is a healer,' she said. 'He will care for your wounds. I will come later, after I speak to the Kuwaini.'

'I am sorry—' began Jax but Anahera silenced him with a finger to his lips. 'We are Ahi,' she said, ignoring Tamati's stony stare. 'I will come later,' she repeated.

Tamati and Malo escorted Jax away and she turned to see Airini's sympathetic face. 'You have had such an awful time,' murmured Airini. 'Finding Jax, looking after him . . .'

'It isn't Jax, it is Tamati and Malo,' said Anahera shakily. 'They are Ikaika and Ikaika are supposed to . . .' She choked to a stop. 'Maybe I am not deserving of their care. Maybe someone who has failed their ohaku isn't entitled—'

Airini pulled Anahera into her arms. 'The Ikaika care for *all* Iolani,' she said firmly.

'Malo barely speaks to me, while Tamati seems to think I should have left Jax to die!'

'Jax is Kawai Alanui but even had he been opala, you did as you should.' Anahera said nothing and Airini smoothed her hair back and kissed her forehead. 'Come, the Kuwaini are waiting.'

The Iolani gathered at their fires but Anahera kept her gaze on the ground until they reached the Kuwain and then Airini hugged her again. 'The Kuwaini are concerned only with your welfare, Anahera. You have nothing to fear.'

'And yet I fear everything.'

'Come to my awin afterwards. You shouldn't be alone.'

'I need to go to Jax,' said Anahera, and managed a small smile. 'He shouldn't be alone either.'

27

*D*avi started the proceedings, as he usually did then sang the song of thanking, normally reserved for new Ikaika. Miru added her voice, grateful like the rest of the Kuwaini for Anahera's safe return. Anahera sat before them, her gaze straight ahead, her clenched hands on her knees.

The song came to an end and there was the usual hiatus to allow any Kuwaini to speak. It was Cheren who took the opportunity and Miru winced but Cheren simply asked Anahera to recount what had happened up to the present. It was a sensible way to begin and Miru closed her eyes to concentrate.

Anahera's ohaku had held no surprises until she had come across Jax in the Cloud Crown. *I thought he was dead at first and when he wasn't, I didn't know what to do. He was terribly injured but I could see he was Ahi, even though I didn't know him. And he shouldn't have been there, with me, in the Cloud Crown, but he was. To aid him, would be to break my ohaku, not to aid him, would be to let him die.*

And so she had aided him despite knowing the cost. Their return journey had been slowed by Jax's injuries and Anahera's need to *shift* to warm and feed him, until Airini, Malo and Tamati had found them at Kohatu, and then Malo and Tamati had hastened their return.

There was a subtle change in Anahera's voice when she spoke of her former *Ahi* friends, and Miru glanced up. It was natural Anahera was upset they were Ikaika, while she remained Ahi, but there was something else at play and Miru's skin pricked.

Davi spoke next, asking who Jax was and why he had come but Anahera's answers raised even more questions. Apparently Jax was one of two survivors from Rua and had returned because there was some sort of threat to Iolana, but Anahera did not know what it was and nor did Jax.

Anahera was clearly exhausted and Miru cleared her throat. 'You have had a difficult few days, Anahera, and should rest now. We will speak with Jax tomorrow and then the Kuwaini will decide what is to be done.'

Anahera nodded and went out, and most of the Kuwaini followed, keen to escape the Kuwain's disturbing news for the company of friends around the fires, but Davi lingered. 'I know you miss Shenrin, Miru, but I am willing to listen,' he said.

Miru nodded, grateful for his offer. 'Ahi must find their skin-spirit in the Cloud Crown and yet Anahera found Jax,' she said slowly.

'And so failed her ohaku,' confirmed Davi.

'Unless she *did* find her skin-spirit.'

Davi blinked. 'Are you saying Jax is Anahera's skin-spirit?'

'I don't know what I am saying,' admitted Miru, 'although I wonder if the skin-spirit *has to be* an animal. We are all Whetu's creatures and if Jax ties Anahera more securely to Iolana, he would serve the same purpose. Anahera obviously hasn't considered the possibility either because, like the rest of us, she expected to find an animal skin-spirit.'

'It is possible,' said Davi doubtfully.

'But too shocking to share with the rest of the Kuwaini, at least for now. What we do know is that Anahera saved Jax despite knowing it would destroy her ohaku.'

'As she should have,' said Davi vehemently.

'Indeed, but it means she is an Ahi who entered the Cloud Crown but remained Ahi. Is she to enter it a second time?'

Davi shrugged helplessly.

'Are there no songs to guide us?' asked Miru.

'Not that I know of and yet it would be cruel to force her to remain Ahi.'

'For her and for others. If Tamati does seek her as a mate-pair, he might resent Jax's intrusion.'

'Tamati is Ikaika now,' said Davi dismissively. 'He owes care to all Kawai Alanui, including Jax, presuming Jax *is* from Rua.'

Miru sighed. 'I wish Anbros were here. With Shenrin gone, I wonder if there are too few of us now to properly consider these things.'

'He will be here tomorrow, as will the Ahi from Rua, if he is well enough. Then we might have the answers we search for.'

'Or more questions,' said Miru heavily.

Jax clenched his jaw as Anbros methodically worked the paste into his gashes. The mixture burned but its scent and the old man's touch, took Jax back to Rua, to when Wiremu had salved his foot. Jax and Matiu had been searching for *tio* along a rocky ledge on Rua's shore, when moana had sent a wave that had knocked them onto the jagged reef below.

Jax had sliced his foot and Matiu had helped him hobble to Wiremu's awin where the healer had applied one of his pastes. Wiremu had hummed as he had worked and Anbros hummed the same tune. It was a healing song and Anbros gifted kindness as well. When he had finished, he set roasted kumara next to Jax, and a bowl of fela, and kissed him on the forehead. 'You will heal better if you rest,' he said, and went out.

The single cup-lamp added more familiar scents, as did the seeli-grass sleeping mat and heavy flax cover. Fire-smoke drifted in from outside too, along with old and young voices, chatting and laughing in Kawai Alanui.

Jax swallowed convulsively and surveyed the awin's dim interior. There were other sleeping-mats and covers, a small bench stacked with bowls and baskets, and a rack hung with cloaks. There were no chairs or tables. The Kawai Alanui ate together around their fires or together in their awins when the weather was wet.

Jax must have dozed and woke to Whetu's light streaming through the doorway. It illuminated Anahera's slender form as she came in and settled on the mat next to him. 'How do you feel?' she asked, taking his hand.

'Better, thanks to Anbros's care. And how do you feel?

'I am well,' she said in surprise.

The starlight transformed her hair into a silvery halo but left her face in darkness. 'I meant since being questioned by the Kuwaini,' said Jax.

'To guide us well, the Kuwaini must know what happened.'

'Will they allow you a second ohaku?'

'They will talk with you tomorrow and then decide what to do.'

'If I hadn't—'

'Don't,' she ordered, and kissed him. Her mouth lingered on his and then she sat back on her heels and surveyed him. 'You are beautiful, Jax, except for your *short* hair,' she added and playfully

151

pushed her fingers through it. 'It is strange you share the Elders' silver.'

'It was the same color as yours before Rua blew. The Off-islander healers said shock changed it to grey but it never changed back.'

'It might now you are home.' She kissed him again, her scent and softness intoxicating, and he turned his head aside. 'You find it hard to show affection,' she said softly. 'Is that because Off-islanders have no care for each other?'

'They care for each other.'

'Then you don't want closeness with *me*.'

He reached up and caressed her face. 'I want closeness with you, Anahera. You are beautiful and kind and giving. I have never known anyone like you.' He tried to smile and failed. 'I haven't shared affection since Rua blew but it isn't only that. On the Off-islands, your affection would be seen as a lead-up to sex.'

'*Sex*?'

Jax dredged his memory for the Kawai Alanui word. 'Joining,' he muttered.

'We are Ahi,' she said in bewilderment. 'Mate-pairs aren't formed until Ikaika.'

'The Off-islanders don't have Ahi, or Ikaika, or Elders, and joining can happen outside of mate-pairs and sometimes at a very young age. People join with many others and don't necessarily stay together.'

'Opala,' she muttered, her disgust plain. 'But we are Ahi,' she repeated. 'I *need* to be near you, Jax. I *need* your closeness.'

Because her friends were *Ikaika* and, thanks to him, she was not? 'Anahera,' he murmured and drew her into his arms. She kissed him again and he returned her kisses, this time delighting in their intimacy. His want of her had not diminished but he forced himself to think of it in Ahi terms, and as she nestled in the crook of his shoulder, he pulled the cover over them both.

'I am glad you came back, Jax,' she murmured, and as Jax felt the tension drain from his body, he realized that he was too.

As soon as Anahera had gone to the Kuwain, Airini went in search of Tamati, and found Malo taking his meal outside Tamati's awin. 'Is Tamati resting inside?' she asked.

'He has gone to Anahera's awin.'

'Why?'

'Why do you think?' said Malo, as he retrieved fish from the coals.

Airini settled beside him. 'Anahera is distressed, Malo.'

'That is to be expected,' he said offering her fish.

'Why?' she asked, waving it away.

'Obviously because a stranger has destroyed her ohaku.'

'It is because you refuse to speak to her.'

Malo's eyes flashed in the firelight. 'What is there to say? That it doesn't matter? That tomorrow she will be Ikaika like the rest of us?'

'There is plenty to say, Malo, such as you love her, that you understand the hard choice she had to make, that she was right to save a fellow Ahi.'

'*If* he is a *fellow Ahi.*'

'You have seen him and heard him speak, Malo. Tell me what he is.'

'*If* he is an Ahi from Rua, he should have come when Rua exploded, not now, and *not* to the Cloud Crown.'

'It isn't Anahera's fault he ended up in the Cloud Crown,' said Airini heatedly, 'yet you and Tamati act as though it is. It isn't how Ikaika behave.'

Malo tossed the remains of the fish into the fire got to his feet. 'I don't need instruction on how Ikaika behave and neither does Tamati!'

Airini rose too. 'He does if he lets anger rule his thoughts!'

'You can instruct him yourself then,' said Malo, as Tamati stepped into the firelight.

'About what?' asked Tamati.

'About how to be Ikaika,' said Malo sourly. 'Apparently we remain ignorant.'

'In what way?'

'In how to comfort an Ahi who has failed her ohaku,' said Airini.

Tamati's hands came to his hips. 'The failure affects more than her,' he said tersely.

'Without our love, she suffers alone,' said Airini.

'She agreed to mate-pair with Tamati,' broke in Malo. 'He has good reason to be upset.'

Airini shook her head. 'You know as well as I do Ahi can't agree to anything as serious as mate-pairs. Whatever is said as Ahi is erased by ohaku. We die as Ahi and are born as Ikaika.'

'Understandings can still be exchanged,' countered Tamati.

'And gifts can still be returned,' retorted Airini.

There was a strained silence. 'Do you know where she is now?' asked Tamati.

'With Jax. She didn't want him to be alone, as she is.'

'In Anbros's awin?'

'Probably.'

'I saw Anbros return to the Kuwain.'

Airini's face hardened. 'What are you suggesting, Tamati? That Anahera and Jax might behave like mate-paired Ikaika?'

'Jax has lived with opala. Do you know how *he* will behave?'

'I know how Anahera will behave, which is enough!' Airini took a steadying breath. 'Anahera needs our love, *as Ikaika*, and if we won't give it to her, she will seek what she needs elsewhere. And given what they endured together in the Cloud Crown, she will seek it from Jax. If you can't act like an Ikaika, Tamati, at least ask yourself whether that is what you really want.'

28

Miru woke with a start, the dream still stark in her head and despite its beauty, she was fearful it heralded her death. She slipped through the sleeping Kuwaini and out into the early morning air, needing its chill to anchor herself to the living world. It was Whetu's will when death visited, she reminded herself, but her heart continued to hammer.

Stars still dusted the sky but two other early risers sat by a fire and she made her way over. One was Anahera and the stranger obviously Jax, the Ahi from Rua. His hair was the color of a white-wolf pelt and her mouth dried.

They rose at her approach and nodded formally. Jax looked pure Kawai Alanui, despite his short hair, but it was odd to see an older Ahi she had not watched grow from a baby.

'Please share our food,' said Anahera politely, as they settled on the mats.

'I will eat later,' said Miru.

'This is Miru of the Kuwaini,' Anahera told Jax, and he nodded, his amber eyes catching the firelight making him even more wolf-like.

Anbros's handiwork was obvious too but no salve could disguise Jax's wounds and Miru winced. 'How did you injure yourself?' she asked.

'Off-islander military bases have fences made of sharp metal. I climbed over one.'

Anahera's horror told Miru Jax had not shared that information with her. 'You were a prisoner?' asked Miru, then wondered if she should save her questions for the Kuwain.

'Not in the way you mean,' he said.

Miru eyed him, aware that opala lied and that Jax had lived with them for many years. 'In what way then?' she pursued.

'After Rua blew, I felt I had no place to go, so I stayed with the Off-islanders, despite knowing I had no place with them either.' Anahera's hand closed over Jax's but Miru did not need to see the gesture to know that Jax struggled. 'I came to Iolana now because

I was told it was under threat,' he added. 'I wanted to complete my ohaku too. I thought it would help but all I did was ruin Anahera's.'

Anahera shook her head. 'Jax, don't,' she whispered, but Jax ignored her.

'Is there *any* way I can undo the damage?'

'The Kuwaini will discuss Anahera's ohaku, as we will discuss the news you bring,' said Miru. 'But I will say this: you have not caused *damage* in the way you were damaged by your time away from us. Anahera remains Ahi, and Ahi are a loved part of the Kawai Alanui, and as Ahi, you are also a part of us, despite your long absence. Nothing changes that.'

Miru was content to simply watch Jax later that morning as the Kuwaini questioned him. He could not provide details of the threat to Iolana due to his *unauthorized* departure from the Off-islands and it was a measure of his lost years that he believed being Ikaika would have made him more trustworthy to the Iolani than being Ahi.

Miru's silence drew the Kuwaini's puzzled glances and it was Davi who finally asked why Jax had not come to Iolana immediately after Rua's destruction. Jax had thought himself the sole survivor, he said, and had not argued with the military over where he was to be sent. He had only learned of a second survivor, *Matiu*, recently, but Matiu had been so injured by the explosion, he could no longer *shift*.

Miru did not believe that Jax lied, for a younger Ahi who had lost everything would have been in no state to argue against the opala, but watching him reminded her of the ice that clothed Wairere's higher lagoons in winter. The ice was motionless but the water beneath continued to swirl and she sensed there was a lot more to Jax than met the eye.

Jax had lived with the Off-islanders almost as long as he had lived on Rua, and yet the need to return to Kawai Alanui had suddenly been so great he had inflicted terrible injuries on himself and then crashed into the Cloud Crown at the precise moment Anahera was on her ohaku. It would be understandable if Anahera resented Jax, but the opposite seemed true, and as Miru considered it, her latest dream started to make sense.

Once Jax had gone, Cheren wasted no time in turning on her.

'You said nothing *at all*,' she exclaimed in exasperation.

'I spoke with Jax earlier,' said Miru mildly.

'Without us?' asked Davi.

'He sat with Anahera at the fires before dawn.'

'And?' pursued Davi.

'He told me what he told the Kuwaini now.'

'Which was very little,' muttered Cheren.

'There is more if we consider Anahera and Jax together, as I think we must,' said Miru.

'And your dreams and feelings,' added Davi.

Sairin, Anbros, and Cheren's attention was suddenly as intense as Davi's, and Miru licked her lips. 'We need to know more if we are to safeguard Iolana and for that, Jax needs to return to the Off-islands and take Anahera with him.'

The Kuwaini stared at her in shock and Sairin was the first to recover. 'The Iolani do *not* visit the opala!'

'We need to learn of the threat, *if* there is one, through the eyes and ears of an Iolani,' said Miru.

'And Anahera is the best candidate,' said Davi slowly.

'She didn't even complete her ohaku,' exclaimed Cheren. 'If we must send someone, it should be an Ikaika.'

'Ikaika are tied to Iolana,' said Miru.

'Do you sense this is why Anahera failed her ohaku?' asked Davi.

'It is possible.'

'*If* she is to go, she must *choose* to go,' said Cheren.

'No one is suggesting anything else,' said Davi tersely. 'And we have yet to consider how she is to complete ohaku.'

'I would prefer to leave that discussion for later,' said Miru.

'I—' began Davi, and stopped as he noted her expression. 'Perhaps we should summon Anahera and discuss the possibility of her accompanying Jax to the Off-islands.'

'Yes,' said Cheren. 'Because if she refuses, we must find another way forward.'

Jax had not been back with Anahera long before the message came for her to return to the Kuwain. He hoped it meant she was to be granted a second ohaku and he fidgeted in Anbros's awin and then, tired of the gloom, went outside. Smoke hung in the trees and people chatted as they breakfasted. Jax resisted the urge to retreat to the awin but he swallowed repeatedly.

The Iolani burned rero, as they had on Rua, and the smoke held the scent of kumara and fish, as it had on Rua. Food arrived in cartons and tins on the Off-islands, or if fresh, by truck from far away. He could choose hundreds of different foods there but none of them tasted like casberries or buri-nuts, or coal-crisped kumara.

More than one group invited him to share their breakfast but he politely declined, not wanting to answer their inevitable questions.

'Jax?' He started, having not noticed Airini's approach. 'Come to my fire.'

She had taken his hand which made it hard to refuse. 'Anahera is with the Kuwaini,' he said, as Airini led him away.

'She will guess where you are,' said Airini 'Lani isn't so big that you can hide,' she added with a smile. 'How does it compare to Pana? Bigger or smaller?' she asked, as they walked.

Pana; he had not heard the name of Rua's settlement for ten years. 'I don't know,' he said. 'I was twelve. Everything seems big at the age.'

'And now you must be twenty-two,' said Airini, as they settled on mats outside an awin and she passed him kumara. 'Anahera and I are nineteen, Tamati and Malo twenty. We complete ohaku any time from eighteen to twenty or twenty-one.'

'As did those of Rua. We came here.'

'The songs speak of it. There must have been a time when those on Puha and Ke-one came too. Four islands of Kawai Alanui and now only one.'

Airini's words seemed ominous but they might be a hint. 'Did Anahera tell you why I came?'

'No.'

Jax didn't want to speak of the threat to Iolana either; it was probably up to the Kuwaini to make it public anyway, *if* they chose. 'I wanted to complete my ohaku but I destroyed Anahera's instead.'

'*Destroyed* is a strong word, Jax. No Ahi knows what they will find in the Cloud Crown. You were in need of aid and Anahera provided it. The Kuwaini understand that.'

'And what did I provide for Anahera?' he challenged. 'Just a ruined ohaku.'

'The Cloud Crown's mysteries don't always reveal themselves on Tihi's slopes. Sometimes they take longer.' Jax said nothing and she glanced down at the slashes on his torso. 'Were you attacked by a screech-cat?'

'I was hurt when I left the Off-islands. I am in the military. You can't walk away when you feel like it.'

'The *military*? The ones who fill our skies with weapons?'

'Yes.'

'Why are you with *them*?' she demanded, her distaste plain.

'I didn't care who I was with after Rua blew.'

'But you are here now,' she said, her gaze as piercing as Anahera's. 'It would be best if you stayed.'

Jax shook his head. 'Completing my ohaku wasn't the only reason I came. I need to return to Samarak for orders.'

'Samarak? I wondered which of the Off-islands you came from. Our songs speak of their hatred for each other.'

Jax bristled but what Airini said was true. 'After the last war, an Exclusion Zone was agreed to around Kawai Alanui. Off-islanders are prohibited from approaching the islands.'

'Yet you came.'

'I am Kawai Alanui,' said Jax curtly.

'*And* military. Can you be both?' she murmured.

'Perhaps I can be neither,' said Jax, unable to hide his bitterness. 'Perhaps you converse with a wairua.'

Airini touched his arm. 'I am sorry I spoke my thought aloud. You *are* Kawai Alanui wherever you choose to live. Nothing changes that. But you *do* need time to heal.'

Time again, thought Jax. The one thing he did not have.

Davi sang a brief song of welcome when Anahera arrived and then Miru spoke. 'You told us what happened on your ohaku, but we would like to know more about how you discovered Jax.'

Anahera nodded. 'It was still raining but the Cloud Crown softens everything. It is like but unlike Wairere. The bird-calls . . .' She stopped, and flushed at having spoken of the world inside the Cloud Crown.

'We have all experienced the Cloud Crown,' said Miru gently. 'Just describe how you found Jax.'

Anahera nodded and moistened her lips. 'I saw his hair first. It was silvery but I could see no eyes, snout or brush, so I thought I was looking at a white-wolf's back, which meant it was lying down. I waited but it didn't move and I circled around and saw it was the back of a male's head.

'He had the short hair of an Off-islander but the silver of an Elder. Then I saw his face. He looked Kawai Alanui but I had never seen him before.' She shook her head. 'I didn't know what to do. He was terribly hurt and broken rero branches told me he had crashed through the trees which meant he had been in shift-form. He was unconscious and cold, and I feared he would die. I *shifted* to white-wolf to warm him.'

'When did you realize you had broken your ohaku?' asked Miru.

'I thought even seeing him might have broken it but . . .' She looked down at the floor. 'I had to decide whether to pretend I *hadn't* seen him and continue my ohaku or help him.'

There was a long silence.

'What is the *main* difference between the Ahi and the Ikaika, Anahera?' asked Miru abruptly.

Anahera looked up in surprise. 'The Ikaika have found their skin-spirit and the Ahi haven't.'

'And the Ikaika care for *all* Iolani while the Ahi primarily care for each other.' Anahera nodded. 'We have summoned you to request you do what the Ikaika do on Iolana, but cannot do elsewhere.' Anahera stared at Miru in mystification. 'We ask that you accompany Jax back to the Off-islands and learn the nature of the threat that confronts us.'

Anahera stared at her in horror and Miru gentled her voice. 'You broke your ohaku for Jax and that frees you to do what the Ikaika cannot, but you don't have to do it, Anahera, and refusing won't affect any future ohaku. You do not have to do this.'

'I want Jax safe,' she said slowly. 'I will go with him.'

Cheren was the first to speak when Anahera had gone. 'Well that proves she wasn't ready for her ohaku.'

'How?' asked Davi in surprise.

'*I want Jax safe. I will go with him,*' repeated Cheren. 'Anahera isn't thinking of the Iolani; she is only thinking of her fellow Ahi.'

'Perhaps,' said Miru, although it could be argued Anahera's want to protect Iolana by leaving was an Ikaika trait, but Miru did not want a quarrel and held her tongue. She had hoped Anahera's description of finding Jax would share the profound resonance Miru had felt in finding her own skin-spirit, but if it had, Anahera had not revealed it.

'When do you think Jax will be strong enough to leave?' Davi asked Anbros.

'He should wait a few more days,' said Anbros.

'It will give Anahera time to prepare,' said Miru.

'How do you prepare for the opala's lands?' murmured Sairin sadly. No one replied. It was not a question they could answer.

29

*A*irini was still considering Anahera's shocking news the next morning when Tamati appeared. He nodded formally as he sat next to her and she poured him a bowl of fela and topped up her own. 'I have considered your words,' he said. 'You were right to remind me of what it means to be Ikaika.'

It was the closest she was likely to get to an apology but she had no right to feel superior, given her own reaction to Anahera's impending departure. No one knew how corrupted Jax had become by his life on the Off-islands or by the military but the opala's dangers were well known.

'I thought ohaku would make me feel different straight away,' she admitted, 'but it seems to take time.'

'I want to mend my argument with Anahera,' he said, 'but she isn't at her awin or at Anbros's.'

'She has taken Jax to some of her favorite places along the cliffs before they leave for the Off-islands tomorrow.'

'*They* leave for the Off-islands?'

'The Kuwaini have asked Anahera to go with Jax. They want to know why he came.'

'Asked or *ordered*?' demanded Tamati.

'*Asked*.' Airini placed a restraining hand on his arm. 'Tamati, it makes no difference. She agreed to go.'

He shrugged her off and scrambled to his feet. 'Her place is here! The Kawai Alanui stay *here*, not go off with opala!'

'Jax is Kawai Alanui,' Airini reminded him, but Tamati had already stormed off between the awins.

Jax gazed out over moana's glittering expanse, the cliff-top giving him a good view. The waters were an ever-moving blend of blue and grey, aqua and teal, slashed here and there by the waves' brilliant crests. The sun was warm on his skin, despite the nearness to winter, and the air fragrant with the lush growth behind him and the tang of moana's salt. For once his muscles were relaxed, having no need to mimic, but then he stared south and his sense of well-being evaporated.

'Rua is hard to see when the tide is high,' said Anahera, coming to his side. 'But when moana drops, foam marks the stone below.'

Jax swallowed hard and shifted his gaze to the gulls' wheel and dip above. The blackgulls were striking but there were redgulls there too, less eye-catching but warmer somehow, their plumage bronzed by the sun.

Anahera slipped her hand into his. 'Maybe it wasn't a good idea to bring you to Tupari,' she said.

Jax forced a smile. 'Tupari *is* a special place and you should stay here to enjoy it.'

'The Kuwaini asked me to go with you and I agreed. We don't need to discuss it again.'

It had been more of an argument than a discussion, conceded Jax. He could not even guarantee Anahera's safety on the journey, let alone once they arrived.

'Speak to me again in the Off-islanders' tongue,' said Anahera. 'I need to practise.'

'URZOL is a research unit that studies the Zoaides' oceans and lands,' said Jax in English.

'*URZOL is a research unit that studies the Zoaides' oceans and lands*,' mimicked Anahera.

'Which means?'

'*Which means?*'

Jax laughed. 'I was asking you to tell me the *meaning* of what I said, not mimic it.'

Anahera smiled at him, the sunshine turning her amber eyes to gold. 'That is the first time I have seen you laugh. I like it when you are happy.'

'And I like it when you are safe,' he said, and smoothed the hair from her face. 'Stay here, Anahera,' he said softly.

'Ahi stay with Ahi,' she said, and kissed him.

'I will come back,' he said, and returned the kiss.

'And I will come back with you,' she said, her kiss lingering.

He brought his arms around her and held her close, enjoying her warmth and scent. 'The Off-islands aren't a good place for you.'

'Then they aren't a good place for *you*. You shouldn't go back.'

He sighed. 'I fear the loss of all this,' he said, gazing around them.

'What is the Off-islander word for *aroha*?' she asked suddenly.

'*Love*,' said Jax, 'although it has a smaller meaning. Why do you ask?'

'I see *love* in your face when you look at Iolana.'

Hope surged that he could reclaim a place for himself as Kawai Alanui then he noticed Anahera was intent on him and forced a smile. 'And what do you see when I look at you?' he asked lightly.

'Aroha, as is fitting for Ahi.'

'And if I were Ikaika and looked at you with aroha?' he asked softly. 'What would it mean then?'

'The Ikaika have aroha for everyone.'

'But not equally or they wouldn't mate-pair.'

'The Ikaika mate-pair for lots of reasons. Were I to mate-pair with a male Ikaika, it would be to share a mate-pair aroha with him *and* a child. If I were to mate-pair with a female Ikaika, it would be to share a mate-pair aroha only with her.'

'And male Ikaika who mate-pair?'

'Males are different to females and their mate-pair aroha is different too, as a redgull is different to a blackgull, or a shia to a sun-eagle.' Jax's thoughts went to Matiu and Carter, and Carter's efforts to protect Jax from Briggs. 'You don't look happy anymore, Jax,' said Anahera.

Jax shrugged. 'You can't be happy all the time.'

'You could be if you stayed here,' she said and kissed his cheek.

'We have discussed that and don't need to discuss it again,' he said ironically.

'*After* we return and the threat is over, you will be happy here,' pursued Anahera.

Jax doubted it would be that simple and he wondered what, exactly, Keli wanted him to do. More than to act as a conveniently winged messenger, he guessed, and as there was only one of him, other military would be involved. But who? Matiu? Carter? Keli himself?

A shadow passed overhead and he looked up. A sun-eagle, its magnificent plumage gold in the sun, a whitiki clutched in its talons. It dropped vertically to land a short distance away. 'I am guessing that is Tamati,' said Jax.

There was a blur as the sun-eagle *shifted* and Tamati barely paused to wrench on his whitiki before he was less than a length from

Jax. Had Jax been on the Off-islands, he would have slumped his shoulders and dropped his eyes to defuse the situation, but he met Tamati's furious gaze steadily.

'I have heard Anahera intends to leave Kawai Alanui for your stinking lands and I am here to tell you that she won't.'

'My *stinking lands* are to the south, under moana, but my preference is that Anahera stays on Iolana too.'

Tamati's eyes narrowed. 'You don't want her to go?'

'No.'

'The Kuwaini asked me to go, Tami,' said Anahera.

Tamati's furious gaze flicked to her. '*Asked* not ordered. You aren't going.'

Anahera made no reply, for which Jax was grateful. Tamati's anger was as potent as an Off-islander's, and angry Off-islanders were not given to reason.

'I want to speak to you alone, Anahera,' snapped Tamati.

'There is nothing you can say to me you can't say in front of my fellow Ahi,' said Anahera.

'Jax isn't *true* Ahi!'

Anahera flicked back her hair. 'What do you want to say, Tamati?' she demanded.

'It isn't for Jax's ears!'

'Then it isn't for mine either!'

Tamati glared at her and then at Jax, and when neither said anything, strode off into the trees, and a moment later, a sun-eagle powered away.

Anahera perched on a nearby stone and stared out over moana. 'I am sorry for Tamati's words,' she muttered.

'He wanted to mate-pair with you and then I turned up and ruined everything. I understand why he is angry.'

Anahera shook her head. 'No you don't. You still confuse us with Off-islanders, Jax. Tamati thought he was ready to mate-pair *before* he became Ikaika, but Ahi don't even consider it, and he certainly isn't ready now, despite being Ikaika. Showing anger, disputing the Kuwaini's wisdom, denying a fellow Ahi . . .' Her face hardened. '*If* I become Ikaika and *if* I decide to mate-pair with a male, Tamati is the very last male I would *ever* consider!'

Jax stared out over moana too but he was not thinking of its restless surge but of Tamati's outburst. Tamati might be the most vocal of Anahera's friends but the others probably thought the same and the longer he stayed, the more upset he would cause. 'I think we should leave tonight,' he said.

Anahera surveyed him shrewdly. 'Why?'

'It will be safer to travel in darkness.' Anahera's gaze was piercing and he stared back towards where Rua had been. 'And I fear for Iolana,' he said, which was true.

Anahera nodded. 'Waiting until night will give you more time to rest,' she said and smiled. 'There are buri-palms nearby and casberries too. It is a good place to spend the day.'

Malo was waiting at Tamati's awin when he returned and they embraced. 'I am glad to see you, Tamati,' he said feelingly.

'And I you. Has Airini told you Anahera intends to go off to the Off-islands with Jax?'

'Yes.'

'And?' demanded Tamati.

'Obviously, I want her to stay here but it is the Kuwaini's decision.'

Tamati broke from his arms and took several paces up and down. 'It is *Anahera's* decision,' he said, swinging back. 'She goes because she feels sorry for the *opala* she helped.'

Malo's eyes narrowed. 'Jax is from Rua, Tami. That makes him Kawai Alanui.'

'He has lived almost half his life with opala! And even worse, he is part of the military. You know the military, Malo? The ones who send their stinking weapons over our heads! He *thinks* like them, *acts* like them. He risks Anahera!'

'The Kuwaini must have good reason to ask her to accompany him.'

'It will achieve *nothing* and I am going to tell them so.'

Malo caught his arm and tightened his grip as Tamati tried to shrug him off. 'You can't do that! You are Ikaika!'

'Ikaika must speak when the Kuwaini err, although I notice that *you* make no such objections,' said Tamati, eyeing him. 'Your love for Anahera must be less than I thought.'

'I loved her as Ahi love each other and now I love her as Ikaika love the Kawai Alanui.'

'So the rest of it was to goad me, was it?'

'We were *Ahi*,' said Malo, stroking Tamati's arm.

'And now we are Ikaika, you are content for her to go off into danger?'

Malo dropped his hand. 'If you think me *content* to risk *any* Kawai Alanui, you know me less well than I thought.'

'Mate-pairing changes everything!'

'You aren't mate-paired!' Tamati said nothing and Malo gentled his voice. 'Mate-pairing changes *some* things but Ikaika obligations remain.'

'Which are to care for *all* Kawai Alanui, which includes Anahera, and that is exactly what I intend to do,' he said and strode away.

Miru rested back against the weave of her awin's wall, turned her face to the sun, and took a long, slow breath. The sky was cloudless and moana calm but she was chill, despite her flax cloak. Winter was near and she wondered suddenly if it would be her last.

'Perhaps it is my time too, Shenrin, my friend,' she murmured as she pulled her cloak close. Lani was quiet as it always was before the Kawai Alanui returned from their day's work. Blue-chuffs sang in the surrounding trees and she noticed a topaz-moko sunned itself on the mat beside her. It skittered away and Miru looked up to see Tamati heading towards the Kuwain. 'Tamati,' she called.

He nodded and would have passed on by but she patted the mat beside her. 'Sit with me a while.' His reluctance was clear but politeness required he sit.

'I wish to address the Kuwaini,' he said.

'Not all are in Lani. It will take time to recall them.'

'I don't have time. Anahera will be gone soon.'

'And back soon too.'

Tamati shook his head. 'The Off-islands are dangerous. She must remain here! I need to speak to *all* the Kuwaini.'

'Iolani can speak with us any time, as you know, but first I want

167

you to do something for me.'

'What is it?'

'Fly to Tupari and look south over moana, then turn and look north. Return and tell me what you see. I will wait.'

'Then you will summon the Kuwaini?'

'If you wish.'

30

*L*ani was crowded by the time Tamati returned and he settled by her side again. She passed him a bowl of fela, and then buri-nuts and kirirua, and they ate for a time in silence. 'I took shia-form and went to Tupari as you asked,' he said, his gaze on the fire. 'I looked south and I looked north.'

'And?'

'I saw the waves break over Rua's ruin and I saw Iolana's beauty. I felt horror that Rua had gone and gratitude Iolana was still here.' He licked his lips. 'I felt sorrow for Jax.'

'Jax told us Iolana is threatened, and while he couldn't tell us how exactly, his fear for us is genuine,' said Miru, her gaze on the fire too. 'We asked Anahera to return to the Off-islands with him to discover more. She has spent the most time with Jax, and is the most familiar with his Off-island ways. She is also an older Ahi. The dangers would be greater for a younger Ahi and Ikaika must remain on Iolana.'

Tamati's breath emptied and he looked at her for the first time. 'I have been worse than a fool, Miru, and less than worthy.'

'You didn't know these things.'

'I knew how an Ikaika should behave.'

'It is easier to *know* than to *do*,' acknowledged Miru. 'We think we enter the Cloud Crown one thing, and exit another, but it is rarely so simple. Changing how we think *and* behave takes time. You are not the first Iolani to discover that.'

'I need to make amends with Anahera and Jax before they leave.'

Miru nodded. 'The Ikaika understand the importance of harmony,' she said, and smiled.

Jax waited until stars had filled the skies before he slipped off his whitiki and shifted to sun-eagle. Sun-eagles saw better in daylight but were fast and he wanted speed for his sake and for Anahera's. Anahera shifted and then they launched from the cliff, their clothes in their talons.

Jax's tension increased as they flew. Samarak's west coast was dotted with bases and he worried he would land at the wrong one and, confronted with something large in the darkness, guards might shoot first and investigate later. He did not know how Keli would react to his return either.

Given Jax's record, Keli might throw him in the cells, and then it would be safest for Anahera to return immediately to Iolana. She had not shown any fear but she must be frightened, given Iolana had been stuck in the middle of the *opala's* wars for years uncounted.

They flew on, staying high to minimize the risk of being shot at, but it reduced moana to a black pit broken only by the occasional yellow light of a patrol boat. Lights twinkled in the distance too but too brightly to be URZOL, and he used his sun-eagle senses to shift their course more southerly. Time slipped away and the next smudge of light suggested fewer buildings. His confidence grew but he circled several times to confirm it *was* URZOL before he guided Anahera down to land.

Keli still worked at his desk when the phone rang and he immediately summoned Connel and Matiu. Keli had ordered all animal sightings to be reported and had accumulated a thick dossier on bats, birds, lizards, snakes, rats and a lone stray cat. It helped URZOL's data banks, he supposed, but the appearance of sun-eagles was a very different matter.

Sun-eagles were seen over the Fayo, but not at night, and they certainly didn't land near URZOL's chopper pad. It could only mean Jax had returned with a second shifter and Keli's mind raced at the possibilities of having *two* shifters at his disposal. Given the question mark over Jax's psychological state, another shifter could be very useful indeed.

Connel arrived with Matiu hard on his heels and both looked as anxious as Keli felt. Keli had kept Matiu grounded in the hope of Jax's return, and had requisitioned Alanui food. It galled Keli to prepare a welcome rather than a disciplinary hearing but he did not have time to deal with Jax as military protocols demanded. Force had not worked in the past and he had been obliged to discuss with Connel and Matiu ways to *encourage* Jax to *better* serve the military, hence the food.

They waited in silence, Keli at his desk, Connel on the edge of the couch, and Matiu pacing. It was a ten minute walk from the pad to Keli's office and it was about that time, when there was a knock at the door.

Connel swiveled and Matiu froze as Keli issued the order to enter. The last time Keli had seen Jax, he had been bandaged and strapped flat to an Infirmary bed, and while his body still bore the stark red of gashes, everything else about him had changed. He was virtually naked, but it was not the brief loin-cloth of reeds that struck Keli, but his ease of movement. He no longer mimicked Off-islander posture, realized Keli, but whether that was a good or bad sign, he didn't know.

Jax's gaze lingered on Matiu but he continued to Keli's desk, came to attention and saluted. The second *female* shifter remained at his side, and Keli hid his disappointment as he took in their tightly clasped hands. He needed a male who could shift for Operation V, not Jax's love-interest.

The female Alanui wore an equally brief loin-cloth but at least she covered her breasts with a woven band. She was almost as tall as Jax, and lithe like him, with Jax's wolf eyes, and a great mane of auburn hair that fell past her hips.

'At ease, Airman,' said Keli. 'Who is your companion?'

'This is Anahera, a Kawai Alanui Ahi like me, sent by the Iolani to learn more of the threat to her island.' Anahera seemed to have understood because she nodded. 'This is Commander Keli,' continued Jax, then half turned to the others. 'And this is Professor Connel and Senior Airman Matiu, the Kawai Alanui from Rua.'

Anahera broke from Jax's side and enclosed Matiu in an intense hug. Matiu's face mirrored Keli's surprise and his arms stayed slack at his sides, but as the hug went on, he reciprocated stiffly. Connel's fascination was clear but Keli was more interested in Jax's reaction. He expected to see jealousy but Jax's expression had softened and it struck Keli it was the first time he had seen Jax betray emotion other than anger or fear.

'We will continue less formally in the meeting room, at least tonight,' said Keli, gesturing to the door. 'And Connel, you might like to fetch some food.'

Keli contemplated the three Alanui as they ate the baked fish and sweet potato, and drank the concoction called fela. It tasted like grass-clippings to Keli and he stuck to coffee, as did Connel. Anahera had immediately sat on the floor next to the fire, and Jax had joined her, and then Matiu.

Keli let Connel do the talking while he tried to gauge how useful the Alanui might be to Operation V. It was unheard of for any Alanui to be beyond the Exclusion Zone and he was determined to exploit the opportunity of having three. Connel seemed determined to exploit the opportunity too but for different reasons, and his early questions were all about Iolani cultural practices.

Jax and Anahera seemed happy to describe them, Jax using English and switching to Alanui to translate for Anahera, but her mimicry and deduction of meaning grew with astonishing speed. Matiu spoke little but he stared at Jax and Anahera so hungrily that Keli felt sorry for him.

It was close to midnight before Keli called a halt to the meeting. They had an early start when the real business of Op. V would be discussed but he wondered where to billet Anahera in the meantime. 'Ahi stay with Ahi,' she said, when he suggested she join the female Airmen in their quarters.

He nodded, not wanting to waste time arguing over military *etiquette*, and as soon as the three Alanui had gone, grabbed beers from the fridge, handed one to Connel, and sprawled on the couch. 'There is no fear of *inappropriate* behavior,' said Connel, as he took a long gulp. 'Mate-pairing happens *after* Ikaika.'

'We are talking sex not a marriage-like arrangement,' said Keli, swigging his beer. 'I hope she is of age. I don't need any more complications.'

'Sex and mate-pairing are the same thing in Kawai Alanui culture. It's one of the reasons they go about wearing next to nothing, that and the fact the islands are a lot warmer and more humid than here.'

'I did notice the lack of clothing,' said Keli shortly.

'Are the mics still in their quarters?'

'Yes, but they aren't much use if they speak Alanui.' Keli contemplated his beer. 'Anahera's acquisition of English was phenomenal.'

'Jax probably tutored her before they left, but I agree.' Connel looked at him thoughtfully. 'I got the impression Jax fled the Infirmary to complete his ohaku but he introduced Anahera as Ahi, *like him*.'

'She made the same point. *Ahi stay with Ahi*, which begs the question what he did in the nine days he was away.'

'I am guessing he learned to be Kawai Alanui again,' said Connel.

Keli nodded. 'He *has* changed.'

'Yes,' said Connel, 'And I wonder whether he will fit back in here.'

Keli's lips thinned. 'He has never *fitted in* but he remains military. The choice isn't his.'

Connel cleared his throat. 'It is strange they sent a *female* Ahi with him.'

'You said the Alanui don't differentiate sex-roles,' said Keli.

'They don't, but they would know females face greater risks in the Off-islands than

 males.'

'She will certainly have to wear more than she wore tonight and so will Jax.'

'Clothing isn't conducive to *shifting*,' pointed out Connel, and yawned. 'And I really want to see one of them *shift*.'

'I will make sure you are there when they leave,' said Keli, and drained his beer. 'And if things go to plan, that will be within the next few days.'

'So soon?' asked Connel in surprise.

'Not *soon*, Professor. I am just hoping it isn't too late.'

'Where are the brack and rero?' asked Anahera as they made their way to Jax's quarters. Her grip on his hand told him she was frightened and he was glad Matiu walked on her other side.

'The Off-islands are different to Kawai Alanui, and bases are different again,' said Jax. 'URZOL studies our islands, but it is still a military base and trees are cleared for security.' She looked at him blankly. 'So you can see the approach of enemies,' he explained. 'There are bases all along Samarak's coast to protect us from Makena.'

'Makena is the Off-islands to the west? The lands you are always fighting?' she asked, staring at the buildings they passed.

'Yes.'

'Why do you fight? Are your Ikaika and Elders silent?'

Jax did not know how to answer. There were millions of Off-islanders led by *Elders* of little interest to those they led, or familiarity, but it was too complicated to try to explain.

'That is a good question,' said Matiu, speaking for the first time. 'Off-islanders don't have Ikaika and Elders like the Kawai Alanui. Most wars are fought over land or what the lands hold.'

'Or over seas, and what the seas hold,' added Jax.

'But don't you have *enough*?' asked Anahera. 'Our songs tell of weapons that dimmed even Whetu's light but I have not seen them, though I have heard your machines. They are terrible,' she said, and shivered.

'Have you heard them recently?' asked Matiu sharply.

'Yes. *Thud-thud-thud-thud-thud* overhead.'

'A chopper,' muttered Matiu. 'Makena breaks the Exclusion Zone.'

'So does Samarak,' said Jax. 'Macy all but clipped Tihi when he delivered me. But if Makena—'

'I am cold and tired and want to rest,' said Anahera. 'Is this our awin?'

'Yes,' said Jax, thoughts still whirring as he led the way in. It was massive after Lani's awins and unwelcoming, with its hard plaster walls, polished floors and shining benchtops. Anahera flinched as Matiu flicked the switch and doused them in harsh white light. 'Maybe we can do without the lights,' said Jax, and opened the blind as Matiu flicked them off again.

'It smells like the other awin,' said Anahera, and wrinkled her nose.

'Off-islanders use a lot of *products*,' said Jax. 'Cleaning gels, polish, soap, deodorant, toothpaste. They all have strong odors.'

'I might turn in,' said Matiu, heading towards his room. 'I will say goodnight.'

Anahera's hands came to her hips. 'Where are you going?'

'To my bedroom, where I sleep,' he said in surprise.

'Ahi sleep together,' said Anahera. 'I had to remind Jax of that on Iolana, more than once,' she added tersely.

Matiu said nothing but even the room's dimness failed to hide his discomfit. 'Anahera *did* have to remind me,' confirmed Jax. 'I had forgotten what it meant to be Kawai Alanui or had chosen to forget. I had forgotten that Kawai Alanui love and care for each other, and might sleep together, skin to skin, for comfort. I had forgotten the special love Ahi have for each other that endures, regardless of place and circumstance.'

The dark made it easier to acknowledge the hurt he had inflicted and he might have said more had he and Matiu been alone.

'I will drag my mattress out,' said Matiu thickly, 'and Jax will bring his. It will make a comfortable enough bed.

Jax pushed the table and chairs to the side of the room and they set the mattresses together and a cover over them both. Anahera crawled under it and Jax lay down beside her but Matiu did not move and Jax knew why. Taking the place next to Anahera meant putting her between them to make what the Off-islanders called a *threesome*.

'I am tired,' said Anahera impatiently, and patted the mattress.

'Off-islanders don't sleep like this unless they are mate-paired,' explained Jax. 'It would be best if Matiu slept on my other side.'

'We aren't Off-islanders. Matiu needs to remember what it is to be Ahi too.'

That was clear enough, thought Jax dryly, as Matiu maneuvered himself onto the bed. 'You need to get rid of your Off-island clothes,' she said. 'They smell.'

Jax suppressed a smile as Matiu stiffly stripped to his underwear but Jax's humour gave way to shock as the dim light revealed the full extent of Matiu's scarring. His reluctance to bare himself was not only about modesty but about shame too and again Jax wished they were alone.

Matiu lay down and Anahera enclosed him in her arms. 'Jax told me you were hurt and could no longer *shift*,' she said softly, 'but Ahi are Ahi, whether in birth-form or shift-form.' Matiu said nothing and Anahera wedged herself onto her elbow and kissed Matiu as she had kissed Jax to start *his* healing. 'Ahi are Ahi,' she repeated fiercely. Matiu remained silent but Jax sensed his tension ease.

It was not long before Anahera slipped into sleep, her arms still wrapped about Matiu, but Jax remained wakeful and after a while, Matiu reached his hand across the pillow. 'I am glad you are back, Jax,' he whispered.

Jax caught his hand and their fingers locked. 'So am I.'

3/

The room was bathed in pre-dawn light when there was a sharp rap at the door and Jax crawled from the cover to answer it. He did not recognize the airman who bore a box of food, a kit-bag, and Keli's orders for Jax and Anahera to report to his office at 06:00 hours. The airman's eyes slid past Jax to where Matiu still slept in Anahera's arms, to Jax's dinted side of the mattress, then to Jax's whitiki.

Jax nodded his thanks, took possession of the man's burdens, and kicked the door shut behind him. Anahera did not wake but Matiu did and took in Jax's anger. 'What is it?' he whispered.

'Off-islander ignorance,' muttered Jax, as he set the food on the bench. The kit-bag held a female Airman's uniform and Jax's clothes from Rilo. Keli's reminder that Jax was in the military clear enough.

Matiu gently disengaged himself from Anahera and donned his clothes. 'It is hard to live between two worlds,' he said softly, as he finished buttoning his shirt.

'You seem to manage.'

Matiu shook his head. 'I only live in the Off-island world. I spent a year confined to a bed like you were confined to the Infirmary, but unlike you, I couldn't *shift* to escape. I never had any choice.'

Jax gripped his arm. 'You have a choice now, Mati,' he hissed. 'You can go back. They will welcome you there, even as Anahera welcomed you here.'

'I can't *shift*, Jax, and Iolana's in the Exclusion Zone. How would I get there?'

'There are always ways.'

'And you?' demanded Matiu. 'Where will you live when this is over? Here with me or there with her?' Matiu's green eyes were intense but Jax did not answer. The Boys' Home, Arozi and the military, had all taught him to *never* plan ahead. 'I guessed as much,' muttered Matiu, and turned away.

'Mati, I—'

'I need to bathe,' said Anahera sleepily as she stretched and then shrugged herself free from of the cover.

'No lagoons here,' said Jax with forced cheerfulness. 'Maybe Matiu can show you the shower and the toilet *and* how they work, while I sort us some breakfast.'

Jax managed to keep the smile in place until the bathroom door closed behind them. The more time Matiu spent with Anahera the better, he concluded grimly, as he tore open the box and rummaged through its contents. Matiu had lived in isolation long enough.

The box contained the sort of food Jax had eaten on Iolana and that Keli had provided last night but Jax was under no illusion that his commander's *benevolence* would continue. Keli had plans he was determined Jax would execute, not that Jax needed any encouragement. Having been to Iolana, he was probably even keener than Keli to protect it, but above all, he wanted Anahera safe.

Anahera donned the *smelly* Off-islander clothes under sufferance, but she left most of the shirt buttons undone, its tails loose, and rolled up the military issue trousers just below the knee. She refused to wear the boots at all and with her long tousled hair, looked more like an Off-islander's sexual fantasy, than the modest young woman Keli had probably envisaged.

She did not like Jax's clothes any better. 'You look like one of *them*,' she said, as they made their way back to Keli's office.

'Maybe I am one of them,' he said, still troubled by his exchange with Matiu.

Anahera's hand caught his. 'You and Matiu are Ahi,' she said firmly. 'Why isn't he with us?'

'Commander Keli only ordered you and me to his office.'

'Why do you have to do as Keli says?'

'It is the way the military works.' Jax had explained military hierarchies to her several times already but she remained confused, probably because such rigid hierarchies were so alien to her. The Kawai Alanui had Elders and the Kuwaini, but blind obedience was not expected.

The chill air was heavy with the smell of rain and Jax was glad of his uniform, despite its constriction after days of being virtually naked, but his tension built as he neared Keli's office.

'Commander Keli's orders only apply to me,' he told Anahera as they walked. 'You don't have to do *anything* he says, especially if it is dangerous.'

'But you have to do dangerous things, don't you?'

'I will do whatever is necessary to keep you and your people safe.'

'*Our* people, Jax. And it will be the Kuwaini who decide what we will do.'

Jax made no reply. One way or another, it would be the military who decided Iolana's fate. All Jax could do was ensure it was Samarak's military and not Makena's.

They were ushered into an interview room which seemed too small for the number of bodies that filled it, and Jax was taken aback to recognize men from Rilo, including Carter. Anahera shrank against Jax and he did not blame her, shocked by the contrast between the heavily muscled, crew-cut military and the lithe, lightly clad Kawai Alanui. Keli called the men to order but he need not have bothered. A hush had settled over the room as soon as Jax and Anahera had entered. They took their seats at the table while Keli took up position at its head.

'You have had a preliminary briefing on Operation Vesuvius,' he began without preamble, 'but the full briefing was delayed until Airman Jax's return from the Zoaides. The Alanui have sent an envoy, Anahera, to liaise with us,' he said, and nodded in Anahera's direction.

'*Kawai* Alanui,' she corrected.

'Which brings me to a necessary point clarification,' continued Keli smoothly. 'With apologies to the Alanui envoy, we will continue to use accepted terms to avoid confusion. Anahera is a member of the *Kawai* Alanui people, as is Airman Jax, as is Senior Airman Matiu, who some of you know. The Kawai Alanui use the same name as their islands, which we know as the Zoaides, and which originally consisted of four inhabited islands: Iolana, Rua, Ke-one and Puha.

'As you are aware, Ke-one and Puha haven't been inhabited in recorded history, and Rua was destroyed in an explosion ten years ago. Anahera is from the island of Iolana, while Airman Jax and Senior Airman Matiu are the only known survivors of Rua.' No one spoke but Jax sensed a ripple of surprise move through the room.

178

'We will continue to refer to the Kawai Alanui islands as the Zoaides and their remaining inhabitants, on the island of Iolana, as the Alanui.'

Anahera bristled and Jax laid his hand over hers where it rested on the table. The men opposite noticed but Jax was more intent on heading off another interjection than dispelling any impression they were lovers.

'I also need to clarify that, while the Alanui don't speak English as a first language, they are expert mimics and highly sensitive to the non-verbal communication that creates meaning in *any* language,' continued Keli. 'Anahera has already acquired proficiency in reproducing sounds and some level of understanding of meaning, but I continue to rely on Airman Jax to translate where necessary.'

Jax nodded. He just hoped Keli also realized Anahera had *no* understanding of military protocols and no interest in acquiring it.

Keli picked up a pointer and turned to the chart behind him. The first of the flip-sheets showed a map of the four islands Jax was already familiar with. The men probably were too because Keli wasted no time in flicking to the second chart, which showed the Exclusion Zone, Makena and Samarak's bases, and their respective ocean patrols. Keli did not linger on it either. The third chart was a geological survey of the islands Jax had never seen before. It must have been taken from old data because it showed Rua and Jax had trouble looking at it.

He mimicked calmness but Anahera's fingers suddenly locked with his. The next few charts showed the geology of each of the islands in turn, which were the same. Keli obviously made the point they had all been created by volcanic activity, and so shared the same mineral composition.

The next chart showed the mineral analysis in greater detail which Keli spent little time on too, except for two minerals, anilrite and theralin. Jax had never heard of either. The first was shown in black on the chart, and the second in red, and small black and red circles dotted the Fayo seabed within the Exclusion Zone and clustered around the islands.

The first, anilrite, was important in particular types of weaponry, Keli explained, and scarce in Makena and Samarak. Both nations sought new reserves and it had been a consideration in negotiating the Exclusion Zone, that neither had access to the Fayo's reserves.

The second mineral, theralin, was not sought by either nation because it was highly volatile. A single spark could set off a catastrophic explosion which made mining any mineral extremely hazardous. Keli continued to speak but Jax's brain had stopped. All he saw were the over-lapping black and red circles that covered Rua and Iolana, and the lands of Makena and Samarak to either side, hungry for minerals.

Bile surged and he shoved back his chair and managed to reach the overgrown garden outside before he vomited. His stomach continued to heave and sweat poured off him, and he was barely aware of Anahera by his side, or of Carter lowering him onto the step.

'Keli has called a half hour break,' said Carter, as he settled beside him.

Anahera sat on Jax's other side, her hand clamped over his. 'I don't understand what the Off-islander meant,' she said tremblingly. 'What did he mean, Jax?'

Jax still struggled to breathe and it was Carter who answered. 'Commander Keli doesn't *mean* anything yet,' he said. 'He outlines the present situation which is that there is a highly explosive mineral mixed up with another mineral which both we and Makena need.'

Anahera's hand shook and Jax managed to raise his head. 'If Makena illegally mined the seabed near Kawai Alanui, they might have set off the explosion that destroyed Rua,' he said in Kawai Alanui.

'And did they?' asked Anahera in horror.

'Probably,' muttered Jax, and turned to Carter. 'And Makena is still mining the seabed, isn't it?' he demanded in English. 'And this operation is about stopping them blowing Iolana and its people sky-high like they blew Rua and *my* people sky-high.'

'Keli hasn't said that.'

'Yet,' said Jax bitterly. 'And how the hell do we to stop them without triggering another war which would probably destroy Iolana anyway?'

Anahera shook his arm. 'Tell me, Jax!'

That was the last thing he wanted to do but he switched to Kawai Alanui and gave her the kindest version he could. 'I don't know any of this for sure,' he added. 'Keli didn't get up to that part before I left.' Anahera said nothing, but she hugged herself and Jax pulled her close. 'I will do *everything* in my power to stop this,' he pledged. 'Everything!

The briefing resumed as if Jax had not fled the room and he forced himself to focus on Keli's actual words but his shirt was soon soaked with sweat and Anahera sat with her head in her hands as if to fend off the horror.

Jax yearned to *shift* and speed back to Iolana but it would be worse than useless. Keli obviously had some plan or Jax would be in the cells instead of in a room with highly trained military personnel being briefed on Operation Vesuvius.

Keli confirmed that intelligence pointed to Rua's destruction being caused by Makena's covert mining but it could not be proved. The Zoaides were volcanic and even dormant volcanoes could erupt again, although not without warning. Seismographs picked up vibrations caused by mining but governments could shrug them off as volcanic in origin *if* they chose, which is what Makena did.

The mining had ceased after Rua's destruction, as if Makena had been as shocked as everyone else, but had started again in the last eighteen months and to have any hope of stopping it, Samarak needed solid proof of it, and even that might not be enough.

No one wanted another war, which gave both sides a lot of leeway to gnaw away at the edges of the last treaty *and* at the Exclusion Zone, as long their actions could be denied or explained away. And if Iolana blew? It would be just another volcanic event, unfortunate but not unexpected, given Rua's demise.

Keli adjourned early for lunch and Jax guessed it was to give him and Anahera a break. He loaded a plate of food for them both and led Anahera outside. They perched on the step in the wintery sunshine and Jax set the plate between them. Keli had provided kumara and fish but Anahera simply stared ahead.

'Eat Anahera,' he said. She shook her head. 'Did you understand what Commander Keli said?'

'Some of it.'

'Do you want me to translate?'

'No.'

He shifted the plate of food aside, pulled her close, and kissed her. The men from the briefing enjoyed the fresh air too and probably already knew of his *threesome* with Matiu.

She pressed against him and he tightened his arms around her. 'I spent ten years trying to forget Rua ever existed after it blew up,' he said softly. 'It was so unbearable the only way I could draw breath was to pretend I wasn't Kawai Alanui. And then I came here and saw Matiu again. I tried to pretend he didn't exist too, because if he existed, Rua and everyone on it had as well.'

He ran his fingers gently down her face. 'Matiu's love pulled me back, Anahera, and your love for Iolana is the reason you came here. Horror is a hard thing to look at but to save Iolana, we *must* look at it.'

'I just want to go home,' she muttered.

'So do I, but you have to have a home to go back to first.'

32

Jax found the afternoon session easier to bear than the morning one, and Anahera seemed to as well. She sat with her attention on Keli and occasionally whispered for Jax to clarify something. The morning had dredged up appalling memories of Rua's destruction and raised the possibility of Iolana's, but the afternoon was all about how Operation V would tackle the threat.

The men Keli had selected were military divers but would be confined to Samarak's waters *for the time being*. Keli's orders prohibited him risking an *incident* by breaching Makena's territorial waters or the Exclusion Zone, and Jax did not need to be a mimic to pick up Keli's anger. He also saw why Keli had been desperate to have a *shifter* at his disposal.

Jax could go wherever he wanted, *in shift-form*, although not without risk. His military status would be clear if he had to *shift* back to birth-form, and in shift-form, he risked barbs and bullets from Makena's military, and predation from other creatures.

'Patrols will continue as usual and divers carry out reconnaissance at night, using dinghies deployed from the patrol boats. Airman Jax will carry out more extensive reconnaissance from below the Fayo and deliver regular reports to the divers. Operation V's longer term direction depends on those reports.'

Keli's attention swung to Jax. 'Your *shifter* heritage has been discussed at the earlier briefing, Airman, but it is important those of Operation V understand *fully* what a *shifter* heritage means. I would like you to demonstrate *shifting*.'

'Yes, Commander Keli.' Jax pushed back his chair and took up position at the side of the room where there was more space. The men present had last seen him tear himself to pieces on the perimeter fence, which was hardly the sign of a *dependable* person they might have to risk their lives for, and he wondered how they would react to him *shifting*.

'With your permission, I will summon Professor Connel, who wishes to see a *shift* for research purposes,' said Keli. Jax nodded though they both knew Keli did not need his permission for anything.

The men's feet shuffled under the table as if nervous they were about to witness an embarrassingly poor party trick, but Jax kept his attention on Anahera's rigid face.

The Kawai Alanui had never hidden their ability to *shift* but nor had they used it to sate Off-islander curiosity or appetite for the bizarre. Connel came in and Jax stripped down to his underwear and sensed the men's distrust increase as his part-healed gashes were revealed.

The men showered together so being naked was less of an issue than Anahera's presence. Her body reeked of anger at her predicament and she glared at Keli.

'Anahera?' he prompted.

She rose and the men's heads swiveled in her direction. They probably thought they were in for a double party trick, but she turned her back.

'We are both older Ahi,' explained Jax evenly, 'and older Ahi do not look upon each other naked.' He enjoyed a moment of grim satisfaction as the men struggled to reconcile the news with the rumours of sexual hijinks at his quarters last night, then considered which shift-form to take as he removed his underwear.

He resisted the urge to choose a snake to test *their* mental strength by slithering around the room with tongue flickering, and chose a white-wolf instead. Off-islanders admired what they saw as a wolf's noble savagery, but he mainly wanted to reassure Anahera he had not changed into an Off-islander.

He *shifted* and remained motionless for a long moment to allow the shocked men to make sense of what they had seen, then padded around the table to Anahera. She still stood but had turned again and he put his front paws on the table beside her, so his head was level with hers, and faced the men as she did.

Jax had intended it to be a declaration of oneness with her but as she brought her arm around him and stroked his pelt, Carter's gaze sharpened. The message could be read two ways, Jax realized, as he continued his circuit back to his neat pile of clothes. Anahera turned away again and he *shifted* back. His gashes burned but he masked the pain, requested permission to dress and was granted it.

Then he returned to his seat and sat down. The door closed behind Connel but no one seemed to notice and it was a while before Keli cleared his throat. 'I understand from Professor Connel that Alanui can assume countless forms. Is that correct, Airman?'

'Yes, Commander Keli.'

'For Operation V, it is likely you will need to assume fish form. Is that going to be a problem, Airman?'

'No, Commander Keli.'

Keli nodded. 'At first light tomorrow, you and the Alanui envoy are to return to Iolana to liaise with those there. You may pass on what has been discussed here. You will spend a rest day there, Airman Jax, and return here ready for the following morning's briefing. The remainder of the men will report here at 06:00 hours tomorrow morning. Dismissed.'

Anahera wrenched off the Off-islander clothes as soon as they got back to his quarters. 'Get rid of yours too, Jax,' she ordered.

'I am military, Anahera. I have to wear them while I am here.'

She scowled as she prowled around the kitchen. 'Where is Matiu?'

'Carrying out his piloting duties most likely. The military doesn't have its members sitting around doing nothing. He was probably only here last night because Keli expected my return.'

'You act like *them* when you are with them,' she accused, rounding on him. 'Why did you have *shift*?'

'Keli ordered me to.'

'It didn't sound like it.'

'When a commanding officer *suggests* you do something, it's the same thing.' He paused, but her expression remained stormy. 'The Kawai Alanui have never hidden their ability to *shift*,' he said, but she shook her head impatiently. 'Why are you angry with me?' he asked directly.

'Because I don't want you turning into *them*. You are Kawai Alanui, not opala!'

There it was: the same fear that haunted him. Us and them, Kawai Alanui and Off-islander, with only the place of the lost in between.

'To stop Iolana blowing up like Rua, I have to work with the military.'

'And afterwards?'

In truth, there might not be an *afterwards*. Operation V was not going to be easy, and Makena wouldn't hesitate to *disappear* witnesses to their operations. Jax swallowed convulsively. And even if they were all killed, including Keli, it would be explained away as a training accident. Operation V's men would be sacrificed to avert another war and they knew it.

'Jax?'

She was very close and he considered the lies he might tell to soothe her fears but Iolana was her home and she deserved the truth. 'Operation V is going to be dangerous, Anahera. There might not be an *afterwards.*'

'I don't want you involved,' she said angrily.

'I am under orders.'

'Leave with me now and never come back!'

Her anger probably stemmed from fear but his own anger ignited. 'I don't have that choice, Anahera, in fact, no one has choices anymore! You, your fellow Ahi, the Ikaika, the Elders, the Kuwaini have *no* power over what happens to Iolana, as Rua had *no* power over what happened to it. Iolana's future will be decided by two nations whose greed feeds war after war.'

'I hate the Off-islanders and I hate what you become when you are with them!' she exclaimed. 'I am going home!'

'Commander Keli ordered us to wait until tomorrow.'

'You told me I don't have to do *anything* that male says!'

He caught her arm. 'The flight over the Fayo is safer together,' he said urgently. 'Ahi stay with Ahi. You taught me that.'

'It's *moana* not *the Fayo*,' she said furiously, 'and I am leaving now! Turn your back, Jax!'

'Anahera—'

'Turn your back!'

He did so reluctantly and only turned back when he heard the scrape of claws on the polished floor. At least she had taken sun-eagle-form but her eyes retained their amber glare and he opened the door and watched her hop through then take to the air. Every instinct screamed at him to follow but he was part of the despised military and under orders.

He went back to the table and threw himself onto a chair. At least if she returned alone there would be time for her and Tamati to patch things up, and she could stay there then, in Iolana's *relative* safety.

His thoughts went to Rafi, who he had listed as next of kin. If

Jax did not survive Op. V, Rafi would continue to receive money to cushion the garage's back-breaking work. As for Matiu . . . Jax rubbed his face. He did not know why Keli excluded him from Operation V, but it meant Jax could not explain why he was about to desert *again*, although he could say goodbye this time.

He sat and watched the wall clock's hands crawl around the dial. Five o'clock, six o'clock, seven o'clock. He should be doing something more productive then sitting there but he felt paralyzed. If Matiu were still at URZOL he should be back soon but he might be flying out of Rilo instead, or some other base, which meant there would be no goodbyes after all.

The door barged open, making Jax jump, and Matiu staggered in. He had been drinking and even the smell churned Jax's gut. The boys at the Home had once smuggled in beer but even a couple of mouthfuls had laid Jax low for days and he had not touched alcohol since.

Matiu lurched to the table and Jax sifted his breath through his teeth in an attempt to avoid the stench. 'Where's your girlfriend?' slurred Matiu.

'Anahera has gone back to Iolana and she isn't my girlfriend.'

'Lover's tiff?' sneered Matiu.

'Matiu—'

'Carter told me all about it,' he said, 'although don't worry, he didn't tell me *anything* about Op. V.'

'We need to talk, Matiu.'

'I seem to remember once saying the same thing to you *and* I remember *exactly* what you said in reply.' He leaned forward over the table and Jax struggled not to avert his face. '*Don't bother. We have nothing to say.*' Matiu's mouth twisted. 'And you know what? You were right, Jax. We have nothing to say.'

He staggered away from the table to where his mattress lay on the floor and clumsily dragged it back to his room. The door slammed behind him but Jax stayed where he was. He did not think of Anahera, Rafi or even of Matiu but of Arozi's silent emptiness. Life had been simple there, but it had not really been a life at all, just an escape into nothingness.

The clock's hands continued their crawl. Eight o'clock, nine o'clock, ten o'clock, eleven o'clock, eleven-thirty. He pushed his chair from the table, carried his mattress back to his room, and made up his bed with a military precision that would have passed the strictest inspection. Then he undressed and folded his clothes into an equally neat pile, placed his kit-bag next to his clothes, and set his boots at right-angles to the bed. He reclaimed his whitiki, went back to the kitchen and opened the door just wide enough for a sun-eagle to squeeze through.

He had considered leaving Matiu a letter during his long night of waiting, but Matiu was right to claim they had nothing to say. What bound them went beyond words and that meant Jax could not leave Matiu as he had left Rafi, and as Anahera had left him.

He *shifted* to sun-eagle, plucked a feather from his breast and set it on the table. It glimmered gold in Whetu's faint sheen and Jax slid through the door, launched into the air, and flew west.

Anahera looked angry when she emerged from between the awins but Tamati felt an immense relief she was back. He had waited outside her awin in the hope she would return and would have embraced her had he not been constrained by their last words together. 'I am glad to see you, Anahera,' he said instead, and glanced around. 'Isn't Jax with you?'

'He is still with the opala.'

'He is staying there?'

'He can't leave until tomorrow because he is part of the *military* and has to obey *their* orders,' she snapped.

'So,' said Tamati carefully, 'did you learn anything apart from the fact Jax acts like an Off-islander?'

'Yes, but it isn't for your ears.' Tamati bit back a retort and she wearily pushed the hair from her eyes. 'I am sorry, Tamati, I didn't mean it to come out that way. I meant it was the Kuwaini who asked me to go and that I must speak with them first.'

'At least let me brew you some fela,' he said, keen to end the ill-feeling between them. Anahera did not argue, which was gratifying, just slumped on the mat beside the fire. Tamati raked the coals back into life and repositioned the pot. 'Tell me about the Off-islands,' he said, as he stripped leaves from a bunch of fela.

'I only saw what they call a *military base*. Their awins are many times bigger than the Kuwain and filled with polished wood and stone. They smell awful.'

'What? Like rotting fish?'

'No, like things I have never smelled before. Jax called them *products*. He didn't like them either.'

'Yet he has been content to live amongst them,' Tamati could not help saying.

'Jax lived amongst them because he didn't think he had anywhere else to go.'

'He could have come here,' said Tamati, dropping the fela leaves into the water.

'Maybe he didn't think he would be welcome.'

'I am sorry for my earlier behavior, Anahera,' said Tamati formally. 'It was unworthy of the Ikaika and hurt Jax and you.'

'I have hurt him too,' she muttered.

Tamati frowned. 'How?'

'By being impatient and bad tempered.' She smiled wryly. 'You are doing better than me, Tamati. *I* have lost none of my Ahi flaws.'

'There is time yet,' he said softly.

Anahera half shook her head. 'I met Matiu, the other Kawai Alanui who survived Rua. He is part of the military too.'

'What is he like?'

'He has your eyes and my hair.'

'I mean, is he more Kawai Alanui or more Off-islander?' asked Tamati, pouring the fela into a bowl and handing it to her.

'I didn't spend enough time with him to know,' she said, and sipped the fela. 'He loves Jax though.'

Tamati shrugged. 'Of course he does. They are Ahi,' he said, and filled his own bowl.

'Yes, the only two Kawai Alanui from Rua to survive,' she said, and took a gulp of fela. 'Imagine that Tamati,' she said tremulously. 'Iolana gone and everyone on it, except for me and you.' Her voice cracked and she closed her eyes.

'Anahera …'

She set the bowl down and scrambled up. 'I need to sleep,' she mumbled, and disappeared into her awin.

33

*J*ax felt exhaustion seep into his shift-form as he flew but even after Iolana appeared beneath him, he circled Lani several times before he landed. He wanted to remind himself what Pana had looked like from the air, but his sun-eagle night eyes were not keen enough. He came to ground in the rero and *shifted*, the pain in his gashes still sufficient to make him gasp.

Most of Lani's fires had dwindled to coals but one had been rebuilt and he wondered if it were Anahera's. He had no idea where her awin was and even if he had, he did not think he would be welcome, presuming she had arrived safely. His gut tightened but it was pointless setting out on search. He would have to knock on every awin wall to see whether she slept inside.

The fire was warm and he stretched himself out on the mats beside it, cupped his hands behind his head, and stared up at the stars. Whetu's light faded, as it did before dawn's approach, but the stars remained brilliant. They had been brilliant in Arozi's clear night air too but there was the smell of rero smoke here and moana's tang.

It allowed him to imagine he lazed by one of Pana's fires and that the events of the last ten years had not happened. He was Ikaika, knew his skin-spirit, and at twenty-two, had mate-paired with an Ikaika who loved him for what he was, and who Jax loved too.

The notion was as fanciful as the beer-fueled tales of Off-islanders' sporting triumphs, and he closed his eyes to shut out the stars. He needed to sleep. In another day he must make the long flight back to URZOL, to Keli's next briefing, to his duties in Op. V, and there would be no chance to sleep then, just countless *shifts* to navigate moana's night-time waters alone.

Tamati loitered in the awins' shadows, too restless to go to his own awin and sleep, and was surprised to see Jax arrive and lie down in front of Anahera's awin. Anahera had been angry when she had arrived, so they may have argued but Ahi were quick to forgive. Whatever the case, the Ikaika owed Jax care which included food and shelter.

Jax's eyes were closed and as Tamati looked down at him, he wondered if he were already asleep. It was a long way to the Off-islands, especially for someone who carried injuries, and he grimaced as he surveyed Jax's body. The gashes were part-healed but still looked terrible.

Whetu's light gilded the shape of Jax's face and beyond the horror of the wounds, the slim line of his torso and hips. Jax was beautiful and Tamati thought of his long exile amongst the Off-islanders and that of the other Kawai Alanui, Matiu. If Jax remained in the Off-islands, his chances of mate-pairing were virtually zero unless he mate-paired with opala.

Jax's eyes opened, wolf-like in the star sheen, but he did not move, just contemplated Tamati staring down at him.

'I saw you come back,' said Tamati. 'Have you eaten? I can bring you food.'

'There is no need. Thank you.'

Tamati squatted and put more rero on the fire. 'Anahera is back,' he said, and nodded towards the awin. 'She is sleeping.' Jax's face showed relief then his gaze returned to the stars. 'There is plenty of room in my awin, if you would like to share it,' said Tamati. Jax looked at him again but said nothing, and Tamati didn't blame him for not leaping at the invitation. 'Rest will help you heal,' he added.

'Thank you but I am enjoying the stars.'

Tamati settled on the mat and peered up. 'There is a lot to enjoy,' he agreed, and shifted the fela back onto the coals. 'At least let me make you a drink. You have had a long flight.'

Jax winced as he sat up but Tamati resisted the urge to ask how he had been injured. 'I made this for Anahera but it shouldn't be too over-brewed.'

'She experienced no problems on her return journey?' asked Jax.

'Not that she mentioned.'

'I intended to travel back with her but she wanted to leave immediately,' said Jax apologetically. 'My orders meant I had to delay until after midnight.'

'She said you had to obey orders,' said Tamati, passing Jax the fela.

Jax nodded his thanks and took a sip. 'It is the way the military works. I must speak with the Kuwaini today and be back in the Off-islands by tomorrow's dawn.'

'And then?' asked Tamati, wondering if Jax intended to stay there.

'My orders prevent me from saying.'

'What about Anahera? Is she under orders too?'

'Anahera is free like Kawai Alanui *should* be.'

Tamati recalled what Miru had said and glanced at Jax sideways. 'Why *is* Iolana in danger?' he asked.

'That is for the Kuwaini to tell you and your people.'

'We are *your* people too,' corrected Tamati.

'I can't be Kawai Alanui *and* military at the same time,' said Jax, his gaze now on the fire, 'and for the time being, I must be military.'

Tamati shrugged. 'Their ways are more familiar to you I suppose.'

Jax set the bowl down and rose. 'Yes, very familiar to me,' he muttered, and walked away.

Jax returned at dawn to find Anahera pacing up and down outside the Kuwain, and as soon as she saw him, she rushed to him and enclosed him in an intense hug. 'Tamati said you were back but I didn't quite believe you were safe,' she said. 'I am sorry for the way we parted. It isn't your fault you have to obey the opala's orders.'

The lonely hours he had spent pacing about in the rero had convinced Jax he had no place amongst the Kawai Alanui, but Anahera's touch dispelled his doubts in an instant, and he tightened his arms around her. The Kawai Alanui used physical contact as much as words to convey their feelings, something he had forgotten in the years away, and he wondered how he had endured being alone.

'You were upset,' he said, and kissed her hair. 'I am just glad you are back.'

'Only for a while. We need to carry the Kuwaini's response back to the Off-islands.'

'*I* will do that. There is no reason for you to risk the flight again.'

Anahera's clear eyes narrowed. 'Ahi help each other.'

'This is different,' said Jax, glancing to where Kawai Alanui were emerging from their awins. Fires were being stirred to life and fela brewed and he shifted his grip to her hand. 'We need to speak with the Kuwaini,' he said quickly. 'They might prohibit you from leaving anyway.'

The first thing the Kuwaini did was to ask Anahera to outline what she had learned in the Off-islands and Jax was pleased by how well she had understood Keli, although her account was peppered by contemptuous asides about the smell of the opala's awins, their lack of choice about how they lived, and their need for evidence that Kawai Alanui could *shift*.

But her demeanor changed when she spoke of Rua's destruction and its implications for Iolana, and so did the Kuwaini's. Their attention switched to Jax, and while he saw compassion in their faces, he saw fear too, and a hunger for information, especially about the military's intentions.

'No one wants another war,' said Jax, 'so Samarak can't just accuse Makena of mining in the Exclusion Zone without solid evidence.'

'And how do you intend to get such evidence?' asked the Kuwaini called Davi.

'By using shift-form to spy on their operations. If I can see where they are mining, the military can bring in divers to take photographs. Like pictures,' he added, in response to their blank looks.

'And then they will stop?' asked Miru.

Jax had hoped no one would ask that question and he wondered if it were a coincidence that Miru had asked it. Anahera said she was a Dream-traveler which suggested some sort of prescience.

'I don't know and I suspect the military doesn't either,' admitted Jax. 'Any evidence will probably be discussed by Samarak's leaders who will decide what action to take, and then order the military to take it.'

'And so there might be another war,' said Miru slowly, 'and Iolana will be destroyed anyway.'

The Kuwaini's fear was palpable and he caught Anahera's hand as she drew a ragged breath beside him. 'I will do *everything* in my power to protect Iolana,' he pledged, 'as will the military I work with.'

'But it won't be enough,' murmured Miru, staring into space, and then her piercing gaze fixed on him. '*You* won't be enough.'

She said it with such authority Jax wondered if she *were* prescient but it was worse than that. Her doubt laid bare every one of his flaws. '*You* must have help,' she continued. 'Iolana cannot leave its future in the hands of others, no matter how well-intentioned.'

It took Jax a moment to understand her meaning and for his gut to unclench. 'Are you saying other Kawai Alanui can work with me in shift-form?'

'Yes. *Shifting* takes strength, as you know, and your injuries still weaken you. But even had you been whole, moana is immense. You will have more chance of *pictures* if you have more taniwha, wheke and hiri in its depths to help you.'

'It will be dangerous,' said Jax.

Miru nodded sadly. 'Everything is dangerous now.'

The Kuwaini sat in silence after Anahera and Jax had gone and not even Davi seemed capable of dredging up anything to say. 'It would have been better had the Kuwaini agreed to send Kawai Alanui to aid the opala *before* you offered it,' grumbled Cheren.

'I can withdraw the offer if the Kuwaini prefer,' said Miru.

'No, we have no choice. And whatever we do, the opala might still destroy us as they destroyed Rua,' said Cheren.

'We could evacuate,' said Sairin.

'To where?' asked Cheren.

'Puha and Ke-one still exist. There is room there.'

'There is room because the Kawai Alanui abandoned them,' said Davi gently. 'There wasn't enough to sustain them.'

'And they don't have Tihi,' pointed out Miru.

Silence fell again as the Kuwaini considered the loss of the Cloud Crown. Without its mysteries, there would be no Ikaika; no one to care for the young and Elders; no one to keep the old songs and make the new ones.

'How much of this have you dreamed, Miru?' asked Davi.

'Most of it, one way or other, not that it has proved much help.'

'Whetu might still guide us,' said Davi thoughtfully. 'You dreamed that Anahera, Tamati and Malo might tread different paths to other Kawai Alanui, and you dreamed of Rua's destruction.'

'Which might portend our own,' said Cheren darkly.

'Or offer us a warning denied to Rua,' said Davi. 'Knowing the danger gives us a chance to act and I think we are agreed that we *must* act. Jax returns to the Off-islands tomorrow and he must take with him the Ikaika who will search, as he will, for what Samarak needs.'

'We will call in the Ikaika and see who is willing to go,' said Cheren.

'Not those mate-paired,' cautioned Davi, and the Kuwaini nodded grimly. No one needed Jax's warning to understand that those who left might not return.

Jax went to Anahera's awin and slept, and it was late afternoon before he woke. She had left food for him and he ate and then wandered outside, surprised she was at her fire with Tamati, Malo and Airini.

'Join us for some fela,' said Airini, patting the mat beside her. She managed a smile but the rest of them looked grim.

'Most of Lani knows what we know,' said Anahera, 'and the Kuwaini have asked for Ikaika to help you. We have volunteered.'

Jax glanced at Tamati's set face. 'You aren't Ikaika, Anahera.'

'I know the Off-islander tongue and how Off-islanders behave. Ikaika will need someone to tell Off-islanders what the Ikaika see.'

Anahera was right. Ikaika would learn fast, as she had, but not fast enough and miscommunications could prove fatal for everyone.

'There might be more volunteers but we won't know until later tonight,' said Airini. 'Rawiri is keen and so is Maia, but they are close to mate-pairing. I think the Kuwaini will ask them to stay.'

Jax resisted the urge to look at Tamati again and forced himself to think in military terms instead. A group of Ikaika in shift-form could cover more ocean *and* rotate to allow for rest breaks, but they were a greater logistical challenge. Apart from the language gap, military systems such as rigid hierarchies and obeying orders were alien to the Kawai Alanui and there was not time for them to become familiar. Keli's orders were for Jax to report at the dawn briefing which meant Op. V might begin later that day or first thing the next.

As the night deepened, more Ikaika joined them at the fire until there were ten gathered. As well as Anahera, Malo, Tamati and Airini, there were three more females: Hana, Tiare and Kaea, and two more males: Tai and Anaru. Anahera would probably remain on one of the boats to interpret, Jax guessed, which gave Keli nine shifters to find evidence of mining so Carter and his friends could take their precious photos.

Jax described the route they would take to URZOL as they ate, the necessity of flying high, and what to expect on their arrival, then they finished their meal, separated to *shift*, and flew east.

34

*K*eli was relieved at the sighting of two sun-eagles flying high in the predawn light. There were still lots of question marks over *Air-man* Jax's loyalty and it was a good sign he had returned in the time ordered, although Keli was surprised he still had Anahera with him.

The mics had picked up their argument *and* that Anahera had *shifted* and left, and they had picked up the second argument with Matiu too, although this time, Jax had not said much. Both exchanges had been in Alanui, and while Connel had not been able to decipher what had prompted the first quarrel, he had speculated the second was triggered by Matiu's jealousy of Anahera, and *that* vindicated Keli's decision to exclude Matiu from the Op.

Operation V's sensitivities meant Keli had to justify every man's inclusion and Matiu was neither a diver nor, for all practical purposes, a *shifter*. There was also the issue of *romantic attachments* which were dangerous to missions where orders might require men to act against the welfare of their comrades and *personal* wishes.

A second phone call told him the sun-eagles had landed and he was considering what Jax might report when he learned five more sun-eagles approached. He barely had time to grapple with that news before yet another call told him three more headed their way. He rubbed his hand through his hair and grinned. Either URZOL was under attack by the Zoaides' largest bird, or the Alanui had sent help.

He made a quick call to Connel, then one to organize food, and paced around his office, his mind abuzz with the possibilities of having ten *shifters* at his disposal. *If* that were the case, he would need to rejig some of his plans.

A knock heralded Connel's arrival, his eyes gleaming with excitement. 'Ten Kawai Alanui,' he said. 'Seeing how they interact will be fascinating.'

'Unless we actually have ten *sun-eagles*,' muttered Keli, taking another turn around the room, 'which might almost be preferable.'

Connel's eyebrows shot up. 'I thought having more shifters would make your job easier, Commander.'

'It makes it a hell of a lot more complicated. If they are as inclined to go their own way as *Airman* Jax, they could risk the whole Op. along with the lives of my men.'

'Jax seems committed now and his liaison will help.'

'Or hinder.'

Connor frowned. 'You still distrust him?'

'It isn't a matter of trust, *Professor*, but of dependability, hardly Jax's strong point, and the more he mixes with his own kind, the stronger will be the pull to Iolana's more relaxed life-style.'

'The Kawai Alanui *life-style* is far from *relaxed*, Commander Keli,' said Connel tersely. 'No peoples can meet their needs for food and shelter by *lounging in hammocks under palm trees* all day. As for his *own kind*, Jax has spent almost half his life here, but if that *is* a concern, then add Senior Airman Matiu to your team. He should provide a powerful incentive for Jax to stay with *our* kind, *if* their argument last night is anything to go by.'

'It was in Alanui,' Keli reminded him briefly.

'I think the nub of it was pretty obvious, as was Jax's attempt to mend things.'

'We don't—' began Keli, and then broke off as a second knock sounded at the door. 'This is going to be *fascinating*,' he muttered, and gave the order to enter.

Having ten Alanui shifters crowd into his office, clad in the barest of clothing, was indeed *fascinating*, conceded Keli. Jax came to attention and saluted, but Keli barely noticed. Five men and five women, he counted quickly, and all as striking as Jax. The women had long hair like Anahera, black as well as various shades of auburn, but accompanied by odd eye-color combinations of green, grey and amber. The men's coloring was similar but their hair was cropped to shoulder-length.

Their lack of facial and body hair and slim physiques reminded Keli of lanky teenagers, but there was an intensity about the males in particular which had nothing to do with adolescence. Apart from Jax and Anahera, these were initiated adults, and it showed in their demeanor.

After brief introductions, Keli directed Jax to take them to the interview room where the food would be delivered. The fire had been lit there too as the weather had turned chill, and after Connel had escorted them out, Keli ordered coats from the stores. The Alanui would need them out on the Fayo, even if they refused to wear them here.

They were eating by the time Keli arrived, some standing, but most sitting on the floor. Connel was speaking with Anahera and Jax, and a black-haired, green-eyed male, but Keli called Jax aside to get his report.

Jax outlined the Kuwaini's meeting and their decision to call for Ikaika volunteers to aid the Off-islanders. Four of the volunteers were Anahera's closest friends who had been on ohaku with her when Jax had arrived on Iolana. 'If I hadn't needed aid, Anahera would be Ikaika too and probably mate-paired to one of them,' he said, then added that the Kuwaini had excluded mate-paired Ikaika from leaving, and those close to mate-pairing.

Keli had not taken much interest in the last piece of information, although he was sure Connel would; Keli had more pressing things to worry about such as how the *shifters* were to be deployed. He wanted to divide them between three patrol boats to cover more area but that left Jax and Anahera as the only interpreters and he needed a third. The obvious candidate was Matiu, who flew reconnaissance further north, and as Op. V started that night, he would have to be winched onto a patrol boat out on the Fayo.

It might be useful to have Connel out there too, to smooth over any *cultural* hiccups, but Keli would need permission to involve him and that would take time. He swore under his breath. He had already postponed the dawn briefing to late morning to give the Alanui time to rest, eat and get used to their surroundings.

Keli returned to his office to set about securing the necessary permissions, which took even longer than he feared thanks to the paperwork, and he was considering how to best use *ten* Alanui shifters to supercharge Op. V rather than scuttle it, when Connel returned.

'And how are our Alanui recruits?' asked Keli, as he dropped the last of the files into the cabinet.

'Very interesting indeed,' said Connel. 'I had to get Anahera and Jax to translate at first but it is astonishing how quickly they pick-up English. Word perfect.'

'But not *understanding* perfect. I am bringing Senior Airman Matiu in to help Jax and Anahera interpret.' For once *the Professor* looked pleased with something Keli was doing, but Keli did not tell him he intended to keep Matiu well away from Jax. He had enough problems without adding that particular one.

'And I have permission to include you too, if you are willing.'

'Me?' asked Connel startled.

'I have nine *non-military* Alanui to coordinate, Connel, and while I have learned less than you would like, I *have* learned that Alanui aren't like us. You being there to *manage* their behavior would be useful.'

'I might not have the knowledge *or* skills to *manage* eight Ikaika and two Ahi,' said Connel.

'Perhaps *monitor* is a more accurate description for what I have in mind,' said Keli. 'I need someone who can identify the first signs of *Alanui* trouble.'

'Such as?'

'If I knew that, I wouldn't have gone to the trouble to include you,' said Keli shortly. He produced a wad of papers and a pen. 'Are you joining us?'

'Of course. No researcher would pass up such an opportunity.'

'Then sign these,' said Keli, and deposited the batch in front of him.

Connel took a seat and eyed the paperwork. 'This is to ensure I remain silent?'

'Yes, and arrangements for the repatriation of your body, should the need arise, and procedures should you fall into enemy hands.'

Connel's eyes jerked to his. 'Which are?'

'Pretending we don't know you.' Connel stared at him, as if to gauge whether Keli was joking, then worked his way through the papers. 'Not going to read before you sign?' asked Keli ironically.

'There doesn't seem much point and I get the impression you are in a rush,' said Connel, without looking up. 'We leave tonight, I presume?'

'You presume correctly. I will brief you as you write.'

The interview room was filled to capacity and Keli allowed himself a moment of detached amusement as he observed his men's reactions to nine near-naked Alanui and the Alanui's distaste at being hemmed in by *opala*.

Jax looked almost military in his uniform compared to the others, but his transformation caused consternation amongst the Alanui and Keli saw them weigh where his allegiances might really lie as his men had at the earlier briefing.

Anahera stayed close to Jax which told Keli their argument had been resolved but he sensed she also sent a message to her fellow Alanui that Jax *was* one of them despite his opala clothing. Keli hoped she was wrong for all their sakes. Op. V's success lay in military discipline not Alanui instincts.

Keli went through the flip-sheets again from the earlier briefing with Jax translating for the new arrivals. It made the process frustratingly slow but Jax's determination to eliminate miscommunications was a good sign.

The tension ramped up when Keli outlined the routes used by Samarak's ocean and aerial patrols, the Alanui making no attempt to hide their distaste for all things military. Makena monitored Samarak's activities as Samarak monitored theirs, he explained, so it was vital they did nothing to trigger suspicion such as increase patrols, change routes, or leave boats stationary.

It meant divers and Alanui would be dropped off and picked up under cover of darkness, using dinghies, although he supposed the Alanui could *fly* back to the boats if necessary. It was risky though given bullets traveled a long way.

The blacked out dinghies would be in radio contact with the patrol boats and remain at the drop off points. Submerged beacons would guide divers and Alanui back to the dinghies although he knew certain shift-forms, such as octopus and sharks, had their own navigation systems.

The dinghies *must* be stowed on the patrol boats before first light which meant they could not delay. If divers or Alanui missed the dinghy's departure, they must wait for the next patrol boat's sweep, and hope it saw them, or survive until the next night's pick-up.

Keli paused to let the men digest the last piece of information and for Jax to translate. Given the Alanui could swim back to the boats in fish-form, it only affected the divers, and he had no need to explain to them the risk of spending the entire day in the Fayo.

The divers and Alanui would live on the patrol boats for the duration of Op.V in accordance with their usual deployments. The Op. was authorized to run for up to ten days but he hoped they would have what they needed in far fewer.

Keli called a short break to let the men and Alanui discuss the briefing amongst themselves, and to run his proposed division of Alanui past Connel. Keli needed a translator on each of the three boats and while he had good reason to keep Jax and Matiu apart, separating Jax from Anahera should help keep Jax's focus military as well.

Anahera's understanding of English was the weakest of the three so he wanted Connel with her to help identify any confusion *before* the Op. unraveled. It had been harder to divide up the newcomers because he knew nothing about them beyond them being Ikaika, although one friendship group was already apparent.

Tiare, Kaea, Tai and Anaru kept together and as they looked a bit older, Keli toyed with the idea of splitting them between the younger Alanui but in the end, he put them all with Matiu.

He put Tamati and Hana with Jax because although Tamati had not attempted to speak English, he had kept close to Jax which suggested friendship, and he put Malo and Airiri with Anahera.

'I can't see any obvious problems,' said Connel, as he perused the list. 'The only Kawai Alanui we know *anything* about are Matiu and Jax, and they seem very different to each other. Even having nine Kawai Alanui doesn't tell us much about typical Kawai Alanui behaviour, because the nine have *volunteered* to leave the islands, and their Elders have, for various reasons, *permitted* them to depart.'

Keli thanked him but given Connel's *disclaimer*, did not feel much reassured he had made a good decision. He could rearrange them later if need be, he supposed, but by then the damage might be done.

*J*ax was glad of the coats they were handed as they boarded the truck for the coast. He did not take a seat because none of the Iolani had ever seen truck, let alone endured their fumes, racket, and bone-shaking movement. He stood where they could see his face and ensured he never showed alarm, even when the truck picked up speed and howled along the coastal road.

The patrol boats were scarcely better, their chugging motors deafening after Iolana's birdsong, and filling the air with fumes, but at least moana was familiar. Keli had briefed him about the split between the three boats and handed him a list of the names, but Jax waited until they were off the truck before he explained the groupings to the Alanui.

Tamati's face showed his displeasure at his placement but Anahera was vocal in hers. 'I want to stay with you and Tamati, Jax.'

'Commander Keli put you with Malo and Airini because you have the greatest familiarity with English. Every group needs someone who can communicate with the Off-islanders.'

'Tiare, Tai, Kaea and Anaru don't,' she pointed out.

She was right but it made no difference. 'These are Commander Keli's orders which we are bound to carry out.'

'You said I didn't have to before.'

'That was *before,* Anahera, but we are *all* in danger now,' he said, and glanced around the rest of the Kawai Alanui to include them. 'Unless we act *together*, some of us might die. We are *all* in danger, including our *friends* from the Off-islands. We are *all* doing this so Iolana doesn't end up the same way as Rua.'

Jax's words seemed to quell dissent and they shuffled into their groups and were led off to their boats, but then Keli pulled Jax aside. 'Some second thoughts amongst the Alanui, Airman?' he asked.

'No, Commander Keli. I reminded them of the dangers of what we did, and of the importance of obeying orders to keep us safe.'

'Including keeping the *opala* safe?' asked Keli acerbically.

'*All* of us are fighting for Iolana, Commander Keli.'

Keli nodded and Jax followed Tamati and Hana onto their boat.

Below deck had the same odors of fuel and Off-island food Jax had become accustomed to, but Tamati and Hana struggled and despite the chill, he suggested they go back up on deck. Men sprawled on the metal seats there and he recognised Carter.

Jax nodded but Carter rose and gripped his shoulder. 'It is good to see you looking better,' he said, his eyes searching Jax's face.

'I *am* better,' said Jax, almost in surprise.

'We are all better when we are with our *friends*,' said Carter.

Captain Briely, the Commanding Officer, found them more sheltered seats but Jax hunkered down in his coat as he watched the sun set across moana. Tamati sat nearby but it was Hana who kept up a steady stream of conversation, wanting to know how the boat moved through the water, how the military organized themselves, and how Jax had spent his time on the Off-islands.

Tamati had made more of an effort to be *Ikaika* since Jax's return, but his antagonism was strong and Jax had no doubts as to its source. He wondered if Keli had picked up on it too and so put Anahera on another boat.

He watched Whetu rise and then the boat slowed and the dinghy was lowered. They clambered in and the patrol boat disappeared into the night. There were three divers with them, including Carter, who started the motor and steered the dinghy west.

It carried equipment to identify areas of possible drilling but Keli's orders prohibited divers from entering the Exclusion Zone until the Kawai Alanui had pin-pointed the source of suspicious activity.

'What shapes will you take?' asked Carter, as he cut the dinghy's motor.

'Taniwha,' said Tamati.

'Shark,' translated Jax, in response to Carter's blank look, 'although if we sight enemy divers, it might be best to be in octopus-form. They are less likely to shoot an octopus, and octopus are adept at camouflage.'

Carter nodded and Jax translated for Hana and Tamati, but Tamati shook his head. 'Taniwha are faster and stronger than wheke,' he said, and Hana nodded.

'Opala have powerful underwater weapons that even taniwha

can't outswim but they won't see wheke as a threat,' countered Jax.

'If we see anything suspicious, we can *shift* to wheke,' said Hana, glancing between them.

'Not without *shifting* back to birth-form which means surfacing and risking being seen. Then they might shoot us to get rid of any witnesses *or* take us prisoner.'

'We can *shift* underwater,' said Tamati.

Jax did not know if Tamati argued because he resented being told what to do by an Ahi, or by Jax, or genuinely believed taniwha were the safest shift-form. Jax didn't have the authority to tell him what to do anyway.

'What is it?' asked Carter.

'A disagreement over the safest animal form,' muttered Jax.

'Commander Keli doesn't want shifters to risk their lives,' said Carter. 'Tell your friends not to hang around if they find anything suspicious. Just get a fix on where it is, so it can be located, and we will do the rest.'

They shrugged out of their coats, and Jax asked the divers to look away as they discarded their clothes and slid into the water. It was cold and Jax shifted to wheke. He was aware that Tamati and Hana had disappeared into the darkness in taniwha-form, and he followed more slowly to let his skin orientate to Whetu's light.

Keli had outlined a broad search area that Captain Briely had gone over in detail, as well as a convoluted system for converting shift-form sensibilities into the geographical locations the military needed. Taniwha used magnetic fields to navigate and wheki underwater features, but they also used currents and tides, *and* the moon and stars that the military could use as well.

Briely had reinforced Keli's orders to report *everything* they saw, no matter how inconsequential, and Jax scanned as he jetted along, his birth- and shift-form sensibilities making him acutely aware of potential predators. Large taniwha ate smaller taniwha, *and* wheke, and then there was Makena's weaponry.

Jax stayed close to the ocean floor where his wheke-senses knew he was safer and where it was easier to recognize landmarks, given he must find his way back. The water was crossed by icy currents and his speed almost doubled when he strayed into one that pulled him west.

It was hard to judge time but when his skin picked-up Whetu's shifting light he turned back. His wheke memory kept him on course but it was exhausting swimming against the current and he turned north to escape its pull and made good progress, until he came upon a second current.

The Kawai Alanui were highly familiar with moana's flows particular to their island but this was different from Rua and to what he had learned in the military. He struggled on, his weariness exacerbated by the cold and was relieved to finally see the beacon suspended beneath the dinghy. He came back to the surface and *shifted*, so tired Carter and Tamati had to haul him on board, towel him off, and help him in his coat.

The radio crackled as a diver communicated Jax's return to a patrol boat, co-ordinates were exchanged, and Carter started the motor.

'You must have gone further than us,' said Hana, as the dinghy bounced over the waves, dousing them with spray.

'I was in wheke-form,' said Jax, still shivering. 'They are slower.'

'You should have used taniwha-form,' said Tamati.

'We had an easy swim,' added Hana.

'Did you notice anything?' asked Jax.

Tamati shook his head. 'The Off-islanders have been talking on their radios though, so maybe someone else has.'

They were given hot showers as soon as they were on board as well as coffee and meal of the usual military fare, and Jax was hungry enough to choke it all down. Tamati and Hana ate too, but the coffee was too much for them, and they ended up with a weak brew of tea before Captain Briely escorted them below decks.

The interview room was metallic-smelling and, along with the boat's roll over the waves and the throb of its engine, was enough to clench Jax's gut. Hana leaned against Tamati who took her hand but Tamati managed to hide whatever he felt.

'This isn't an easy environment for a Kawai Alanui, Captain Briely,' said Jax.

'I will try not to keep you long,' said Briely. 'The Operation requires a thorough and consistent reporting regime to allow your observations to be integrated with existing data and the reports of your colleagues on the other boats.'

'I am happy to be interviewed last,' said Jax. 'I am more used to Off-island environments.'

Briely nodded but his questioning of Hana and Tamati didn't last long. Hana had seen nothing that suggested a disturbance such as cloudiness, strange bubbles or human-like shapes in the distance, or felt pulses of water at odds with the prevailing flow, or sensed vibrations, and neither had Tamati.

Briely completed his notes, then Tamati put his arm around Hana and helped her from the room. The door closed behind them but the image of Tamati's comforting embrace stayed with Jax and his thoughts swung to Anahera.

'Airman Jax,' said Briely, and Jax straightened. 'You also took the shape of a shark?' he asked, pen poised, his gaze on his notes. Jax knew he had not enjoyed asking Hana and Tamati the question about *shifting* either.

'I *shifted* to octopus-form,' said Jax.

Briely's head jerked up. 'Why not shark?'

'They are a more likely target for the Makena military. I pointed that out to Tamati and Hana, but it is a Kawai Alanui's decision which shift-form to take.' Jax paused but knew Briely had no interest in Kawai Alanui culture *or* quarrels. 'The advantage of us using different forms is that octopus spend more time on the ocean floor.'

'And?'

'I saw nothing out of the ordinary but I did experience some strange currents.'

'Strange in what way?'

'Strong and very cold currents running east-west. They took me towards Makena with a speed I couldn't match in octopus-form, but it was a struggle to come back. I swam north for a time but was caught in a second current of similar strength. It took me a long time to reach the dinghy.'

'I was aware of that,' said Briely, turning the pen over in his hands. 'We wondered whether you *would* come back.'

'I am military,' said Jax curtly.

'I didn't mean it in that way, Airman. We both know Makena has no interest in its activities being curtailed.' He frowned down at his notes again. 'Your colleagues made no mention of currents, so they seem confined to the sea floor, but how or why, I don't immediately know.' He gave a quick smile. 'Make sure you sleep today, Airman. You will be back in the Fayo tonight.'

Keli perused the reports from the first night's dives, noting that only Jax and Anahera's experiences stood out and that only they had been in octopus-form. He wondered briefly whether octopus-form distorted human senses, *if* the Alanui could be classified as human. URZOL's work told him octopus were highly intelligent, their vision excellent, and their skin extremely sensitive. They also favored the ocean floor where the effects of any drilling would be more obvious. But what Jax and Anahera reported did not fit drilling.

He retrieved the geological surveys and spread them out on the table. Captain Perry's navigators had been busy all day mapping the shifters' routes, which was no mean feat, but Keli had asked them to prioritize those of Anahera and Jax.

The first night's dives had been completed without incident, except for Jax's late return. It had woken Keli's doubts about him again especially as Anahera had been late back too, for the same reason, as it had turned out.

His fingers drummed the table as he wondered whether the currents they fought were a natural part of the Fayo. There was no record of them in the logs, so they were not discernable at surface level, although it was odd the divers had not picked them up either.

He was on his second cup of coffee when Perry appeared with the plot of Jax and Anahera's routes. They had been transcribed onto clear plastic to over-lay the geological chart and Keli stared at them for a long moment. 'Can that be right?' he asked eventually.

'There is always a possibility of error,' said Perry. 'Divers can confirm its accuracy or otherwise.'

'Jax and Anahera were further south than I thought,' said Keli. 'Closer to Rua, in fact, or where Rua was.' He glanced up at Perry. 'Has Rua's crater been surveyed?'

'It is in the Exclusion Zone, Commander,' said Perry briefly.

'I understand that, Captain.'

Perry's expression became bland. 'I cannot advise you, Commander Keli,' he said, which was military-speak for the information being classified.

'Is it possible the currents are caused by sea-floor fractures from Rua's destruction?'

'It is possible.'

'Thank your men for the speed of their work,' he said. Perry nodded and Keli heard his footsteps recede. It would be a neat explanation, he thought, as he stared down at the overlay but given what Op. V had so far cost him, a bit too neat.

36

Jax found it hard to sleep, despite knowing he needed to, and was still weary when they boarded the dinghy again. Keli's orders were to retrace the previous night's route and search for the source of the currents, especially things like fissures. Tamati and Hana were to swim deeper this time to identify the currents' vertical extent, while Jax, Carter and the diver called Thompson were to take measurements on the sea floor.

Jax didn't know why Keli was interested in the currents but he supposed the commander of Op.V had to be interested in everything. There was certainly a lot more gear in the dinghy now and an extra diver Carter introduced as Darly.

'Thompson and Darly have a *fascination* for ocean flows,' Carter added with a grin.

Carter started the motor and Jax stared over moana as they powered along. The moon was full but veiled by cloud which gave the ocean an eerie glow. It meant he would need to rely more on submarine features to navigate in wheke-form.

Carter cut the motor and Tamati and Hana *shifted* to taniwha and sliced away, but Jax waited in birth-form until Carter and Thompson joined him in the water, laden with instruments. 'Stay with us, Jax,' said Carter, and Jax nodded and *shifted*.

The divers slowed Jax which gave him more time to search for landmarks. Jagged lumps of coral-encrusted stone lay on the sandy bottom, some so large he had thought them reefs on the first expedition, but he now realized with a shiver were actually fragments of Rua. There were no bones fortunately, for a blast big enough to rip an island apart, left no sign of its peoples.

The currents seemed more powerful than the previous night and just as cold, and Thompson had trouble staying stable enough to take his measurements. Carter braced him, but in the end, Jax wrapped tentacles around him and around a lump of stone to anchor them both. It was exhausting and he was glad when Thompson signaled he had what he needed and they turned back.

Jax led them north again to escape the flow but it was still a struggle to swim east and it again took a long time to reach the dinghy.

Carter and Thompson disappeared into it and, once Jax had shifted, they hauled him in, helped him dry, and bundled him into his coat. Darley passed around a flask of coffee and Jax was so cold he took a scalding gulp.

'That was hard,' said Carter.

'Harder than last night,' said Jax, and glanced up at the moon. The cloud had shredded under a small breeze to slash moana's choppy surface with light.

'I have never felt anything like it,' said Thompson. 'It's the sort of surge you get in a very narrow strait where water is forced through a constriction, not on the Fayo.'

'And which has nothing to do with drilling,' said Carter, voicing Jax's thoughts. 'It just makes our job a hell of a lot more difficult.'

Jax said nothing, too busy searching the waves for Tamati and Hana. 'How long?' he asked.

'They should be back soon,' said Darley, checking his watch.

'What does it feel like to be an octopus?' asked Carter as they waited. 'Do you think like an octopus?'

'You think like a Kawai Alanui but are aware of the shift-form's senses. Whetu's creatures do not *think* like you or me. Their world is different.'

'But what happens if *you* think one thing and *they* feel something else?' asked Carter. 'Who wins?'

Jax had always avoided questions about *shifting* but Carter's interest was genuine. He did not gather bizarre information about *flash-monkeys* to later laugh over with his friends. 'Your Kawai Alanui form must always be in control, but it gets harder the longer you stay in shift-form. Stay in shift-form too long and you can't come back.'

Darly and Thompson looked shocked. 'You mean you can't shift back to your human form?' asked Carter.

'You don't want to.'

'So, some of the animals on Iolana, or even the sharks or octopus in the Fayo, could be human?'

Jax nodded. 'We call them *wairua*, ghosts who are no longer Kawai Alanui nor truly the creatures whose form they take.'

'Why would a Kawai Alanui *choose* to become a ghost?' asked Carter, his gaze intense.

'It might seem preferable to other choices,' said Jax, and stared back over moana.

Carter fell silent and Jax was relieved when a taniwha fin sliced the water. The fin circled the dinghy and while no one spoke, Carter pulled a weapon from the dinghy's side pouch. 'It will be Tamati waiting for Hana,' said Jax, although he had no proof it was not a taniwha in birth-form looking for dinner. A second fin appeared and then both were replaced with Hana and Tamati.

He helped Hana into the dinghy then averted his gaze and held up her coat while she toweled off, donned her clothes, and then the coat. Tamati looked after himself but kept his back turned. The Off-islanders were as polite as they could be given they were jammed in a dinghy together.

'Did they notice anything?' asked Carter.

Jax translated the question, unsure of how much Tamati or Hana understood. Hana had made more attempt to use English than Tamati but mimicry was not the same as comprehension. 'Same as yesterday,' said Tamati in Kawai Alanui.

'So the current seems localized,' said Thompson, after Jax had translated Hana and Tamati's observations. 'And given the dip in temperature, flows under the warmer surface water, as expected.'

Carter started the motor but they had not gone far before the radio crackled and Darly gestured him to cut it again. Tamati and Anahera seemed unconcerned as they bobbed on the water but Jax's tension ratcheted up. Carter and Thompson were intent on Darly's conversation and given the *yes sirs, no sirs*, Jax gathered it was Keli or Briely on the line.

The exchange ended and Darly muttered something to Thompson and Carter, before turning back to the rest of them. 'We have a missing member of Op. V and are to stay here as long as possible. Captain Briely will slow the patrol boat but can't stop it. Thompson, lower the beacon again.'

Jax translated for Tamati and Hana but they seemed more interested in the private conversation they were having, unlike Jax, whose heart had started an uneven thump. 'Who is it?' he asked Darly softly.

'I am not permitted to say.'

Jax swallowed convulsively. The only reason Keli would withhold the person's identity was if they wer*e* Kawai Alanui and Anahera in particular, in case Jax and Tamati broke ranks to search for her, or the other Kawai Alanui did.

Hana had taken more interest in the exchange than Tamati, and Jax forced all expression from his face as he passed on that he did not know who was missing, which was true, though everything pointed to it being Anahera.

He had no idea what form Anahera had taken, where she had been, and whether she had been alone. Nor did he know if she had been closer to the suspected drill sites. She could have been murdered by Makena's divers, taken prisoner, killed by a predator or simply be lost. And Whetu's fading light meant they had less than an hour to guide her back before the beacon was hauled up and the dinghy removed.

He spat over the side and glanced back to see Tamati's gaze on him. 'What troubles you, Jax?'

'Nothing,' he said, and looked away. Tamati still watched him as did Carter but even if they all launched themselves into moana, they had no hope of finding her without knowing her shift-form and route. It would also risk Op. V too and the lives of its members.

Time dragged on, made worse by the silence in dinghy, and Jax scanned the waters for *any* sea-creature at all. Anahera had mainly taken white-wolf and sun-eagle form on land, but he had no idea what form she favored in moana.

The dark faded and Carter hauled up the beacon and started the motor. A stiff breeze capped moana's waves with white but Carter kept the motor at full throttle and they had to cling on to the roped sides avoid being hurled out. At least it meant Tamati had other things to occupy him.

They clambered back onto the patrol boat and Jax was aware of it picking up speed even as Briely escorted them below deck. Yesterday they had gone to the showers first and eaten, but this time Briely took them straight to the interview room where Keli and Connel waited.

Jax saluted but his dread was not helped by Tamati's glare. Tamati had learned enough about the military to know Keli's presence meant something was amiss and he guessed Jax knew what it was.

Keli sat at the head of the table with Connel and Jax watched Briely take up position near the door. The only other exit was a porthole sealed with Perspex. Keli's expression was bland but he saw Jax scan. Keli probably thought Jax would abscond, but Jax knew Tamati was more likely to; Jax understood that more than Anahera's life was at stake.

'My apologies for bringing you here before you have eaten,' said Keli briskly, 'but the matter is urgent. As you know, a member of Op. V failed to return for reconnaissance last night and the more we can discover of the possible reasons, the more likely we are to retrieve her.'

Hana translated for Tamati before Jax had the chance and Tamati half rose from his chair. 'Who?' he demanded.

'Anahera,' said Keli.

Tamati's chair grated and the next moment his furious face was a hand span's from Jax's. 'You knew!' he grated. Jax stood too but did not move; the last thing Op. V needed was a brawl.

'No one was told,' interjected Hana quickly.

'Jax knew! It was clear on moana and he did *nothing*! We *could* have searched for her then! We *should* have searched for her then!'

'Tamati—' began Hana.

'Jax knew,' he fumed. 'He's one of *them*! He's opala filth!'

Jax thought Tamati was going to strike him but Keli, Briely and Connel remained motionless, which was just as well. 'I guessed it was Anahera,' Jax confirmed, 'and all I wanted was to dive back into moana. Anahera saved me in the Cloud Crown and made me feel that I might have home again, but you are right, Tamati. I *am* opala filth, because being *opala filth* is the only way I can stop Iolana suffering the same fate as Rua.'

'So you traded Anahera's life! You should never have come to Iolana! You will *never* be one of us!'

Jax leaned in until their faces all but touched. 'There is *no one* on this boat or on *any* of the boats, whether Kawa Alanui or *opala filth*, who isn't willing to trade their lives for Iolana's survival!' he gritted. 'It is why *you* volunteered, why *Anahera* volunteered, why the other Iolani volunteered. We are here in this room to find Anahera before time runs out, and it is running out *now*, Tamati!'

Tamati threw himself back into his chair but turned so his back was to Jax. Hana sat again too, her worried eyes darting between the two of them, but Jax stayed on his feet, knowing Keli required an explanation.

'We are all distressed by Anahera's disappearance, Commander Keli,' he said evenly, 'but Tamati perhaps more so for the reasons we discussed.'

Keli frowned. 'What reasons?'

'I informed you that Anahera had interrupted her ohaku to save my life,' said Jax, confused in turn.

'Yes, but—'

'Pardon my interruption, Commander Keli,' said Connel, 'and correct me if I am wrong, Airman Jax, but I gather your arrival on Iolana prevented Anahera from completing her ohaku?'

'I know that,' snapped Keli.

'Pardon me again, Commander, but it means Anahera stayed Ahi while her friends like *Tamati* and Hana, and I believe Malo and Airini, became Ikaika. Ahi must be *Ikaika* to mate-pair,' he added more softly, and glanced towards Tamati.

Keli followed Connel's gaze. 'I see,' he said tersely. 'Sit, Airman, you must be tired,' he said to Jax, and Jax sat. 'If Anahera became disorientated, we hope she will be there for pickup tonight or find us in shift-form,' said Keli crisply.

'If she were captured, we will learn of it by other channels. If she became a casualty of some natural or *unnatural* event, we may never know what happened to her.

'She took octopus-form to investigate the currents as Airman Jax did and my understanding is they were colder and stronger last night. She and the divers were swept towards Makena, but the divers managed to escape the pull.' He paused to let Hana completed her translation for Tamati.

'My preliminary advice is that such cold, strong currents must flow from some sort of tunnel, or several tunnels in fact.'

Hana translated again but this time the effect on Tamati was completely different. He straightened and stared at Keli in astonishment. 'I think I know,' he said in Kawai Alanui.

'Tell me,' said Jax quickly. 'We don't have much time.' Tamati nodded and Jax concentrated on his description of an underwater tunnel that exited into a subterranean cavern on Iolana.

'The charts, Captain Briely,' ordered Keli, after Jax had passed on the information. Briely brought them to the table and they crowded around them. 'Ask Tamati whether he knows where the tunnel was,' ordered Keli but Tamati already pointed to a spot on Iolana's south-west coast.

'They might be the remains of lava tubes,' said Briely thoughtfully.

'You mean tunnels formed by lava when the Zoaides' volcanoes were active?' asked Keli.

'Or when Makena's were,' said Briely. 'The Zoaides are similar to Makena *geologically*. Given the currents, there might be tubes running east from Makena towards the Zoaides too and terminating in the depths of the Fayo, unless there was a really big lava run, in which case the tubes might all but join like an underwater highway.'

'That's what *Kawai Alanui* means,' said Jax. 'Water-road.'

Keli rubbed his chin. 'Does Tamati remember what the stone looked like in the cavern?' he asked.

Jax translated, listened to Tamati's description, and turned back to Keli. 'There was a beach made up of small red and black pebbles. The back and walls were black stone with bigger chunks of the red.'

Keli exchanged looks with Briely. 'It sounds like anilrite mixed up with a nice smattering of theralin,' he said.

'Yes,' said Briely grimly. 'Just waiting for a spark from a drilling bit to blow.'

37

$\mathcal{T}$he day seemed to go on forever, the tension on the boat worsened by Tamati's silence and Hana's upset. She had tried to make amends for Tamati's outburst with mundane conversation but Jax could not dredge up anything to say and she had fallen silent too. The only reason Tamati was still with them was because to have any hope of finding Anahera, they had to enter the same current at the same time, and that meant waiting for nightfall.

Perry's men had completed calculations based on the reports of those who had been with her, the tides, and the Fayo's *known* currents, and Op. V's focus had swung to the location of lava tubes between Makena and Iolana, *and* any that ran east from Iolana towards Samarak.

If lava tubes *did* crisscross the Fayo's floor, the force of any blast could be funneled west to obliterate Makena's east coast, or east to destroy Iolana, or if big enough, even impact Samarak's west coast.

Jax hoped the risk to Makena would be sufficient for them to stop drilling, but if they needed proof of the lava tubes' ability to channel an explosion, Rua's destruction would probably be enough.

They set off as soon as it was dark, accompanied by Carter whose brief was to collect mineral samples. Jax was glad to be with Tamati despite his antagonism, because Tamati was as desperate to find Anahera as Jax was *and* he had experienced a tunnel before.

The change in Op. V's focus meant Keli had increased the breadth of the search by splitting the groups and Hana now swam further south. Jax and Tamati's orders were to investigate the current that had swept Anahera and the divers west towards Makena. Keli had probably decided it would be pointless ordering Tamati to do anything else but it was also logical to assume that if Anahera *were* still alive *and* free, that she had been pulled into a tunnel.

They took wheke-form as Anahera had and descended into moana's darkness, and were not far from the bottom when the temperature plummeted. Jax saw Carter's eyes widen behind his mask and then Tamati abruptly disappeared into the murk. There was a brief hiatus before the current seized Jax and he flung out a tentacle and managed to hook Carter's arm.

If they *did* end up in a tunnel, Carter needed to be with them but as they were swept along, Jax was horribly aware that Carter could not *shift* and only had two hours of air. He pulled Carter closer as the blackness closed in and his wheke-skin picked up small flicks in the current where it glanced off the uneven surfaces of stone that now surrounded them.

Jax had no idea how long they had been in the tunnel before he sensed the constriction give way and jetted water to slow himself as he sent up an explorative tentacle. He felt no stone overhead and propelled himself upwards, taking Carter with him, and broke the surface. The absence of the moon and stars confirmed he was in a cave but not as much as the reverberations that thrummed around its walls.

He *shifted* then spun as a garish light struck the water. It was Carter's torch. The beam swept the cave and Jax started as it illuminated Tamati and Anahera perched on a ledge. Tamati's arms were wrapped around her but she shuddered uncontrollably and Jax's heart raced.

He swam over and clambered up beside them, then helped Carter up. If it had not been for Carter's torch, they would have been in complete darkness and the drill's bone-jarring thud would be even worse.

Carter unclipped the bag from his waist and set his instruments on the stone but Jax's concern was for Anahera. 'Are you hurt?' he asked urgently, aware of Tamati's arms tightening around her.

'Just cold,' she croaked, teeth chattering.

'Why didn't you swim out?'

'I tried to but then I saw divers like him,' she said, nodding jerkily towards Carter.

'Divers like Carter?' repeated Jax in English.

Carter's head snapped up. 'Op. V are accounted for,' he growled. 'They had be Makena. Ask her where.'

'Further in the tunnel,' said Anahera, understanding his question. 'They had lights like yours and weapons like the Off-islanders at URZOL. I came back here but they did too. I shifted to kirirua and hid but I got cold, so cold, and wasn't strong enough to swim out.'

'They came *here*?' echoed Jax in horror, and even as he spoke, a glow appeared in the water. They all stared at it and he heard Carter swear but all he could think of was Carter and Anahera's awful vulnerability. 'I need to drive them off,' he said, and slipped back into the water.

'No, Jax!' cried Anahera. 'They have weapons!'

'I'll take taniwha-form,' said Jax.

'They will have spear guns or concussion guns or both,' warned Carter, as he wrenched a weapon from his belt. 'No one likes sharks but Makena won't tolerate witnesses of *any* kind.'

'Get the samples, Carter,' said Jax hurriedly as the glow strengthened, 'and Tamati, get Anahera out of here,' he added, but as he *shifted*, he was aware that Tamati had joined him in the water and taken taniwha-form too.

Jax's keen taniwha vision pierced the murk to see three divers and he charged. He had surprise on his side, but little else. Their reactions were quick but as they raised their weapons, he smashed into the first diver, then swerved into the second. He had no idea what Tamati did behind him, there had not been time to talk tactics. He spun back and then there was a flash and the world imploded.

Jax's first awareness was of bone-numbing cold, and then blackness intruded and time seemed to jag. He was still cold, when he next became aware, but taniwha smacked against him and terror surged as he imagined he was about to be torn apart. It woke the last vestiges of his birth-consciousness and he *shifted* and screamed as pain slammed through his body.

'Get him in!' a voice ordered, and he was hauled over the rubbery lip of a dinghy, his breath emptying as pain burned. He curled into a ball in the slosh of water in the dinghy's bottom, so cold that his teeth rattled.

'We need to warm him.'

It was Tamati's voice and Jax was desperate to know whether Anahera was there too *and* Carter, but as pain lashed him like a storm, he was grateful to escape into oblivion.

The third time he roused, the pain was a dull throb and he was wondrously warm. For a while he simply luxuriated in it, but then the dull rumble of an engine intruded. It told him he was on the patrol boat and the bed's regular roll told him it moved. Memories of Tamati being in the dinghy but not of Anahera or Carter hammered and he dragged his eyes open.

'About time you stopped lazing about.' It was Carter, his face split with an uncharacteristic grin. 'And in case you are wondering, your friends are in a lot better shape than you. I've never known anyone survive a concussion blast but then I've never been closely associated with sharks.'

'Where?' croaked Jax, his eyes searching beyond Carter.

'Almost back to port where I will be departing. You have been out of it for thirty-six hours, Jax, thanks to the medics pumping you full of pain-killers and muscle relaxants, so let me fill you in on a few details before they throw me out. After you were blasted, your Kawai Alanui colleague took a chunk out of one of our Makena friends. Not enough to kill him mind, but enough to make *his* friends pretty keen to get him out of there.

'But we had to wait for the tide to turn to get *you* out. Your friends took shark-form to keep the water moving over your gills or else you would have drowned.' Carter's face sobered. 'To be honest, I am surprised you are still with us.'

'Did you get the samples?'

Carter smiled grimly. 'We have what we need.'

Keli was on his second beer with Connel when the call came that told him Jax had regained consciousness 'We still have our shifter,' he said, as he came back to the couch.

Connel shut his eyes in relief. 'Congratulations on a successful operation, Commander,' he said. 'All personnel accounted for and mission accomplished.'

'Half right; the latter is out of our hands.'

'It is interesting that a concussion gun isn't fatal to humans in shift-form,' said Connel.

'Airman Jax might have been lucky, or a taniwha's cartilage skeleton might absorb impact better than bones, or shifters might not be human.'

Connel grinned. 'A good answer, Commander.'

'You taught me well,' said Keli dryly.

'Now what?' asked Connel.

'The Alanui have returned to their islands and when Jax has recovered, I will send him too. The Alanui's governing council, *the Kuwaini*, need a formal report of Op. V's outcome. Hopefully by the time Jax is well enough to leave, we will have something useful to say.'

'And until then?'

'We wait.'

Jax slept again and woke to discover he had lost another two days and that new orders awaited him. As soon as the medics signed off on him, he was to return to Iolana to inform the Kuwaini of Op. V's outcome.

Briely briefed him later that day on exactly what they were. The threat to Makena had been deemed so great that the usual machinations of diplomacy had given way to expediency and it was not long before Makena's divers confirmed what Op. V's divers already knew: that a lethal combination of minerals had the potential to blast Makena's eastern seaboard into oblivion.

There were no assurances drilling would cease because that would confirm it had begun but the pause in the seismographs' activity suggested Makena understood the risk. The anilrite and theralin that riddled the tunnels could not be separated, at least with existing technology, and even plugging the tunnels would not limit the force of a blast like the one that had destroyed Rua.

Keli's orders required Jax to report back to URZOL within ten days of his departure. It was a generous break and as Jax took his breakfast, he wondered if Keli expected him to return at all. Given Jax's history of absconding *and* that Iolana was in the Exclusion Zone, there was not much Keli could do about it if Jax did not come back and Iolana's pull was stronger now Op. V had reinforced how precious it was.

The Kawai Alanui and divers had already gone by the time Jax made it up on deck, and he rattled around the patrol boat exchanging pleasantries with the crew until it was dark, then took leave of Briely, *shifted* to sun-eagle, and flew west. The night was mild but the moon small and he was glad when he saw the twinkle of Lani's cooking-fires below.

Anahera was outside her awin, as he hoped she would be and, despite Tamati, Malo and Airini keeping her company, she rushed to his arms and it was a long time before he could bear to let her go.

'They said you were recovering,' said Anahera thickly, 'but they wouldn't let us in to see you.'

He settled by her side and gratefully took the fela Tamati offered. No one asked any questions but the firelight showed the intensity of their gazes. 'My orders are to speak with the Kuwaini first,' he said, between gulps.

'They are waiting for you,' said Anahera. 'Come back to us afterwards, Jax.'

Jax nodded and smiled. 'We should all sleep well tonight,' he said, and felt the group's tension ease.

The Kuwaini said little after Jax had delivered his report but their relief was palpable. 'So, the western Off-islands will never drill again,' murmured Davi.

'I cannot promise that,' cautioned Jax, 'but they understand the threat to themselves and that it won't go away.'

'And if it weren't for that, they would be happy to destroy us, as they destroyed Rua,' said Cheren bitterly.

Miru's piercing gaze settled on him. 'And what of you, Jax? Will you stay here amongst your own or return to them?'

It was a question that had haunted Jax for weeks. 'I need to complete my ohaku,' he said slowly. 'Then I might know.'

'We will think on your ohaku,' said Miru, and glanced at the other Kuwaini for confirmation. 'And speak to you in the morning.'

'And will you think on Anahera's ohaku too?' pursued Jax.

'Yes,' said Miru. 'Sleep now.'

And Jax *did* sleep. Anahera was warm in his arms and when he woke, he lay motionless, savoring the dry-leaf smell of the awin and the bird song outside. He had nine days before he must return to URZOL, *if* he returned, and he wondered if Keli had given him such a lengthy break to make a choice. Jax was military but he saw for the first time that an Airman who spent half his life in the cells was not much use to Keli, or to URZOL, or to the military more broadly.

The Kuwaini summoned them later that morning, and Jax settled with Anahera on the mats and bowed his head as Davi led a song of welcome. It was painfully like those of Rua and Jax found it hard to raise his head again.

'We have spoken of you both, of how you came together, of all that has happened since,' said Davi. 'We have spoken of our songs, of how they record our ways, of how Ahi are born and grow, and of how, in the Cloud Crown, Ahi become not just protectors of their friends, but of all the Kawai Alanui.

'Our songs tell of how ohaku unfolds so that Ahi die and Ikaika are born to ensure the Kawai Alanui endure.' Davi paused. 'No song tells of an Ahi entering the Cloud Crown and remaining Ahi. That is not the Kawai Alanui way.'

Jax's heart sank as he realized he and Anahera were to be denied ohaku and be left like wairua. He had grown used to the emptiness in the space between being Islander and Off-islander, but the consequences for Anahera of not being either truly Ahi or Ikaika would be devastating and he reached for her hand. 'I understand why you refuse me the chance to be Ikaika,' he said harshly, 'but it is wrong to punish Anahera for something that wasn't her fault.'

Anahera's hand tightened on his. 'Don't, Jax,' she whispered.

'We do not speak of punishment,' said Miru, 'but of how our songs record our ways so that new Ikaika understand what has gone before. You have been to Kohatu, I believe.' Jax nodded curtly. 'If we were to make a song of Kohatu it would tell of its blackness, of its mighty slabs, and of their jagged edges, because that is true of Kohatu *now*. Some of our oldest songs tell of the Kuwai Alanui on Puha and Ke-one, and others of Rua's broad stony beaches. These songs are no longer true but still we sing them.'

Jax stared at her in confusion. He had considered Miru the most lucid of the Kuwaini but not even she made sense now.

'If we were able to sing of Kohatu in the endless years ahead, it might be a song of round-edged boulders, softened with lichen and moss,' continued Miru. 'Nothing remains the same. Each wave that breaks upon our cliffs changes them, Jax; each droplet of rain the falls

223

upon Wairere adds something and carries something away.'

Jax's thoughts whirred but Cheren spoke before he had a chance to say anything. 'Anahera returned here as Ahi because she chose to save you,' she said. 'Ahi aid Ahi; it is what *Ahi* do. But Anahera also set off to the Off-islands to save us all which is what *Ikaika* do. As for you, Jax, you entered the Cloud Crown without proper preparation. You completed no ohaku-sai and heard no songs and yet you also went to the Off-islands to save us, as *Ikaika* do.'

Jax still had no idea of the Kuwaini's intentions but he managed to hold his tongue and it was Davi who spoke next. 'You are both Ahi yet have acted as Ikaika. New songs will tell way it is so, but *all* songs are important, even those that tell of things that are no more.'

Davi's attention shifted to Anahera. 'You must know your skin-spirit, Anahera. We ask you to rest today, think on the lessons of your ohaku-sai, and set out on ohaku tomorrow. As for you, Jax, your time away robbed you of the songs you *must* know as Ahi, and we ask you to spend time with us over the next two days, in readiness to die as Ahi must to be reborn as Ikaika.'

Jax was too stunned to say anything but Anahera rose and bowed low. 'I thank you,' she said tremulously, and Jax managed to do the same and followed her out. His head was so full of what had happened it took him a moment to speak. 'They are going to let us complete ohaku,' he breathed.

'Yes,' she said thickly.

He brought his arms around her. 'I am so glad for you.'

'And I am glad for you.' She looked up at him, tears wetting her cheeks. 'It was never your fault, Jax. If you hadn't come, we wouldn't have known about the tunnels or what they meant. The older songs tell us what we *were* and the more recent songs what we *are*. Only Whetu knows what we will *become* and the songs to be made of that time.'

'You should tell Tamati you are to complete ohaku, *and* Malo and Airini,' he added.

'You still think I want to mate-pair with Tamati, don't you?' she said, as they turned back towards her awin.

'He certainly wants to mate-pair with you, Anahera.'

Her head swiveled, her amber eyes intense. 'And who do *you* want to mate-pair with, Jax?'

'I can't think of *anything* beyond ohaku,' he admitted.

'You are right,' she said slowly. 'Ohaku changes everything.'

Jax spent the rest of the day with the Kuwaini, and only returned to Anahera's awin to eat and sleep. She was not there and nor was she at dawn when he went back to the Kuwain. The Kuwaini wove songs around him like moana wove waves around the islands and, like moana, the songs were sometimes dark with storm and sometimes as light as sunshine.

Most songs were new to him but a few he recalled from his childhood, the Kuwaini's hoarse voices like sparks to coals he had thought long dead. The songs brought pain, but joy too, and Jax let them wash over him and the Kuwaini's kindness heal wounds so old he scarcely knew he carried them. And the longer he sat in the Kuwain's dimness, the more remote his Off-islander life became.

He slept heavily that night and at dawn, trekked away upslope through Wairere's lush valleys. Anahera was ahead of him somewhere, and he hoped she journeyed in safety, but he thought of little as he walked, just drew the fragrant air deep into his lungs and let the chill moss imprint the soles of his feet. He was glad when he crossed Kohatu and then as night fell, he jogged across Makariri's frozen whiteness.

It was as chill as he remembered and he welcomed the Cloud Crown's shelter and slept in a hollow under a fallen brack until the dimness brightened again. The bird-calls were the same as on his first visit, sometimes far away and sometimes astonishingly close, and the owls, blue-chuffs and hawklings he glimpsed were strangely plumaged.

He paused only to drink from streams and to listen for sounds of threat. The Kuwaini had warned him of the Cloud Crown's perils but he was less fearful than on his first visit. He had been injured then and running from Briggs, and Iolana had seemed as hostile as the lands he had fled. And then Anahera had found him.

He thought of her amber eyes, the fall of her auburn hair, and her tenderness. She might still be somewhere in the Cloud Crown but he hoped she had discovered her skin-spirit, looked upon Iolana's shining peak, and was on her way back.

Jax had thought little about his skin-spirit, so unsure about *what* he was and *where* he belonged that he had left his future up to Whetu, but he saw nothing but the occasional bird as he climbed. No scuttle of moko, no flick of scarlet-tongued frog, no slide of white-wolf through the leaves. Jax did not know how long it took to clear the Cloud Crown but as his hunger grew, he worried the shifting mists would suddenly dissipate, leaving him the same opala intruder as when he had arrived.

As he trudged on, he wondered whether the perils the Kuwaini had warned him of were less obvious than savage animals and plunging cliffs. He knew from his military training that a man could kill with his bare hands and Rua's destruction had taught him that threats could be as amorphous as appalling memories and crippling guilt.

The cloud's clammy greyness grew increasingly dreary and when moana's voice strengthened, he turned in its direction until he reached the edge of the cliff. A small breeze roused, not enough to dissipate the cloud, but enough for him to catch glimpses of moana below. The sun's westering rays gilded its waves and showed the usual collection of black- and redgulls on the wing.

The cloud muffled their cries so that it seemed they flew in silence, rising and falling in the space between sky and sea. They broke from their flocks but always returned and, as he watched, the last of the sun caught the redgulls' plumage so that they shone bright too.

A shiver ran over his skin and he went on and then finally he was in clear air, Huna's brilliant peak rising before him. The first stars haloed it like a second crown and as Jax stared, he felt oddly light, as if his cares lay amongst the Cloud Crown's detritus below.

He turned back into the mists and, despite being bone-achingly weary, walked on through the night. When he could go no further, he found another hollow under a brack and slept. It might be the same one he used on his ascent but it did not matter. That version of himself no longer existed.

The Cloud Crown ended with its usual suddenness to reveal Makariri and, despite being light-headed with hunger, he broke into a jog. He was staggering by the time he reached Kohatu and collapsed onto a stone and lay spread-eagled as moko did to warm himself in the midday sun. He had half-hoped Anahera would be waiting for him but he was glad she was not. Her ohaku would not be complete until she reached Lani and received the Kuwaini's final songs and he wanted nothing to delay her this time.

He gorged on frost-damaged casberries in Wairere and reached Lani as the Kuwai Alanui gathered for their evening meal. He was tempted to skirt the awins and reach the Kuwain unseen but straightened his shoulders and went on through the settlement instead, nodding to those who stopped to stare. He was no longer *Airman Jax*, but Ikaika, or soon would be.

The Kuwaini's greeting was warm and the Kuwain filled with the familiar scents of cup-lamps and seeli-grass. Jax sat with his head bowed and when the last of the songs had been gifted, rose and thanked them. They embraced him in turn, and then he was back in the evening air, surrounded by *his* people.

38

Jax was relieved to see Anahera safely at her fire and back in Tamati, Airini and Malo's company. These were the friends Anahera had grown up with and with whom she had been briefly out of step, but she was not now. They rose and nodded formally and Jax quelled the urge to hug Anahera.

He gratefully accepted the food Anahera offered but the sureties of his place the Kuwaini had gifted suddenly seemed tenuous. Weariness made thought difficult and Anahera's exhaustion was plain too, and it was not long before she wished them goodnight and disappeared into her awin.

'The ohaku is long and hard,' said Tamati, 'and we know how tired you must be. Please share my awin.'

Jax nodded his thanks and followed him through the awins, Malo by his side. 'Malo has been sharing my awin,' said Tamati, as they walked, 'so if we choose to mate-pair, it will be other Ikaika.'

Jax nodded but it took his tired brain a moment to work out that Ikaika only shared awins with those they had no intention of mate-pairing with. Jax sensed Tamati wanted to help him understand Ikaika ways but as he curled up on the sleeping-mat and pulled the flax cover over himself, all he wanted was sleep.

He slipped out of the awin before Tamati and Malo woke, *shifted* to sun-eagle, and flew north to Tupari. The sky was clear but a chill wind whipped off moana and ruffled his breast feathers as he perched on the stones. He had first come here with Anahera but moana was lower now and he could see where foam marked Rua's ruins.

He launched from the cliff and gulls scattered as he snatched up a silverfish and then with powerful wingbeats, returned to his perch. The silverfish was sweet and his keen eyes sought out the gulls' plump bodies but he realized the danger and *shifted* to birth-form, then strode away into the trees.

He had been too hurt to really look at Wairere when he had first arrived in Iolana, and too jarred later, but now he saw how similar the forests were to Rua. The emerald mosses, the dance of golden-flies, the brilliance of scarlet-tongued frogs; all stirred memories that were still exquisitely raw.

A stream tinkled and Jax made his way through the tangled foliage until he found it, then followed it down. Rua's streams had often ended in lagoons as this stream did, and like those on Rua, it was bounded by rero and pan-reeds. He stripped of his whitiki and swam out to its centre, flipped onto his back and floated. It was as if he were suspended outside time, beyond his cares and worries. He did not want to think about Anahera or Matiu or the military, or whether he was Kawai Alanui or Off-islander, he simply wanted to be.

The lagoon provided drinking and bathing water, the pan-reeds a snug bed, and a thick stand of buri-palms gave him nuts. The days slipped past broken only by long walks under Wairere's trees and *shifts* to kirirua and sun-eagle to feast on water-snails and silverfish.

He came to know the shia that hunted nearby; the nesting-sites of black- and redgulls; the haunts of snow-goats and hares; and the trails of white-wolves. There was a rhythm to eating, sleeping and hunting that required no thought, and then one day, when he returned from his fishing expedition to moana in sea-eagle form, another sea-eagle occupied his perch.

There was a blur as it *shifted* and he glimpsed long auburn hair before he turned away.

'Jax?' He turned back reluctantly but did not *shift*. 'Jax, I was worried about you. *Shift*, I want to talk.'

He *shifted* grudgingly, having grown used to his solitary life, and slipped on the whitiki he had left nearby.

'You have been gone a long time,' said Anahera, coming to him. 'I thought you had left.'

'I wouldn't leave without saying goodbye.'

Her brows drew in an intense frown. 'Why are you here, Jax? The Ikaika don't live alone. You should be in Lani.'

He shrugged. 'Maybe I'm not Ikaika.'

Her eyes searched his face. 'But you found your skin-spirit, didn't you? And the Kuwaini gifted you the songs of Ikaika?' Jax nodded. 'Then you *are* Ikaika.' The breeze blew her hair into her eyes and he might have smoothed it away had they still been Ahi but he stepped back instead. 'Why are you behaving like this?' she demanded.

'Because I don't know what it means to be Ikaika,' he said in frustration. 'Can I touch you? Hug you? Or does that mean something else now? I need to be sure my *opala* ways don't offend you.'

'The Ikaika care for all and that means they show affection to all.'

'But not aroha.'

'We have discussed the nature of aroha.' she said, impatience creeping into her voice.

'Yes, but ohaku changes everything, doesn't it?'

'It doesn't change aroha.' He said nothing and she lay her hand on his arm. 'Your skin-spirit is *here*, Jax. You are part of *us*.'

He glanced back to where the gulls wheeled above moana's waves. 'My orders mean I must return to the Off-islands in the next two days.'

'But your skin-spirit tethers you *here*!'

'My skin-spirit tethers me,' he repeated slowly, then shut his eyes as the understanding washed over him. He opened them again to see Anahera watching him anxiously and smiled. 'You have saved me in more ways than you will ever know,' he said softly, 'and for that I thank you. But maybe the gap was always too big.'

'What gap? What are you talking about?'

'I am saying goodbye, Anahera.'

She swallowed convulsively. 'Forever?'

'That is up to the military.' He kissed her formally on each cheek. 'Farewell Tamati for me, and Airini and Malo,' he said, and walked back towards the lagoon.

Anahera sat by her fire, her chin on her knees, her gaze on the flames. Whetu lit the skies but she did not look up, even when footsteps crunched nearby.

'Did you find Jax?' It was Tamati and the mat rustled as he sat beside her. 'Yes.'

Tamati peered about. 'He's sleeping in your awin?'

'He has gone back to the Off-islands.'

'Permanently?' he asked in surprise.

Anahera looked at him sideways. 'Isn't that what you wanted?'

'Jax's place is here. He is Ikaika.'

'Do you really believe that?'

'Yes, but I understand why you doubt me.' He smiled sourly. 'I let jealousy blind me to how Ikaika should behave, to how *I* should behave. Jax knew the risks in that cavern, Anahera, and did what he did to protect us *and* Iolana. He acted as an Ikaika should.'

'He said his orders were to return to the Off-islands.'

'He is Ikaika wherever he is,' said Tamati, and sighed. 'Iolana lies between lands that hate each other and we know what that means. Having an Ikaika there might help keep us safe.'

Anahera said nothing and Tamati touched her hand. 'Shall I go to the Off-islands and ask him to return?'

'You need to be here,' she muttered.

His eyes glittered in the firelight. 'Because I am Ikaika or for some other reason?'

His attention on her was intense but Anahera's thoughts had gone to the cavern too, to how Tamati had fought the Off-islanders with Jax, and fought with her to keep Jax alive. 'I want you here, Tamati.'

'And you already know what I want.' She said nothing and his face gentled. 'You told me that ohaku changes things. Has it for you?'

'Yes.'

He opened his hand to reveal the pearl shell wolf-head. 'You accepted this from me once before, Anahera. Have things changed enough for you to accept it from me again?' She looked from the carving back to his face, her head full of the Cloud Crown's soft swirl, of Jax's silver hair through the foliage and of all that had followed; of her second ohaku and of the white-wolf that had paused and for a tingling moment, turned its amber eyes to hers. 'It is the first step to a mate-pair,' he said softly. 'Is it a step you want to take with me?'

She took the carving from his hand and for a moment simply held it. 'Yes, it is,' she said, and slipped it over her head. 'Thank you, Tami. It is beautiful.'

Jax left when the first stars blossomed in the sky and headed to where the redgulls nested. They abandoned their nests in fright but he sought something other than their chicks and when he found it, he sped off over moana.

Whetu outshone the stars before he reached URZOL and he landed as close to his quarters as he could, *shifted*, and donned his whitiki. The building was dark which meant Matiu could be sleeping, or at Rilo, or on reconnaissance but Jax's hopes rose as he smelled the bitter taint of coffee.

The small kitchen looked exactly as he had left it, right down to the sun-eagle feather on the table. The blinds were open and the feather glimmered in Whetu's light, but the sight of it there, untouched, left Jax as cold as moana's depths.

He placed the redgull feather next to it and collapsed onto a chair. He was tired from the flight but mostly he was tired from the never-ending struggle to decide where he belonged, yet none of it mattered if he were to spend the rest of his life alone. He folded his arms on the table and rested his head on them, and then a door creaked and Matiu was there.

'You came back,' he said.

'Yes.'

'Are you Ikaika?'

'Yes.'

Matiu's face twisted, his ability to hide his feelings less than Jax's. 'Did you mate-pair with Anahera?'

'No.'

'Why not?' he demanded.

He seemed as angry as when Jax had left but he had been drunk then and he was not now. He wore only Off-islander underwear and as Whetu's light played over the scars on his body, Jax realized Matiu was in two halves too.

'Mate-pairing isn't entered into lightly, Mati. It needs a love strong enough to survive separation, distrust, and anger; a love strong enough to forgive; a love strong enough to hope.'

There was a long silence and then Matiu lowered himself onto the chair opposite. 'You brought back a redgull feather,' he said thickly.

'For you,' said Jax. 'But I am guessing since you didn't want the sun-eagle feather, you won't want the redgull one either.'

'You would be guessing wrong.'

Jax searched Matiu's face. 'It's where I left it.'

'To remind me that for a precious time, you were here and that one day, you might be here again.' Jax shut his eyes and Matiu reached for his hand. 'I live because of you,' he whispered.

'And I *want* to live because of you.'

Matiu's eyes glistened in Whetu's light. 'Can a sun-eagle live with a redgull?'

Jax struggled to his feet and pulled Matiu into his arms. 'My skin-spirit is the redgull,' he whispered.

'Ikaika don't share their skin-spirits,' muttered Matiu, and looked away but Jax gently turned Matiu's face back to his.

'They might with their mate-pair.'

'I will never visit the Cloud Crown, never be Ikaika, never be able to pair,' said Matiu raggedly.

'The Cloud Crown reveals many things, Mati, but you already know the most important one without having set foot there, and that makes you Ikaika. When I stared beyond the Cloud Crown and saw the redgulls flash above moana's waves, I *knew* you had led me away on that day when everything ended but us, and then I *knew* where I must be.'

'But can you *live* here, Jax?' cried Matiu.

'There will always be a threat to Iolana and a need for what I can offer as Kawai Alanui *and* as military. It will be enough for me, if I am enough for you.'

'You were *always* enough for me,' said Matiu and, with utter tenderness, met Jax's kiss with his own.

End of I Heard the Wolf Call My Name

Enjoy fantasy with diverse romances? Take a peek at two of my other stories.

Messenger

Luke came to the fireside, his arm still around Severine and draped his other arm over Saul's shoulders. He smiled at Jeph ironically and Jeph managed to keep his face expressionless. At least he still had that stinking skill!

'Well man,' said Luke, 'Severine has declined my invitation to join my wain. What about you? Would you like to make a life as a Traveler?'

'I thank you for your hospitality but I go where Severine goes.'

Luke's smile did not falter. 'That is a shame, Jeph. There are many in the wain, like Saul here, who will be most disappointed.' He sighed theatrically but his gaze was intense. 'Then again, love's journey is seldom as smooth as we would wish, is it, Jeph?'

'Time runs on,' said Severine hurriedly as she picked up the seethe of Jeph's thoughts. 'We must make a start.'

'Yes, you must, as you insist on going,' said Luke. 'May good fortune light the way ahead,' he said formally and kissed her on each cheek.

'And the wain-circle remain unbroken,' responded Severine, nodded to Saul, and set off through the wagons.

Heart Hunter

Mist's attention was on something ahead and, as Tor hastened after him, he saw it was a pack. And then, before Tor could stop him, Mist launched himself over the gully's edge. Tor cursed but Mist completed the descent safely on his backside and Tor wasted no time in following.

Snowhawk lay at the bottom, his perfect face motionless in death. Grief was like a knife in Tor's heart and he staggered, while Mist sobbed out endearments and covered Snowhawk's face with kisses. Swamped by his own agonising loss, Tor barely registered what he saw and then, beyond hope, Snowhawk's eyes flickered open.

There was no awareness in them but Mist's sobs turned to exclamations of joy. More of his kisses found Snowhawk's mouth and Snowhawk turned so that his lips met Mist's. The kisses of lovers, not friends, realised Tor, unable to look away. Mist's cheek pressed to Snowhawk's and his fingers twined in Snowhawk's hair, and there was such tenderness in Mist's embrace that Tor's eyes burned. This was what he had wanted with Serest, *craved* with Serest, but it was not what she wanted with him *or* it appeared, enjoyed with Snowhawk.

I hope you enjoyed *I Heard the Wolf Call My Name.* **Authors need reviews!** It is how our readers find us. I would love you to leave me an honest review on Amazon, Goodreads, or another of your favourite reader sites. Read on to discover my other books.

Works by K S Nikakis
Available on Amazon KDP and a range of digital platforms.

Non Fiction

Journey: Seeking the Sacred, Spirit and Soul in the Australian Wilderness

When we set out into the wilderness, what is it we *really* seek?

Do we seek new sights or do we seek new selves? And are we *really* on one journey or on two?

Journeying fifteen thousand kilometres into Australia's blood-red heart, Nikakis discovers that every journey is perilous, for travellers risk carrying the clutter of their outer lives with them; a clutter that blinds them to the other journey they crave; that of the inner *soul-journey* into a deeper understanding of self.

To enter Australia's vast Outback wilderness, is to enter a place of endless horizons; a place doused with brilliant gold dawns and dazzling sunsets; a place silvered by star-encrusted night skies and, most importantly, a place of hidden sacred places in whose deep stillness our inner journeys can at last unfold.

In the spirit of travellers like Robert Macfarlane and Scott Stillman, Nikakis asks what it is we really see, feel and understand when we follow in the steps of those who have gone before us deep into the wilderness.

Drawing on her Ph.D. in Joseph Campbell's hero myth, and using original poetry and novel extracts, Nikakis takes us on this second journey; a journey of the sacred, spirit and soul, where our inner selves finally have the time and space to gift us richer and more fully-realised lives.

Fantasy Novel Series

Angel Caste 5 Book Series – available complete in one book or as five individual books: Angel Blood, Angel Breath, Angel Bone, Angel Bound, Angel Blessed.

Angel Caste – Complete 5 Book Series - *A modern female hero on a timeless quest*

A troubled half-angel, a beautiful angel guide, a binding promise . . .

Viv is on day release from jail to attend the funeral of the thug she thinks is her father, when she comes face to face with her real father, the powerful angel Archae Kald. If finding out she's a half-angel isn't shocking enough, Viv discovers her mother isn't dead after all but lost somewhere in the tangle of worlds called the Rynth.

Determined to find the only person who has ever truly loved her, Viv goes to Kald's angel world where he appoints the beautiful Thris as her guide. Thris is kind and caring, unlike the males Viv has known before, but after living on the streets, Viv finds it almost impossible to trust.

Friendship grows as Thris trains her to travel the rifts, but the Rynth is a dark and dangerous place, even for angels and, as Thris grows increasingly tempted by Viv's emerging angel traits, disaster strikes.

Viv journeys on alone and stumbles into a war zone where she finds a lost child. She pledges to take the child to safety but, as the war rages on, deciding who is friend and who is enemy becomes a deadly game of chance.

Bound by his promise to guide Viv to her mother, Thris embarks on a desperate search for her, but a greater threat confronts them both and, in the end, they must fight not just for their own lives, but for the lives of those they love.

The Kira Chronicles - 6 Book Series – available complete in one book or as six individual books: The Whisper of Leaves, The Silence of Stone, The Secrets of Stars, The Thunder of Hoofs, The Crying of Birds, The Music of Home.

The Kira Chronicles – Complete 6 Book Series – *traditional fantasy with deep forests and high stakes*

A gold-eyed Healer, a prophecy, two brothers at war.

In seasons long past, twin gold-eyed princes sundered a kingdom. Rejecting his brother Terak's warrior ways, Kasheron led his people deep into the great southern forests and established the healing settlement of Allogrenia. The Tremen flourished, upholding Kasheron's legacy of peace and healing, and protected by the vast, trackless trees.

All Tremen delight in the healing arts, but Kira is the greatest Healer of them all.

To the north of Allogrenia, drought ravages the Shargh's land, and as their suffering escalates, the chief's younger brother seizes on an ancient prophecy to snatch the chiefship for himself. The prophecy links the Shargh's doom to a gold-eyed Healer, and Kira has gold eyes.

The Shargh attack with devastating consequences and Kira must fight to save the wounded, but the Shargh wounds rot, no matter her skill, and Kira finds herself in a deadly race against time. As the slaughter continues, she makes the horrifying discovery that the Shargh hunt *her*. To halt the attacks and save her people, she sets off for the North to seek aid from her long sundered warrior kin.

But the dangers beyond the forests exceed even the Shargh attacks. The Tremen detest their warrior kin but Terak's descendants have inflicted a worse fate on the Tremen. Kira's new-found love is torn apart by ancient hostilities and when trust turns to betrayal, it risks everything she has fought for.

Fantasy Novels

The Emerald Serpent – *the Celtic Fae in a fight for survival*
Book trailer: https://www.youtube.com/watch?v=bGpKxnpCEMg

Betrayal, torture, death: Etaine lives on only to destroy those who robbed her of everything she loved.

Seven years before, Etaine met fellow Ranger Cormac, the he-Eadar she believed was her longed-for true-mate. Emerald-eyed, white-skinned, and black-haired, the Eadar had formed into Ranger bands to fight the Fada, invading religious zealots determined to replace the Eadar's Serpent Goddess with their own gods of stone.

The pure blood of the ancient Eadar runs strong in Etaine and Cormac's veins, and their joining had the potential to open the Emerald and Serpent Ways to them, old worlds only true Eadar can enter. But their love affair goes tragically amiss, with catastrophic consequences.

Etaine flees and as the years pass, slowly rebuilds her life, but the Fada's attacks grow more ferocious, and the Eadar are forced to fight for their very existence. When the Fada mass to commit yet more bloody slaughter, and the bands join in a final, desperate effort to defeat them, Etaine comes under Cormac's command, the very last Eadar she ever wants to see again.

Together they have a weapon that can destroy the Fada, but to use it, Etaine must learn to trust again and Cormac to Remember. And time runs short: the Serpent rises.

Heart Hunter – *a female hunter on an impossible quest*

Fleet is a young Sceadu hunter: skilled, strong, and fast. She hunts deep into the icy mountains, seeking meat for her people, for the rains have failed and plunged the Sceaudu into hunger.

Her hunts are hard, but she has much to look forward to. Soon she will be gifted her air-name by the Sceadu's shaman, and then she will be a full adult, and free to marry the man she loves.

But while Fleet is on hunt, the old shaman dies, and the new shaman visions a very different future for her: cross the frozen, ice-locked mountains and complete a perilous quest or lose the man she loves forever.

In a moment of anger and frustration, Fleet commits a terrible wrong and sets out into the frigid mountains to atone with her life. In a journey that takes her deep into the earth's darkest places, into strange new worlds, and even into Death itself, she discovers that only she can save her people. To survive, she must draw on every shred of her hunter strength, and doing the impossible, it turns out, is just the beginning.

The Third Moon – *Science fantasy with a very human quest*

Where does the past end and the future begin?

Haunted by inherited memories of his people's dispossession and theft of their children, Warrain is just twelve years old when the nightmare repeats. But Warrain isn't living on Earth in the 21st Century, he is living on the planet Imago in the far flung future.

Five years before, Station One's Mech's got high on the opioid arrash, and in the bloodshed that followed, Warrain's scientific community were expelled from the Station, his father murdered, and his mother and unborn sibling lost to him.

The scientists carve out a rudimentary Station high in Imago's ranges, and Warrain's friends get on with their lives. Not Warrain; he climbs the Tors to stare down at Station One, dream of his mother and sibling, and plot revenge.

And then one day, everything changes. A third moon appears in the sky, one of Imago's life-forms calls him by name, and disease breaks out at Station One.

When the Mechs visit to seek help for their ill, Warrain seizes the opportunity to deal them a blow they will never forget. But the third moon brings changes that threaten them all and, to aid the life-form whose kind is being dispossessed and slaughtered, he must turn his back on the hate that has long sustained him and find another way to live.

Messenger – *a dystopic future filled with hope*

In a world made deaf by hatred, who will hear the messenger?

Severine's world ends the day her family is murdered. Being raised in the loving community of gay Travelers always marked her as an outsider, but being female puts her in mortal danger. Women are scarce, precious, and hunted.

When chance brings Severine face to face with the father she has never known, he assigns the son of his murdered best friend to guard her. They soon clash. Severine believes all men are violent brutes and Jeph resents his freedoms being curtailed.

An uneasy understanding grows but Jeph is glad to deliver her to the Enclaves, a sanctuary her father has carved out in the mountains for his women and children. But there is no safety in a world broken by war and sickness and when violence follows her, Severine flees to the northern city of Andhaka in search of a home amongst her mother's people. Jeph follows, bound by loyalty to her father, but the north holds terrible dangers for him.

It's been years since Andhaka has welcomed outsiders with anything but bullets, and to survive and to protect Jeph, Severine must learn to use her enemies' weapons against them. As the stakes rise, she comes to understand the horror of her mother's loss, and what drove her father north seventeen years before. His quest becomes her quest, but she hasn't counted on the savage legacy that war and sickness have left behind, or on falling in love.

Fantasy Short Stories

Available on Amazon KDP

The Gift – A Deep Fantasy Short Story #1 – free on my website at
www.ksnikakis.com

Excerpt:

Thariel sat for a long time, surveying all around her, as if she ate the
world that would soon be memory. Then she took the harness from
the mare, and with soft words, thanked her and bade her farewell. Her
own feet she turned towards the forest, tossing her face-plate aside as
she went, so that her hair fell loose to her waist, then she discarded her
chest-armour, the sword and dagger, her bow and quiver.

The trees closed in and she came at last to the lake Men call
Menios and stood for a while on its shore. An owl cried and a mouse
shrieked, and all around her the souls of the newly dead jostled in their
journey to the void. She stepped into the water and the new life inside
her quivered.

'Fear not, little one,' she whispered, in her own tongue. 'We are
going home.'

The Tale of Prince Anura – A Deep Fantasy Short Story #2 – free on my website at www.ksnikakis.com

Excerpt:

I should have been happy, for she was beautiful. Dark rivers of curls, skin as white as moonlight on water, breasts softer than spawn, and she loved me well. But her chamber was small, no matter the comfort of her bed, and the old feelings of entrapment rose, as persistent as gas that bubbles from rot below still waters.

I sat at the casement and listened, as I had once loitered near the watery skin of the second world and waited. The moon grew large and small many times, but it came at last, as I knew it would. The soft lament on the night-time air, the song of a soul as confined as mine. It took me a journey of many days through the depths of a massive forest to find her tower.

Stone it was and sheer, and as remote as the third world's glimmer had once been. I sang to her and she answered with sweet melodies of her own and we made love as frogs do, with our voices. And when trust had built, she let down her shining ladder of golden hair.

Glass-Heart – A Deep Fantasy Short Story #3

Finalist Best YA Short Story, Aurealis Awards, 2019.

Excerpt:

Geth moved amongst his band, exchanging quiet words while they waited. Some he had fought with since the Tallon's foul ships had first found their shores while others had come later, when the burn of cot and kin had sent them from their valleys.

Hate drove them but hate was no shield against arrow and knife. It was fighting skills that kept them hale, and Geth ensured they had them aplenty. He needed them living, not just for their own sakes and his, but for what would come later. When the Tallon's stain had been scoured away, the destroyed must be rebuilt.

Kyth sat alone and he went to her and gazed about. 'The glass-heart's fled, has it?'

'I sent her to a place of safety. She will come to me when it is over.'

'Safety was what I wanted for you!'

'And what I wanted for Nyar.' Her eyes caught the star-sheen as she looked up at him. 'But you can't always have what you want, can you, Ceannasai?'

Dragon Sprite – A Deep Fantasy Short Story #4

Excerpt:

Genn rocketed straight upwards, not just because she enjoyed seeing the limitless blue sky before her, but because a Waiwin's wing shape made vertical flight harder for them. Orin didn't try to catch her but swept in circles around her, gaining height in an ever-narrowing spiral. It was a clever tactic and one Genn didn't believe he had thought of in the instant she had cleared the trees. He had obviously studied her strategies and developed a plan to counter them *or so he thought*.

Genn waited until the spiral narrowed to *axeel*, the minimum distance a Waiwin must keep from a Velven unless she *accepted* him, then swerved towards him, narrowing the distance between them. Orin's eyes flashed to black, shocked she *had* accepted him, but before he could act, she folded her wings and dropped.

The strength that had driven Orin's pursuit had surged to his wing-tendrils in anticipation of locking them with hers and he would struggle even to stay airborne until it flowed back.

www.ingramcontent.com/pod-product-compliance
Lightning Source LLC
Chambersburg PA
CBHW071831020726
47502CB00004B/1317